Fornax didn't care for tight spaces, and certainly none was tighter than a passageway onboard a spaceship.

He was being held prisoner, held against his will. Behind him in that narrow passageway was a burly guard. Fornax turned to address the man, thinking that perhaps he could talk his way out of this.

No sooner had he twisted his head to speak to the man though, than his weary eyes caught the glimmer of an upraised blade. Suddenly horrified, the adrenaline shot through his system like a bolt!

Fornax spun to face his attacker, raising his arm to deflect the impending slash. But the man was already in motion, thrusting his blade at Fornax with evil intent.

Trapped inside that narrow corridor without any room in which to maneuver, it was impossible for Fornax to avoid being cut by his assailant.

The killer's knife ripped through his shoulder, its point penetrating deeply, all the way to the bone. Yet, even before the searing pain had a chance to hack its way through his central nervous system and on up to his brain, Fornax gave free rein to his self-preservation instincts.

Using the only thing available—the toothbrush in his pocket—Fornax responded with extreme violence. He plunged the hard plastic hilt of the instrument into his attacker's left eye like a dagger.

The gelatinous orb popped bloodily, its milky-white contents spewing like a geyser into the zero-g atmosphere around them.

Stunned by the attack, the assassin staggered backward, releasing his grip on the blade still jutting out from deep within Fornax's flesh.

When the pain from his ruptured shoulder was finally acknowledged by his beleaguered brain, Fornax screamed icily. Only it wasn't over, not yet anyway.

Drawing on his last ounce of resolve, Fornax took a deep breath and jerked the blade from his upper arm. Then, summoning all his strength, he rammed it into the belly of his opponent. It was a deep and lethal blow, and just for good measure, he gave it a vicious twist.

Grimacing, the man collapsed in a heap on the floor, the toothbrush still protruding from his head where his eyeball used to be. Droplets of blood filled the air between them.

Fornax sank to the floor as well. On Earth, even with the helpful tug of her one-g of gravity, arresting the flow of blood from a deep laceration was tough. But in space, with no gravity whatsoever, it was difficult raised to a power of two. He had but seconds to live . . .

Other books by Steven Burgauer:

- **THE BRAZEN RULE** — a viral killer on the loose
- **THE LAST AMERICAN** — a country on the brink of disaster
- **IN THE SHADOW OF OMEN** — Mars at its best!
- **THE GRANDFATHER PARADOX** — a time-travel story
- **NAKED CAME THE FARMER** — a round-robin murder mystery written by 13 of the looniest minds in central Illinois
- **THE WEALTH BUILDER'S GUIDE** — an investment primer

Available at finer bookstores everywhere, or

write: zero-g press, 6605 N. Rustic Oak Ct, Peoria, Il 61614

phone: 309-692-2953

e-mail: SCIFI20@prodigy.net

online: www.amazon.com
www.barnesandnoble.com
bradley.bradley.edu/~dlb/steven.html

Treachery On The Dark Side

Treachery On The Dark Side

by

Steven Burgauer

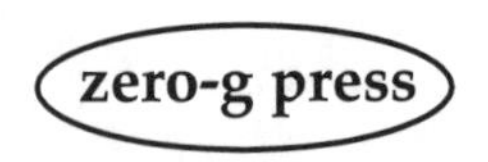

Treachery On The Dark Side

This is a work of fiction. All characters and events portrayed in this book are fictional, and any resemblance to real people or real situations is purely coincidental.

Printing History
First Printing 2000

ISBN 1-892086-03-4

PRINTED IN THE UNITED STATES OF AMERICA
10 9 8 7 6 5 4 3 2 1

To my son, Scott, who taught
me the meaning of a bad guy.

PRELUDE

Farah District, Afghanistan
Daybreak, Tuesday, October 4, 2425

His boots heavy and caked with mud, Fornax Nehrengel marched zombie-like through the bleak and raw dawn. He wore the face of exhaustion, wincing as each step brought forth a fresh dose of pain from the untreated blister oozing puss from between his toes. His dark skin and hair were grimy, his legs and arms sore. From deep within his belly an unheated breakfast of gruel protested its confinement. Indifference deadened his spirit, and his eyelids drooped with fatigue.

Like the other foot soldiers in his unit, Fornax Nehrengel was outfitted in a tattered, drab-colored uniform, wearing poorly-fitting boots, and carting a handmade, breech-loading rifle of irregular calibre. Suffering privation, the Afghan army could not afford to equip its men with recoil blasters like the enemy had, or even with force guns. Their chances for success were slim, and Fornax knew it. Surely the black scowl etched into his face said it all. Fear. Exhaustion. Pain.

Through chapped and broken lips Fornax Nehrengel silently cursed his plight. He was not a brave man. Indeed, he found it curiously ironic that he should be fighting to defend a flag he paid scant allegiance to or risking his life in support of cherished ideals he barely endorsed. Fornax Nehrengel resented being here and desertion was on his mind.

This was not his war, this was his father's war. Nevertheless, Fornax found himself stranded in its midst, laboring to discharge a hastily-made promise to serve in uniform so he might gain entrance to his beleaguered country's finest university. And yet, it was a promise which he now held in contempt.

Fornax resented the war's inconvenient disruption of his studies. He resented how his grandiose schemes to achieve great things at a young age had all of a sudden been thrown askew. But more than anything else, he resented being under the thumb of Pasha Norandu, the feeble-minded young officer heading up his platoon. How this inept buffoon ever earned his command was anybody's guess, but by impatiently pressing his men forward without first waiting for an updated recon report, he was needlessly endangering every last one of them. What should have been a simple and straightforward scouting operation had suddenly become a new and more dangerous game in the less-than-capable hands of Pasha Norandu.

To a recruit as green as Fornax, it was all a bit unnerving, and he was beside himself with fear. Turning to speak to the dark-skinned soldier marching directly behind him in line, Fornax vented his bitterness.

"He's gonna get us all killed," came the hoarse whisper. "And the bastard doesn't even give a damn!"

"Me-thinks you worry too much," Vishnu chided, trying to maintain a visage of calm. Though Vishnu would probably have been the last one to admit it, he too had been wrestling with the same troubling thoughts. He and Fornax were like two peas in a pod: they thought alike and wanted much the same things from life. And well they should. The two of them were not only distant cousins, they were close friends as well. They had both grown up in the same, desperately poor village; they had both seen war ravage their tiny, landlocked country.

"I *do* worry too much," Fornax admitted. "Especially about staying alive."

"Unless you want Pasha to hear you, you had better quit bitching," Vishnu cautioned, brushing back a lock of rain-soaked hair from his eyes.

"Look," Fornax grumbled, "all I want is to come out of this thing alive. Alive and with all my body parts still in working order. Is that so much to ask? I'm no hero, you know—not like my father anyway. Now there was the genuine article—the original army hero—but not me."

"I promised your mother I'd keep you safe. But you'd better quit griping or else . . . "

"Quiet back there!" Pasha shouted, bringing the line of soldiers to a halt and interrupting their harmless banter. "If you two pains in the butt don't shut up, and I mean right now, I'll have you both drop right here in the mud and give me twenty. Is that understood?"

"Oh, yes sir . . . perfectly," Fornax parroted, suppressing an irreverent snicker. "Whatever you say, sir."

"Enough already!" Pasha boomed, determined to have the last word. "Not another syllable."

Rubbing the black stubble of an untended beard, Fornax shrugged his shoulders in resignation and hiked dejectedly on. Through dark, brooding eyes he surveyed the landscape, his field of vision obscured by the unrelenting rain.

The eleven-man unit he was attached to was tramping through a wasteland of barren hills in a single-file line, taking the utmost care not to uproot the scruffy mountain vegetation as they went. Outgunned and outnumbered, the tiny band of freedom-fighters couldn't risk leaving behind a trail of upturned moss or broken twigs an enemy patrol might follow back to their main camp.

The wet ground over which they trod was dotted with outcroppings of immense boulders. Every so often they would come upon a stunted bush clinging tenaciously to what little topsoil it could find. Like an unlanced boil, the terrain was swollen with one butte after another. And, had the turf been sandy instead of rocky, it might well have passed for a desert rather than a meadow. But, decimated by centuries of unrelenting war, the formerly fertile prairie now supported only a few scrawny sheep per acre.

Hardly worth fighting over, Fornax reflected, stomping his feet to stay warm. But then what was?

A moment later, he had his answer. It stared them in the face when they crested the next rise.

"Oh, my Lord!" Pasha groaned, his panic-stricken voice serving to focus their attention on the open expanse before them. There, just sitting in the neighboring valley waiting for them, was a heavily-fortified Chinese detachment. Raised over the camp were Overlord Ling Tsui's colors, and adorning the cadre of armored vehicles was his coat-of-arms.

"Damn you, Pasha!" Fornax spat, his face going white. "This is your fault, you stupid mongrel! You were more concerned with keeping us on schedule than with keeping us safe!"

Even as he spoke, Nehrengel's sinewy arms tightened with rage. The bloody fool had led their small company into harm's way; unintentionally perhaps, but into harm's way just the same. And now they were in big trouble. The mechanized Chinese column they had accidentally stumbled upon was obviously engaged in a search and destroy mission—and the emir's main camp was almost certainly Ling's intended target. Only, before Overlord Ling ever had a chance to move his big guns into place, Pasha had obliged him by giving his artillery a target to practice on ahead of the main attack—*their tiny platoon!*

"Oh, my Lord!" Pasha groaned again, shrinking from his responsibility. "There's so many of them . . . "

"I don't think they've spotted us," Vishnu said, bravely mustering a full dose of courage. "Maybe we ought to strike while we still have the element of surprise."

Fornax couldn't disagree more. "We've got to get out of here!" he shouted, diving for cover behind a huge boulder. "And I mean right away!"

"Shut up!" Pasha screamed, clearly out of his head. "Shut up or else . . . "

"Or else *what?*" Fornax hollered back, the foul wind tearing the words from his mouth. "You'll make us drop and give you twenty? Don't you get it? We don't stand a chance out here in the open like this. For God's sake, Pasha, they outnumber us fifty to one!"

Still crouching low for protection, Fornax stole a glance in the direction of the enemy camp spread out in the canyon below. Along with hundreds of battle-hardened soldiers, a dozen or more fearsome-looking artillery pieces were assembled right there beside the road.

It made for a chilling sight, one Fornax would never forget. Without exaggeration, the grim truth was that once their platoon was spotted, it would be only a matter of minutes before the yellow-skinned heathens ordered in their deadly airchops to bushwhack them from above. Scattered across the open hillside the way they were, there was almost nothing they could do to defend themselves against an aerial assault like that. Plus, instead of taking charge of the situation and giving orders, all their squadron leader could manage to do was point and grunt.

Seeing Pasha fidget with indecision, Fornax coughed out a desperate, freakish sort of plea. "We've got to get out of here!" he implored, repeating his earlier entreaty.

But when Pasha didn't respond, when he just stood there frozen in his tracks staring blankly off into space, Fornax stepped in without hesitation, issuing but one forceful command.

"Hit the dirt!" he yelled. "Everybody down!"

But it was too late. The murderous ordeal had already begun.

The words scarcely out of his mouth, the men in Fornax's platoon barely had time to scramble for cover before the Chinese perimeter-gunners began pounding their position with a vicious round of shelling. The results were brutal and devastating.

No sooner had Fornax himself dropped to the muddy ground to avoid the sudden barrage of small-arms fire, than the hair on his neck stiffened. A bullet whizzed by, perilously close to his head. Sprawled as he was, face down on the rocky earth, it was difficult for him to judge how many of his comrades had fallen prey to the merciless spray of gunfire, but the air around him was filled with pained cries of agony.

Instinctively scurrying along the ground on his belly to shield himself behind one of those massive boulders the Afghan steppe was so famous for, Fornax closed his eyes and curled himself up into a ball to protect his vitals. As he lay there mortified, hugging the wet dirt for dear life, an anguished moan reached out to him from the scraggy bushes to his left. He didn't have to see the man's face to know who it was. Commander Pasha had been standing at the head of the line when the attack began. Apparently, he hadn't been as adept as Fornax at dodging bullets.

Deep down, Fornax was glad. And he had no qualms about admitting it. If not for Pasha, if not for his brazen attitude, this senseless slaughter would never have taken place. The man was responsible, damnit—he *deserved* to die!

Unfortunately, no matter how satisfying Pasha's death was to

Fornax personally, it didn't improve his own, rather precarious situation one little bit. Indeed, he was busy devising a way out of this quagmire when the inflection of a familiar voice reached his ears from across the hillside.

"Heh, Fornax!" his buddy yelped from the safety of a nearby escarpment. "The bastards have got us pinned down here! What the hell should we do?"

"How the devil should *I* know?" Fornax snarled, unable to camouflage the raw fear in his voice. Dipping his head in contrition, he watched as a drop of rain trickled off his brown-skinned face and rolled onto his tattered parka. It joined a hundred other such raindrops in a pool at his feet.

Vishnu stared at him through expectant eyes, waiting for an order. But none was forthcoming.

"What should we do?" he repeated. Vishnu was disappointed that Fornax hadn't moved a muscle to exercise his prerogative as second in command.

When Fornax looked up to see his friend's dour expression, he shuddered. "You of all people should appreciate that I'm no leader. Hell, I'm not even a very good follower! All I want to do is come out of this thing alive and . . . "

"I know, I know," Vishnu interrupted, exasperation coloring his voice. "All you want to do is come out of this thing alive and with all your body parts intact. Well that's just not good enough, damnit! With Pasha dead, *you're* in charge now. You had better think of something! And darn quick!"

Making every effort not to panic, Fornax locked his teeth with indecision. He felt totally unqualified to make these sorts of decisions; yet, with Vishnu and the others depending on him, he dared not shirk his responsibility either. But what did they expect him to do?

Staring down the length of his drab uniform in quiet terror, Fornax contemplated his poorly-crafted pistol and ill-fitting boots. His feet were already swollen with blisters; how far would he be able to get before being cut down?

Again came the question. Only this time, it was everything Vishnu could do to be heard over the staccato whine of incoming tracers. "What the hell are you waiting for, Fornax? We can't just sit here all day doing nothing!"

Vishnu was a short, unremarkable fellow with a temperament to match; yet, there was a certain finality, a certain determination to his words. As a perplexed Fornax looked on, the other man drew his archaic weapon from its battered holster, peered cautiously around the boulder he was hiding behind, and then, without even taking aim, let loose a couple of rounds.

Watching this whole process unfold would have been comical if it hadn't been so dangerous. But no sooner had Vishnu unloaded his sixshooter in the direction of the opposite valley, than the ground at his feet was peppered with return fire. Charting a hasty retreat, he quickly ducked his head back behind the giant outcropping to avoid being hit. His wet, black hair twisted crazily in the wind.

"Are you out of your mind?!" Fornax boomed at the top of his voice. "Put that silly six-gun of yours away before it misfires and blows off one of your damn fingers! For God's sake, all you're doing is drawing their attention!"

Lowering his eyes, Vishnu mouthed an apology. But his words were lost in the din as the almond-eyed demons made the switch from light guns to heavy shells.

With the contentious roar of artillery thundering in the background, Fornax realized he had to make a decision. And it had to be the right one! If they stood and fought, they'd almost certainly die. Their only chance was to run for it, and he said as much.

Vishnu's response was immediate and blunt. With an astonished look plastered across his weather-beaten face, he grunted out a bitter objection. "Begging your pardon, cousin, but what in Allah's name can running accomplish? If we retreat now like cowards, we'll be stripped of our honor. Shame will follow us wherever we go; it will haunt our every waking moment."

"So what?" Fornax retorted, crouching on one knee, his sights set on a distant grouping of rocks. "Better shame than an unmarked grave! Better long life than kudos!"

"I don't understand you, Fornax—it's considered honorable to die for one's country." It was an exacting, matter-of-fact statement; one given without hint of fear.

"I fail to see the honor in dying," Fornax returned, flexing his muscles in grim anticipation. "Not for my country—not for *any* reason."

Clearly agitated, Fornax trembled uncontrollably. It was everything he could do not to suddenly lose his nerve. His dark eyes spoke only of fear. They were out of time—and out of choices. No matter how cowardly it might seem, escape was their only hope. Nothing could change that now, even if quitting the battlefield meant violating their vaunted Afghan Code of Honor.

Poised to make a wild dash to safety, Fornax flushed the adrenalin from his system with a single, sharp deep breath. "Honor is not the issue here, my good friend—body parts are. I want to keep them all in proper working order."

"And the emir? What will he say?" Vishnu quizzed, his bandanna grimy with sweat.

"The emir? He can go to blazes!" Fornax vented at the height of disrespect. "Now, are you with me or not?"

There was resignation in the other man's reply. "You're the boss,

Fornax. Lead the way."

Though disappointed by Vishnu's tepid show of support, Fornax steeled himself for action. With a wave of his hand, he signaled the others to follow suit. And then, as if on cue, the two men sprang to their feet and began scrambling towards the next ridge as fast as their cramped legs would carry them.

Hobbled by their shoddy boots, hindered by the rough terrain, the going was torturously slow. So slow, in fact, that they hadn't covered more than a dozen meters when an artillery round struck the very boulder Fornax had taken refuge behind earlier. Under the force of the impact the giant stone disintegrated, spewing razor-sharp fragments of dirt and rock in every direction. To Fornax's unspeakable horror, one particularly lethal shard of rock struck his friend in the back, mortally wounding him.

At first, when Vishnu grunted out a barely audible outcry, Fornax didn't even realize that his cousin had been hit. Indeed, if not for the sudden explosion of blood, he might not have known how serious the injury actually was. Certainly, the truncated gasp which issued from Vishnu's mouth seemed insufficient given the true extent of his wounds.

Aghast, Fornax stopped dead in his tracks. For a long instant, he thought to administer first-aid to his friend, but it would have been a futile gesture. *There was no possible way he could save the man!*

In the first place, Fornax was no medic. Yet even if he had been one, such a remarkable amount of blood had already hemorrhaged from the fist-sized cavity blown out of Vishnu's back, it was doubtful whether he would have been able to keep the man alive. Aside from comforting Vishnu in his final moments, there was nothing Fornax could do now to prevent his cousin's death.

Gently slipping his hand beneath Vishnu's shoulder, Fornax drew him close, letting the man's head come to rest in his lap. Had the morning sun not been held captive by the gray mist, it might have witnessed a bitter tear roll across Fornax's dirty face and fall to the earth.

"You were right," Vishnu sighed, the life nearly drained from his body, "there is no honor in dying for your country. None at all."

And then, after coughing once or twice, he expired, his head still cradled in Fornax's arms.

Squatting on the wet ground, the sounds of mortar-fire raging all around him, his clothes and hands splattered with the fresh blood of his only friend, Fornax was sickened by this horrible turn of events. Never before had he seen death at such close quarters. Never before had he seen death at *any* range!

His eyes still fixed on Vishnu's ashen face, Fornax struggled unsteadily to his feet. Clenching his fist in rage, he wanted to shout obscenities at the heavens. He wanted to shout obscenities at the heavens and ask who the hell up there was to blame for this travesty.

But he didn't say a word. What was the use anyway? There was nothing to be gained by it. Vishnu was dead and no amount of cursing at Allah could change that. Vishnu had paid the ultimate price and the only question still remaining to be answered was: had it been worth it?

Dying for the preservation of vague ideals had never made much sense to Fornax, and from where he stood now, defenseless on that craggy hillside, his future looked awfully dim.

If death was the price to be paid for victory, then he would just as soon lose. If death was all he had to look forward to out here on the battlefield, then he would much rather make a stand elsewhere, at another time and in another place.

Whether he succeeded or whether he failed was no longer of consequence; whether his nation survived or whether it was overrun no longer mattered. With Vishnu dead, all that he had once held dear was now gone, and existence had lost its very meaning! All Fornax knew for certain now was that his heart was no longer in this. *His short career as a soldier had come to an end!*

If Fornax was to have a future, if any of his lofty ambitions were to have even a prayer of being fulfilled, he had no choice now but to try and make a run for it. As much as Vishnu might have disagreed with his decision, Fornax knew that the only possible way for him to escape from the crosshairs of this nightmare would be to desert!

Caught-up in this moment of introspection, Fornax failed to notice the menacing blotch swelling ever larger against the horizon. Not until its ominous whine reached his ears, shocking him back to the present, did he focus on the airchop closing in swiftly on his position.

Approaching at high speed, the killing machine hugged the ridge, its short, stubby wings glistening in the rain, its overhead rotors slicing effortlessly through the cold air.

Even at this distance, Fornax could plainly see the bomb bay doors hanging open from its steel belly. Like perhaps no other, this was an unambiguous sign of its eagerness to do battle.

Then too, Fornax could make out the silhouette of a giant eagle affixed to the underside of its stubby wing. Appropriate to his methods, this bird of prey was the heraldic symbol of Overlord Ling Tsui, their avowed enemy.

Armed with a phalanx of deadly nitro-projectiles, each capable of incinerating an entire battalion in the blink of an eye, these highly-maneuverable, flying war-wagons were well-suited to strike at soldiers in a mountainous district such as this one. And when they were done with their killing and their maiming, they would leave nothing behind in their wake but twisted metal and charred bones.

"Oh, my God!" Fornax exclaimed, a lump forming in his throat. "The bastards are gonna fry us right where we stand!"

With a wave of panic rising up to engulf him, Fornax mechanically began to wipe Vishnu's hardening blood from his hands. Black and white pictures of death formed in his head as he visualized the pain these incendiary weapons would visit upon the few remaining members of his unsuspecting platoon. Once the scorching nitro ignited, his men would suffer a most grisly and painful finish.

Yet, even in the face of a death more horrifying than anything he could possibly imagine, a determined look took hold between his eyes. There was no way he was going to meet his maker without first putting up some sort of a fight!

Ignoring his improbable chances for success, Fornax calmly reached down and drew Vishnu's antiquated handgun from its holster. It felt heavy in his palm.

Dauntless, Fornax took deliberate aim. Nothing but a hundred meters of cold, wet air separated him from the glassed-in cockpit of the incoming airchop. Nothing, not even the threat of imminent harm, could deter him now. All he heard was the whine of the airchop; all he saw were the charcoal-black eyes of the sneering pilot.

Steadying his grip on the gun, Fornax waited. Even as the pilot guided his deadly, jet-propelled craft directly at him, still he waited. And then, when the craft was almost right on top of him, he squeezed off a single round. This act he did with the cold dispassion of a man who was going to die anyway.

What happened next, happened in slow-motion. He heard the crinkle of glass as the bullet hit home. He saw the airchop pilot's wounded look of anguish as he slumped over the control-stick. He heard the roar of the engines as it screamed by, just overhead.

All at once, as if Fornax had deliberately planned it that way, the enemy airchop veered obligingly off to the right, away from his beleaguered platoon and straight down into the valley where the Chinese garrison was bivouacked.

But the best was yet to come, for no sooner had the airship dipped below the horizon, than the ground at his feet was rocked by a horrendous explosion! An instant later, a fierce firestorm leapt skyward, the pillar of flame choked with smoke and debris. The white-hot flash of combustion was so bright, Fornax had to shield his eyes to avoid being blinded by it.

It took him a moment to figure out what had happened, but then it hit him—the nitro-projectiles onboard the airchop must have exploded on impact, unleashing an inferno which consumed everything—and everyone—in its wake!

As the dank wind carried the stench of seared flesh across the mesa to his nostrils, Fornax committed the entire gut-wrenching scene to memory. Even though the putrid odor was nauseating, even though the smell made a chill run up and down his spine, he found the whole gruesome affair curiously satisfying.

Lingering there on the hillside, his sweat-drenched face baked by the heat of the blast, Fornax felt no remorse at viewing the spectacle of burning enemy soldiers. They deserved to die if only to give honor to Vishnu's death!

Then suddenly, from out of nowhere, came a voice. It was the voice of one of the other soldiers from Fornax's decimated platoon.

"Well done!" the burly Afghan said, slapping Fornax on the back in a hearty, congratulatory fashion. "Hitting that pilot must've been the luckiest pistol-shot in the history of the world! You're a hero! Just like your father! Honor shall follow you all the days of your life!"

But Fornax wasn't having any of it. He simply shook his head in annoyance and started to walk away, heading off in the opposite direction. From the moment Vishnu died in his arms, his mind had been made up, and nothing this overexuberant comrade of his could say or do was going to change it.

"Your bravery spared all our lives!" the husky man shouted after him as Fornax set off across the steppe at high speed. "Mark my words—the emir'll give a banquet in your honor."

Slowing his pace just a little, Fornax chuckled with derision. It was all he could do not to laugh. "A banquet, eh?" he said, speaking over his shoulder even as he continued to meander further afield. "And I suppose if I hang around here long enough to collect it, my rash act will win me a commendation. Perhaps even a promotion. I can just hear the emir now: 'For your bravery and quick thinking, I present you with the coveted Afghan Medal of Honor. We're all so very proud of you.' Hah!"

"Are you out of your *head?*" the big Afghan bellowed as Fornax walked away. "Where in the blazes do you think you're going?"

But this time, Fornax didn't answer. Exhausted by his ordeal, he staggered from the field of battle and just kept right on moving.

If it occurred to him that by his actions he would be disgracing his father instead of making him proud, his face didn't show it. If it occurred to him that by taking flight he would be sullying his family name rather than elevating it, his expression didn't reveal it. On that day and at that moment in time only one thing could be said with certainty—the man who once called himself Fornax Nehrengel deserted, never to be heard from by that name again.

Now, as this man without a country moved with dispatch across the muddy land, he cocked his head skyward. A thin sliver of last night's moon still hung in the western sky. Though he didn't know how, he was certain his future lay up there among the stars!

PART I

1
Fornax Engels

Launch Pad 4, Sri Lanka Spaceport
Five Years Later

A pained look creasing his forehead, Fornax Engels winced under the pressure of a throbbing headache. It was all he could do not to cringe at the memory of the horrible night just ended. Everything about it had been intolerable, beginning with his sagging bunk and his filthy bunkmates.

Though Fornax had tried off and on for hours, falling asleep inside the DUMPSTER barracks had been all but impossible. Like a big metal pot that had been cooking all day long in the blazing sun, the seedy dormitory still supported an insufferable temperature well into the night. And then, as if to add insult to injury, the hot, bitter air of Sri Lanka had been uncommonly still, its taste fouled by the fumes of the ever-present rocket fuel.

Refusing to be outdone by the vexing heat, all manner of irksome noises had shamelessly competed to keep him awake. There was the incessant scratching of roaches as they scurried hungrily across the concrete floor, the aggravating door-slamming of his residence-hall mates as they came and went the whole night long, and the amorous moaning of a bimbooker one of the lugs had rented for a few hours' pleasure. Each had taken its turn keeping him from sleep.

For hours he just lay there, wide-eyed and furious, his blade tucked tightly beneath his pockmarked pillow, his buttocks wallowing in a pool of sweat. It was a sweat which had begun earlier in the day, that afternoon in fact, when his taxi-driver first left the cool air along the coast and turned inland towards the spaceport. In startling contrast to his adopted Auckland, here on this island there was hardly ever any relief from the crippling mugginess.

When daybreak finally arrived, no man in the compound had been more happy than he. In defiance of a pounding migraine, Fornax had been literally overflowing with anticipation. This was the day he had been looking forward to since before he boarded the tubes in Auckland; this was the day he was scheduled to go into space!

Pinned now by thick leather restraints to the contoured launch-chair, he stared lethargically through blood-shot eyes at the unfamiliar dials and switches which crowded the ceiling of the spacecraft. In front and beside him, strapped into the other seats like papooses to a board, were four men, all filthy, all intoxicated. Doing what he could to shut out the smelly foursome from his mind, Fornax wondered whether his clammy hands revealed the trepidation he felt deep within his knotted stomach.

After last night's dreadful heat and humidity, the purified air of the launch-vehicle was a welcome relief. Even so, he found himself sickened by the unpalatable stench of tortan-beer reeking from the sweat-clogged pores of the hulking shipmate occupying the seat closest to his own.

This big dense man who, for obvious reasons went simply by Red, was an irreverent bully; and judging by his slovenly dress and unshaven face, he barely made it from paycheck to paycheck. Compared to Red, Fornax was a short, scrawny fellow given to timidity. But much in the same way that a luxury yacht might seem puny or impotent in the company of a battleship, it was only in the side-by-side comparison that Fornax appeared of diminutive stature. In fact, he was an agile man of medium build, a man who had been blessed with intelligent good-looks and a quick wit to boot. Crammed in there amongst this bunch, he couldn't have seemed more out of place!

Whereas Red and his DUMPSTER brethren—veteran space-monkeys all—sat there in the capsule waiting impassively for the countdown to commence, Fornax was so agitated about what was to come next, he made the first of what would be several miscues this trip, gulping down air so fast he was soon on the verge of hyperventilating.

Around him the others sneered. To them, Fornax was nothing if not the greenest of tenderfoots. And as for space-travel, to them it was little more than a boring and commonplace business unworthy of their sober attention. And who could blame them? After all, a DUMP shuttle was little more than a glorified garbage scow piloted by a rough and tumble captain and manned by a crew of five not-so-very bright fellows. Not to put too fine a point on it, but there was nothing whatsoever about their lives, or even their jobs, worth getting excited over. But to Fornax—who had never been inside a spaceship before, much less one headed for the moon—the prospect of making this trip was at once exhilarating and terrifying!

Not only did it mark the culmination of a far-reaching personal journey which began with his desertion from the Afghan army five years ago, it also represented his first real chance to make a grab for the wealth he coveted so badly. Tracing his steps from the blood-stained battlefields of Afghanistan to the idyllic fjords of SKANDIA to the alps-like mountains of Zealand to the present tarmac at Sri Lanka, Fornax Engels had been on a lengthy, meandering quest—an odyssey, really—in search of success. And he was impatient to get on with it!

Fighting an uphill battle now against claustrophobia, Fornax nervously questioned how much longer he could stand to be confined inside the cramped capsule. There seemed to be barely enough air for him, much less for him plus a foul quartet of delinquent knaves. Just seeing the four of them together made him wonder whether or not he had made the right decision by coming here. Even his friends back home had thought embarking on this hazardous flight was a pretty bold step. Just how good were his reasons anyway?

The idea had hatched itself one evening, a month ago, under the most unusual of circumstances. Legend had it that if the horizon was totally cloudless at the spot where the sun was setting, and if the atmospheric conditions were just right, it was possible for the last visible edge of the sun to flash with a brilliant green light. Fantastic tales were told about this phenomenon, especially by sailors, and for a long time many people considered it a myth, just like that of the mermaid. But the phenomenon was genuine, and for several years now, while he was finishing up work on his doctorate, it had been Fornax's ambition to actually witness the "emerald flash," as it was called. On that particular day a month ago, conditions were as close to optimum as he had ever seen them.

Though the sky was by no means totally cloudless that evening, there *was* a completely clear and open stretch of it at the horizon precisely where the sun was going down. When nearly all of the sun's elliptical disc had disappeared beneath the horizon, he put his eyes to the sight of his trusty telescope and, for the hundredth time in two years, excitedly followed the sun's fast-shrinking terminus.

As was ordinarily the case when the air was dry and there was hardly any water vapor in the atmosphere, the sun was a blinding, orange-red almost to the very end. But for the tiniest fraction of a second, right before it disappeared, the color of the last visible luminous line of the sun changed to a brilliant green!

The explosion of green happened so suddenly and was gone so quickly, Fornax was quite dazed by the effect. Stunned, he found himself at a loss for words, and for a long moment afterwards, he just stood there, mouth agape.

Comprehension dawned slowly, but when it did, he realized that what he had actually seen was the kernel of an idea!

In the minutes ahead, as the blue sky became darker and darker, and as the fixed stars appeared overhead in blinding succession until the whole sky was ablaze, a sixth sense told him to point his telescope in a new direction. Though the Milky Way spanned the sky above his head like a luminous arch stretching from horizon to horizon, what inexplicably drew his attention now was not the constellations, but the moon. Like a moth to the light, Fornax was seduced by the glow, and as he burned the midnight oil that night studying its pitted surface, he began asking himself why.

Why had so few people taken up residence there? Why had no industry—none whatsoever—ever taken hold there? Why, despite generations of trying, had so few of the moon's resources ever been exploited? All burning questions, all deserving of an answer.

The earliest of lunar enterprises, indeed the only one to endure to his day, was the moon DUMP. Once each week, a mammoth shuttle—its cavernous cargo-bay laden with red-hot nuclear wastes—detached itself from Earth orbit and engaged a trajectory which would convey it towards the far side of the moon. Its load was nothing less than the most toxic poison known to man—the radioactive sludge which spewed out like an unending stream from Earth's many hundreds of fission reactors.

Because no cost-effective method had ever been devised to completely drain these spent fuel rods of every last ounce of their radioactive energy, they were all still dangerously hot even after their output had declined below commercially-acceptable levels. With no satisfactory locations left on Earth for their safe storage, and with environmental issues always a point of contention, the uninhabited moon had beckoned early on as the most logical place for their internment. Over the centuries, tons-upon-tons of the deadly refuse had been shipped to the moon, then discarded there in one of three centrally-located craters the Council had earmarked especially for the warehousing of such wastes.

"Outta sight, outta mind." Those were the words that had come to him that evening as he contemplated the moon's mottled face from the darkened balcony of his utilitarian flat. When the almost too obvious truth suddenly occurred to him, it took his breath away!

Whereas the amount of energy salvageable from each *individual* fuel rod was no longer sufficient to turn a turbine back here on Earth, *collectively*, the energy being sloughed off uselessly into space by hundreds of thousands of these rods had to be enormous!

Peering once again down the long, dark neck of his telescope, Fornax saw his opportunity for wealth staring back at him through the aperture!

Why hadn't it occurred to him before? Why hadn't someone else seen it first? There could only be one conceivable explanation—it had to have been that "emerald flash!" What other possible reason made any sense?

But simple inspiration wasn't enough. Figuring out a profitable means for harnessing that massive flow of wasted energy meant doing some serious research. Beyond that, he would have to see the DUMP site for himself, if only to verify whether or not his plan was even workable. Clearly, what was called for here was an atomic storage cell or a battery of some sort, but what . . . and how?

Deciding right then and there that this was something he simply must do, Fornax set out for Sri Lanka two weeks later to hire on as a DUMPSTER. Considering the job's pitifully lowbrow qualifications, landing a berth as an indolent DUMPSTER wasn't much of a challenge. The hard part proved to be securing passage to the island.

Getting to the spaceport on Sri Lanka meant either surviving an arduous days-long voyage by ship or else shelling out enough of a bribe to hustle a certified passport for the tubes. When it came right down to it, Fornax actually had less of a choice than one might think. As susceptible as he was to motion-sickness, an ocean trip was simply out of the question! It had to be the tubes, or nothing at all!

Hocking his moped and hitting up a few of his friends for a loan, Fornax had managed to scrape together the necessary funds. Now, at long last—after the boring ride in the tubes from Auckland and after the unexpected complication of nearly being turned away at the DUMPSTER employment office by some fat Chinaman—he was finally here, on the launch-pad, staring at the endless collection of strange gauges and buttons which filled the ceiling of the spacecraft right above his head.

Fornax was about to count his blessings for having made it safely this far, when, without any warning, a teasing, sing-song voice intruded in upon his private thoughts.

"Heh, Fornucks!" the big, red-haired man taunted from the leathery comfort of his g-couch an arm's length away. "I'd be lying to you, man, if I didn't tell you the truth—you are one'a the *ugliest* velcroids I ever did see!"

Before Fornax could open his mouth to object, the crowded capsule echoed with derisive laughter as the other three hooligans joined in to boisterously ratify Red's disparaging opinion with a few of their own.

Fornax cringed uneasily. He was totally out of his element here and quite unaccustomed to dealing with slugs as crude as these four. But rather than debating his swarthy good-looks with them, he decided instead to keep his mouth shut and play blithely along. Unfortunately, this only served to whet their appetite!

Catching the scent of an easy mark, the four DUMPSTERS circled like sharks at a kill. Slinging slurs at him and meting out a fusillade of cutting remarks, the jackals ridiculed Fornax with adolescent vigor. And when he refused to stand up for himself in the face of their verbal barrage, it only made things worse!

It was everything Fornax could do not to respond to their taunts with his fists. Indeed, he thanked his lucky stars they were all strapped into their seats for takeoff. Lord knows what kind of a pommeling he might otherwise have taken at the hands of these morons! After everything he'd already been through thus far just to get here, about the last thing Fornax wanted now was a physical confrontation right before lift-off.

Though Fornax wouldn't have put it past these cretins to beat him up just for the fun of it, help was at hand. Much to his relief, Butch, the crew member seated directly in front of him, jumped to his defense, promptly silencing the pandemonium before it could get any further out of hand.

"Leave the poor sap alone!" Butch instructed sternly, twisting around in his seat to address Red over his shoulder. "If you don't settle down, and I mean right now, I'll have no choice but to report you to launch control!"

Infuriated at having been told by Butch what to do, for an instant it looked as if Red might burst free of the restraints holding his giant hulk of a body in place. But then, to Fornax's dismay, Butch qualified his order. "We'll get 'im *later*, when the Cap's asleep!"

Again the four cretins howled with laughter, and again Fornax held his tongue. He was perfectly aware that his doctorate in physics would not impress this bunch of hyenas in the slightest. Considered the dregs of the world, they were contemptuously referred to by outsiders as DUMB-sters, rather than DUMPSTERS. They had a reputation for being a dangerous lot and Fornax had come prepared to defend himself should matters deteriorate that far.

Anticipating that he was now but moments away from being assaulted, his palm slid smoothly across his abdomen and came to rest just above his belt. Holstered snuggly beneath his cotton shirt was the comforting length of a long, steel blade. Firmly grasping the hilt with fingers that spoke of strength, Fornax was on the verge of drawing it into his palm when the threatening banter suddenly died down.

In the background, a mechanical whine penetrated the hull of the ship as if a large, geared wheel had begun reeling in a heavy cable.

"Heh, ugly!" Red taunted again, his breath still reeking of tortan. "Try real hard now not to wet your diapers . . . main engine is 'bout to kick in!"

Then, with a belch of bright-orange flame, the giant thrusters burst to life, sending a shudder of acceleration coursing throughout the ship. As the thunderous roar of the engines reached his ears, Fornax clenched the padded arm of his launch-chair in exuberant terror.

He was on his way to the moon!

• • •

Hong Kong Province, China
10:00 a.m., same day

The self-proclaimed monarch chewed the long whiskers of his flowing mustache as he gazed unseeingly out the picture window of his palatial drawing room. Although the stately, royal gardens spread out in front of him were exquisitely manicured and the lawns immaculately well-groomed, it wasn't with an air of satisfaction that he surveyed their expanse. To the contrary, a joyless scowl colored his tawny face.

And why should this be? Did he not possess practically everything in the whole world? Did not hundreds of millions of loyal subjects humbly address him as "Overlord"? Was not unspeakable wealth his to do with as he pleased? Was not unfathomable power at his beck and call?

All true, and yet it wasn't enough! The status quo never was, especially for a man of his ambitions, a man who had never once been content with the size of his dominion, a man who sought nothing short of world hegemony!

Indeed, bored and frustrated by the lack of recent triumphs on the battlefield, Overlord Ling Tsui had spent many an unhappy hour these past few months plotting out how to expand his empire further. To that end, he had paraded one general after another through his luxurious parlor to listen to and weigh their often less-than-brilliant ideas for new conquests.

But as of this morning, he had heard nothing to suggest that even a single one of these supposedly-great military minds had given the matter so much as a second thought. And, in the case of one particularly pompous naval officer, Overlord Ling even questioned whether or not the man had ever even *had* an original thought! Having reached the pinnacle of their careers unscathed, having long ago lost their taste for danger, the only thing his pathetic flock of generals cared to do now was play it safe until retirement. *This,* however, was definitely not what Overlord Ling had in mind.

The Chinaman was hungry for power and did not wish to be ministered to. He ached to risk it all, if need be, that he might extend the borders of his kingdom. He would let nothing stand in his way—and certainly not his very own people!

What Overlord Ling was searching for was a new class of weapon, a weapon unlike any the world had ever seen, one whose effectiveness had not already been blunted by his enemies' equally awesome defenses.

In this era of unending stalemate, guns and bombs were impotent. And with each nation shielded against attack by its own protective umbrella of missile-killing satellites, even missiles and the like were redundant.

Biological weapons weren't much better. Though they had proven themselves successful far beyond their users' wildest dreams, the simple truth was, they accomplished nothing. While mass genocide guaranteed an almost certain victory, with no subjects left standing in the vanquished nation for the victor to lord-over, the triumph was rather hollow. For a man of Overlord Ling's ego, that took quite a lot of the fun out of winning!

No, what Overlord Ling needed was something new, something no one had thought of before, something more powerful than missiles or guns, yet something more pervasive, more sinister—something along the lines of a massive power-cell.

Like a Zeus sitting astride Mt. Olympus, Overlord Ling Tsui had reached the conclusion that if he was to have any hope of ruling the terra firma below, he would first have to dominate the high ground of space above. In defiance of the odds, the moon seemed the only logical place for him to start.

The sudden buzzing of the comm jarred him from his self-indulgent daydream. Thee emperor growled irritably as he opened the contact. "Who in the blazes is it?" he roared.

A familiar voice greeted Overlord Ling from the other end. The speaker was a fat and unusually gruff man; only today, the disagreeable man began almost apologetically.

"Sire, I beg your forgiveness for this most untimely interruption, but I have just hired a most unusual fellow."

As the sweaty man spoke into the comm, his eyes slanted more noticeably, crinkling at the corners. Unlike the Overlord in his ornate and polished surroundings, this man was calling from a spartan, poorly-lit room harbored in the corner of a dilapidated building just inside the main gate of the DUMP compound. An electric window-fan clanged noisily behind him in its timid struggle to move the heavy air around the muggy room.

When Overlord Ling spoke now, he made no attempt to hide his impatience. This bothersome flunky calling him from the Sri Lanka spaceport was a man he held in low regard. "Tell me, Chou, in what way is this man you hired unusual? Isn't every DUMPSTER a misfit? Aren't they all unusual in *some* way? Aren't they all muggers and rapists and the like?"

"Admittedly so, but this chap was different," Chou Kim replied, shifting his bulk to try and get comfortable. Even as he spoke, the caller couldn't help but remember the sober, intelligent eyes and the clean, well-manicured hands of Fornax Engels. "In fact," Chou Kim continued with forced politeness, "I almost *didn't* hire the man for that very reason. He seemed so . . . so . . . well, honest. He was bright-eyed and cleanly shaven and . . . "

"Let me see if I have this straight. You are calling me in the middle of the day—and on my private line no less—just so you can tell me you have hired a man who knows how to *shave?!*" the Overlord exploded, outraged that one of his lackeys would bother him with such a triviality. "You fool! I should send Whitey and that deranged daughter of his down there to extract your goddamned fingernails!"

"No, sire, I beg of you," the underling whimpered, a bead of sweat forming on his Cro-Magnon brow. "Anything but those two!"

Screwing up his courage before he continued, the fat Oriental labored to swing his rolling bulk ever closer to the impotent fan. "This bloke I hired was traveling on an Auckland passport. Now, before you get mad and start shouting again, I'm well aware that, taken alone, an Auckland passport is not all that unusual; only, judging by the color of the man's skin, this fellow was almost certainly *not* a Zealander. I made a point of interviewing the taxi-driver who brought him up here from town, and he confirmed my suspicions—the man's an Afghan."

"Is that a fact?" the despot chirped, his pointy ears suddenly perking up. At the mere mention of the word, Overlord Ling began climbing out from beneath the folds of his overstuffed chair. He sat, perched now, on its edge like a falcon. "I detest Afghans!" he roared. "My eldest son was shot down by one of those mongrels. In the uprising. Five years ago."

"I had heard that," the almond-eyed Chou replied, feigning sympathy.

"The airchop my son was piloting crashed, killing not only him, but wiping out most of his battalion as well. It was a terrible loss," the Overlord groaned painfully. "Eventually we turned it around, overrunning the emir's mountain stronghold and taking most of the rebels prisoner, but it hardly made up for the death of my son. In retribution, I ordered the captives tortured, but they were tough, tougher than I expected, and not a single one of them would give up the murderer's whereabouts. To a man, I had the insolent bastards put to death."

The Overlord's normally-forceful voice drifted off, and his next words were but a whisper. "Though I've never been able to trap the scoundrel responsible for killing my boy, I will never forget the man's name so long as I live."

The potbellied man from Sri Lanka protested vigorously. "A thousand apologies, sire—I had no idea his being an Afghan would resurrect such painful memories for you. But the truth is, that is not what I found particularly unusual about this man."

"Get on with it, then!" the annoyed Overlord demanded, his temper rising.

"According to that taxi-driver I told you about, the bloke arrived here on the island by tube."

"By tube, eh? Now, that *is* interesting."

The Overlord's fu-manchu mustache moved sideways from a mouth formed by restless suspicion. He knew perfectly well that no one less than a citizen carrying a certified passport could gain access to the tubes. But more to the point, it would only be under the most extraordinary of circumstances that a citizen of such affluence would find himself desperate enough to seek employment as a DUMPSTER. Chou Kim was right! There was indeed a glaring incongruity here, one that needed resolving.

"Maybe I misjudged you," the Overlord harrumphed, offering the lumpish Sri Lankan a feeble compliment. "What is the name of this Afghan dog, anyway?"

"Fornax Engels," came the muted reply.

There was a protracted silence as the Overlord digested this new information. When finally he did speak, it was with deliberation, as if he were carefully selecting each and every word.

"Fornax is a rather curious and odd-sounding name; indeed, in my entire life I have only come across it on one previous occasion. Engels, on the other hand, is fairly common among Zealanders, though certainly not among Afghans."

"My thoughts exactly! But, sire, if I may—I would wager Engels is but an alias!" Chou bubbled triumphantly, as if he were the only one smart enough to have figured it out.

"Oh, would you now?" the Overlord sneered, his voice laced with sarcasm. "Sometimes, your intelligence overwhelms even me," he added cruelly.

Then, before Chou Kim could respond, Overlord Ling abruptly changed his tone and began issuing orders. "I must know more about this Fornax Engels," he said.

"Your wish is my . . . "

"Of course it is, you tubbalard, and don't you ever forget it! Now, this is what I want you to do: radio the Captain onboard the ship and instruct him to learn why this Fornax Engels is posing as a DUMPSTER. Tell him to apply whatever amount of pressure is necessary and then to report his findings directly back to me. Is that understood?"

"Why, yes, my Overlord," the slit-eyed underling obediently replied, his jowls quivering loosely.

"And you, my chubby friend, you are to hire someone to trace this man's steps backward to Auckland. Maybe we could use our old friend Lester Matthews for the job—he's based in Melbourne and he's always in need of a fast buck. And be quick about it, Chou—I have little patience in such matters. I want to know what this Fornax Engel's real name is, and I want to know right away!"

His instructions given, the Overlord slammed the comm down into its holder, shattering the receiver in his fury.

"Fornax Engels, indeed!" he muttered, staring at the two broken pieces in his hand. "After five long years, at last my son's death will be avenged!"

And with that, the die was cast.

2
To The Moon

Slammed into his seat by the thunderous roar of acceleration, Fornax broke out into a cold sweat when the rocket leapt skyward. Thrown to one side by the twisting, thrusting yaw, an involuntary tear streamed out of his eye and across his cheek.

The explosive ride up through the atmosphere was unnerving. Yet, as abruptly as it had begun, it was over just as quickly. In under a quarter of an hour the launch-vehicle had reached docking orbit, and then—in only a matter of a few minutes more—had coupled with the waiting DUMP shuttle. As Fornax would soon discover, on the other side of that docking ring lay a strange new world.

While the shuttle itself was enormous, the crew's actual living quarters were absurdly small. Nearly all of the ship's mammoth size was consumed by the giant cargo-bay and more than half of what little space remained was given over to the navigational and life-support systems. The five of them would be gone approximately one week, and during that time, would have essentially no space they could call their own. Most of their time would be spent either in the miniscule galley or else in the adjoining commons. Outside of a tiny cubicle that doubled as a toilet and showering stall, that was all there was to the ship. And even that space was so cramped as to hardly be functional. Plus, with potable water at a premium, one two-minute shower per person per week was the absolute maximum. As for the toilet, it was equipped with so many belts and straps, figuring out how to use the darn thing properly was a mystery Fornax would not solve for at least several days.

Though Fornax might have preferred it otherwise, he had to make do as best he could. The crew members lived literally right on top of one another, with no hope whatsoever of even a moment's privacy. By night, they slept stacked up like steaks in a freezer; by day, huddled around a tiny table in the galley sipping tortan-ale.

Not that his modest flat back home was roomy or even vaguely luxurious, but here onboard the ship, each man had little more than a narrow bunk and a tiny desk to himself. Fornax found the crowding unconscionable, and for perhaps the first time since he arrived, began to appreciate what drove men like Red to drink until they couldn't see straight. Only a measure of tortan could dull a man's senses sufficiently to permit him to endure these jam-packed conditions for long.

Until Fornax stood in the galley staring out through one of the ship's two porthole windows, he had no sense of the spacecraft's wicked spinning motion. But then, several times in rapid succession, he observed the Earth flash briefly into view, and then just as quickly, back out again. Even in the space of those few blurred instants, his propensity for motion-sickness began to get the better of him.

Though Fornax judiciously averted his eyes from the twirling scene almost immediately, the damage was already done—his stomach had begun doing somersaults and a cold, clammy sweat had broken out on his forehead. With his head woozy and his heart pounding crazily, Fornax was just about to beat a hasty retreat for the toilet when an authoritative voice suddenly boomed out to him from across the room.

"Now listen here, you dirty bastards!"

Sweating profusely, Fornax turned to greet the first cleanly-shaven, sweet-smelling person he had encountered in several days. The newcomer was a big man; yet unlike Red, he was rock-hard muscular. The sour look on the new man's face said it all: he didn't think much of the sight—or the *smell*—of his fresh crew.

"My name is Captain Michael," he roared, "and you are my meat for the next seven . . . "

Increasingly disoriented by the deleterious effects of the micro-gravity, Fornax reached out for a handhold, finding small comfort in a knob protruding from the bulkhead. Summoning every last ounce of willpower, he held fast, trying to concentrate on what the Captain was saying to him and the rest of the crew. But the room was spinning swiftly out of control!

His skin flush, Fornax sagged weakly to one side. As he stood there ailing, the blood slowly draining from his face, he had the dreadful sensation of drowning in deep water.

Struggling valiantly not to go under, Fornax held on for as long as he could. But it was useless. As soon as he caught one further glimpse of the whirling Earth through the viewport, the Captain's voice faded to nothingness. In the next instant, his cement-like legs began to buckle beneath him, and, stricken with nausea, he began a slow, miserable descent to the floor.

"Hah!" Red sneered to everyone's delight as he went down. "Ugly *and* weak-kneed, eh?"

Collapsing in a crumpled heap upon the deck, a trickle of drool oozing from his mouth, Fornax was already too far gone to hear Red's sardonic remark.

• • •

When Fornax came to, the viewport had its face turned away from the Earth and towards the Milky Way. Transfixed by the wondrous scene, he stared hard, striving to gain some perspective on the vast distances of the void, to gain some appreciation for the family of strange objects which inhabited the cosmos. It was a boundless ocean of dark planets, white comets, and bright stars. He wondered whether the universe had an end—an edge, really—or whether it went on forever. Perhaps it even curved back upon itself as Durbin had claimed. If so, what lay beyond?

Captain Michael's stern voice interrupted his musings. "So, Earth-lubber, have you found your space-legs yet?" he asked, openly referring to Fornax's fainting spell.

"Yes, sir, I think I have," Fornax answered gravely. When he spoke, his dark eyes reflected their owner's exceptional intelligence.

"Listen, boy—you're not at all like the sort I usually get 'round here. Just who the hell are you anyway? Some sort of government inspector? An industrial spy?"

The question caught Fornax completely off-guard, and before he could even fashion an answer, the Captain had already grabbed him by the shoulders and thrown him roughly up against the bulkhead.

"You don't look much like a DUMPSTER to me, boy!" the Captain declared, turning Fornax's hands palm up. "Your hands are too clean. And you don't talk much like one either. You've been to high school . . . or beyond. I'm giving you fair warning, whoever you are—stay outta my way or else I'm gonna slit your throat with *this!*"

Into Fornax's still up-turned palm, the Captain slapped the steel blade he had happened across while Fornax was out cold on the deck.

"Captain," Fornax stammered, his dark complexion reddening as he reholstered his blade, "you have got to believe me. I don't work for any government agency, and I'm certainly not an industrial spy. The truth is, I'm a graduate student doing research for my dissertation."

That statement, while a total fabrication, was nevertheless still close enough to the truth to cover his likely questions throughout the remainder of the trip.

Eyes narrowing in disbelief, Captain Michael hesitated to accept Fornax's story. "You're a lousy *college* student?" he declared, quite unconvinced. "I don't believe it. And even supposing that you were, what kind of research would lead a soft-bred Zealander like yourself to risk his gonads with an infernal bunch of degenerates like us?"

"Well, sir," Fornax stuttered, doing everything he could to maintain his self-control. "I took this trip so I could have a firsthand look at the DUMP. All that energy is going to waste out there and I'd like to have a chance to measure the ambient level of radioactivity for myself. My treatise will examine whether or not some of that waste-energy can be put to any practical use."

Still doubtful, Captain Michael said, "Son, those are some mighty hot rocks you've come here to study. The radioactivity out there is so high, we've had to switch to dee-dees just to protect ourselves while working out at the site."

"Dee-dees?"

"Double-density suits," the Captain explained. "I've told the Sri Lanka brass that the moon will melt down one of these days, but they just don't seem to give a damn."

"Are you serious?" Fornax exclaimed, suddenly interested.

"Do I look like I'm kidding? Even the surface rocks three kilometers away are throwing off heat! They're warm, I tell you—four degrees Fahrenheit. I measured them myself," the Captain boasted proudly. "Don't forget, college boy, the rest of the moon's hindside is several hundred degrees *below* zero. I'm talking four degrees *above* zero. Put that in your thesis and smoke it!"

Confused, yet excited by the implications, Fornax queried the Captain further. "May I quote you on this?" he asked.

"Hell, no! I'd lose my bloody job!" Captain Michael stormed. "When I informed Chou Kim of my temperature readings, he told me to mind my own damn business. When I asked him why, all he said was that if the Greenies ever caught wind of it, they'd shut down the moon DUMP for sure—and then we'd *all* be out of a job."

"The man's probably right," Fornax conceded, remembering the fat Oriental who had practically refused him work when he first arrived on the island to apply for a job.

"On the other hand," the Captain reflected, scratching his head shrewdly, "if your research could find a way to sop up some of that excess energy, well, that would be another story, now wouldn't it? In that case, my job would be secure. I might even earn a promotion."

Fornax gave the man a knowing smile. "I catch your drift, Captain."

"I prefer, Michael. Or, Captain Michael."

"Okay, Captain Michael, thanks. My friends call me Fornax."

"You'll have no friends here, Fornax. Keep that blade of yours close. And don't wander too far afield once we land."

With that sobering piece of advice still hanging in the air, Captain Michael excused himself to attend to other matters.

Staring after him, Fornax could barely contain his excitement. He was ecstatic about what the Captain had told him, and there was absolutely no hiding it! Already mesmerized by the prospect of converting mounds of worthless nuclear wastes into untold riches, Fornax sat cross-legged on his bunk, and—notepad in hand—eagerly began sketching out a picture of the battery-like contrivance which had been brewing in his head since that insightful night with his telescope a month ago.

While it was admittedly true that what he conjured up on paper now fell short of being a detailed drawing, it was also true that the design he penciled was comprehensive enough to include all the major elements of the atomic storage cell he had already dubbed the "Fornax Battery."

Over and over again he thought of it as he worked—one man's garbage is another man's dinner! What Earthlings threw away with careless abandon could perhaps still have some value! This battery of his—if it worked (and who would be naive enough to doubt that it would?)—just might be powerful enough to propel a freighter across the ocean or even send a shuttle hurdling through space! It could be worth a fortune! Corporations—even governments—would stand in line to buy his invention! No price would be too steep, he confidently predicted, still hastily etching the lines on his pad in a delirious bout of greed. He could charge whatever he wanted!

It wasn't all wild-eyed avarice, though; his hypothesis was firmly grounded in the little-known phenomenon of "halo" nuclei. As far back as the twenty-first century, particle-physicists had discovered that, in certain nuclei, some of the constituent neutrons would venture out beyond their normal positions to form a misty cloud, or halo, around the nucleus. Whereas normal nuclei were difficult to excite or break apart, halo nuclei turned out to be rather fragile. They were larger than normal nuclei and interacted with them more easily. In fact, the halo was a quantum phenomenon which did not obey the laws of classical physics in any way. Indeed, the exotic-metal durbinium was one of the few stable substances known to regularly exhibit halo properties.

As a general rule, only those nuclei containing roughly equal numbers of neutrons and protons were stable enough to occur naturally on earth. Yet, strangely enough, nuclei having *unequal* numbers of neutrons and protons were known to exist as well, though their lifetimes were somewhat limited. That is, although they were bound—meaning, energy was required to remove one of their nucleons—they were unstable. Beta radioactivity could change them into a more stable species by transforming some of their neutrons into protons, or vice versa. It was *this* property—a remarkable effect called "tunneling" in the lexicon of quantum mechanics—which made halos possible. Without it, there could be no Fornax Battery.

According to his calculations, a razor-thin strip of the specialty-metal durbinium ought to be susceptible to saturation by precisely the sort of high-energy neutrons the Captain had suggested were streaming out of the DUMP craters in great quantity. Though there was no way to predict in advance how long this neutron-absorption process would take, once it was concluded, the delicate, fully-charged durbinium strips could then be inserted into a modified energy-exchanger. To control the rate of neutron release, a standard regulator would have to be linked to the exchanger using an improvised O-ring coupler of his own design.

Conceptually, anyway, the picture was complete, and upon lifting his hand from the paper, Fornax proudly surveyed his finished sketch. Seeing it made his mind race with nervous anticipation. After months of uncertainty he had finally identified all the key elements required to make this fascinating jig-saw puzzle a reality! The real task, the one which lay before him now, was how to go about collecting up all the separate components.

The problem wasn't so much in securing a standard regulator; they were inexpensive and manufactured in great numbers for use in the newer generation fission reactors. Even modifying an energy-exchanger to suit his purposes, while somewhat more of a challenge, wouldn't be all that difficult. No, the formidable obstacle would be in acquiring the finely-machined strips of durbinium he needed. *That* was going to be the real problem!

Not only was durbinium expensive, the military had classified it as a strategic alloy. For all practical purposes, the metal was off-limits and unavailable to a civilian such as himself. Though Fornax hated to admit it, the harsh reality was that the metal's inaccessibility represented a stumbling block he couldn't easily circumvent. For a man of his intelligence, this was damn aggravating!

All Fornax really had thus far was a smudged sketch of an unconfirmed hypothesis. It was all so much theory until he could actually build the thing—and that would be impossible without an ingot of durbinium!

Suddenly demoralized by the seeming futility of his enterprise, Fornax slammed his notepad down on his tiny desk, then stomped dejectedly off towards the galley for a stiff mug of tortan-ale.

It never occurred to him that someone might take an interest in his unattended pad of paper.

• • •

Later That Evening

Muffling the sound of the latch, Captain Michael gently pressed his cabin door shut. As the crew had already retired for the evening, only Red, the night officer, was still up and lurking about at this late hour. Even so, Captain Michael wasn't taking any chances; privacy was essential for what he had to do!

Hoping to avoid drawing any attention to himself by using the comm in the forward cabin, Captain Michael had no alternative but to place the two calls from the extension back in his cramped quarters. Except for the telltale green light on the main console adjacent to the galley, no one onboard the ship would even know he was on the comm. Even Red, as inquisitive as he normally was, was unlikely to notice the console light—

the Captain had just spoken with the man and, night duty or not, Red was already in a tortan stupor. Now, if Captain Michael could just keep his voice down, he should be in the clear.

Lights dimmed and door shut behind him, Captain Michael encoded the first number into the comm. He wore a face of impatience as he waited for the call to be patched through to its destination. The ship was a third of the way along its looping trajectory to the moon, and there was an audible crackle on the headset as the radio signal raced at the speed of light from the shuttle to a relay satellite orbiting high above the Earth. From there the signal would be routed through a bundle of switches to a receiving dish on the ground, and then passed on by cable to the recipient's handset at the other end.

Despite his many years as a shuttle commander, Captain Michael had never quite gotten used to the sluggish response of the comm at such a distance; tonight it seemed like an eternity until a voice finally came on the line.

Though the voice was clearly audible over the headset, the Captain recognized at once that the speaker was not addressing him, but was instead talking to someone else there in the room with him. There was no mistaking what was going on at the other end—while the Overlord was fumbling with the broken comm in his hand, he was scolding one of his servants for some grievous error.

"How in the world am I supposed to hold the damn thing if the handle is busted? Didn't I tell you yesterday already to have this damn thing fixed?" he yelled, obviously taking a great deal of pleasure from rebuking his domestic. "Who the hell is on the line, anyway?"

"I have no idea, sire," the Captain heard the female servant reply meekly. "You instructed me never to answer your private line."

"Insolent dolt!" the Overlord boomed. "If I've told you once, I've told you a thousand times: I hate it when a subordinate insists on telling me what I have already told them! Why can't you get that through that pretty little head of yours?"

"Well . . . I don't know . . . I mean, I'll try . . . really, I will," she groveled humbly.

True to his character, the Overlord wasn't about to break off his attack just yet. He was unrelenting in his pursuit of servility. Shaking a bony finger at the cowering woman, he said, "I know a man who will teach you the meaning of obedience, young lady. If you are not more attentive to my needs, I will arrange for you to spend a long, unpleasant night with my friend Whitey and that crazy daughter of his. How would you like *that?*"

Cringing with fear, she pleaded. "I *will* try harder; I promise I will! May I be excused now, sire? . . . Please?"

"Go!" he bellowed, his voice echoing down the great hall. "Be gone from my sight!"

Turning his attention from the house-servant, the Overlord barked into the comm. "This had better be important!" he said. "I'm not in a very good mood today."

"My Lord, this is Captain Michael. Reporting as ordered."

The Captain spoke softly, not wishing to upset the Overlord further. Then too, he didn't want to risk being overheard by an eavesdropping member of his crew. Butch, especially, had impressed him as a double-crossing scoundrel, but then Fornax was a question mark besides.

"Well, if it isn't my good friend, Captain Michael!" Overlord Ling declared graciously. "I certainly didn't expect to hear from you so soon. A convenient lull onboard, perhaps?"

"By ship's clock it's nighttime here," the Captain replied. "Which means I can speak to you without any prying eyes looking over my shoulder. Besides, this might be my only opportunity for days—once we insert ourselves into moon orbit, things get awfully busy 'round here."

"Very sensible; as always. So tell me: did Chou Kim reach you with my message?" the restless tyrant asked, nervously chewing on the tail of his mustache.

"Yes, he did, but I cannot imagine what was going through Mister Kim's mind for him to bother you with such a nonsense. Near as I can tell, there is absolutely nothing to this Fornax fellow—nothing at all. The boy's merely an overeager preppy intent on impressing some thesis committee with his own daring first-hand report detailing the activities taking place up here at the DUMP."

"You expect me to *believe* that?" Ling suddenly exploded, his almond-shaped eyes dark with fury.

"Yes, sir, I do," the Captain gulped, a lock of blond hair slipping across his worried forehead. He had no wish to be caught in a lie, and suddenly he found his stomach churning. "I know Chou Kim is a good man, but I think he has us chasing a shadow this time," the Captain added, shifting uneasily in his cramped cubicle.

"You do know how my son died, don't you?" Overlord Ling Tsui asked, a tinge more reserve in his voice now than before. "The bastard who killed him was named Fornax Nehrengel. My intuition tells me that this is one and the same man."

"That's preposterous!" the Captain exclaimed, surprising even himself with his sudden boldness. "This has got to be a case of mistaken identity! This Fornax fellow you're talking about here is no war hero, for Chrissake—he's a pantywaist! What makes you think this is the same man who killed your son?"

"I could be wrong, of course, but I have my reasons. Either way, I want you to keep a tight watch on him," Ling commanded. "And just to be certain, I want you to fax me a copy of his gene-prints right away. I'll have my people in Afghanistan compare them against Nehrengel's army records as soon as we can locate them."

"Consider it done," the Captain obliged, almost too quickly.

"You might be interested to know that Chou Kim has hired your colleague, Lester Matthews, to run a background check on our enigmatic Mister Nehrengel. Thus far, Matthews has learned that a Fornax Engels landed in Auckland three years ago onboard a freighter en route from SKANDIA. The ship's skipper remarked that he had never seen a man with a worst bout of seasickness in all his life. That's as far back as Lester has been able to track him, but it did make me wonder."

"About what?"

"People who get seasick typically get spacesick as well, don't they?"

"Usually," Captain Michael agreed hesitantly.

"Has your Fornax fainted?" the Overlord quizzed. "Has he been nauseous or sick to the stomach?"

"Not in the least," the Captain lied. "Healthy as a horse."

"Curious," the Overlord grumbled in what could only be described as a disbelieving tone. "I look forward to a full report upon your return."

"Until then," Michael stipulated, throwing the switch and breaking the connection. Already his mind was focused on his next call. Compared to the one he had just completed, this one was going to be a walk in the park!

• • •

"Couldn't this have waited until you returned?" the hefty, gray-haired gentleman challenged, his heavy British accent camouflaging his displeasure.

Like a big, carnivorous beast, the man was hunkered down behind an enormous wooden desk. The pale glow of a Victorian-style lamp illuminated the desktop in front of him. An umbrella-stand stood in the corner by the door. His office, simple yet elegant, was buried deep within the bowels of a giant complex of red-brick government buildings. Bulletproof glass darkened his windows.

"Considering what I'm paying you, Michael, I should have hoped you'd have more sense than this. Calling me on an open line—indeed, from a shuttle of all places—seems rather shortsighted to me."

"Some days it hardly seems enough," Captain Michael griped, making a fist of his muscular hand and rapping it vigorously against the steel bulkhead. The thump could be heard reverberating throughout the entire hull of the ship.

"What's not enough?" the man from London asked.

When silence answered him from across the miles, he rephrased his question. "Tell me, old friend: *what* isn't enough?"

Lamenting on the hazards of being a double-agent for a man as unforgiving as this one, the Captain frowned before answering. "The pay. That's what isn't enough."

"You are free to resign whenever you please," the man Captain Michael knew only as "J", coldly returned.

Even after all his many long years with the agency, Captain Michael was still uncertain whether the initial his boss went by was short for a proper name like John or James, or whether it might be an abbreviation for an official title such as Judge. For all he knew, the initial might designate that J was the tenth man to sit behind that desk, just as a name beginning with "D" might be used to designate the fourth hurricane of the season.

"Resign? You must be joking!" Michael protested, inadvertently raising his voice. "I have no wish to resign; but then I never took you for much of a comedian."

"The head of Commonwealth Intelligence has to be a comedian," J pointed out, his voice flat. "This is an exceedingly funny business."

"Yes—very funny," Michael admitted cynically. "Hilarious, in fact." Then, as if to add emphasis to his sarcasm, he forced out a strained, "Ha, ha, ha."

"Quit dancing about!" J ordered, his tone suddenly stern. "What is so bloody important that you had to risk blowing your cover for?"

"It couldn't wait, sir. I have a most urgent need for a set of gene-prints to be located and destroyed."

"Just like that?" J asked, taken aback.

The Captain chuckled lightly, picturing in his mind how distressed J must have looked, stranded like an ex-marine behind that swimmingly huge desk of his, an astonished frown plastered across his grizzled face. Like a mountain gorilla, J was a stout man with a dense mat of hair gripping his arms, the back of his thick neck, and even the tops of his swollen knuckles. Michael imagined that beneath the man's shirt his chest was like a gray forest, the hair on his legs, like an untended lawn.

"Just like that?" J repeated, his temper rising.

"Hear me out," Michael urged. "The gene-prints I need you to lay your hands on belong to one Fornax Nehrengel, a soldier loyal to the Afghan resistance some five years back. Unfortunately, I have no idea which sector he was headquartered in at the time."

"Finding those damn things sounds like an awfully tall order to me; that is, if they even still exist! Perhaps you have forgotten, my good friend, but you work for me—not the other way around."

"I haven't forgotten."

"Well then, perhaps you might explain why I should waste a valuable field-operative's time to track down and destroy some long-forgotten gene-prints?"

"Because that man—that Fornax Nehrengel—killed the Overlord's son in the uprising of '25."

"Good for him!" J congratulated. "But that still doesn't answer my question!"

"Even today, Overlord Ling still holds a grudge against the man who killed his son—and understandably so. That man may be onboard my ship even as we speak."

"Damnit!" J swore. "Get to the point! Why should I give a *hoot* about keeping this Fornax fellow alive or protecting his identity from Ling Tsui?"

There was a long pause as the Captain enjoyed his moment of sway. When he spoke, it was with cool detachment. "Within the hour I will fax you a copy of a sketch I found in his quarters. Once you have studied it, I'm confident that you'll agree we must keep this man alive."

"Sketch? What sketch?"

The Captain didn't answer; he had his own agenda now. "I insist the gene-prints be done away with, J. Plus anything else your people come up with down there which might connect *my* Fornax to this Nehrengel fellow. If there *is* a link between the two, I want it severed!"

"I'll take it under advisement," J murmured quietly.

"Oh, and one more thing. Rumor has it that one of our operatives is on deep cover inside Lester Matthews' organization."

"Is that a fact?" J replied noncommittally.

"Yes, boss, and it could be a very painful one," Captain Michael retorted just as curtly. "It would help matters a great deal if that agent were made aware that Ling Tsui had hired Lester Matthews to nose around in Fornax's past. Any co-operation in throwing Matthews off the scent would be much appreciated."

"I'll take it . . . "

"Yeah, I know," the Captain interrupted testily, "you'll take it under advisement."

"Listen, smart aleck!" J boomed in uncharacteristic anger. "In case you've forgotten, this is a dangerous business we are in here—very dangerous!"

"I thought you said this was a *funny* business," Michael snapped, unable to hold his tongue any longer.

This time, J let the Captain's crack go unanswered; he was ready to move ahead to new business. "Do you think he's on to you?" he asked.

"Who? The Overlord? No, sir, I don't believe he suspects a thing," Michael answered, leaving out the inevitable word "yet." Captain Michael was not the sort to admit that discovery was only a matter of time.

3
Dumping

As the moon's craggy surface came into sharp relief, Fornax's heart started pumping faster. The breathtaking panorama he knew almost by rote from his telescope back home, was now so close he could nearly reach out and touch it. Though the shadows played havoc with his depth perception, once the shuttle swung around to the far side of the moon, it wasn't difficult to pick out the DUMP site from orbit. Fired by the heat of a hundred thousand radioactive fuel rods, the three craters were seething cauldrons of energy bubbling on the surface below.

Adjacent to the most prominent of these three glowing orbs stood an odd collection of buildings, including an equipment shed, a quonset-hut which served as the crew's sleeping quarters during their short stay on the moon, plus a rather well-stocked armory packed with enough force guns, manual firebombs, and Tovex explosives to fend off a small army. In the event of a shuttle malfunction, there was even a tiny, two-man rocketsled outfitted for an emergency return-trip to Earth.

Once they landed on the moon, the lax and indolent mind-set of the crew shifted noticeably. While it would have admittedly been too strong a statement to say that their attitude became businesslike, it would also have been a fair assessment to say that, after three days of excruciating boredom onboard the shuttle, the DUMPSTERS became practically earnest about getting the job at hand completed with a minimum of horseplay.

Prompted by the emphatic glare of two, red warning lights mounted above the radiation-monitors next to the airlock, each crewman urgently gathered his tools and donned his dee-dee. Nothing less than a double-density spacesuit could shield a man from the harmful rays while working outside. As Fornax slipped on his own protective garb, he silently reveled at the neutron readings displayed prominently on the screen of the nearest monitor. The ambient levels were even higher than he had hoped—certainly high enough to make his Battery a reality! Armed now with this knowledge, Fornax was as impatient as the next man to get started.

The essence of unloading the cargo-hold was fairly straightforward, beginning with the correct positioning of an enormous funnel directly over the center of one of the glowing craters. Then, in orderly succession, the shuttle's maneuvering rockets would be fired to flip the spacecraft over, and—while the ship hovered overhead—the cargo-bay doors would be flung open and the "hot" load dumped into the outstretched mouth of the waiting funnel.

Though the process was simple enough in principle, problems invariably arose in the actual execution.

To begin with, the funnel was neither lightweight nor easily transported. To the contrary, hanging as it did by cables between the legs of an immense tripod, even moving it required the utmost care. At the base of each independently-actuated leg was a cab, and in the expert hands of the three cab-drivers, the tripod could be guided slowly across the moon's uneven surface riding on a trio of giant caterpillar treads. As the funnel was gradually filled from above, the leg-control operators had to continuously adjust the hydraulics to keep the whole assembly from becoming unbalanced and toppling over.

With Captain Michael at the ship's helm steadying the shuttle, the load was discharged. Three of the five DUMPSTERS sat in the leg-control cabs, while the remaining two (in this case, Fornax and Red) labored with shovels inside the cargo-bay to insure that all the fuel rods were directed into the funnel's gaping throat. Although gravity did most of the work, spillage was a constant threat, and rods were prone to slip out the side between the walls of the rectangular cargo-hold and the lips of the circular funnel.

Suspended by elastic safety-tethers, Fornax and Red toiled in the hold under the watchful eye of Captain Michael. Because the two men had been at each other's throats all day long, and because the Captain had two unforgiving bosses to answer to, he figured it only made good sense to keep both Red and Fornax in plain view. It wouldn't do the Captain's credibility any good to suddenly have Fornax suffer some unexplained "accident." Besides, Captain Michael had decided to do some sleuthing of his own.

He began innocently enough. "So tell me, Fornax," he said, his voice crackling through the comm from the main console where he sat. "All kidding aside, where are you *really* from?"

Wondering why the issue of his background should suddenly arise, now of all times, Fornax stopped work a moment to catch his breath.

"I'm from Auckland," he answered, puffing heavily. "Just . . . like my . . . passport says."

Near exhaustion, Fornax found himself stumbling clumsily about in the cargo-bay. Even with the benefit of the moon's low gravity, unloading the shuttle had turned out to be a mammoth job, one he was barely up to. Clad in their bulky spacesuits, he and Red had been working feverishly at it for nearly an hour now, and Fornax had become winded by the effort. These unwieldy double-density spacesuits, while impervious to radiation, were uncomfortable to wear and cumbersome to work in.

Not only was his body drenched in sweat, Fornax was beginning to suffer the ill-effects of working for a long stretch inside a suit. No matter how many improvements had been made in pressure-suits over the years, there seemed to be no escaping the bloating or constipation which accompanied their long-term wear. The worst of it, however, was the sweat. It rolled off his brow in an unending stream, dripping down the inside of his suit to places he did not know existed, and could not reach to scratch in any case. And now, as if to add insult to injury, Captain Michael's sudden interest in his nationality threatened to take an uncomfortable situation and turn it into an intolerable one.

"I know what your passport *says*," the Captain retorted. "But passports can be forged . . . even bought."

From where he stood, shovel in hand, face-mask clouded with sweat, Fornax could not see the Captain's face. He could read the man's tone, however, and it put him on his guard. Except for this morning's briefing in preparation for today's landing, the Captain had been uncommonly quiet since their last talk yesterday evening. Now, all of a sudden, there were all these questions! Clearly, something had happened in the interim, but what? Why should the Captain suddenly have a reason to be snooping around asking him about his nationality? Of what possible difference could it make?

Though Fornax couldn't fathom the reason, it occurred to him that perhaps someone, somehow, had informed the Captain that his certified passport wasn't genuine. If that were the case, Fornax might have a lot of explaining to do. Putting up a brave front, he said, "For Heaven's sake, why would I travel on a forged passport?"

"Why *indeed!* You tell me!" the Captain instructed, gazing out over the work area. From where he was stationed up in the cockpit of the ship, he could supervise the entire unloading process.

Suddenly a new voice entered the conversation. "Do you mean to tell me this ugly Fornucks is some sorta 'scaped *convict?*" Red exclaimed.

"Not at all, my dimwitted friend," the Captain remarked, knowing how his crack would rile the big man. "But he might be working undercover for some enviro group—or else for the union. For all I know, he's here to check up on you. To see whether or not you're doing your job properly."

"Mother of God!" Red cursed. "A union *scab?* I shoulda known! I didn't like the bastard from the start!"

"Nor I, you," Fornax snapped angrily back. "Like I told you before, Captain, I'm a college student, here doing work on my thesis!"

By this time Fornax was thoroughly confused by the whole treacherous turn of events. He kicked himself for having ever thought of the

Captain as a friend and made up his mind that until he had a better handle on the reason for this puzzling interrogation, he would reveal as little as possible about his true identity to these people.

"You may be a college student," Captain Michael granted, though Red grumbled in the background, "but you're certainly not from Auckland as you claim, are you?"

"No, I am not," Fornax confessed, attempting to be as circumspect as possible. "If you must know, I arrived in Zealand from SKANDIA."

"A dark-skinned runt like you from SKANDIA? No way!" Red exclaimed.

By now Fornax had decided that this conversation had gone off in the wrong direction long enough. It was about time he took the offensive—not only against this line of questioning, but against Red himself.

From the moment the two of them first met, Red had done everything in his power to make Fornax's life miserable. And after yesterday's humiliating episode in the toilet, Fornax figured he owed the man one. This seemed as good a time as any for payback.

Wrapping his powerful hands around the shovel-handle as if he meant to strangle it, Fornax thought once again of the preceding day.

In the micro-gravity of space, satisfying basic human needs was often difficult, if not annoying. Going to the bathroom, for instance, was nearly an impossibility, for the simple reason that, whether it was a wooden outhouse at the edge of a forest or a lovely ceramic privy on the second floor of a suburban home, Earth toilets depended on gravity, as did the people who sat on them. Here in space, therefore, certain conventions had to be observed before sitting down.

Yesterday's episode was a prank, pure and simple, and Red had set the stage over lunch by regaling them all with gross and disgusting stories of toilets-past and accidents narrowly averted. By the time Fornax made his way to the shipboard toilet for his first visit, he had already been primed for disaster.

Though there had apparently been some minor improvements in space-toilet technology over the years, to hear Red tell it, there had not been many. Early astronauts employed a plastic bag with a band of adhesive around the top which stuck to the circumference of the astronautical butt. To guide the fecal matter into the plastic receptacle, the bag was constructed with finger pockets. Although this method was antiseptic, the procedure was unsettling just the same. So much so that, on one pioneering flight, an astronaut was reputed to have "held it" for eleven excruciating days rather than use the facility.

Although urination for the all-male crews of early space ventures was a simple matter by comparison, the influx of women into the astronaut corps, plus widespread dissatisfaction with the fecal-bag system, brought a unisex toilet into general use. It was outfitted with a seal which was lodged between the toilet seat and the toilet-sitter's seat, a safety belt which was meant to be wrapped around the squatter's abdomen, and restraints for the occupant's feet. Once all the straps were secured, a suction device was engaged to pull the waste to the bottom of the toilet bowl.

Unfortunately, keeping a tight seal often proved impossible, and, as Red pointed out to an increasingly nervous Fornax, restraints weren't always up to the job of holding the sitter firmly seated. Accidents and their attendant messes were more common than the early astronauts would have liked to admit.

Thus, yesterday, it was with more than a little trepidation that Fornax approached the ship's lavatory for the very first time. Though not particularly worldly in any sense of the word, Fornax had encountered a great many privies in his day, from the muddy pit-toilets dug into the rocky battlefields of Afghanistan, to the utilitarian splendor of SKANDIA's finest kohlers, but never once had he confronted one as unlikely as the awkward-looking lavatory onboard the shuttle. It was a nightmare to behold, one made even worse by the childish antics of his vexing shipmate, Red.

No sooner had Fornax dropped his pants and completed the arduous task of strapping himself down, than the ship's fire-alarm went off. This was cause for panic, and he reacted accordingly. In the confined area of a spacecraft, even a small fire could consume the limited oxygen in a matter of minutes, killing everyone onboard. The only hope for survival lay in immediately donning an oxygen mask while the blaze was being extinguished.

After Red's harrowing tales of bathroom disasters-past, Fornax had to quickly ask himself which was more terrifying—bursting to his feet to grab an oxygen mask (and perhaps causing an unsanitary mishap in the process) or dying from asphyxiation. Neither choice seemed particulary attractive.

Torn between running to safety from the supposed fire and remaining perfectly still until he was done, the wailing klaxon lent a note of urgency to what was already a daunting challenge. Straining as hard as he could to finish, Fornax was all too aware that one false move could unleash a torrent of unpleasant and foul-smelling events.

Then, just in the nick of time, the scream of the siren began to wind down. For Fornax, it couldn't have come one second too soon; only, much to his dismay, a peal of laughter exploded in the hallway to take the siren's place. Unbeknownst to him, while he had been anxiously fidgeting on the john, Red and the others had been watching him through a small gap in the bulkhead. He had been duped!

That's why now, after three days of being the butt of every dimwitted joke his uncouth cohort could think of, after thirty-six hours of being the mark for every stupid antic this nitwit could conjure up in his head, Fornax was delighted to be standing across from Red with a shovel gripped tightly in his gloved hand.

"Heh, runt!" Red exclaimed, invading his consciousness in a teasing, sing-song voice. "You still with us?"

"Yeah, ya big oaf, I'm still here. You wanna make something of it?"

When Fornax spoke, it was with a haughty, determined tone. He'd been pushed around long enough, and it was about time he stood up for himself. Firmly gripping the shovel with both hands, he intentionally scooped up a fuel rod and chucked it into his partner's face-mask as hard as he could.

"You bastard!" Red screamed, enraged by the other man's temerity.

With anger-filled eyes, Red took hold of his own shovel, turned, and smacked Fornax across the abdomen with all the strength at his command. It was an incredibly powerful blow and the swipe sent Fornax reeling. In fact, under the force of the wallop he was flung clean out of the cargo-bay and into open space!

Fortunately for him, the safety-tethers were up to the task as they stretched tight, arresting his outbound trajectory. Drawn out to their limit, the elastic tethers recoiled, causing him to rebound like a missile. With his legs deliberately extended out in front of him like a pair of battering rams, he struck Red front-and-center with a full body-blow.

By now, all the DUMPSTERS were hooting and howling for one or the other combatant as a clumsy scrap exploded between the two men right there in the cargo-bay. First came the uppercut from Red, then the jab from Fornax, then the slam from Red.

Encumbered as they were by their protective dee-dees, it was practically impossible for the quarreling pair to have a credible fistfight. Nevertheless, in the minutes ahead, the two antagonists did their level best to beat the tar out of one another anyway. Seemingly unconcerned, Captain Michael let the fracas run its course, knowing full well that, wrapped up inside their suits as they were, Red and Fornax could hurt little more than each other's feelings. Indeed, for the next several minutes the two men wrestled with one another in among the spent fuel rods until they were both hopelessly winded by the drill.

When they were both so worn-out that neither one of them could even budge, their anger was replaced by laughter. They weren't exactly friends now, but by standing up to him, Fornax had successfully ended Red's reign of terror. More importantly, by breaking the tedium, he had put a stop to the Captain's cross-examination as well.

By the time the torturous job of unloading the cavernous cargo-bay was finally finished several hours later, the crew was exhausted and ready to retire to their bunks for the night. Unlike the carnival atmosphere in Sri Lanka three nights ago, this evening everything was much quieter and a bit more sedate. The quonset-hut here at the moonbase was a vast improvement over the Sri Lanka dormitory in yet another respect—without the bugs and the humidity, it was all that much more palatable and antiseptic. Not only that, but compared with the crowded accommodations onboard the ship, these quarters—though spartan—were refreshingly roomy and soothingly clean. It almost made life worth living again!

After an abbreviated shower to wash off the sweat of a day's hard labor stuffed inside a pair of dee-dees, sleep was foremost on everyone's mind.

As Fornax used the toilet in preparation for bed, he was comforted by the gentle tug of gravity against his bottom. He took that blissful, uninterrupted moment to gather his thoughts—so much had happened to him since that first day nearly a week ago when he set out from his tidy flat in Auckland for the Sri Lanka spaceport.

Though this undertaking had begun with uncertainty, whatever doubts he may once have harbored were now all but erased. If ever in the past he had had any misgivings about what he was up to, he was confident now that his Battery could be made to work. But to build a prototype, to construct a working model, he would need permits. And engineering assistance. And money—lots and lots of money! That, plus enough high-grade durbinium to run a proper test. Beyond that, he would have to return to the moon with the prototype, if only to be sure that the metal strips would take up a charge as he predicted. As for the permits and the rest of it, he would just have to see.

Securing a permit to transport durbinium onboard a shuttle might not be so easy. Even under the guise of doing lunar "research," he might not be able to satisfy the powers that be. The DUMP was administered, after all, by a quasi-governmental corporation which had little official interest in experiments or scientific pursuits. Its only agenda was to dispose of nuclear wastes for the four major terrestrial powers, plus a handful of minor monarchies. Space and space-exploration were ancient ideas, long since forgotten.

Even before the Great War, mankind's efforts to colonize the solar system had all but failed. The harshness of life on Earth's moon had easily cracked the will of its eager immigrants, and, despite a handful of noteworthy successes at the outset, disgusted terraformers had eventually given up on Mars as well. The once hopeful vision of man in space had all but evaporated, and might well have been extinguished, if not for Fornax's hungry ambition for wealth. Only *he* could serve to resurrect it!

As Fornax slipped towards the edge of sleep that night, such deliberations rolled through his head like a massive tsunami, a veritable flood of ideas which served to drown out every other thought. Over and over again they came, these waves, that night and on the long trip home. Fornax was eager with the prospect of making something of his idea, and each minute of the return flight seemed like an eternity!

• • •

Overlord Ling Tsui fiddled nervously with the hairs of his long mustache. Watching him fidget, an observer might have concluded that patience was not one of his virtues. Indeed, since learning that, centuries ago—in a world considerably less provincial than his own—comm service was quick and reliable, nothing spiked his anger quite like waiting fretfully for a long-distance call to go through. A man of his station and enormous ego just didn't like to be kept cooling his heels!

For one anxious minute after another, as the operators passed his call from one antiquated exchange to the next, he restlessly paced the marble floor until finally he was patched through to the city-state of Johannesburg.

The erstwhile Republic of South Africa was little more than a loose confederation of sprawling metropolises, each too weak to go it alone, yet each too powerful to willingly surrender their sovereignty to a central authority. On account of this power vacuum, these gritty urban centers had—like giant electromagnets—sucked in villains of every sort, from the White Brigade to the Lynch Brotherhood. Indeed, over the course of the last century, these garrisoned municipalities had become convenient havens for the world's finest assassins, its most notorious drug lords, and the most cutthroat of high-seas pirates.

Overlord Ling Tsui, the exalted monarch of China, had frequent uses for all three classes of scoundrels—pirates to harass and rob his trading rivals, drug lords to peddle his poppies, and assassins to eliminate his political opponents. It was a member of this last vocation who was on his mind today.

After several rings, an unexpectedly pleasant female voice answered the comm. "Good-day," she began politely. "Deaths-Are-Us, how may I direct your call?"

"Goodness gracious," the Overlord exclaimed, recognizing the woman by her accent. "Is this Marona?"

"It is," the tall, attractive female acknowledged, her well-kept hair bouncing sprightly as she spoke. Although on first glance she gave one the impression of being a soft-bred lady more interested in preserving her splendid fingernails than in soiling her lily-white hands, Ling knew better—he had seen this deadly femme fatale in action! Marona was rock-hard muscular and nearly as ruthless as her own father, a man who, rumor had it, was also her lover. This incestuous, sadistic pair was not to be taken lightly.

Marona identified the Overlord's familiar voice right away. "I assume you want my father," she suggested, her tone that of a professional. Not only was Marona as seductively beautiful as one of the mythical sirens, she was as cunning as a fox.

"Is Whitey home?" he asked with mixed emotions.

There were few men on the planet Ling feared more; fewer still that he needed as much. Though Ling had never met the man face-to-face, he imagined that Whitey's country estate was every bit as palatial as his own.

"Papa!" he heard Marona yell irreverently across the room. "Ding-a-Ling's on the comm!"

The Overlord cringed at the disrespectful nickname. Under any other circumstances he would have flown into a rage. But not today. Today he figured, why be critical of another man's daughter, much less his lover? There was nothing to be gained by it.

"Marona!" her father scolded in the background. "You ought to know better than to address His Highness that way. Really, honey, you know how he hates being called a ding-a-ling."

Marona giggled wickedly.

"That'll be quite enough, young lady!" Whitey barked, trying to sound stern for Ling's benefit. "Now hand me that comm."

"Yes, papa dear," she snickered, grinning at her father like a Cheshire cat.

"Overlord Ling, what a pleasure," the sinewy man declared, hoping to smooth over his daughter's rudeness.

"Cut the crap, Whitey!" the Overlord spat, irritated that the man hadn't apologized for his girl's impudence. "Let's face it, it's only a pleasure when I have a job for you."

"And do you?" the white-haired man inquired. Though his hair was white, it wasn't from years; nevertheless, those who knew him, and those who feared him, were unsure of his actual age. Even Commonwealth Intelligence, with all the resources at J's command, had little more than a vague idea how old the man was, or even what he looked like.

"Do I what? Have a job for you? Perhaps. But I must caution you, dear friend, this is a follow—not a kill."

Whitey reacted vehemently. His piercing black eyes blazing with passion, he exclaimed, "Forget it, Ling! We've been through this before—I only do *kills*, you know that!"

"Yes, of course, but I need you on this one," the Overlord pleaded, groveling about as much as his ego would allow. "The kill might come later," he added, offering up something of a carrot.

Whitey answered him, cool and detached. "Perhaps I would consider it," he said. "*If* the target were challenging enough, and the paycheck big enough. Who is the mark anyway?" the assassin asked, straining that raspy voice of his.

"Captain Michael," came Overlord Ling's matter-of-fact reply. The Overlord knew that Whitey and the Captain were well-acquainted and was curious to see how Whitey would react to the news.

Swift and unflinching would be the only way to describe his

response. When Whitey spoke, it was with an unconcerned, professional air. His intonation never revealed his inner feelings—if he had any.

"Captain Michael, eh? Well that's too bad. He is quite the pilot, you know."

"Didn't you two fight together in the war?" the Overlord asked. "Isn't he your friend, for God's sake?"

"Yes, of course, but this is business, isn't it?"

"Aren't you even the least bit interested as to *why?*"

"Not really."

Whitey's cool indifference was unsettling. Everything about him said: "Danger—stay away!" Like no other man alive could, Whitey rattled the usually unflappable Ling. The man was aloof and impassive, even more evil than Ling had imagined, certainly more evil than others of his ilk. This was not a man to be trifled with.

An anxious bead of sweat forming on his knitted brow, Overlord Ling became cautiously insistent. "Like it or not, I think you should know. Since you were both once friends, I feel an obligation to tell you."

"Knock yourself out, Ling," Whitey said quietly. "But do hurry—my Marona awaits me on the couch."

"I suspect Michael of being a double, working for me as well as for the Brits," Ling patiently explained.

"What's so unusual about *that?*" the assassin questioned. "I myself do jobs for your enemies all the time. It all depends on who pays the best at any given moment. Must I now live in fear of *you?* Do you intend to put out a contract on *me?*"

The Overlord gulped tensely. "Of course not! You're different."

"How so?"

"I'm *afraid* of you," the emperor confessed in shameful resignation.

"Good!" Whitey cackled with obvious glee. "Let's keep it that way, shall we?"

All else equal, Whitey preferred if his clients had a healthy fear of him. Much better for business that way. And to encourage that dread, he never hid the fact that—if the terms were right—he'd gladly accept a contract to kill anyone, including a previous employer. Yet, having said that, his favorite employer by far was Overlord Ling. Not only did the Chinaman pay well, he also regularly provided him and Marona with fresh young girls to torment.

Whitey continued. "So you suspect Michael of being a double. You might be right, you know—those boys over at Commonwealth Intelligence pay pretty well. Still, what makes you so sure?"

In the background, Marona could be heard cooing romantically for Whitey to come join her. Just the thought of father and daughter together on that couch sent a shiver down Overlord Ling's spine. As far as Ling was concerned, this conversation couldn't be concluded soon enough.

"Whitey, I can see you have other matters to attend to, so I'll be brief and not bore you with the details. Let me only say this: I very much wanted to put my hands on a set of gene-prints belonging to a suspected enemy of mine; yet, just hours before my people arrived on the scene, the district armory where the prints were being stored burned to the ground."

"And let me guess: Captain Michael was the only other person who knew you wanted those gene-prints."

Mortified, Ling mumbled his assent. "Not to put too fine a point on it, but yes."

"So he double-crossed you—what of it?"

"Enough already, damn it! Quit jousting with me!" Overlord Ling bellowed, momentarily forgetting his fear of the assassin. "Do you want the job or not? If so, you will follow the son-of-a-bitch until I tell you different. If he turns out to be a double-agent as I suspect, you get the kill."

"And if he doesn't? Then what do I get?" the killer probed, still angling for the upper hand.

"Yeah, ding-a-ling, what do *we* get?" Marona echoed from across the room.

"If, by some miracle, it turns out that your dear friend, Captain Michael, is *not* a double, I will ship you a truckload of little ladies to torture," Ling assured them both, gritting his teeth as he spoke.

"Ah, yes, more goodies! But include a red-head this time," Whitey urged, a sadistic smile filling his face.

"With freckles, dad. Please get me one with freckles this time," Marona yelled in the background.

"You heard the lady."

"Yes, I did," the Overlord panted, anxious to break the connection. "Count on me. Whatever will make you two happy."

"Now that's what I like to hear!"

4
Prelude To Chaos

Wellington Auditorium was one of those grand old lecture halls one might expect to find on the campus of a venerable ivy-league school. And, while the University of Auckland could not match the finest the Commonwealth had to offer, it certainly ranked among the very best in the southern hemisphere.

The four hundred and fifty student-desks were arranged in the amphitheater as they might have been in an ancient Roman senate, with each of the several dozen steeply-banked rows providing an unobstructed view of the podium, and of the wall-sized projection screen behind it. And, except for a single, wide aisle splitting the classroom in two from its entranceway at the back to the rostrum at the front, the closely-spaced, parallel lines of wooden desks were otherwise unbroken.

Exhausted by yet another fitful night without sleep, Fornax pressed himself into a seat in the eighth row and folded the aged desktop down across his lap. Twisting around nervously, he settled in for what he feared might be an hour or more of struggling to stay awake. He had purposely sat close enough to the podium that Dr. Sam might recognize his face, yet far enough away from it that he might escape notice should he happen to inadvertently close his eyes and fall asleep during the lecture.

Taking steps not to doze off just yet, Fornax examined the auditorium's ornate lines in a way he never had as a pupil. Though Fornax had spent untold hours sitting in this very lecture hall during his tenure as a student, he had never given the classic architecture a second thought. Not the oak-paneled walls, not the intricate wood molding which framed the ceiling, not the elegant light fixtures which hung from the canopy like so many pregnant apples on a tree, none of it—it had all escaped his notice until now. How could he have been so blind? Old or not, Wellington Hall was truly a magnificent place in which to conduct the mundane business of learning!

Feeling his eyelids grow heavy now, Fornax shook himself awake, remembering once again why—after returning home from the moon—

he had dared return to his alma mater, and why being in this particular room at this particular time was so important to his plans.

What had drawn Fornax here like a moth to the light, was money—or more precisely—the utter lack of it. Fornax was not a wealthy man; indeed, he was acquainted with only one person who was—his one-time college professor, Dr. Samuel Matthews.

Dr. Sam, as he preferred to be called, was a part-time economics instructor at the university. And among Dr. Sam's abundant idiosyncrasies, his obsession with the medieval practice of taking a vitamin each day had made a lasting impression on Fornax. Yet, despite his eccentricities (or perhaps because of them), Dr. Sam was considered an excellent teacher by most, and his classes were almost always booked to capacity. Only Wellington Hall was of sufficient size to hold them.

Fornax supposed that Dr. Sam's peculiar accent might also have contributed to the students' fascination with the man. While it was admittedly true that Dr. Sam spoke the language with absolute clarity, he was almost certainly not a native Aucklander.

More than two decades ago, driven by forces Fornax weakly understood, Dr. Sam had emigrated to Auckland from Alberta, Canada, his then-infant daughter bundled tightly in his arms. Rumor had it that even earlier than that, even before the Great War, he had escaped to Canada from somewhere in the former United States. Hence his unusual accent.

It was at the Calgary Institute that Dr. Sam had studied finance, and it was there that he presumably learned how to think as well. From the stories Fornax had heard circulating around campus, he had decided that it was this skill, Dr. Sam's ability to think, which accounted for the man's considerable wealth today.

Not only had Dr. Sam foreseen the Great War, correctly anticipating that in a desperately poor world America's immense affluence would make her the envy of nearly every other nation, he had also correctly gauged that the national currencies of the undamaged economies—like Zealand—would rise once the war was over. Dr. Sam's boldness in acting upon his convictions saved not only his life, but explained his financial success as well. As he was so fond of telling his students: "Good men predict, but great men act."

Fornax knew next to nothing about currency trading, but from what little he'd gathered, Dr. Sam had sold short the currencies of the countries he expected would lose the war, while simultaneously accumulating the currencies of the nations he expected to be victorious. Apparently, he'd won big on several of his speculations, and by the end of the war was reputed to be worth millions. In fact, the only misstep the man ever admitted to making—and the source of yet another one of his pet sayings—was the stand Dr. Sam had taken on the Commonwealth pound. He had bet against the Brits being among the victors—and lost. "Never count the British short," was the lesson he repeated ever so patiently to those who sought his counsel.

Despite his great wealth, Dr. Sam endured a lonely existence. He had lost his family to the war—his brother, his parents, and, as far as Fornax knew, his wife as well. Fornax didn't know the circumstances surrounding her death, but she had been dead at least twenty years, maybe longer.

With nothing else to keep him busy other than doting on his now full-grown daughter, Dr. Sam had taken refuge in his enormous estate up on the North Cape. They had met once, she and he, at a university function. Fornax had found her to be pretty in a tomboyish sort of way, though she'd also struck him as being somewhat aloof. He had put it down as an attitude which no doubt resulted from having grown up without a mother around to make a proper lady out of her. Damn shame, Fornax thought. What good's a woman if she doesn't know her place?

Yet, he also remembered her as being shapely, and now, as he sat fidgeting in Wellington Hall waiting for class to begin, Fornax struggled to picture the woman in his mind. Short on sleep and barely able to hold his head up any longer, he thumped his tired brain trying to match name to face. Was it Cathleen? Or perhaps, Katrina? No, that couldn't possibly be it! Maybe it was Corona? No, that wasn't it either!

When none of the names he conjured up seemed to fit her quite right, Fornax grew flustered. Finally, as the students began to file into the auditorium, he gave it up altogether, redirecting his attention to a much more pressing matter.

By coming to Wellington Hall early, Fornax had hoped to do more than just get a good seat, he had hoped to have a chance to scrutinize the face of each and every person who entered the room as it filled. Someone had been tailing him since immediately after he landed, and a crowded classroom seemed the perfect spot to ferret out that sinister someone.

The long, boring ride back home from the moon had undoubtedly put him on edge to begin with, but from the moment Fornax first stepped foot out of the return-pod back on Earth, he had had the impression of being followed. It wasn't merely that after a week of breathing the rarefied air of the shuttle that the "fresh" air of Sri Lanka had been thick with jungle humidity or choked with noxious exhaust fumes, there had also been an unmistakingly evil atmosphere surrounding the pudgy-faced Mister Kim. Fornax had been unable to avoid Kim's cruel, accusing stare—and that bothered him.

In the unhurried light of day, the launch-complex lacked the aura Fornax once imagined a spaceport should have. Trying to identify the source of his uneasiness, he found himself intrigued by the weird mixture of buildings which ringed the grounds. Some were framed with rust-pocked steel, others with paint-splattered stucco, still others with gleaming glass, and yet still others with dull-red brick. Sri Lanka's proximity to the equator had favored its continued use, and the facility had been in more or less continuous operation for more than two hundred years. But, having been completed piecemeal over the course of two centuries, its architecture lacked any grand design.

Unable to put his finger on what was out of place, Fornax was eager to put the spaceport behind him as soon as he cleared security. He left in the company of Red, and for probably the first time since they met, was glad for the big man's companionship.

Red was primed for a big night out on the town. His pockets were overflowing with a week's wages and his cheek was bulging with a plug of tobacco. Red insisted Fornax join him in paying a visit to Jaffna's glamorous Corkscrew Pub and the city's finest bimbooker-house next door. He dragged Fornax from the launch-compound and into a waiting taxi. Indeed, Red made the whole excursion sound so inviting, Fornax forgot all about rushing back to Auckland to start work on his Battery project and decided to have a go instead at bedding one of Jaffna's dark-skinned delights before he left.

By the time the taxi had wound its way across the hot, dry red earth of Sri Lanka and the spaceport had disappeared in the distance, Fornax suddenly found himself in a world far different from the quiet, civilized one he had left behind in Auckland just a week ago.

The downtown was dominated by a noisy bazaar where scruffy specimens of humanity peddled dubious bargains and questionable herbal cures. He and Red had come into the city during the Hindu festival of Nallur, and they were both astonished by the noise and mayhem in the marketplace. Even so, blinded by the prospect of being with a woman for the very first time, Fornax had ignored the unswept streets and unkempt people as the two of them elbowed their way ever deeper through the throng and towards the docks where the whorehouse was located.

Nearly engulfed by the mob of unruly celebrants, Fornax was soon separated from Red. Without the big man at his side, he felt utterly defenseless. And now that he was alone, the size of the crowds made him uneasy. On top of that, he had the distinct impression of being watched by some unknown hidden from view within the horde of rabble-rousers.

Unable to shake off the feeling of being followed, Fornax checked to be sure his blade was securely holstered beneath his vest. Then he shoved his precious passport even deeper down into his pocket. The man couldn't risk having the certified passport stolen because, without it, he'd never be permitted to board the tubes for the long ride back home.

As the neighborhoods Fornax drifted through became more and

more unsavory, and as he looked nervously over his shoulder time and again, the man found that he ached less and less for the sex he had come here for. Indeed, by the time Fornax caught up with Red again at the Corkscrew Pub, he'd changed his mind altogether about the tryst.

His ardor more than adequately cooled now by the seamy surroundings, Fornax promptly excused himself without so much as a swig of tortan. Then, to the jeers of his compatriot, he threaded his way back across town and towards the tube-station. There was no turning back: he simply had to get home!

Station security was tight, far tighter than usual—and with good reason. With the Nallur festival still in full swing, and crazies everywhere, a terrorist with a simple concussion-grenade could wipe out miles of tube in an instant. As a result, Fornax had to endure a long delay before clearing customs. As he stood there, anxiously marking time in line, waiting to be inspected, he tried to commit every face in the departure gate to memory, wondering all the while who would follow him—and for what purpose.

When he was finally permitted to board, Fornax literally bounded for the tube-car. Magnetology wasn't his field, but Fornax understood enough of it to appreciate that the magnetic pulses which coursed through the network of steel tubes connecting the major metro areas of the southern hemisphere would rocket his tube-car from here to his destination in a matter of hours. All things being equal, other modes of transportation in 2430 were slow-moving and dirty by comparison; the tubes were exceptionally fast and clean. And seeing as how his only other choice would have been to travel aboard a coal-burning steamship—something Fornax knew from experience he simply could not stomach—the man was thankful to have been able to afford the tubes at all.

Encoding the four-digit code for Auckland on the travel monitor, he settled in for the silent, underground ride back home.

Within minutes, the exhausted traveler was fast asleep.

5
Chaos

When the eleven o'clock buzzer sounded signaling the start of class, Fornax was jerked to attention. Like a fool, he'd fallen asleep practically the moment he settled into his seat in Wellington Hall.

As he shook himself awake now, it all came rushing back. Someone was following him—of that much he was sure—but who? Unfortunately, the "who" would have to remain a mystery a while longer. Fornax had made the mistake of nodding off for a short nap, thus missing a golden opportunity to figure out who that someone actually was.

Shaking his head with extreme irritation, Fornax glanced quickly around the room looking for anyone familiar. Though he had probably just blown his single best chance of matching up one of the students with the faces he had memorized back in the departure gate of the tube-station, maybe, just maybe, he would recognize someone. After thirty seconds of trying, however, he gave it up—the lapse couldn't be helped now, and there was no way for him to see everyone in the room without making it obvious that he was looking.

Judging by the number of empty seats in the auditorium, a fair number of students had begun the long weekend early. Fornax wondered whether Dr. Sam would be disappointed. Then again, for a warm spring Friday in September, it was a turnout most professors could be proud of.

As the ding of the bell faded in the background, the room grew quiet and Dr. Sam cleared his throat to speak. He looked a little older than Fornax remembered him, his uncombed hair somewhat grayer at the temples, his lean body a bit rounder than before. Nevertheless, his voice was powerful and his presence commanding.

"As you are no doubt aware by now," he asserted, "the name of this course is 'Advanced Micro-Economics.' However, the title of today's lecture is, 'When Butterflies Cause Tornadoes.' The connection between the two should be apparent shortly."

As he spoke, Dr. Sam wrote four words on the overhead transparency:

CHAOS INITIAL CONDITIONS FEEDBACK

"The word CHAOS lacks the poetry to properly describe what it is all about. CHAOS is about beauty. It is about symmetry. It is about ugly. It is about economics, the stock market, the weather, emotions, evolution, leaf shape, snowflakes, and war. In fact, everywhere you turn, there is CHAOS. Not chaos as in disheveled, but CHAOS as in a theory which helps us bring order to a seemingly disordered world.

"The first CHAOTIC system discovered corresponds exactly to a mechanical device—a waterwheel. This simple device proves capable of surprisingly complicated behavior. Imagine that water pours onto the wheel from the top at a steady rate and each bucket on the wheel leaks steadily from a small hole in the bottom of the bucket. If the flow of water onto the waterwheel is slow, the top bucket never fills up enough to overcome friction, and the wheel never starts turning. It remains motionless with the water leaving and entering the bucket at the same rate. If the flow is faster, the top bucket begins to fill, and its weight sets the wheel into motion. The waterwheel settles into a rotation which continues at a steady rate.

"If, however, the flow is made faster still, the rotation can become CHAOTIC. As the buckets pass under the in-flowing stream of water, how much they fill depends upon the speed of the spin. If the wheel is spinning rapidly, the buckets have little time to fill. Moreover, if the wheel is spinning rapidly, buckets are apt to start up the other side before they have had sufficient time to empty completely. As a result, heavy buckets on the side moving upward can cause the spin to slow down—and in some instances—even reverse! Over long periods, the spin can reverse itself many times, never settling down to a steady rate, and never repeating itself in any predictable pattern.

(Suddenly fascinated by the images of spinning waterwheels, Fornax found himself captivated by Dr. Sam's lecture.)

"The same properties can be applied to rotating cylinders of fluid as a result of convection. In a fluid, if heat is applied at too low of a rate to overcome viscosity, the heat will not set the fluid in motion. At the other extreme, fluid in a fast-turning convection-roll has little time to absorb more heat. CHAOTIC properties govern not only waterwheels, but also pots of boiling water, the spinning of Jupiter's Great Spot, Earth's weather patterns, the mutation rates of chromosomes, sunspot activity, and even the currency and stock markets.

(So that's why the man makes so much money trading the markets, Fornax told himself excitedly. He's learned *how* to think, not what to think!)

"The behavior of a dynamo like the waterwheel provides a good model, though not quite a full explanation, for many of the peculiar reversing-phenomena we see in the world around us. Take the Earth's magnetic field, for example. This 'geo-dynamo' is known to have flipped many times during the Earth's history, at intervals which seem both erratic and inexplicable. Theorists typically look upon outside causes, such as a meteorite collision, to explain these anomalies, but perhaps the flip-flopping waterwheel is a better model of this seemingly CHAOTIC behavior.

"Perhaps motion in the nearly fluid, molten iron core of the Earth explains the flipping magnetic field; perhaps motion in the gases of Jupiter's atmosphere explains the behavior of her Great Red Spot; perhaps motion in the currents of the oceans' waters helps explain low pressure areas. The concept of CHAOS might also help explain such seemingly erratic phenomena as changes in the stock markets. Water falling onto the waterwheel at certain speeds produces explosive changes in the waterwheel's velocity much akin to sudden weather explosions like tornadoes, or explosive changes in stock prices like investment panics.

"The rate and direction of rotation of the waterwheel depend upon the rate of flow of water onto the top bucket. The surface conditions of a pot of boiling water depend upon the rate of flow of heat into the pot. The rate of mutation of genes depends upon the rate of flow of radiation into the biosphere. Lurking everywhere is a quality of sensitive dependence on the initial conditions of the system. Small perturbations can have large consequences. A man leaves the house in the morning, thirty seconds late, a flowerpot misses his head by centimeters, and then he is run over by a gtruck. An unimportant Duke is shot, and the world is plunged into war.

"But CHAOS requires more than just a set of initial conditions. Feedback is also required. All the buckets are attached to a single waterwheel; thus, the information each bucket contains—as gauged by its depth—impacts the depth of the water in each of the other buckets by changing the rotation speed of the wheel. The murder of that Duke in the central Europe of the early 1900s would not have led to world war without the feedback effect of treaties which required reactions based on others' actions. If the selling of stocks reduces prices sufficiently to trigger margin calls in enough accounts lacking adequate equity, investors will be forced to sell even more stocks depressing prices further, and triggering stop orders which bring on yet another round of selling. INITIAL CONDITIONS. FEEDBACK. Both are required for CHAOS.

"Nearly five hundred years ago . . ."

(The lecture continued on, but Fornax was no longer paying attention. He had come here to the university for one reason, and one reason only, and that was to ask Dr. Sam for money, money to cover the probable expenses of his Battery project. It was high time Fornax rehearsed his lines, because no matter how many times he went over them, this wasn't going to be an easy sell. For openers, Dr. Sam was an eccentric man. He held unorthodox views on life. Indeed, his cavalier attitude towards dress said it all. The man believed life had value and didn't want to squander it thinking about clothing. Dr. Sam couldn't imagine anything more boring than fashion. Professional sports, perhaps. Grown men swatting little balls around while the rest of the world paid money to applaud. On the whole, though, he found fashion even more tedious than sports, and as Fornax thought about it now, it suddenly occurred to him that, being the abstract thinker that he was, it might not be in Dr. Sam's nature to speculate on newfangled gizmos. If trendy clothes didn't faze the man, would something as farfetched and unproven as the Fornax Battery? Had Fornax come all this way for nothing?

(Suddenly fearing the worst, Fornax sat there for a long time afterwards wrestling with his doubts. Twenty minutes passed before he again tuned in to what Dr. Sam was saying.)

" . . . but, folks, consider this: it may be all wrong! Linear thinking implies that with enough data and a big enough computer, you can solve for all the unknowns in all the equations and arrive at all the answers. And so, in *theory*, you can find the tax rate which optimizes growth and employment. In *theory*, you can find the market clearing price for a good, or choose the level of output which maximizes profit. But, alas, the world isn't linear, and you have ignored all the feedback effects. Higher profits attract more producers who flood the market producing *lower* profits. Technology invents substitutes for high-priced goods in short supply. In reality, economic activity does *not* align itself on smooth lines. In fact, economic activity is turbulent and uncertain. There *are* no equilibriums in the real world. Only in the *models* of the real world are there equilibriums. And there are no predictions! The only way to know the future is to watch it unfold!

"The business climate is as difficult to predict as the weather—and for much the same reason. Both weather and business cycles exhibit CHAOS. Will a tax cut increase economic activity? Or will it precipitate some secondary effect in the bond and currency markets which cascade into a result quite different from what was expected, in fact causing a *decrease* in economic activity? This is what we in economics call the 'butterfly effect'—a severe, but very localized hail storm triggers rumors that the corn crop may fail in a remote corner of the Ural, which sets off sell programs on the Hong Kong Mercantile Exchange leaving a South African floor trader caught short on a huge unhedged corn contract, which causes a run on his clearing bank in Melbourne, setting off a stock selling panic on the floor of the London Stock Exchange. Feedback may cause small, even inconsequential, events to be magnified in a series of cascading steps which produce completely unexpected changes in the outcome.

"CHAOS theory also has implications for the introduction of new technology. For instance, why doesn't the best technology always win in the marketplace? Frequently, technologies become de factò standards not because they are better, but because they get *marketed* better, or marketed *sooner*. High expectations often fulfill themselves as customers buy an expected standard, leading investors to invest their money in it, and third parties to write software for it, and schools to instruct their students about it. There is a favorable chain reaction which reinforces itself to implant this new technology as the 'standard.' And once implanted, it will not be dislodged except by another, even more powerful, cascade of events. This same type of interlocking critical mass, or self-reinforcing chain reaction, may help explain take-offs triggering such things as the Industrial Revolution, or meltdowns leading to the Dark Ages, or even the mob psychology propelling a Hitler or a Rontana to power.

"Well, folks, time's up. We have come from waterwheels to weather to economics. There are no straight lines in nature. There are no equilibriums and there are no predictions. However, CHAOS theory *does* open the door for men of insight to harness such cascades to their advantage. Remember: Good men predict, but great men act.

"Class dismissed."

6
No

The students shifted nervously in their seats as they gathered their belongings and quickly headed out the door. Although Dr. Sam had given them plenty to think about over the weekend, it was lunchtime for most and the spring-like weather was rather inviting.

Fornax lingered in his chair as the crowd thinned. He was still stunned by Dr. Sam's final words. They echoed back at him syllable by syllable: *CHAOS theory opens the door for men of insight!*

Of course! Fornax exclaimed silently. It all made perfect sense! Dr. Sam relished pitting his wits against the markets! Stocks, bonds, precious metals, currencies, you name it—the man spent his time playing out a cascade of events and speculating on their outcome. Such was the nature of his intellect! That's what the man was all about! That's how he'd made his fortune; that's how he intended to keep it. By investing in what he knew best, and avoiding all the rest.

Making his way down the center aisle and up towards the front of the lecture hall, Fornax glumly swallowed his rising fears. While Dr. Sam undoubtedly understood the forces which moved markets, he clearly wasn't a venture capitalist. He wasn't the sort to take a chance on the Fornax Battery!

Thinking that perhaps it wasn't too late for him to turn back, Fornax stopped mid-step. But then he changed his mind. Even if his chances were slim, he still had to try.

Undaunted, Fornax summoned all his courage and pressed forward to the podium to present his case. Extending his hand out in front of him, he opened the conversation with a smile.

"Hello, Dr. Sam. My name is Fornax Engels. I doubt if you remember me, but I was once a student of yours. It's been several years, though."

At first, Fornax was unaware of the pleasant-looking girl approaching the rostrum from behind him, but as he stood there waiting for a reply, Dr. Sam acknowledged her presence with a nod and a toothy grin. It was the sort of look a loving father would give his only daughter.

Dr. Sam made no attempt to accept Fornax's outstretched hand, but he did take a moment to study the young man's face. After an instant, he declared, "I remember you. You were that very bright and overly-ambitious boy who was pretty impressed with his own prospects. As I recall, you were preoccupied with making money. 'As much as I can, as fast as I can,' I believe you once told me. And now, am I to suppose that things have suddenly changed? If not, then to what do I owe this pleasure? What am I to make of your being here today? It has been perhaps four years since the last time you sat before me as a pupil, and since I haven't seen or heard from you even once in all that long time, I assume you are here today to ask me for money, money to fund some harebrained scheme which will make you—and perhaps me as well—richer than Midas. Does that about cover it, boy?"

Dr. Sam's bold comments unnerved the younger man, and it took Fornax a moment to rein in his surprise. "Doc, your intellect is as keen as ever," he stammered. "And, yes, that does about cover it. Will you listen to my harebrained scheme anyway?"

"Son, I am already richer than your legendary King Midas. Besides, I am having lunch with my daughter today. Maybe some other time," he snapped tersely, brushing back a swatch of uncombed hair from his forehead.

Fornax stood his ground. "Sir. If I may. This will take just five minutes of your time."

"You have ninety seconds," Sam advised. "Do get on with it."

As Sam's daughter drew nearer, she nodded a silent hello to Fornax. Instantly enchanted, he took the lead, praying that he had remembered her name correctly. "Why hello, Katrina. If memory serves, we met once at a BeHolden Day rally."

Carina ignored the incorrect moniker. "I do not recall," she said smugly.

Glancing impatiently at his watch, Sam barked sternly, "Ninety seconds!"

Thinking to himself that she was still every bit as shapely, still every bit as aloof as he remembered her, Fornax began his explanation: "Dr. Sam, for generations now we've been dumping nuclear wastes—used fuel rods mainly—on the moon's far side. These fuel rods, while still lethal to us and to the environment, lack sufficient kick to power our turbines here at home. Up there," Fornax went on, pointing towards the heavens, "there are three craters just *filled* with the stuff. Believe me, sir, when I tell you. I've been to the moon; I've seen the DUMP with my very own eyes. These craters are emitting absolutely *prodigious* amounts of energy!" he announced, brimming with excitement.

"And, except for what's being absorbed directly into the moon itself, most of that energy is being uselessly sloughed off into space. If I can get the funding, I propose to capture some of these highly-energized neutrons using a lattice-work of finely-machined durbinium strips. Once they have been charged, these strips can be inserted into a modified energy-exchanger and, voilà—a battery powerful enough to do some really heavy lifting. It might even be able move a shuttle!" he said, concluding with a proud flourish. "I call it the Fornax Battery. So, there you have it, and all in under ninety seconds!"

Giving Carina a quick once-over as he wrapped up his speech, Fornax briefly wondered what she might be like in bed. But when she caught sight of his lustful stare, her eyes shouted emphatically back: "Not a chance, buddy!"

Having listened intently to Fornax's presentation, and having just witnessed the quiet exchange between his daughter and this swarthy-looking man, Dr. Sam abruptly exclaimed, "You are still a very bright young fellow; still very ambitious; and still have little more than making money on your mind. I am not a scientist, mind you, thus I do not understand the physics of your battery. And I will not invest a farthing in something I do not thoroughly understand. My apologies to you, sir, but no thank you, and good day."

Fornax was crushed. His eyes followed Dr. Sam as he turned, linked arms with Carina, and started to walk away. Then, all of a sudden, as if he had changed his mind, Dr. Sam stopped, took out his pen, and wrote a name and address on a slip of paper.

Handing the slip of paper to Fornax, he said, "Though I will not invest a dime in your damn fool idea, he just might. Tell him I sent you."

"Thanks for the referral," Fornax said, frantically studying the name and address. "And nice to see you again, Katrina. Until next time!" Then, happy as a clam, he went merrily on his way.

"He seems like such a weasel," Carina remarked to her father once Fornax was out of earshot. "Who *is* he? And to whom did you send him?"

"He *is* a weasel, but he is a damn smart weasel. I sent him to your uncle Lester, who is an even *bigger* weasel."

Linking arms, Carina and Dr. Sam strolled down the wide corridor of Wellington Hall and out into the sunshine with lunch foremost on their minds. A butterfly danced in front of their eyes and then across the schoolyard.

"Oh look, daddy!" Carina clucked gleefully. "It's a Tikkidiw!"

He just smiled. "Butterflies and little girls."

"What does *that* mean?" demanded Carina with an impish grin.

"Oh, just something your mother used to say. 'Butterflies and little girls don't need a reason.'"

• • •

The speaker was a stout, gray-haired man. From where he sat, hunkered down behind that big wooden desk of his, he managed to keep his fingers on the pulse of the world. And well he should, for he was perhaps the third most powerful man on the planet! Except for a map tube on the floor and two file folders on his desk, his office was tidy, almost pathologically so. He spoke with a heavy British accent, but loudly, as if, by itself, his voice had to carry the entire distance from London to the party waiting at the other end of the line. Today, his voice had a rare, congratulatory tone to it.

"Agent Cornwall," he said, "you and that fellow you hired—what was his name again?—did a wonderful job for me down there in Afghanistan. Fornax's gene-prints were destroyed just in the nick of time."

"Gandu. The man's name was Harsha Gandu. And thanks boss," the young recruit answered, gripping the comm with newfound confidence. "But, if I may, the Overlord's no dummy. It won't take him long to figure out who torched that armory, *or* that it was burned down on Captain Michael's recommendation. Which means that . . . "

"I can't fault your logic, of course; only, I'm too busy just now to take time out to worry about Captain Michael." By now J's voice had taken on an uncaring, condescending tone which caught Cornwall off-guard.

"But, sir, this will put him under suspicion!" Cornwall argued. "We must warn him!"

"I caution you not to get yourself too worked up over the good Captain. Rest assured, Michael can take care of himself. Besides, I pay him handsomely to recognize the risks *without* being babied. Now what about the rest of your report?"

Agent Cornwall swallowed hard, his sandy-colored hair underscoring his youth and inexperience. Endeavoring to please his boss even in the face of J's cold disregard for Captain Michael's safety, he made his report:

"As you ordered, I followed Fornax from the spaceport back to Auckland. At one point, I thought I had lost him in a crowd, but by staying with that red-headed buffoon he came into town with, I caught up with him again at the Corkscrew Pub."

"Did he make you?"

"Gosh, I really don't think so, boss," the clean-cut young man said.

"Did he take in a bimbooker?" J asked, snickering crudely into the comm.

"Believe it or not, he never entered the place."

"A strange fellow, this Fornax," the older gentleman remarked, squinting at the hurried notes spread open before him. Overhead, an ornate, nineteenth-century lamp splashed light across his desktop. In his hands was the dossier his people had compiled for him thus far on Fornax Engels, a.k.a. Fornax Nehrengel.

"Strange indeed," Cornwall muttered. "And between then and now, all he has done so far is to sit in on a lecture over at the university."

"Durbin Physics?" J guessed, glancing at the sketch Michael had faxed him from the ship that day.

"No, sir," Cornwall answered politely. "Interestingly enough, economics. Something about giant butterflies causing tornadoes, only . . . "

"A class in economics? Who'd have guessed it?" the head of Commonwealth Intelligence exclaimed in a disbelieving tone. "Curiouser and curiouser!"

"Sir, if I may," Cornwall volunteered, eager to impress his boss with everything he had learned. "The instructor was one Dr. Samuel Matthews. He seemed . . . "

"Good God!" J declared, his chiseled face suddenly looking more haggard. "That instructor—that Dr. Samuel Matthews you're talking about—he's Lester's brother!" Even as he spoke, J reached across his desk for a second, much thicker file folder.

"I don't understand," Cornwall stammered. "You mean *Lester* Matthews? As in the pirate who runs guns for the Overlord? As in the man whose organization BC has been working so long and hard to *infiltrate?*"

"Yes, yes, and again, yes!" Cornwall's demanding boss answered. "One and the same."

"But how can that be?" the younger man returned, his voice trembling. "This cannot be a coincidence."

Staring down at his dossier on Lester Matthews, J chuckled. "Our Mister Engels is quite the operator. He probably went to Dr. Sam with his hand out—Sam's quite wealthy you know—but given the man's reputation as a tightwad, he undoubtedly sent the boy packing."

"So, then it *was* a coincidence!" Cornwall said, a boyish grin leaping across his face.

"Maybe. And then again, maybe not. It is impossible to say for certain. Only time will tell."

"Oh, I nearly forgot," Cornwall conceded bashfully. "There is one other thing."

"And what might that be?" J asked, a hostile quality suddenly entering his voice.

"After Fornax and the professor were done talking, Sam handed the man a piece of paper. From where I was standing it was impossible for me to see what was scribbled on it, but when Fornax looked at it, he seemed genuinely delighted to have it," Cornwall said, his bright eyes beaming. "What do you suppose Dr. Sam gave him?"

The comm was silent a moment as J pondered the question. "An address," he answered, his clever mind churning. "Lester's address, no doubt."

"So, it wasn't a coincidence *after* all!" Cornwall exclaimed as if he had just unearthed a remarkable archaeological find. "So you think Sam's an Overlord agent just like his brother?" The way Cornwall put it, it sounded more like a statement than a question.

"Don't be silly!" J carped. "There are precious few men about whom I can say this with absolute assurance, but Samuel Matthews is one of them. I promise you—the man is above reproach."

"What then?"

"Lester has forever been obsessed with newfangled devices; anything which would make him wealthy beyond his wildest dreams. He has always coveted his brother's material success, a fact I am sure has not been lost on Dr. Sam. According to our information, Lester has repeatedly asked his brother for money and Sam has repeatedly turned him down. So I figure it is only natural that, no matter how promising Fornax's proposal may have sounded, Dr. Sam would have sent Fornax to Lester, if for no other reason than to assuage his guilt for having always refused to lend Lester any money. Either way, Sam lacks the entrepreneurial bent to exploit the device; he's a speculator, not a roll-up-your-sleeves businessman."

"I see," Cornwall mumbled even though he really didn't.

"I would wager that at this very minute Fornax is on his way to Melbourne to see Lester, a development which worries me a great deal. Too much is at stake here, Cornwall—Fornax mustn't be allowed to fall into the Overlord's clutches. I'll advise BC of our interest in this matter at my earliest opportunity, but I'll need you to stay on Fornax's tail no matter what."

"Yes, boss, whatever you say," Cornwall submitted meekly.

7
Traitor

"Yes, boss, whatever you say."

Agent Cornwall's timid words warmed J like no fire ever could, his ego feeding like a piranha on the carrion of a servile underling.

In his own way, J was just as lawless, just as ruthless, just as powerhungry as his rival, the Overlord. Both men made it their practice to employ others to do their dirty work, and each ruled his respective fiefdom by means of intimidation and bullying. Neither man felt so much as a tinge of remorse concerning the welfare of the people they puppeted—or of the people their puppets killed. Oh, there were some subtle differences between the two—the titles they bestowed upon their subordinates, for one; the phraseology they applied to rationalize the heinous acts they set in motion, for another—but aside from these nuances in style, both men were in fact broken from the same hideous mold.

Whereas the Overlord bluntly referred to his troupe of marionettes as hit men or assassins, J christened his yes-men with much nobler sounding titles, like operative or secret agent. And whereas J's armies slithered stealthily through the murky shadows in elite teams of one or two, the Overlord's armies trampled openly through the cultivated fields of *his* enemies in battalion-sized numbers.

Their only differences were in degree—and in the images they cultivated for themselves. "Do it for the Queen," one man might urge his recalcitrant charge. "Preserve the Emperor's honor," the other might demand. And while the wider public might say that the Overlord was an evil man deserving of their disdain and the minister of Commonwealth Intelligence a godsend responsible for defending the public good, in fact, the two men were both cut from the same piece of wicked and grimy cloth.

"Yes, boss, whatever you say."

Smiling widely, J repeated the words to himself as he hung up the comm. Nicholas Cornwall was one of his newest and most promising rising young stars, a man not yet jaded by the dichotomy of their dirty business, a man affectionately known in the trade as a virgin. If only everything could be that uncomplicated!

Turning again to the thick file which lay sprawled before him on his desk, J undid the elastic band which held it together and separated the cover from the papers inside. The top sheet was labeled, "For Eyes Only," and centered immediately beneath it was the name, "Lester Matthews."

J practically had the contents of the file memorized. Before sending BC in undercover, he had gone over and over it until he knew it by heart. But this time, he was searching for something different—any scrap of information which might help him to anticipate what Lester was likely to do once Fornax landed at his doorstep.

As far as Commonwealth Intelligence had been able to document, prior to the Great War Lester Matthews had been an Ensign assigned to the United States Navy (Southern Command). By the time hostilities broke out in the Pacific, however, he had been advanced in rank to full Lieutenant. In that region of the world the war accelerated rapidly out of control and his naval group was engaged in one pitched battle after another. Casualties were frightful.

Although it was never substantiated beyond a reasonable doubt, naval intelligence had it on good authority that in the fall of 2398 a traitor working a high-level contact within the American defense establishment managed to put his hands on a set of top-secret ciphers which he subsequently sold to the Chinese. These illegally obtained ciphers not only allowed the Overlord's people to crack an entire series of vital American military codes, they also allowed them to target and sink a portion of the unsuspecting American fleet lying just off the Chinese coast. It was a major setback for the United States and a colossal victory for Overlord Tsui.

At the time, Lieutenant Lester Matthews had been at the top of a short list of military personnel believed responsible for the treachery. However, nothing definitive was ever proven. The high-level American contact Lester was using reportedly collapsed and died before he could be interviewed, and Lester's frigate—the *Intrepid*—was purportedly sunk in the attack (along with most of the other warships attached to the Southern Command) before he could ever be brought up on charges. Without a criminal to court-martial and with the war nearly lost, his guilt became a moot point. No formal investigation was ever launched.

Even though it was reported in the American press that all hands onboard the *Intrepid* had been lost, there were in fact a couple of dazed survivors, among them Lester Matthews. Somehow—dehydrated and near death—Lester had washed up on shore somewhere along the Chinese coast. A peasant family from a nearby fishing village found him and nursed him back to health. Stranded halfway around the world from his native land, Lester soon adopted this rustic family and their pedestrian way of life as his own.

Far from the mainstream, Lester knew little of the daily progress of the war until after it was over. By the time the news that America had been defeated made its way upriver to where he was busy mending fishing nets, the former navy man had already forsaken his origins and embarked on a fresh career. Too cold-blooded to care that his parents had perished in the ferocious struggle for the American mainland or that they had died without ever knowing that he, their eldest son, had survived the attack on the fleet, Lester turned his back on the world. He was so bitter and twisted, so filled with resentment for his younger brother Sam, that it blinded any love he might once have harbored for his father or his mother.

To hear Lester's account of it, he had done his duty on behalf of God and country, nearly losing his life in the process, but Sam had risked nothing, nothing at all! In Lester's warped judgment, it was *Sam* who was the cowardly traitor, not himself. Not only had Sam not fought for his country, he had ducked his responsibility as well, by—to use Lester's words—"hiding out in Canuck-land shacked up with some Amerind half-breed."

Of course, J knew that nothing could be further from the truth. Lester's anger at Sam for staying out of the war was, at best, unfounded and at worst, a cleverly trumped-up lie designed to cover-up his own treasonous acts. In actuality, it had been Sam's grandfather—that same high-level American official Lester was suspected of stealing state secrets from—who had been instrumental in getting Sam, his only remaining grandson, to safety in Canada.

As for Lester, with his parents dead, his homeland destroyed, and his only remaining relative a brother not worth his contempt, he made a new life for himself in Asia. A seaman by trade, Lester soon graduated from mending nets to sailing square-rigs for the Chinese merchant marine. His ports of call included such far-flung places as Hong Kong, Tokyo, Shanghai, Brisbane, and Jaffna.

The Chinese merchant marines were little more than an angry army of pirates and mercenaries, and it was exceedingly dangerous for a white-boy such as himself. To survive in that kind of environment, Lester had to become even tougher and meaner than before. Even so, Lester was shrewd, and when he wasn't hatching a scheme to make money, he was out trying to bed any woman he could hold down long enough. Looks were of no consequence so long as he got it regularly.

Afraid that one morning he would wake up dead, Lester ultimately left the merchant marines to start up his own freight business serving southeast Asia. He began as little more than a gunrunner for thieves plundering villages along the Chinese coast, but in time graduated from supplying waring factions with force guns to smuggling stolen freight into blacklisted countries. Then, to provide a legitimate cover for his illicit activities, the man began hauling legal cargoes like appliances and furniture.

As Lester's business grew and his circle of acquaintances widened, he happened upon customers with "special" needs; well-heeled, but circumspect clients who, like the Overlord, had no petty qualms about breaking the law. In time, Lester began concentrating his efforts on the disposal of unsanctioned, illegal wastes at the DUMP. That is how Captain Michael came to be in his occasional employ, and that is how Lester eventually came to be in J's jurisdiction.

In struggling to halt the sickening flow of contraband-garbage finding its way from the Earth to the moon, Commonwealth Intelligence had targeted all manner of shady outfits, gradually narrowing the list of likely rogues down to but a despicable few. Lester's transportation company made the final cut, thanks in no small part to his reputation as an unprincipled double-crosser.

Even though J's people had no trouble accumulating enough damning evidence to send Lester to prison for transporting prohibited wastes, J wasn't really after him. Catching small fry, after all, was not what J was paid for—landing big fish was. And there was no bigger fish in the ocean than Overlord Ling Tsui. That's who J had his sights set on, and that's who J longed to bring down. But to do *that*, he needed his own people on the inside.

Captain Michael had been recruited from the Overlord's ranks precisely for that purpose: to help document the illegal shipments passing through Lester's freight terminal on their way to the moon. Meanwhile, BC, one of J's most highly-regarded special agents, had spent the last eight months working himself into Lester's inner circle.

Lester employed many hardy laborers in his operation and he rarely, if ever, made a delivery himself. So, when he set out alone one morning from his warehouse on the coast to personally gtruck a load cross-country, J's spotters followed close behind. They were excited because this could be the big break they had been waiting for. Thus far, their investigation had turned up nothing whatsoever which could directly link Overlord Ling to Lester Matthews—or to the unlawful refuse being dumped on the moon. J had become frustrated by the lack of progress, and understandably so.

Alas, the meeting Lester attended turned out to be of a sort much different than J's people had expected, albeit one in which Sam's honesty was forever after etched indelibly into J's mind.

It all began when Lester received a bill-of-lading to transport an expensive handcrafted piece of furniture from the manufacturer in Singapore to one Dr. Samuel Matthews on the North Island of Zealand province. As any brother might be, Lester was immediately curious.

The last he'd heard, Sam was living up north in Canada somewhere, keeping house with some swarthy Amerind squaw. That he should now be making his home down under came as a bit of a shock. For the life of him, Lester couldn't imagine how Sam might have ended up in Zealand. But one thing was for certain—Lester had to see for himself whether or not it was indeed his turncoat baby-brother that he had accidentally stumbled upon. And the easiest way for him to do that, would be if he delivered the clothes-dresser to Auckland personally. This he did, and when Lester arrived at Sam's estate, he was stunned by the enormity of the place. The rub was, Lester had spent his entire life trying to hit a financial "home-run" and it never occurred to him that bookworm Sam might be the one who would turn out to be successful.

When Lester introduced himself, Sam practically bit his head off. Here was this smelly, bearded laborer at his door claiming to be his long dead brother! The absolute nerve of the man!

"Listen, punk," Sam barked. "What kind of a cruel hoax are you trying to pull here anyway? So you know my name—big deal! Am I supposed to be impressed? Does that make you some sort of a genius? My name's on the goddamned mailbox for Christ sake! If you are who you say you are, then offer up some proof, man, or be gone. Get off my porch!"

"I have no *proof*, you jackass!" Lester retorted, his pathetic little mustache nothing but a humid smear. "I joined the Navy to serve my country, but *you* . . . you were a coward . . . you fled the country . . . you went to Canada instead."

"Coward? Why you bastard! How *dare* you accuse me of cowardice! I had no choice. If you were still alive after the attack on the fleet, why didn't you contact me? You knew where I was. Hell, we talked just days before you set sail. Don't you remember? I called you. I asked you to look in on grandpa just before he died. If you had wanted to reach me, I would have been easy to find. You know very well I sat out the war at the university."

"You sat out the war all right!" Lester boomed contemptuously. "You'll get no argument from me on that one, little brother."

"Don't be an idiot! Dad wasn't willing to risk a second son to the war and grandpa . . . "

" . . . was an old fool! He never once had a clue what was going on. And as for you, you abandoned your country in its time of need!" Lester said, his accusation downright vicious.

That was about all the needling Sam could take, so he swore, curled his fingers into a fist, and punched Lester in the face. The hard blow knocked Lester to the ground.

"You goddamned bastard!" Sam shouted, his anger driving him close to tears. "You stupid velcroid! They butchered my wife for Christ sake!"

"She was a damn half-breed," Lester said as he picked himself back up. "One of those prairie-niggers."

Sam punched him again, even harder than before. This time, Lester fell backward, spitting blood from his bruised mouth.

"If you were safe, you might have told me," Sam declared, towering over his prone brother. "As it is, you've been 'dead' for more than twenty years now so let's just keep it that way, shall we?"

At that point, Sam turned and slammed the front door shut in disgust.

Lester half-crawled, half-walked away from the encounter, leaving Carina's clothes-dresser on the front porch of Sam's mansion. That night it rained hard in Auckland and the handmade dresser, which Sam had left standing outside his house, was ruined. The next day Sam called the furniture company in Singapore to complain about the rude delivery man and the ruined dresser. A month later, Sam got a dental bill from an orthodontic specialist in Melbourne for repairing the tooth he had apparently loosened with his right hook. He gladly paid it.

Disputes between brothers are rarely solved easily and after that, unless Lester called asking for money, the two of them had infrequent contact.

Pushing back from his desk now, J closed Lester's file. A furrowed wrinkle creased his forehead. He had a pretty good idea now what would happen next, and he didn't like what he saw. Fornax would go to Lester with the plans for his device and Lester would go to the Overlord. Without some sort of miracle, J would be powerless to prevent this interlocking chain-of-events from happening—but then, he wasn't a man given to prayer.

• • •

His feet propped up on his shabby, pockmarked desk, Lester Matthews spoke in a swaggering, almost cocky tone. Clearly, here was a man who didn't know when it paid to put aside his pride and be humble.

"Overlord Ling," he said, "I have just scheduled a meeting with a most unusual young man, a man who has come up with a revolutionary new idea, a man you will almost certainly wish to meet yourself."

"Do tell," the Overlord retorted, his voice laced with sarcasm. Over and over again as they talked, he twisted the whiskers of his fu-manchu between the tips of his long fingers. It was a hideous ritual, and it made the man look as if he literally reeked of evil. "A new recruit, perhaps?"

"Oh, no, not at all," Lester objected, his own swipe of a mustache curling meanly. "This man claims to have made a technological breakthrough of stupendous proportion."

"So you said," Ling replied unimpressed.

"But to build this thing, I will need your help with permits and money and . . . "

"Lord of All Beasts Great and Small, when will it end? Don't you *ever* stop scheming?" the Overlord boomed at the top of his voice.

"But, sir, this isn't *like* the last time. I tell you, this is for real!" Lester said, salivating like a rabid animal. "This man has come up with a remarkable . . . "

"*What* man, damnit? What is the bloke's name already?"

Up to this point, Lester had purposely avoided any mention of Fornax's name, hoping to spring it on Ling at just the right moment. Sensing that he now had the Overlord just where he wanted him, Lester said the words as nonchalantly as he could.

"Fornax Engels."

"Fornax Engels!?" the Overlord yelped, nearly falling from his chair. "Did you say, Fornax *Engels?*"

"You've heard of him?"

"Yes, of course, I've heard of him, you fool! I hired you to find him, remember?" the Overlord thundered. "Have you gone daffy, man?"

"Not at all," Lester answered, enjoying himself.

"Okay, mister, you've had your fun. And all at my expense. Now let's get down to cases, shall we? First and foremost, I want to be kept informed. After you and this Fornax meet, I want to be brought up to speed right away on everything—and I mean everything—the man tells you about this miraculous device of his. Give him whatever he asks for—I will provide all the permits and materials he requires. I am worried, though, about this information leaking out before I've had a chance to act on it. Besides myself, who else knows about this?"

"Captain Michael, for one."

"You have spoken with Captain Michael about this?" Ling asked, his voice cracking as if an old friend had just died.

"Yes, but what's so surprising about that? When I talked with Chou Kim, he told me you had asked Michael to keep an eye on Fornax. Did I misunderstand him?"

"Not in the least. It's only that he never mentioned it, and he should have. Now, besides the good Captain, who *else* knows about this?"

"Well, let's see," Lester said, thinking out loud. "BC, my chief engineer; and my brother, of course. He was the one who originally referred Fornax to me. And maybe my niece as well. Is there a problem? I promised to meet with the boy the day after tomorrow."

"No problem at all," the Overlord said, already focusing his mind on his next move. "Lester, I realize that you and the Captain have worked together for me as a team in the past, but on this one, I have reason to believe he can no longer be trusted. I assure you, Michael will be dealt with in due time. As for you, you are to give him nothing further on this. Not a thing."

"But, sire!"

"I mean it, Lester. You tell him nothing! Disobey me on this—open your big mouth—and I'll have that devil-woman Marona sew it shut for you. I understand she just loves needles."

"Yes, boss, whatever you say."

8
Lights Out

For the third time in less than two months, Fornax Engels was again back on the moon. He was moving slowly from crater to crater, collecting up the thirty razor-thin slivers of durbinium he had set out to be charged on his last visit here a month ago. It was dangerous work, though he took some comfort in being shielded from the intense radiation by the impervious cloth of his double-density spacesuit.

Like a loving parent, he carefully gathered the fragile strips, methodically securing them one by one into the lead-lined pockets which ringed the inside of the three insulated cases he had brought with him from Earth. Unless properly stowed, the radioactive strips posed an extreme hazard to anyone who might accidentally come into close contact with them. Unprotected exposure to a fully-charged strip could be lethal, charring a human's flesh in under thirty seconds and killing an average-sized man in as little as three minutes. Once started, no heroic last-minute injection of Acceleron could hope to reverse the process.

But Fornax wasn't stupid, and he didn't need to be reminded that, given the risks, exercising extreme caution as he worked was an absolute necessity. At any rate, until he got back to the ship and had a chance to run the necessary tests, Fornax couldn't be sure of anything. Out here in the field he had no quick and ready way to judge whether or not the glowing strips had even *taken* a charge. And yet, a great deal was riding on that very question. If the neutron absorption had gone as Fornax predicted it would, Lester had pledged to finance a series of dry runs meant to confirm his Battery's capabilities.

At the time, weeks ago, this arrangement had suited Fornax just fine; now it weighed on him heavily. There seemed to be a yawning gap between the obviously pitiful resources at Lester's command and the sweeping dimensions of what he was promising to do—in fact, had already done—to speed up the progress of making a prototype a reality. Now, as Fornax knelt there in the crater gathering up the last of his precious metal pieces, he worried anxiously about what he had gotten himself into. And with whom!

Thinking back to that rainy day a month ago when he and Lester first met, Fornax resurrected images of how it all began. He remembered standing there in that muddy parking lot, kicking up chunks of gravel and peering through the downpour at the run-down exterior of Lester's warehouse. The condition of the building was laughable, and at the time, Fornax couldn't help but wonder whether his long trip by rail to Melbourne in search of money wouldn't turn out to be another dead end. If the owner of the building couldn't afford to patch up its roof or reattach its gutters, how could he afford to take a risk on a long shot like Fornax's Battery? But then again, did Fornax have a choice in the matter? No! He needed money, and, having come this far, he wasn't about to walk away empty-handed—not this time!

Eager to get out of the rain, Fornax entered the grungy warehouse, only to be met by two steroid-buffed guards cradling force guns in their beefy arms. The musclebound pair led him to Lester's office, a poorly-lit, poorly-ventilated room buried deep within the dark bowels of the musty freight terminal.

There he was greeted by an even grungier, common laborer whose dirty face was slashed by a wisp of a mustache. This scrawny, unremarkable man introduced himself as Lester Matthews and offered him a chair.

Fornax hesitated, unsure whether or not to accept the man's offer. It was all a bit unnerving: the whole place reeked of organized crime with Lester cast in the role of chief mobster!

Doing what he could not to show his fear, Fornax boldly reached out to shake the man's hand. Lester reciprocated, though reluctantly, then once again motioned him to sit. This time, Fornax acquiesced. As he made himself comfortable, though, the first thing that struck him was just how different Lester looked from his very own brother. Despite Dr. Sam's perennially uncombed hair, he always exuded the air of a well-bred gentleman, something Lester clearly was not.

No sooner had the two of them taken a chair than they were joined by BC, Lester's chief engineer. Unlike his seedy-looking boss, BC was a handsome, rugged man. He had the splendid build of someone who trained regularly with weights, someone whose very life hinged on his being fit, someone who endured not solely by his wits, but by his agility as well.

Frankly, Fornax couldn't see how a man of BC's particular abilities fit in with Lester's otherwise pathetic surroundings, and yet, Lester had made it clear when Fornax first scheduled that day's appointment, that he would have to convince BC if Lester was to sign onto the project.

So, without any further prompting, Fornax dove right in, laying out in careful detail the thinking behind his invention. By the time their talks were concluded several hours later, Lester was sold. More importantly, so was BC.

In exchange for being granted the patent rights, Lester agreed to supply Fornax with thirty durbinium strips, each to be milled according to Fornax's precise specifications. For his part, Fornax agreed to ride the shuttle back to the moon, deposit the strips, ten each, into the three red-hot craters, then return four weeks later with BC to recover the precious cargo and bring it home for testing.

Now, clad in his stuffy, close-fitting dee-dee, Fornax was in the process of completing that final step. As he trundled from crater to crater retrieving the rest of the strips, his forehead crinkled with doubt. He was in a quandary, at once perplexed by the abundant incongruities surrounding his partner, and at the same time swamped with misgivings about their entire association.

Take the permits, for instance. To transport hazardous materials onboard a shuttle required special vouchers, yet it had taken Lester only a matter of days to obtain them! At the outset, that speed had impressed Fornax to no end; now it only made him skeptical. In this day and age, no bloated, overgrown bureaucracy worked that fast, not without prodding anyway.

But that wasn't the *only* ambiguity! How to account for Lester's ease in rounding up so much high-grade durbinium—and on such short notice? Durbinium, after all, was a strategic metal. An unsanctioned sale to a civilian was a jailable offense; even military procurements were closely scrutinized by an industry panel. For Lester to have gotten his mitts on so much of it, he obviously had to have a friend in high places. But who?

And what about the money? Where was *it* coming from? Despite Lester's single-minded obsession with making lots of it, he clearly had none—none at all! If nothing else, the run-down condition of his freight terminal bore witness to that! So where was the money coming from?

Since Lester was unquestionably a small-time operator, the durbinium, the funding, and presumably the permits as well, had to have been provided by some mysterious partner, some allusive Mister Big with whom Fornax wasn't yet acquainted.

And if all of that weren't enough to give him pause, there was no longer any doubt that he was being followed. Where, earlier on, he had imagined being shadowed without any proof, now he was sure of it.

The typical DUMPSTER was, like Red, a drunken, unshaven, low-life; but on this trip, in addition to BC and himself, there was one other sober, well-mannered crewman aboard. Fornax knew this was no coincidence; he had seen this good-looking, young fellow with the sandy-colored hair once before.

Eyes never lied, and this set matched a pair he had scrutinized on the way to his first meeting with Lester just last month. That day, after exiting the tube at Brisbane, he had boarded a coal-burner for Melbourne. Between the overcast sky and the singing of the rails, he could have easily been lulled to sleep. But not wanting to repeat the mistake he had made once before in Wellington Hall, Fornax struggled to stay awake, long enough anyway to at least memorize every single pair of eyes riding with him there in that coach.

Masquerading now as a DUMPSTER, that same clean-cut fellow with the piercing blue eyes who had ridden with him that day in the coal-burner, was onboard the shuttle. This bloke who the Captain had introduced to him as one Nicholas Cornwall, was undoubtedly the same man who had been dogging him since the beginning. It was about time they were formally introduced and Fornax put a stop to this cat-and-mouse game! He would confront the man just as soon as he finished gathering the last of his durbinium, a chore which had become ever more strenuous the longer he stayed at it.

Much to his surprise, Fornax now found himself experiencing difficulty staying focused. For the first time since he began work collecting up the slender metal strips, his head had begun pounding from the effort. Immediately he suspected the culprit might be his oxygen/nitrogen mix. In his three trips to the moon and back he'd heard enough stories from Red and the others to know that if his mix was out of balance, that would account for his shortness of breath and slow reflexes.

Determined above all else not to become disoriented, Fornax set his cases down, leaned against a boulder, and took a long hard look at the three illuminated enviro-dials sewn into the sleeve of his dee-dee. The first measured internal suit pressure; the second, temperature; and the third, the ox-ni mix. All three needles were in the normal range, as they should be. But just to be sure, he tapped their pressurized faces several times. The pointers didn't budge.

Confused by the nasty way he felt, Fornax shook his head to dispel the groggy sensation. Maybe he was coming down with a cold. Maybe, if he stopped thinking about it, he'd feel better. Sometimes that helped in the past when he was about to be seasick. Maybe he should forget the whole damn thing and try to figure out what to do about this Cornwall character.

Who was this fellow *really?* And what were his intentions? Why had he followed him all the way to the moon? And what exactly was he after? The durbinium strips? That had to be it—they were, after all, quite valuable!

Almost by reflex, as if someone were threatening to run off with one of his cases, Fornax grabbed them up and held them tightly in his trembling hands.

He had suddenly come to the realization that if he *was* being tailed, that effort had to have predated his meeting with Lester. And if *that* were the case, there was no escaping the fact that no one less than Captain Michael must have been the instigator of this whole sordid affair.

But could it be that simple? It made no sense at all! What could the

Captain possibly hope to gain by having someone stalk him? Had Red or Butch or one of the other velcroids objected to Fornax's interest in the DUMP? Come to think of it, hadn't there been persistent rumors in the press about illegal dumping? Were the Lanka brass afraid he would stumble onto something incriminating in the course of his research? Or maybe the Captain wasn't involved at all! Who then? The fat Mister Kim? Hadn't he acted awfully suspicious when they first met? Or . . . ?

By now, Fornax's head was spinning with intrigue, and he still hadn't figured out who to trust. Fornax sensed that he was in over his head; he just didn't know why.

Captain Michael's words from their first encounter echoed groggily through his brain. "You'll have no friends here, Fornax. Keep that blade of yours close. And don't wander too far afield once we land."

Suddenly aware that he had indeed wandered pretty far afield from the rest of the crew, Fornax instinctively clutched at the pocket of his dee-dee. He had to be sure his blade was still securely holstered there at his side where he'd put it earlier. Though not an expert by any means, Fornax was competent enough with a blade to defend himself in a pinch. Somehow he felt certain that skill was about to be put to the test.

Thinking back now, it occurred to him that Lester must have been concerned about his safety as well. Otherwise, why send BC along? Though Lester had given BC and Fornax strict orders to behave as if they didn't know one another, from the very start Lester had been adamant about BC accompanying Fornax on this flight for protection. Come to think of it, BC himself was an anomaly—just one more in a long list of things that were totally out of sync. Fornax felt certain that, out from under the shadow of Lester's dark personality, BC must be a policeman or an enforcer of some sort, not the mechanical engineer he claimed to be. And yet, whatever he was, Fornax found comfort in having at least one ally along for the ride—just in case.

Eager to interrogate Cornwall personally, Fornax snapped the last of his three storage cases shut, bounded to his feet, and started back towards the shuttle. Right away he felt lightheaded, though he dismissed it as having stood up too fast. But when, a few meters later, the woozy sensation hadn't passed, he paused again to check his air mix.

This time, when Fornax looked at the dials, he knew he was at an impasse. Through eyes blurred by weariness, he was shocked to discover his low-oxygen indicator flashing red! Ordinarily, an imbalance this severe would have been accompanied by an audible alarm. Its absence could mean only one thing—his suit had been tampered with!

Conscious now of the sweat building up on his forehead, Fornax fumbled with the comm, hoping to alert BC that he was in trouble. But his oxygen-starved muscles wouldn't cooperate!

As his mind fogged over and his movements became glacial, Fornax dropped the durbinium-filled cases and sank weakly to his knees.

Just moments from death now, his limp body rolled onto the graveled surface of the moon.

9
Prelude To Battery

When Fornax came to, he found himself strapped into his bunk with nightcords, the same sort of elastic safety-tethers which kept a sleeping crew member from floating free of his bed at night and accidentally hurting himself. Hovering over him like an anxious parent was BC.

Fornax squinted his eyes, staring past BC as if he weren't there. Just beyond him was the starboard viewport. Through it Fornax could just make out the blue and white halo of the distant Earth. Only then did it occur to him that the ship was already out of moon orbit and on its way back home. Hence, the nightcords holding him in place. Clearly, he had been out for quite some time.

"What the devil happened to me?" Fornax stammered, straining against the nightcords.

"You passed out," BC said quietly. "Ox-ni pressure inside your suit dipped into the red zone. You're damn lucky to be alive."

Fornax met the other man's steely eyes with a look of confusion.

Continuing in a low whisper, BC said, "Someone tampered with the enviro circuit in the lining of your suit—someone who knew what he was doing."

"Who?" Fornax asked. Following BC's lead, he spoke in a hushed voice.

"I suspect one of the crew, but it's too early to know which one yet."

Fornax's tone rose in anger as it all came rushing back. "It was Cornwall, wasn't it? He's the one, isn't he?"

"I just told you, damnit, I don't know *who* did it! Now keep your voice down, will you? And remember, we're supposed to hardly know one another."

"Sure, sure, but what's the big deal? You saved my bacon, so naturally I would confide in you."

"Only I didn't," BC declared flatly, "save your bacon, I mean. Nicholas Cornwall did. If Nick hadn't happened by when he did, you'd be pushing up roses by now."

Fornax was aghast. "That can't be!"

"Well sorry to disappoint you, my friend, but it is. Cornwall was straggling in from the DUMP behind you when he saw you collapse. When you didn't get right back up again, he got alarmed and hustled over to find out what the hell went wrong. He saw your emergency light flashing red, so he coupled his reserve oxygen tank onto your auxiliary hose. Believe me—if not for Nick's quick thinking, you would've bought the farm for certain."

"First he tries to kill me, then he tries to *save* me?" Fornax mumbled, shaking his head in disbelief. "It makes no sense, no sense at all!"

"Don't be a dunce!" BC scolded. "Haven't you figured it out yet? Cornwall's one of . . . "

But before BC could finish his sentence, he was cut off by the noisy arrival of Butch and the rest of the crew. Like a pack of rabid dogs they gathered around Fornax's berth snickering and cutting wise. The Captain put an immediate halt to it, then turned to address Fornax.

"I see you've finally come around," he said. "You didn't look so hot when Cornwall first brought you in. Good thing our man BC here is an experienced medic, or else you might not have made it."

"Gee, Captain," Fornax began, his stinging sarcasm self-evident. "Let me say I am thrilled—nay, overwhelmed—by your compassion. But you know damn well, this was no fluke! Some son-of-a-bitch messed with my suit!"

Even as he spoke, Fornax undid his nightcords and sat up in bed. There was fire in his eyes.

"Let's not make accusations we cannot prove," BC urged.

But Fornax wasn't having any of it. "The dee-dees they give us to wear when we're out working on the moon have been rigorously tested!" he roared. "They've been designed to endure literally *thousands* of hours of trouble-free operation. What do you take me for, an imbecile? You know very well there isn't a damn thing wrong with my bloody suit! Someone tampered with it! There's a *murderer* onboard!"

"That will be quite enough, mister," Captain Michael shot back. "I have written this incident up as an equipment malfunction, and that is how it will remain."

"Equipment malfunction, my butt!" Fornax grumbled, getting shakily out of bed. "And speaking of equipment, where are my cases?"

BC and Captain Michael exchanged fleeting glances, but neither one said a word.

Speaking slowly and deliberately now, Fornax repeated his question.

"Where . . . are . . . my . . . cases?" By this time he was on his feet and pacing back and forth across the narrow cubicle.

"Answer me, damnit! Where the hell are they?" He was just fuming.

Captain Michael glanced again at BC before answering. "Your cases are safely stowed away in the cargo hold. When I reported your suit failure to Central, they instructed me to lock up both you and your cases."

Furious now, Fornax banged his fist against the bulkhead. "Lock *me* up? That's absurd!" he spouted angrily. "This is intolerable! I'm a scientist for Christ's sake, not a criminal! Hell, I'm the goddamned *victim!* Besides, why incarcerate me? *He*'s the one who should be locked up!" Fornax yelped, pointing at Cornwall. "He's been tailing me for weeks!"

"Gosh, Captain, the man is delirious," Cornwall carped. "Goodness, I saved his worthless hide, didn't I? What can he possibly want from me now?"

"I want my cases," Fornax said flatly. "I simply must be allowed to see them. It is imperative that I measure their neutron absorption right away. Before they've had a chance to discharge."

"That won't be necessary," the Captain assured him. "I have already done so—and with some mighty interesting results. Two strips showed no evidence of neutron absorption whatsoever, and six more were only partials; the other twenty-two, however, seem to be fully charged."

"Well, I'll be," Fornax exclaimed, momentarily forgetting his anger. "It worked! My experiment worked! I just knew it would," he chuckled excitedly. "But wait a minute. Did I hear you right? Did you say two of the strips didn't take *any* charge? There must be some mistake!"

"No mistake," Captain Michael said, shaking his head.

"Heh, wait just a damn minute!" Fornax said, his voice becoming strident. "Who the hell taught you how to calibrate my monitoring equipment anyway? Damnit, man, you're not being straight with me. Just what the hell is going on around here?"

"You, my friend, are confined to quarters until we make landfall at Lanka," Captain Michael answered. "My orders are quite specific. I am to place you under ship's arrest with a 'round-the-clock guard. Butch here will take the first watch."

"See here, Captain," Fornax objected as he retreated to his bunk. "Who ordered this outrage? Tell me the truth, Michael—who has his hooks in you anyway?"

But this time, there was no reply; only a stern look from the Captain as he shooed the others away.

Recognizing that further argument was futile, Fornax collapsed on his bed grumbling. "This is damn confusing!" he muttered aloud. "Damn confusing!"

Silently contemplating the ominous shadow of the husky, dark-haired guard standing watch just outside his door, Fornax tried to decide whether Butch was there to be sure Fornax remained in his cabin or whether he was there to protect Fornax against another attempt on his life. Either way, it all worked out the same—and none of it made any sense! Fornax wasn't any closer now to figuring out how Cornwall fit in with all this than he was before; and frankly, by this time he was totally baffled!

If Cornwall had truly gone out of his way to save Fornax's life like the man said, and if he had indeed been the one who'd been tailing him all this time, then maybe Cornwall wasn't to be feared after all. Maybe, just maybe, Cornwall was not the enemy, but rather an ally. Maybe, like BC, he was some sort of a bodyguard. But if *that* were true, then for whom did he work?

Circles inside of circles and still no way out! As near as Fornax could tell, the trail *still* led back to Captain Michael, only by this line of reasoning, the Captain once again could be placed on his "should be trusted" list. Framing him as an ally not only made good sense, but Fornax preferred it that way. To have to paint the Captain as his archenemy sent chills down his spine. And yet, the most basic question of all still remained unanswered: If Cornwall worked for Captain Michael, what puppeteer was tugging on the *Captain*'s strings? Surely, he wasn't acting alone! Who was giving *him* his orders?

Fornax rolled the Captain's earlier words through his head: "My orders are quite specific . . . *They* instructed me . . . "

Who, damnit? *Who* instructed him? *Who* gave the orders?

Once again, the conclusion was inescapable—somewhere in the background, hidden from plain sight, stood an unknown Mister Big, a criminal warlord of some standing, a powerful man, one with influence, one who had taken an interest in Fornax for an as-of-yet undetermined reason. But with nothing concrete to go on, this was a particularly unpleasant state of affairs. There was absolutely no way for Fornax to distinguish the good guys from the bad! One thing was for certain, though: If he was going to muddle his way through this thing successfully, he would simply have to rely on his own resourcefulness.

Resigned to keeping as low a profile as possible until he got home safely, Fornax did not talk to anyone, not even the Captain. And except for being escorted to the head once or twice, he never even left his bunk. The guard was changed each hour, and it became such a routine that he paid scant attention to who stood outside his door at any given moment.

His meals were brought to him from the galley, but afraid of being poisoned, Fornax drank practically nothing and ate even less. The man didn't expect to live long enough to see the green hills of Earth ever again—and he was very nearly correct!

That evening, shortly after nine p.m. ship-time, Fornax asked to visit the john so he could go about his nighttime routine in preparation for bed. From outside his door, Butch grunted his assent.

In previous trips to the toilet, the guard on duty had always led the way down the shuttle corridor, instructing Fornax to follow behind. This time, however, Butch stepped aside, motioning Fornax to go ahead of him. Figuring it was late and no one was going anywhere anyway, Fornax paid little heed to the change in protocol.

Carrying his toothbrush in one hand and his toothpaste in the other, he casually sauntered down the narrow passageway in the direction of the bathroom. While it was true that brushing one's teeth in space was a notoriously messy and cumbersome task, it wasn't one to be ignored or even taken lightly. Years of experience had shown that the bacteria which promoted tooth decay literally thrived in micro-gravity. Indeed, to encourage brushing, each ship was equipped with a wall-mounted suction tube, a device not unlike those found in a dentist's office back home. Though the suction tube reduced somewhat the unpleasantness of brushing one's teeth, should the filter became plogged or the vacuum-draw prove insufficient to the task, wet droplets of goop—spit mixed with lathered toothpaste—would spread relentlessly throughout the ship, coating every surface with a disagreeable sticky residue.

Intending to commiserate with Butch about the antiquated gear in the shuttle's lavatory, Fornax turned to address the burly guard walking directly behind him. But no sooner had he twisted his head to speak, than his weary eyes caught the glimmer of an upraised blade. Horrified, the adrenaline shot through his system like a bolt!

Raising his arm to deflect the impending slash, Fornax spun to face his attacker. But the man was already in motion, thrusting his blade at Fornax with evil intent.

Trapped as he was in that narrow hallway, trapped without any room in which to maneuver, it was impossible for Fornax to avoid being cut by his assailant.

The killer's knife ripped through his shoulder, its point penetrating deeply, all the way to the bone. Yet, even before the searing pain had a chance to hack its way through Fornax's central nervous system and up to his brain, he gave free rein to his self-preservation instincts. The swarthy Afghan responded with extreme violence!

Wielding his toothbrush like a dagger, Fornax plunged the hard plastic hilt into Butch's left eye. The gelatinous orb popped bloodily, its milky-white contents spewing like a geyser into the air around them.

Stunned by the attack, the assassin staggered backward, releasing his grip from the blade still jutting out from deep inside Fornax's flesh.

When his beleaguered brain finally acknowledged the pain sprouting from his punctured shoulder, Fornax screamed icily. Only, he knew it wasn't over. Not yet anyway.

Drawing on his last ounce of resolve, Fornax took a deep breath and jerked the blade from his upper arm. Then, summoning all his strength, he rammed it into the belly of his adversary. It was a deep and lethal blow, and just for good measure, he gave it a vicious twist.

Grimacing, Fornax's opponent collapsed to the floor, the toothbrush still protruding from his head where his eyeball used to be. Droplets of blood filled the air between the two men.

By now the sounds of their fight had brought the rest of the crew bounding from their beds and into the passageway. Dressed only in his skivies, BC was the first on the scene. It took him no more than a split second to perform triage. One look at Butch's ruptured gut convinced him the man couldn't be saved; in Fornax's case, however, the prognosis was better. If he acted fast enough, BC might just be able to mend the furrow in Fornax's shoulder before the man bled to death!

Trying to make himself heard over the rancor, BC sprang into action, yelling for Cornwall to get his kit. Time was short!

Arresting the flow of blood from a deep laceration was tough enough on Earth, even with the helpful tug of her one-g of gravity. But in space, with no gravity whatsoever, it was difficult raised to a power of two.

As Fornax lingered at the edge of consciousness, he found it curious that the tatoo of a butterfly should adorn BC's naked arm up near his shoulder, a butterfly which seemed to flap its wings each time BC flexed his muscles to apply direct pressure to the horrible gash.

As anyone with even a rudimentary knowledge of first-aid would know to do, BC pressed a gauze pad over the gaping wound with his free hand. Then, as the sterile pad ripened in color from white to pink to red, he positioned a second pad over the first. And each time, as the uppermost dressing filled with blood, he thrust on yet another layer of gauze, all the while doing his best to maintain maximum pressure on the wound with his free hand. It was a formidable task, and he knew that the gauze was little more than a stopgap measure. Fornax couldn't stand to lose much more blood.

BC barked out instructions to Captain Michael to prepare a hypo with morphine to deaden the pain, and then another with hyprhene to calm his frantic patient. The Acceleron injection, to speed the healing, would come later, as would the surrogate skin and muscle.

By now Fornax was delirious, and when he saw BC warm up an electric searing iron to cauterize the hacked flesh, he went limp. Before he passed out though, he thought he heard the Captain tell BC: You must save this man! My life depends on it!

And then, for the second time this trip, Fornax blacked out. He never even saw the large-bore needle BC had to use to piece his perforated skin back together.

• • •

"Boss, there's been another attempt on his life," Michael reluctantly revealed. He had barricaded himself into his tiny cabin to use the comm in private.

"Good God, what happened *now?*" J groaned from his wood-paneled office buried deep within the City of London.

"This time they nearly got him, but I gotta tell you something boss, this Engels fellow is really quite resourceful. By all rights, he really ought to be working for us! If you can believe it, he disabled the assassin with a toothbrush, then turned around and killed the bastard with his very own blade!"

"Oh, I can believe most anything," J grumbled skeptically. "But a toothbrush? How is that possible? And answer me this: I have three of my best goddamned people onboard that ship to keep track of the man—count them, three: you, BC, and Cornwall—and still the man almost *dies? Twice?* How is that possible?" J asked, totally flabbergasted. "I must say it gives one pause. What in the world am I paying you for, Michael? If I didn't know better, I'd say you were *intentionally* sabotaging this mission."

"Don't be silly, Chief, I could never . . . "

"Have you identified the perp yet?" J brusquely cross-examined.

"All I know for certain is that the cretin's name was Butch. Other than that, I haven't a clue. I've had him onboard several times before, and although he's always impressed me as being a suspicious sort, he never impressed me as being all that bright."

"Bright enough to fool you," the head of Commonwealth Intelligence remarked critically.

"Yes, well, I can't tell you how much I appreciate you pointing that out," the Captain said. "But Butch has got to be one of Ling's men. BC put the corpse on ice so we can take a crack at making a gene-print match once we return."

"Thank goodness at least one of you is thinking straight," J mumbled. "Now tell me: how seriously was Fornax hurt?"

"Blade wound to the shoulder," Captain Michael replied bluntly, leaving out all the gory details. "But BC patched him right up and Fornax is now in stable condition. I'm confident he'll be okay until we reach Jaffna Municipal."

"BC's top-notch, there's no denying that. No matter what else you do, see to it that he stays with Fornax 'round-the-clock until you land. I don't want any more 'incidents.' Also, inform young Cornwall that since he's now managed to blow his cover, I'm pulling him off the case. He's to report to the section chief in Delhi."

"Isn't that a bit severe?" Michael objected, knowing what a rotten assignment Indiastan could be.

"That's none of your concern," J declared sternly.

"Okay, okay," Captain Michael relented, "but isn't it about time you started worrying about *me* for a change?"

"For Pete's sake, whatever do you mean?"

"I have to come in," the Captain pleaded. "He knows, I tell you; Ling knows."

"So? What of it?" J replied indifferently.

"You insensitive bastard! It's my life that's on the line here, not yours! I'm certain the man knows I'm a double! I felt it in his voice the last time we talked."

"*Felt* it?" J said, addressing him in an impatient, almost mocking tone.

"Yes, felt it," the Captain answered, thinking back to his conversation with Overlord Ling, concluded only moments before. "Ling assured me that he could never harm a loyal employee. But, judging by the way he said it, I can only assume the opposite."

J chuckled lightly. "What are we talking about here—woman's intuition? You have not a single shred of hard evidence, not one; and yet, on the basis of nothing more than the man's tone of voice, you have somehow deduced that Overlord Ling has learned of your duplicity? Jesus Christ, Michael, have you taken leave of your senses?"

"Not at all!" Michael objected strenuously. "But consider this: From out of nowhere comes this assassin. First he tampers with Fornax's suit; then he tries to knife him. And to what end? This hit man must have been sent by Ling! And since Ling chose not to confide in me about the killer's mission, that can only mean one thing—*he no longer trusts me.* My cover is blown, damn it! You have to bring me in!"

"I don't give a flying fig whether or not your cover is blown! And, no, I'm not going to bring you in—at least not yet. You simply must see this thing through to the end; at least until we've had a chance to determine whether or not this device Fornax has cooked up really works. Once I have my hands on that Battery of his, well then we'll have to see about you. But not a moment sooner."

"How long do you think that'll take?" the Captain asked, a note of dark desperation crowding into his voice.

"It's hard to say," J answered, a fiendish grin painted on his chiseled face. "A few weeks, maybe. A month at the most."

"A *month?*" Michael echoed with disbelief. "Why you bastard! I'll be dead inside of a *week!*" Even from the other end of the line, there was no mistaking the dread in his voice.

"There, there, Michael—Whitey won't move *that* fast."

"Thanks. Thanks a whole lot," the Captain grumbled, his throat suddenly very dry. "I can't tell you how much better that makes me feel."

10
Gcar

Three days later, with BC at his side, Fornax was wheeled from Jaffna Municipal Hospital in a medi-chair. Although his throbbing shoulder was still heavily bandaged, the delirium of the morphine had finally evaporated, and for perhaps the first time since the attack, his mind was totally clear.

As BC rolled his patient down the handicapped ramp and out towards the dark, strange-looking gcar waiting for them at the curb, Fornax again relived those few terrifying moments in the corridor of the shuttle. He couldn't help but wince thinking what he'd done to Butch's eye with that toothbrush. Yuck!!

Fornax didn't say a word to BC until they'd cleared the hospital's outer doors. Then, in a voice befitting his weakened condition, he spoke up.

"What in the blazes have I gotten myself into?" he asked.

"It's all become rather confusing—I'll grant you that much," BC said as he helped his charge from the wheelchair into the unusual vehicle. The gcar wasn't like the electric models Fornax had ridden in so many times before; it was of a sort he'd only seen in pictures.

"Where to, buddy?" the driver asked hoarsely over his shoulder.

"Central Hotel," BC answered, "but take your time, we have a great deal to discuss."

"It's your dime," the driver answered as the big gcar pulled away from the curb.

"I see now that Cornwall wasn't out to kill me," Fornax said. "But I'm quite certain he was the one who'd been following me from at least as far back as Zealand. What I can't figure out is why?"

"I'm hardly in a position to speculate about motives," BC said, shading the truth. "However, I did learn one thing which might interest you. I took a skin sample from our good friend Butch and had the lab run a gene-print analysis on it. Turns out, the man had quite a rap sheet. Butch was a two-time loser who was last interned in a Chinese prison. Not long ago, he was released into the custody of one Chou Kim."

"That name sounds familiar."

"And well it should!" BC exclaimed. "In case you've forgotten, Chou Kim is the heavyset Oriental in charge of Sri Lanka ground-ops."

"Oh yeah, good ole Mister Kim. A suspicious-looking character, if you ask me. But what's the big deal? So what if Butch was hired by Mister Kim? So was I. Hell, so were you!"

BC gave Fornax a knowing look. "I'm afraid there's more. I have it on good authority that Chou Kim is a known henchman for Overlord Ling Tsui. You know who *he* is, don't you?"

Fornax nodded, but said nothing. He couldn't very well reveal how, as a soldier, a man named Fornax Nehrengel had gone to war against this loathsome tyrant. Or how that same man had lost his best friend Vishnu to that godless fight.

"Have you heard of him or not?"

"Yes, of course I have," Fornax stammered, "but why would he want *me* dead? I mean nothing to him."

"Undoubtedly true," BC agreed, "but consider this: maybe Chou Kim wasn't after you—maybe he was after your *cases*! Stealing so much durbinium at one fell swoop might have improved his standing with the Overlord; it might even have earned him a handsome bonus."

"Let me see if I have this straight," Fornax said, settling deeper into the padded seat of the gcar. "Chou Kim has me killed so he can do what? Get his slimy hands on my *durbinium?* That's ridiculous! What the hell would Ling be able to do with it? The stuff's too hot to handle, and with me out of the picture, how could he possibly hope to assemble a prototype of my Battery? Just what good would a couple dozen strips of energized durbinium do him anyway?"

"How in the world should I know?" BC returned. "Maybe he thought he could build the darn thing without you. Who else have you shown your blueprints to anyway? Besides Lester and me, that is."

"No one. Not a soul. Not intentionally, anyway," Fornax said, scratching his head in thought. "It's remote, but now that I think of it, there is one possibility. On my first trip to the moon, even before you and I met, I made a crude sketch of the thing. I suppose Butch might have seen it sitting there on my desk. It's a long shot I'll grant you, but he just might have had enough brains to figure out what he was looking at."

"Well *somebody* certainly figured it out!"

"Yes. And for somebody to have gone to all the trouble to arrange for my murder—up there in space, no less—my Battery must be worth far, far more than I had suspected. Or even dreamed."

"Don't flatter yourself," BC scolded as the gcar wove its way through the busy streets of Jaffna. "We haven't even built the thing yet. We don't even know if it works!"

"That's just my point! The killer wanted to stop me *before* the cases reached Lester. The scheme had to have been arranged by someone who was acquainted with both Lester *and* me . . . You, for instance."

"*Me*?!" BC erupted, nearly rocking the gcar.

"Yes, you," Fornax repeated calmly, testing BC's reaction.

"For God's sakes man, I stitched you back together! Where did you get such a crazy idea?"

"Back on the ship you were hemmed in by a half-dozen onlookers. Let's face it: you didn't raise so much as a finger to help Butch, and you probably would have left me for dead as well if it hadn't been for Captain Michael."

"That's just plain silly!"

"Is it?" Fornax sneered. "I distinctly remember him ordering you to save me. And with Butch conveniently dead at *my* hand, that spared you the trouble of having to silence him yourself later on."

"You have a vivid imagination," BC grunted in a tired tone.

"Indeed I do," Fornax replied. "Indeed I do."

"Well think what you will, but I've had just about all the crap I'm going to take from you in one day! I'm giving you fair warning, buddy—either shut up or I'll shut you up!"

And then, as if to add teeth to his threat, BC waved a rolled up fist in front of Fornax's face.

For the recipient of the threat, it was a particularly unsatisfying answer. But rather than pressing his luck any further, Fornax turned away, crossing his arms with an arrogant, self-possessed air. However, it was not with pride that he stared out the window now, but dejection.

For a long time Fornax just sat there, casually studying the tenements they passed with unseeing eyes. One block after another rolled by until suddenly he realized they were amid a rabble of people who were standing on the sidewalk gawking in amazement and pointing towards the very vehicle he was riding in! At first, he couldn't figure out what all the commotion was about, then it dawned on him what had struck him earlier as being so strange about this gcar. *It was powered by petrol!*

Like durbinium, oil was an extremely rare commodity, a commodity which had already been in short supply as far back as Rontana's time. Nowadays, what little remained was in the hands of a few select individuals. These were men of unspeakable sway, the most powerful men on the planet, men who were heads of state, or titans of industry, or underworld crime bosses. It didn't take a genius to figure out which of the three categories Lester belonged in!

As they navigated their way through the littered streets of the city, provoking startled glances from commoners who had never seen a gasoline-fueled gcar before—or smelled its odious fumes—Fornax's daydreams were filled with images of gangsters and spies and espionage. Like before, he couldn't help but wonder what he had gotten himself into—or with whom. In fact, he was just about to vocalize his sentiments to BC when the sedan screeched to a halt in front of a seedy, second-rate hotel.

This just keeps getting better and better, Fornax said to himself, staring in wonderment at the ramshackle exterior of the place.

When the driver propped open the door and BC unfolded the medi-chair, Fornax didn't put up a fight. He knew he needed BC's help to get into the chair for the short ride up to Lester's suite. It would be several days yet before he had the strength to get around unassisted.

Lester's room was, without a doubt, the nicest one on the floor; nevertheless, Fornax still found it intolerable. When the door swung open, he and BC were greeted by a man whose grinning face and miserable-looking mustache was an immediate annoyance. True to his barbarous nature, Lester came on hard and fast, like a used-car salesman.

"My business partner triumphantly returns," he said. "Welcome! Please come in!"

Seemingly delighted to see them both, Lester slapped BC on the shoulder as if to say, "Thanks for a job well done!" He was on the verge of subjecting Fornax to the same hearty salutation when he remembered the mangled shoulder that had put Fornax in that wheelchair to begin with. He reached for the man's hand instead.

Fornax rudely waved him off. There was hot fire in his eyes when he spoke. "Triumphant, you say? Spare me the platitudes! I nearly *died* up there, you son-of-a-bitch!"

"For God's sake, get ahold of yourself, man! I did what I could ahead of time to ensure your safety. Why do you think I sent BC along? So you'd have somebody to play cards with? Don't be a fool! He was there to protect you. Besides, even before you two took off, I had a chat with Captain Michael. He *assured* me that every single member of the crew could be trusted. And why shouldn't I have believed him? The Captain and I have been close friends and confidantes since our merchant marine days. That was thirty years ago! If *he* had no idea Butch was a foreign agent, how the hell could I be expected to?"

"Foreign agent?" Fornax barked, fidgeting like mad in his medi-chair. "What in the world are we talking about here? Give me one good reason why our private dealings should have attracted the attention of an outsider?"

Lester said nothing, neatly avoiding Fornax's dark piercing eyes.

"Damn it, Lester! Who in the hell did you leak word of our project to anyway?"

"Well," Lester stammered. "No one really."

"You owe the man an explanation," BC said, speaking up for the first time since they left the gcar. "The enemy we know is not to be feared as much as the enemy we don't."

"Okay, already, but it wasn't as if I'd wanted him dead!" Lester carped. "You want to know who else knew about the project? Well, let's see. Sam knew, of course. Then there was Captain Michael; he verified that you had made that very first trip to the moon. Chou Kim had at least an inkling. Then too, I had to grease a few palms along the way. How do you think I got ahold of thirty strips of durbinium, not to mention three maximum-clearance moon permits? Those things don't come cheap, you know! Plus don't forget, I had to get the energy-exchangers modified like you wanted. So, you see . . . "

"All I see," Fornax said testily, "is that the list of possible suspects is entirely too long!"

Gathering all his strength, Fornax rose uneasily to his feet and hobbled shakily towards the window overlooking the street below. Not until he'd reached the supporting comfort of the wall did he take a breath and finish what he had to say. "It occurs to me that that list might even include the people in this very room!"

"How dare you!" Lester objected strenuously.

"There you go again with your paranoid delusions," BC said. "The answer doesn't lie in conjuring up conspiracies; the answer lies in identifying culprits. With or without Lester's help, any number of people might have been bright enough to put it all together. All we need to do is put our heads together and figure out who."

"BC's right," Lester said. "If your thing works, it could be worth *billions*! In the hands of a foreign power, it could have repercussions around the globe."

Not backing down, Fornax resumed his hard questioning. "You keep using that word. *Foreign* agent. *Foreign* power. Foreign to whom, Lester? To whom do you pledge *your* allegiance?"

"To our nation, of course," Lester grumbled nervously. "And I can't tell you how insulting I find your questions."

"That may be, but you have neatly avoided answering them, haven't you?" Fornax shot back.

"Only because I am unaccustomed to having my motives doubted. Listen, Fornax, you had better make up your mind—and darn soon. Either you're in, or you're out. If you're in, then let's get to it—we have loads of work to do. Before we can secure a patent on your invention, we must first build a working model. It's high time we got started," Lester signaled, a greedy look in his eye.

"Hey, not so fast!" Fornax protested. "If not you, then who? Put a name to it, Lester. Tell me who you think my enemy is."

"Time is your enemy," Lester said, continuing to be evasive. "We don't have enough of it. The longer we sit around here arguing, the longer we wait before building and testing a prototype, the longer our adversaries have to track us down and steal it. Or kill us dead. That's why, first thing in the morning, we'll be boarding a suborb and heading back to my warehouse in Melbourne. We'll be safer there, and we'll have plenty of room in which to work."

Still not satisfied, Fornax became intransigent. "Damn it, Lester, I want some answers! Just who are you involved with? Organized crime? Neo-Rontanians? The White Brigade? Or do you just consort with killers and thieves?"

"Guilty as charged," Lester admitted, a broad evil grin plastered across his otherwise dirty face. "On all counts. I have no political loyalties of any kind, I have no scruples whatsoever, and I freely associate with shadowy persons operating well outside the law. There—are you happy now?"

Listening to this exchange from the sidelines, BC couldn't help but stand there stunned. It wasn't just the boldness of Fornax's interrogation which caught him off guard, but the frankness of Lester's replies. In under thirty seconds, Fornax had unwittingly prodded Lester into spontaneously confessing what BC had been trying for months to prove!

"You ask if I'm *happy?* Well, in a strange sort of way, yes, I guess I am," Fornax replied without enthusiasm.

But the truth was, he wasn't happy at all! And why should he be? To be in bed with an avowed criminal was the cruelest cut of all! And the more he thought about it, the worse it got. Lurking somewhere in the shadows, just out of sight, was the real Lester Matthews, dark and mysterious, a person more dangerous than any Fornax could have possibly imagined!

Was it possible then that Butch actually had worked for Lester? That it was Lester who had arranged for Fornax's two close brushes with death? That once Lester had his hands on Fornax's device that Fornax himself would undoubtedly vanish, never to be seen or heard from again?

No matter how he figured it, it always added up the same—he was trapped in the lion's den with no way out! To stay alive, Fornax would have to delay divulging the secret of his Battery for as long as possible. The longer the technical know-how remained tucked safely inside his head, the longer he was apt to *have* a head!

"Okay, then," Lester said, motioning Fornax back to his wheelchair. "Why don't you sit back down and take a load off?"

"In a minute, but first answer me this: how did you get your hands on that gasoline-powered limousine that brought us here today?"

"Like I told you," Lester smiled, "I associate with unscrupulous people who operate outside the law."

• • •

The brilliance of the early morning sun blazed through the window of Whitey's luxurious Johannesburg home. Oblivious to the splendid spring weather, he sat slumped in his overstuffed easy chair, depressed. Like a drug-starved addict deprived of his regular fix, Whitey was in an especially cranky mood. He hadn't murdered anyone in weeks, and even his daughter's repeated sexual advances hadn't been enough to raise his downtrodden spirits. For hours already, he had been like this, moping feverishly around the house. But now, when the comm rang, everything changed! For the first time in days, his eyes lit up, a rabid glimmer shining forth.

Like any drug-addicted junkie who couldn't escape his chemical dependency without first suffering the debilitating side effects of withdrawal, Whitey was long overdue for a syringe-full of his own special brand of opiate. Nothing fascinated him more than sitting for hours watching his hapless victims as they slowly succumbed to one or another of his singularly brutal methods for inflicting pain. The twitches. The contortions. The spasms. Whitey took incalculable pleasure in his work, a pleasure which buttressed his reputation for ruthlessness while at the same time feeding his sick habit.

In his vile and heinous career Whitey had murdered dozens—heads of state, political aspirants, captains of industry, even pregnant mothers. Indeed, the man's complete disregard for human life was what made his foul services so invaluable.

At the tinny sound of the comm, the killer literally leapt across the room, praying that this would be the call which would bring him an assignment. He was flush with excitement to hear the Chinaman's voice at the other end.

"Overlord Ling, it is indeed an honor," Whitey began, forcing himself to be as polite as possible. Behind him, his daughter wantonly paraded her half-naked body through the living room chanting, "Oh, Daddy, Daddy, is that ding-a-Ling?"

Not wanting to risk upsetting the Overlord and blowing his single best chance to be hired for an important kill, Whitey moved to silence his villainous daughter.

"Shush, Marona!" he ordered, pressing his hand over the mouthpiece. "He may have a job for me!"

Apparently satisfied that Whitey was showing him the proper respect, Overlord Ling explained the reason for his call. "If memory serves, the last time we spoke, you put in a request for a red-head. One with freckles, I believe. Undamaged, and suitable for torture. You'll be happy to know, I have found just such a girl."

"*Damn!*" the white-haired man swore, angrily slamming his fist down on the table. "Of all the luck!"

"I thought you'd be ecstatic. For God's sake, Whitey, what's the matter?"

"You have the audacity to sit there and ask me what's the matter?" the muscular assassin complained bitterly. "*Everything*'s the matter! If you're offering up a pretty young virgin for me to dissect, that means I don't get the kill assignment you promised me after all. And I did so much want to gut a worthy adversary."

The Overlord shivered. Though ten thousand kilometers separated him from the other man, Whitey gave him the creeps. The man never maimed for a cause, political or otherwise, nor did he ever require a reason for any of the terrible things he did. Whitey was just barely human and took infinite pleasure from his bloody craft.

"Don't be too hasty," the Overlord cautioned. "I'm feeling generous today. You may have the red-head *plus* the kill. By the way, she's one of those plucky Irish lasses, fresh off the farm."

"Ah, such a lovely gift! And just before the holidays too," Whitey rejoiced indecently.

"Heh, do me a favor already and drop the dramatics, okay? The girl's my present—you may have her either way—but I want Captain Michael dead by BeHolden Day."

"Any particular place you have in mind?"

"I will see to it that Lester brings him to the Corkscrew Pub . . . "

"In Jaffna? Down by the docks?"

"Yes, that's the one," Ling confirmed. "The two of them are longstanding friends. Lester will invite him to join him for a drink at the Corkscrew during the BeHolden Day commotion. You can do the Captain there. By the way, if you're in the mood, there's a wonderful little bimbooker-house next door."

"My God, what kind of a sicko do you think I am? I could never be unfaithful to my Marona—you know that!"

"Suit yourself, but before I forget, there is one more thing."

"What's that?" Whitey asked, still shocked by Ling's suggestion that he visit a whorehouse.

"Another man may be with them, a man named Fornax Engels. If so, you are to get a good look at him. But even if he interferes, even if he puts up a fight, he is not to be harmed in any way. I have *other* plans for Mister Engels."

11
Testing

When Fornax was finally reunited with his precious hoard of durbinium strips, he was so eager to get started wiring them together into a Battery, he put aside his reservations concerning Lester—at least for the time being.

Shielded behind a radiation-proof barrier he and BC had set up in a remote corner of Lester's warehouse, Fornax carefully removed the thirty red-hot strips from their storage containers. As Captain Michael had warned him, not all of the thirty strips had taken a charge; but using twenty that had, he and BC worked meticulously through the night to wire ten strips into each of two specially-modified energy-exchangers Lester had scrounged up from some utility company.

Then, using a pair of transposed O-ring couplers, each of the two resulting assemblies were joined to a standard regulator and entombed in a protective casing before being fitted with an appropriate mega-capacitor. All that remained now was to see whether or not the thing worked!

Given the abundant inadequacies of a conventional solar-powered battery, Lester was enthusiastic to have Fornax first try out his device on one of Lester's freight-gtrucks. Though solar-power worked well enough for light jobs of short duration, a heavily-loaded gtruck equipped with a solar cell and an electric engine simply lacked the hauling capacity to travel any distance before requiring a lengthy and expensive recharge. Any improvement would be of great commercial value!

Since the leads from Fornax's Battery could be fed directly into a gtruck's electric engine, bypassing the existing solar pack was really quite simple. So simple, in fact, that in order to make a fair comparison, Lester suggested they jack-up two gtrucks on hoists side-by-side for a time trial.

It was an auspicious start. Before sputtering to a halt the next day, the gtruck energized by Fornax's Battery ran for an incredible twenty-seven hours and fourteen minutes—twelve times longer than the one carrying a conventional solar cell! Any doubts either one of them may once have had were suddenly erased—the partnership of Fornax Engels and Lester Matthews had a prodigious breakthrough on their hands, a breakthrough which demanded further exploration!

The second test went much as the first, only using a harbor tender Lester borrowed from one of his merchant marine buddies.

Oceangoing vessels in the year 2430 were either coal-burning steamers or else the much more economical, wind-driven sailships Lester was familiar with. Like all such rigs, the sailship he borrowed was outfitted with a modest, coal-burning steam engine for maneuvering while in port or for locomotion in still winds.

As was the case with the solar-powered gtruck, adapting the Battery to a sailship was a rather straightforward operation. Mounted along a central axle was a series of gears, and acting through these gears was a steam engine which spun a propeller-like contrivance called a screw. It was the twirling screw which drove the ship forward, and it was along this linkage that Fornax and BC made their modifications. Taking the steam engine temporarily off-line, they hooked up the second Battery in its place. Then, sailing out into the bay, they held their breath hoping it would work.

The test was rather short, but quite telling. The torque pressure of the Fornax Drive was so strong and the strength of the boat's drive shaft so puny, within minutes the axle had been twisted totally beyond repair, its gears stripped completely clean of their teeth!

To say that Lester was delighted would have been a gross understatement. The experiment—a success—had not only consumed but a tiny fraction of the energy stored in that second Battery, it was now obvious to them both that with a properly redesigned screw and a more substantial axle, a formidable oceangoing vessel could be engineered and put into service. That Lester now had to make restitution to his friend for the damaged drive shaft seemed a petty annoyance by comparison. To the contrary, he couldn't help but stare in helpless fascination at the knotted heap of metal before him, his greedy little mind in overdrive. Along with making the shipping fleets of the world obsolete, along with changing the future of gtrucking, Fornax's device could change *his* future! It could make *him* wealthy!

Lester smiled. Wantonly. He couldn't help it. All at once he visualized himself atop a bustling, trading empire, the world's oceans being busily plied by his ships. The man literally glowed with anticipation for what was yet to come.

And what was yet to come was test number three—onboard a shuttle!

Compared with a ship or a gtruck, arranging to borrow a shuttle seemed like an utter impossibility to Fornax. But then again, he didn't know everything there was to know about Lester Matthews. It seemed that appropriating shuttles for illegal DUMPING was one of Lester's specialties!

Over the years, Lester had come to make a science of shrewdly manipulating the DUMP bureaucracy to his own advantage, avoiding the rules wherever possible, and circumventing the multitude of safeguards put in place by the member nations. In fact, it was precisely this manipulation which J had sent BC to investigate in the first place. Plenty was at stake here, and as Fornax pressed stubbornly forward with his series of tests, he was unwittingly helping BC to carry out his assignment.

Both the DUMP and the Sri Lanka facility were owned and operated by a consortium of four nations—Australia, SKANDIA, the Commonwealth, and China—four nations so conceited they called themselves "members," four nations so arrogant they referred to every other nation on the planet as "non-members." It was as if the gateway to humanity's country club were open only to a select few—all others need not apply.

The privilege of shipping garbage to the moon was tightly regulated, and all major classes of pollutants—nuclear toxins included—had to first pass through the turnstiles on Sri Lanka before being lifted aloft. Despite the regulations, however, a substantial amount of illegal DUMPING was still going on. It was BC's job to find out the "who" and the "how." The "who" he already knew—that was Lester Matthews. Now—thanks to Fornax—he was about to find out the "how."

Because there were no longer any places on Earth to store such garbage, scores of non-member countries were at the mercy of the self-anointed few. For a non-member nation to launch its contaminants to the moon, it first had to negotiate transshipment rights through a member country intermediary, often paying an exorbitant fee in the exchange. Because the fee was itself tantamount to blackmail, non-member nations had no choice but to engage an illicit operator like Matthews Transportation to covertly dump their harmful wastes for them.

For three or four years already, Indiastan had been one of Lester's regular customers. So, when he got a call from Delhi that they had an illegal load that needed dumping, Lester saw an ideal opportunity to use the trip as a cover for a third and final test of Fornax's incredible Battery. There was one fly in the ointment, however—Captain Michael. He and Lester had had a longstanding arrangement whereby Captain Michael agreed to pilot these loads in exchange for a reasonable cut of the action. Normally, this wouldn't have presented much of a problem, except that under the circumstances there was no easy way for Lester to avoid telling the Captain more about the Battery than he already knew. This entailed some risk because it meant going against the Overlord's strict orders to keep mum where the Captain was concerned. Nevertheless, Lester didn't feel as if he had a choice. For him to handle a shipment of this size and complexity, he simply had to have the expertise which was Captain Michael's stock-in-trade.

Absconding with a shuttle which was temporarily out of service for a much-needed overhaul, Captain Michael rendezvoused with Fornax and the others in docking orbit. By then, all the necessary paperwork had already been filed with the authorities and the shuttle's cargo-bay had been filled to capacity with Indiastan's poisonous freight. But to avoid arousing any suspicions regarding their true mission, Captain Michael had piloted the shuttle from orbit in the normal fashion, engaging the standard trajectory for a conventional three-day voyage to the moon.

Once underway, Fornax went straight to work. It took him the better part of a day to tie into the shuttle's propulsion and guidance systems with the slightly-used Battery left over from the short-lived boat test. Adapting his invention to propel the spaceship forward required that he tap directly into the Battery's prodigious neutron outflow, technologically an altogether different proposition from the earthbound dry runs just concluded. Unlike a gtruck which traveled atop four spinning wheels, or a sailship which was propelled forward by a spinning screw, a shuttle operated according to Newton's Third Law, pure and simple. A stream of tiny particles expelled to the rear of the craft thrust the ship forward.

To complete the installation Fornax was back and forth so many times between the forward cabin and the ship's engine room that when he finally tightened the last O-ring into place and sat calmly down before the main console, no one even gave him a second thought.

For a very long moment he just sat there quietly, his finger poised nervously on the switch he had soldered into place only an hour earlier. Though all the proper connections had been made and all the correct coordinates had been fed into the ship's nav-computer, he forced himself not to throw the switch—at least not yet anyway. One element was missing, and that was the element of surprise.

Twisting around in his seat to where he might have a better view of his companions, Fornax took a quick inventory of what they were doing.

Lester was sitting idly by the viewport, staring in quiet fascination at the splendid sight of the slowly receding Earth; the Captain was crouched over the helm monitoring the ship's lethargic pace, occasionally stopping to recalibrate his arc-sextant as the nav-computer spat out new readings on their position; and BC was standing off to one side running diagnostic routines on an outdated circuit board he had found in the storeroom. Neither BC nor the Captain nor Lester had so much as an inkling as to what was about to take place.

Without so much as a hint of warning to the others, Fornax furtively flipped the switch he had been fingering. What happened next was the stuff of which dreams are made!

In the flash of an eye, the orb which had been the Earth shrank to the size of a half-dollar and the swollen face of the moon glared back at them instead!

The sudden short burst of power from the Fornax Drive propelled Lester from his perch, knocking him first against the bulkhead, and then to the floor. Meanwhile, the Captain frantically checked to be certain he hadn't wet his pants. A wad of chewing gum hung from his disbelieving mouth. Even the stalwart BC stood white-knuckled, holding fast to the railing which ran alongside the raised platform of the command-console. Never had three men been caught more unaware!

Relishing the spectacle of BC's brief moment of fear, Fornax's face twisted into a mean-spirited, almost comical grin. For the first time in weeks, he felt as if he were finally back in control.

The Captain was the first to speak. "I have . . . lost control . . . of the ship," he stammered.

"My readings . . . have gone . . . completely . . . berserk!" BC sputtered, a confused look plastered across his face.

Enjoying himself thoroughly, Fornax chuckled at BC's bewildered look. "Hey, boy," he mocked. "Caught you napping, did I?"

Seeing Fornax's amused smirk and hearing his taunting tone, BC's face shone red, his temper flaring.

A haughty look of, "I dare you," hung from Fornax's face. But this was a mistake; BC was not the sort to be toyed with. Without a moment's hesitation, he promptly rolled his fingers into a fist and decked the other man!

It was a single, well-placed jab to the chin. Only, given BC's muscular build, it was not the sort of punch he would have thrown if he'd really meant to hurt Fornax. It was a neighborly punch (if an uppercut could ever truly be described as such)—one intended to firmly draw a line over which Fornax had better not step again.

Fornax deserved the wallop—and he knew it. And yet, in the space of that muted instant, he became aware of something else, something much more important—BC could be trusted!

Despite all his previous fears, Fornax now felt certain that BC was on his side—if not his friend, at least friendly; if not his ally, at least not an enemy.

Still, Fornax wasn't done having fun with him. "Hah!" he exclaimed, rubbing his chin. "You'll have to do a lot better than that to break *my* spirit!"

As BC cocked his fist to smack him again, Fornax threw up his arms in protest. "Damn it, BC, don't you see? It worked! My Battery *worked!*"

"It *did* work!" Lester nodded, greed literally oozing from his pores. By now he had regained his footing after the jump through hyperspace and was just beginning to digest the full impact of what had happened.

"I can hardly believe it myself," Fornax said, gesturing to the nav-console, "but when I flipped this switch—whoosh—the Drive kicked in just like it was supposed to. An instant later, here we were—at the moon!"

"The commercial possibilities are . . . are . . . God, we'll be rich!" Lester said, panting.

"Well, don't forget, I had to program the computer beforehand with our coordinates so that . . . "

"We have to give it a catchy name," Lester interrupted. "Something with pizzazz."

"I call it the Fornax Drive."

"Not good enough. How 'bout something like 'Warp Drive'?"

"Forget it already and pay attention," Fornax instructed. "If our instruments are to be believed, just two point seven seconds elapsed from the time of ignition until the moment of full stop."

"Incredible!" BC exclaimed. It was suddenly a real question whether cracking Lester's smuggling operation wasn't penny ante stuff compared with this. J would have to be notified right away.

"Which means," Fornax continued excitedly, "our velocity had to be somewhere in the vicinity of 130 thousand kilometers per second."

"Per *second?* That's simply not possible!" Michael blared. "For Christ sake, let me see that dohickey—you must be multiplying wrong!"

Even as he spoke, the Captain grabbed the calculator from Fornax's hand and started punching in numbers. "Why didn't we feel the acceleration? I mean if we actually jumped to something on the order of forty percent of light-speed in an instant, why didn't we get smashed like pancakes by the g-forces? It's simply not possible!"

"Well it may not have been possible yesterday, but it certainly seems so today," Lester said.

Still doubtful, Michael again challenged Fornax's numbers. "A hundred and thirty thousand klicks per second?"

"Give or take a little," Fornax replied tentatively.

"Tell me, how can that be?"

"Ah, the mysteries of Durbin physics! In accelerating through conventional speeds, say from 100 kilometers per hour up to ten thousand kilometers per hour, g-forces work in the conventional way. But when the physics were worked out years ago uniting gravity and quantum mechanics into a single unified Grand Theory, it was hypothesized that there would be a phase-shift at around five percent of light-speed where so-called g-forces would fall away. Just as the sound barrier proved to be purely psychological and not physical at all, so too should be the fear of being smashed at high rates of acceleration."

"Even so," Michael admitted at the conclusion of Fornax's explanation, "for a man who has traveled to the moon hundreds of times before, and never at a speed exceeding forty thousand klicks per *hour,* this all takes a little bit of getting used to. In the right hands, this thing could be worth *billions!*"

"That is, after all, the reason we're out here, isn't it?" Lester asked. "To make money?"

Captain Michael interjected. "Lester, old buddy, in case you've forgotten, I'm just a hired hand. Beyond my per diem for this trip, there's no money in this for me. How 'bout cutting me in on a share of the profits?"

"If it's a cut you want, it's a cut you'll get," Lester suggested darkly. "Maybe we'll have to do something in that regard, eh BC?"

"Whatever you say, boss," BC answered grimly.

"Don't be a fool!" Fornax said. "Instead of threatening one another, we have to concentrate on staying alive. Remember, I've been a target twice already."

"Don't be such a baby," the Captain snapped. "Out here, no one can touch you . . . except us three, of course."

Fornax trembled at the thought, but calmly forged ahead. "Captain, if I were you, I wouldn't be so damn cocky. When knowledge of my invention becomes public, *all* our lives will be in jeopardy, not just mine."

"What makes you so sure?" Michael quizzed, afraid that his own rather precarious position as a double-agent might become even more untenable than it already was.

"For starters, look at the company he keeps," Fornax said, gesturing in Lester's direction. "Are we supposed to believe his underworld buddies are gonna just let us keep this thing for ourselves? Not very damn likely! And if the crime bosses don't get us, and if Indiastan doesn't get us, one of the giant, multinational energy conglomerates *will.*"

"You're not making any sense," Lester insisted. "And as for what I said the other day about associating with criminals, you had to know I was just kidding."

Fornax rolled his eyes in disbelief.

Lester continued. "Who the hell are these unnamed giant conglomerates you're so worried about anyway?"

Fornax ticked them off on his fingers one by one. "It's simply a question of jobs. The coal miners' union, the nuclear fission lobby, the solar-battery cartel, hell, even the DUMP operators themselves; every single one of them is gonna feel threatened by my Battery."

"Why should they feel threatened?" Lester asked, climbing back into the chair he'd fallen out of earlier. "I still fail to see your reasoning."

"Likewise," the Captain said as he contemplated the moon through the viewport. It seemed close enough now to touch.

"Listen, you two. If you don't understand, maybe it's because you don't want to! There are other issues here besides just jobs."

"Like what?"

"Like, if space travel were to become cheap and fast, half the political systems on the planet would unravel! Without borders to hold them, the free thinkers of the world would be able to migrate wherever they chose—

including other planets. The tyrants haunting the Earth would no longer be able to hunt down and murder their opponents. In time, the despots would be dethroned; the oppression would end. And all because of my Battery!"

"Free thinkers? Humbug!" the Captain ridiculed. "I can't believe how naive you are! Anyhow, what does it matter? There *are* no other livable planets to run to. Terraforming failed, remember? Rontana was right, God rest his soul—kill their genes; kill their ideas! The people don't care. Most of them are still living in the burned out cities left behind in the aftermath of the Great War. Places like Sane Lou. Or worse."

"You're wrong! The people *do* care! I know! I've been there!"

Fornax's anger came as a surprise even to him, and for an instant he just stood there glaring, looking as if he might cry. Even after all these years, he was still burdened with unresolved passions over the death of his friend Vishnu. Even after all this time, he was still vexed by the Overlord's subjugation of his people and his homeland. Though he had tried his best to hide it, the anger had stayed with him all this time, lurking there in his subconscious. It was ironic that these feelings should suddenly surface now, but as quickly as they did, he suppressed them once more. What was done was done!

"Well, I think I've heard just about enough," Lester taunted icily. "You're afraid of the company I keep and you're afraid of the energy guilds—you got any more reasons for us to be dead, college boy?"

"No," Fornax admitted in a heavy, tired voice. "I've said my piece. But don't take my words lightly—we *are* in danger!"

"Don't be a pansy!" Lester finally erupted. "This is all a bunch of crap! I want a patent on your damn Battery, and I want it now! In case you've forgotten, we have spent lots and lots of money running all these tests—my money! Not to mention, burning up the drive axle on a perfectly good ship. And so far, I have absolutely nothing to show for my trouble. If marketing this device endangers our lives—so be it! We will buy protection if necessary, but market it we will!"

"*Your* money?" Fornax shot back incredulously. "I seriously doubt that we have been spending any of *your* money. In fact, I seriously doubt whether you have any money whatsoever to spend. The truth now, Lester: Who is funding you? Who is pulling your strings?"

"Look, all your questions will be answered in due time," Lester replied in a conciliatory tone. "In fact, I intend to introduce you to my silent partner as soon as we return. But for now, we should forget all about this nonsense and celebrate our great success! Let's dump this cargo we're carrying, then get back to Jaffna and hoist a few at the Pub."

"Okay by me," the Captain mechanically agreed. Behind him, BC eagerly nodded his head in unison.

Yet Fornax hesitated. He wasn't ready to celebrate, and he certainly wasn't ready to plunge in any further with Lester until he'd taken the time to clear his head. Fornax needed an excuse to delay the project, at least until he could talk to someone independent about it. The only someone he could think of at that moment was Dr. Sam.

"I want to discuss this with Sam before we move ahead," Fornax explained in a firm but steady voice.

"*Sam?*" Lester echoed astonished. "My brother, Sam? What the hell does *he* have to do with it? He's a bookworm for Christ sake, not a businessman. He couldn't be bothered to help you before; what makes you think he'll take the time to help you now? Originally he sent you to *me*, remember?"

"All I know," Fornax replied quietly, "is that I trust him. There will be no patents . . . there will be no celebrations . . . there will be no public announcements . . . until I have spoken with Sam." His tone was adamant.

Lester's eyes narrowed in a hateful glare. "You obstinate son-of-a-bitch!"

At the first raised voice, BC took a step backwards. He had no intention of being between two bullheaded men.

Their hooves dug in, their hairy nostrils flaring, Lester and Fornax squared off. It looked as if they might charge one another, butting their thick heads right there on the flight deck.

Firmly planting his feet, Fornax expected there would be fisticuffs—or worse. His instincts told him the jabs wouldn't be of the gentlemanly sort like they had been with BC.

As the first of several tense moments rolled by, Fornax primed himself to yank his razor-sharp blade from its thick leather holster. He wasn't about to back down now.

Seeing the determination in the other man's eye, Lester relented. "Okay, you win," he said. "If it'll make you feel any better, then go ahead and talk with my baby brother. After you return, we'll all meet in Jaffna to celebrate BeHolden Day—and our good fortune."

"We will need protection," Fornax recommended, lowering his defense.

"I agree," Lester said, "so I'll set up a meeting with my associate in Hong Kong right after the holidays."

"And don't forget the boost in my pay envelope," Michael reminded him. "To keep me quiet, remember?"

"There are other ways to keep a man quiet," Lester threatened, his smear of a mustache wet with sweat.

"Don't even *think* it!" Captain Michael warned, stealing a glance at BC. "I have more friends than you could possibly know."

"Bad joke, my friend," Lester apologized. "You know how I like to kid. Honestly, Michael, I couldn't manage without you. Now let's get back to work—we have lots to do. We still must dispose of this load for Indiastan and deposit the leftover strips back in the craters for recharging."

"Exactly," BC and Fornax said in unison.

12
War

Several Days Later

When Fornax arrived at the massive wrought-iron gate, he was amazed by the colossal, almost park-like dimensions of the estate he saw through the rungs of the fence. Though he knew Sam was a wealthy man by reputation, the size of his property gave Fornax pause. By every common standard the main residence was enormous and without parallel, and the meticulously-kept grounds substantial. On top of that, other buildings dotted the manor, each more unusual than the next. Taken together, it was an impressive, if somewhat eclectic picture of a level of wealth that Fornax could not easily comprehend.

At the sight of such opulence, Fornax's covetous mind descended into overdrive. He imagined that these smaller structures might house anything from personal servants to bio-stallions, that legions of groundskeepers must be on call round the clock to keep the lawns looking so neat. Everything was so foreign to his own experience, Fornax could hardly believe his eyes.

It was early summer in Auckland, and as Fornax stepped from the lawn onto the front porch of the mammoth white mansion, his jaw dropped open yet another notch: red and orange tulips bordered the house by the hundreds! When he reached up to rap on the front door with his fist, he found his very being racked by pangs of jealousy—the porch itself was half again as large as his own miniscule flat back in town!

Given the plush surroundings, Fornax expected to be met at the door by a tuxedo-clad butler or an apron-draped domestic. So when it was Sam himself who greeted him, Fornax was actually disappointed.

For his part, Sam was none too thrilled to see him either. Fornax had come without an appointment, and it was clear from the look on Sam's face that being bothered at home was an affront of some magnitude. Nevertheless, after a word or two of prodding, he politely agreed to listen to what Fornax had to say.

From the front foyer, Sam led Fornax down a long hall and into a great sitting room. The room, exquisite in every detail, was crammed full of museum-quality pieces, including a thousand-year-old suit of armor, a mummy case, a Ming dynasty ornamental fish bowl, and the most erotic bronze sculpture of a naked woman consumed by ecstasy that Fornax had ever seen. Yet, Sam's untidy appearance made a mockery of his own wealth.

The man was simply, even ordinarily, dressed and his light brown hair, which was never combed anyway, seemed especially unruly today. Sam had already gone gray at the temples; nevertheless, he still projected an air of youthful rebelliousness.

A portrait of his daughter sat on the table next to his chair; it was obviously one of his prized possessions. Alongside it was a glass of juice and a bottle of tiny red vitamin pills.

Sam offered his uninvited guest a seat and they talked. Fornax related everything that had happened to him since they last met more than a month ago, culminating with the three successful tests of his Battery.

Sam was flabbergasted to learn how fast the shuttle had gone, and as he digested the full magnitude of Fornax's discovery the expression on his face changed from polite boredom to amazed wonderment. At the same time, though, his forehead crinkled in doubt. Fornax had shown him the scar on his shoulder; he had explained how there had already been two attempts on his life and why he thought there would be others.

"So what do you want from *me?*" Dr. Sam finally asked. "If my brother's a scoundrel, then stay away from him!"

"I guess what I came to ask you is: Do you think there's a way for me to cash in on my invention without endangering my life further? Or should I abandon the whole thing and count my blessings that I've made it this far with all my skin still intact?"

"I see your dilemma," Dr. Sam nodded as he slowly rocked his head back and forth in quiet contemplation of Fornax's question. "But giving up is not the answer. Never, *ever*, abandon your dreams; and certainly not for reasons of personal danger!" he instructed in a fatherly tone. "Remember: good men predict, but *great* men act."

Having spoken so forthrightly, the man fell into a long period of silence during which he took a swig from his glass of orange juice and downed his daily vitamin pill. It was a curious habit which Fornax had never really quite understood. Then Sam squeezed his eyes shut and seemed to nod off into the netherworld.

Frustrated by the delay, Fornax was just about to lean over and wake the old guy when Dr. Sam cleared his throat and began to speak.

"You are right to be worried," he said. "My brother *is* a scoundrel, even worse than I imagined. And the points you've raised are very well taken indeed. Deep down, however, they are but variations on the same basic principle."

"Which is?"

"Which is that the status quo hates to be upset," Sam answered in a scholarly tone.

Though Sam paused again, even longer this time than before, Fornax could see the fire in the old man's eyes as his keen mind awakened to the challenge. At long last he said, "Proposition: The Inevitability of War."

"Sir?"

"What causes a group of relatively peaceful nations filled with reasonably intelligent people to plunge themselves into a murderous, even suicidal, war?"

"I'm not sure," Fornax declared, confused by his mentor's line of reasoning. "Pride? Fear, maybe?"

"Fear is a good answer, but you can do better than that."

"An ineffective deterrent?" a frustrated Fornax offered. "Honestly, I . . . "

"Very good," Sam interrupted. "Inasmuch as effective deterrents are at the very heart of the equation, we'll start there. Remember that day when you first came to see me? Do you recall the subject of my lecture? I was explaining the phenomena mathematicians refer to as CHAOS. That theory has an application here as well. When relations between nations become unstable, they exhibit CHAOS. More often than not, that instability leads rapidly to war."

Silently, Fornax marveled at the man's intellect. No wonder Sam was so rich—he knew how to think, not what to think!

Sam began. "Deterrence is most likely to keep the peace when the costs and the risks of going to war are unambiguously stark. The more horrible the *prospect* of war, the less likely the risk of war actually becomes. Defenders have the advantage when deterrence levels are high because defenders generally value their freedom more than aggressors value a new conquest. But instability—CHAOS—will result where power is unequally distributed.

"Whether there are two superpowers or multiple medium-sized powers makes no difference—both systems are likely to be more peaceful when power is distributed equally among the leading competitors. Yet, the prospects for peace are not simply a function of the number of great powers in a system. Peace is also affected by the *relative* military strengths of those major states. Power inequalities invite war because they increase an aggressor's prospects for victory on the battlefield. In fact, the *size* of the gap in military power between the two leading states is the key determinant of stability. Small gaps foster peace; large gaps promote war.

"Competition for security makes it difficult for states to cooperate. When security is perceived as scarce, states—like brothers—become more concerned about *relative* gains, than about absolute gains. They no longer ask themselves, will both of us gain, but rather, who gains more? When cooperation promises to yield an absolute economic gain to one party, states tend to reject it, fearing that the other party will convert its economic gain into military strength and then use that added strength to win by coercion in later rounds."

"So you're saying there will *never* be a permanent peace? How depressing!" Fornax interjected.

"Depressing or not, there will never be a permanent peace, my friend—never! You can't uninvent the bow and arrow or the force gun or the nuclear bomb. Armed conflict is our evolution. You can't remove that gene. States are principally concerned about their relative power within the system, so they constantly search for opportunities to take advantage of one another. If anything, they prefer to see their adversaries decline, and invariably will do whatever they can to speed the process of decline and to maximize the distance of the fall. Generally speaking, a nation will make war whenever it has a reasonable prospect of gaining anything by it."

"But shouldn't the increasing volume of world trade make countries more dependent upon one another and thus less willing to fight with each other?"

"Not true. Economic interdependence is as likely to lead to conflict as it is to lead to cooperation; states will struggle to escape the vulnerability which dependence creates. In times of crisis or of actual war, states which have come to depend upon others for critical economic supplies will fear being cutoff or blackmailed. They may very well respond to that fear by trying to seize the source of the supply preemptively by force."

"So I *was* right about fear being a driving force."

"Indeed, it is one of the critical elements," Sam acknowledged.

"But doesn't the spread of democracy enhance the chances for peace?" Fornax questioned.

"The idea that democracies are more peaceful is a vision of international relations shared by liberals and conservatives alike. But in actuality, the historical record shows that democracies are every bit as likely to fight wars as are authoritarian states, the only difference being that, in the past, democracies have fought wars less often with *other* democracies."

"Okay, Sam, slow down. This is all very interesting, but just what does it have to do with *me*?"

"I'm coming to that," Dr. Sam replied impatiently. "As you have suggested, your device is destabilizing; but I don't think you know the half of it. Just as most men cannot run a two-and-a-half-minute kilometer, and most gcars cannot exceed a speed of eighty kilometers per hour, the spaceships of our era—that is, if you want to call a DUMP shuttle a spaceship—have a top speed under forty thousand kilometers per hour. Now along *you* come with your Fornax Drive able to deliver 130 thousand kilometers per *second*, and the frontiers of space instantly get closer by a factor of ten thousand! *This* is why your thing is so damn dangerous. As far as our world is concerned, in fact, as far as the entire *solar* system is concerned, all is now within one man's reach—*your* reach. And whoever takes it away from you will be able to subjugate just about everyone else."

"Subjugate?" an astonished Fornax wailed. "I thought this would free people, not enslave them. I'm out to make money, not war. My Battery is not a weapon."

"To the contrary, it is a very *compelling* weapon. And one which will upset the balance of power. Since the four leading nations are essentially equal matches from a militaristic point of view, the world now enjoys a measure of peace. But if any one of them were to sense that another of their number had snuck ahead, or for that matter, fallen behind, the other three would immediately pounce on her and we would suffer an instant replay of the Great War."

"Is that what happened to your homeland?" Fornax asked, unsure of the answer. "Did everyone suddenly pounce on America?"

"Yes, in a manner of speaking," Sam replied sadly. "She became overextended. Isolationist. Unable to meet all her obligations. She unilaterally disarmed, thus making her an inviting target."

"So are you now telling me that I should *abandon* my project?"

"Not at all. There may yet be a way. We have to package your revolutionary breakthrough as if it were neither revolutionary, nor a breakthrough. That's what'll keep us both alive."

"We? Us?" Fornax quizzed. "Since when did *you* get involved?"

"Since you were irresponsible enough to come to my home, and I was dumb enough to allow you to enter."

"Huh?"

Sam lectured as he got up from his easy chair. "If they shadowed you all the way to the moon, don't you think they followed you here? Doesn't it stand to reason that since I sent you to Lester in the first place, they will figure that I'm in on it too?"

"Well . . . yes," Fornax answered sheepishly. "So, how do we camouflage my discovery?"

"I would recommend lying," Sam replied with an uncharacteristic chuckle. "An undeniably huge breakthrough is never believed, or if it *is* believed, it only serves to generate hostility. But don't take *my* word for it, just ask Galileo. Or Durbin. Both of them ended up in prison for *their* trouble.

"On the other hand," Sam continued, pacing anxiously about the room, "a *moderate* breakthrough will not only be accepted by others, it will generate admiration rather than anger. Whereas people will not be envious of, say a ten percent improvement in a product or in another country's standard of living, they might very well go to *war* to neutralize a two hundred percent improvement. It's the *relative* disadvantages which scare people into rash acts."

Fornax screwed-up his eyebrows in a frown. "Your point eludes me, Sam."

"I gathered that from the look on your face, but consider this: If the DUMP operators can presently manage to run the shuttle route in no better than seven days' time round-trip, they might be open to an offer to run it in say, five days. This represents a modest improvement in efficiency, and not only will they believe you can do it, they will agree to let you try. If, on the other hand, you were to tell them that the whole trip could be done in under twenty-four hours—which is the *truth*—they will refuse to consider it out of hand and have you locked up as a crazy instead. If, by some stretch of the imagination they *do* believe you, then they will more than likely use force to separate you from your invention, preferring to steal it for themselves."

"Yes, I'm beginning to see that now."

"Assuming they accept your offer to handle the job for them on a five-day cycle, then you might consider making them a further proposition. If they will agree to finance the construction of a new shuttle according to your exact specifications, then you will knock forty percent off the price that you would otherwise have to charge them if you were forced to use their old equipment for the job."

"You make it all sound so simple."

"Believe me, Fornax, it is. If you follow my plan, you will retain control over the Drive technology, and—of even greater importance—you will *gain* control over the essential element which makes your device so worthwhile—the DUMP itself. That way, no one will be the wiser that the very wastes you are transporting to the moon are in fact charging the Battery which makes the whole trip possible to begin with."

"And," Fornax interrupted energetically, "no one will really know just how long the trip actually takes!"

"Exactly!" Sam exclaimed. "This is the single best way to keep your secret *as* a secret, make some money from the darn thing, and keep us both alive."

"Sam, you're a genius!" Fornax complimented. "But you're also full of it!" he added hastily. "They'll never go for it in a million years! It's much too easy. And it's much too good for *us*."

Dr. Sam shook his head. "Au contraire, my friend, I think they will go for it. In the first place, they don't know how good it is for us because they don't know enough about your Battery or how it works. And don't forget, transporting nuclear wastes to the moon is an expensive, dangerous, and dirty business; one which serves no strategic military purpose and one which is not glamorous in any way.

"Trust me, Fornax, civilized peoples hate to get their hands dirty.

They love their flower gardens, but hate to weed them. They love their flush toilets, but hate to clean them. They love their cuddly little babies, but hate to change their putrid diapers. Mark my words, they'll *pounce* on your proposal. And when they do, and when you get ahold of that new ship, promise me you'll take me along on her maiden voyage; I've never been to space before."

Fornax nodded his head in assent.

"Now," Sam concluded, "you've taken enough of my time. Go meet my brother and his henchmen for that BeHolden Day toast you promised them and leave me the hell alone! My daughter Carina will be here shortly for dinner, and I must get the house picked up before she arrives."

And with that, he showed Fornax to the door.

13

White Is The Color Of Evil

Lodged between two dilapidated tenements in an unsavory corner of Jaffna near the docks, the Corkscrew Pub was probably unique both in its unwholesome reputation and in its gaudy decor. Its reputation as a cowboy-tough bar catering to the ruffians of the high seas was legend from Port Elizabeth to Sydney; and like a bug-light, it attracted every breed of pleasure-seeking vermin one could possibly suppose. In other words, it was the perfect spot for a man of Lester's ilk to want to commemorate BeHolden Day.

Weeks ago, when Fornax was first here in the company of Red, he had judiciously avoided entering the premises—and with good reason. Even now, as he paused once again on the littered street in front of the Corkscrew, everything about the place told him to stay away, beginning with the appalling stench of fire-brewed tortan which intoxicated the muggy night air.

It didn't end there, though. There was also the amorous red glow of lights which bathed him from the doorway of the bimbooker-house next door, plus the growling of an unseen bio-canine which no doubt doubled as a guard dog when it wasn't out chasing stray cats. All of it said danger, stay away!

Suddenly feeling stupid, Fornax scolded himself for ever having agreed to meet Lester and the Captain here in this run-down neighborhood so late in the day. Next time, he would know better!

Though his heart was filled with trepidation, Fornax took a deep breath and shoved open the massive set of swinging doors which hung across the entranceway in the fashion of an American Wild West saloon. As he crossed the threshold into the jam-packed tavern, he was greeted by the nauseating odor of smouldering tobacco and the deafening roar of cack music. It was quite a spectacle to behold!

With the gin mill bursting at the seams with people, Fornax could barely make out the immense, twenty-meter-long bar which dominated the room along one wall or the dozen or so poker tables which were scattered haphazardly throughout the rest of the establishment.

Adjacent to the bar, a row of tall stools provided seating for a lucky few, though most of the drunken patrons had to be content to lean against the brass rail and bang on the tabletop for service. Behind the counter, a half-dozen scantily-clad bartenders struggled feverishly to keep up with the incessant demands of the delirious holiday crowd.

BeHolden Day could count as its antecedents the American tradition of Thanksgiving, as well as English harvest festivals dating back at least a millenium. The religious fundamentalists who had been summarily thrown out of Europe found a cornucopia in the New World, and their Thanksgiving Day was not only an acknowledgment of their good fortune, it was considered by them to be a day of grace as well.

Sadly enough, the holiday had devolved over the passing centuries into an orgy, and by Fornax's time, BeHolden Day was little more than an ugly caricature of its former self. Oh, the turkey was oftentimes still there, along with all the trimmings, but nowadays, it was a carnival of engorgement marked by bouts of excessive eating and drinking. Like the Saturnalia festivals of ancient Rome, it was a period of orgiastic revelry; only in weight-conscious modern times, the overconsumption was often remedied with a round of forced regurgitation. In some circles, this latter event was even a matter of some pride, what with would-be throwers-up lining the streets, buckets in hand, to compete for distance or else for volume.

And if that weren't enough to mar the solemnity of this once holy celebration, by nightfall on this, the fourth Thursday of November, widespread brawling would typically erupt in pubs all across the land.

Having once read of these uncontrollable outbreaks of violent behavior, Fornax cautiously pressed ever deeper into the saloon, warily eyeing the faces in the crowd for the first hint of trouble.

The place was absolute pandemonium—a complete uproar! While he stood there mouth agape, drunken rabble-rousers jostled one another sloshing tortan-ale everywhere, bawdy bimbookers hustled the room trying to sell themselves, and macho revelers busily shouted gross obscenities and boisterous challenges at each other. Never in his life had he been in such a place!

Unaccustomed as Fornax was to the raucous holiday atmosphere, he carefully negotiated his way through the riotous, strobe-lit tavern taking a seat near one end of the grand bar. The cigarette smoke was so thick, and the high-ceilinged pub so splattered with restless shadows, he could barely make out a thing.

From where he sat astride his bar stool sipping the froth off a cold mug of tortan-ale, Fornax searched the throng for any signs of his partners. It was a difficult task, made doubly so by the annoying flash of the strobe. This, plus the mindnumbing blast of cack music and the commotion caused by the holo-people made locating either one of them a near impossibility. Technology had come such a long way, it was now all but impossible to distinguish a virtual image from a real one, that is, unless you reached out to squeeze a cute one on the behind. A virtual woman might give you an electric shock; a real one, a jab in the ribs! It was anybody's guess how many of which were in *this* crowd.

Once Fornax's eyes adjusted to the darkness, however, he spied Captain Michael sitting far across the room looking as if he had just lost his last friend in the whole world. Indeed, it seemed as if the Captain were in a trance, a trance so deep he didn't notice Fornax waving to him from across the bar.

With the number of bar stools at a premium, and with Fornax himself reeling from the dizzying first effects of the potent drink, he was reluctant to give up his seat, at least for awhile. When, an instant later, a festively-clad Jaffnian nymph came up to him from behind and began rubbing her lithe body against his, Fornax forgot about the Captain altogether.

The temptress was real, no holo-image at all, and she laced her arms about his waist, baiting him with her wares, and probing him with her powerful hands. Fornax never saw her face, but her firm breasts left an indentation in his back, her perfume an indelible imprint on his brain.

Before he could turn in his place and begin taking advantage of his good fortune, a fracas broke out at the opposite end of the bar.

Instinctively, the muscles in his abdomen tightened. His eyes narrowed. A sixth sense told him that something was amiss, that the woman was a contrivance to distract him, that the fisticuffs were a cover for something much more sinister!

His survival reflex suddenly triggered, Fornax broke free of the woman's arms. Though the femme fatale tried to hold him back, he fought his way through the mob in the direction of Captain Michael's table. Every step of the way, though, he found his progress hampered by the thickness of the horde.

The scuffle soon became a fight, and the fight, a free-for-all which rapidly engulfed the entire tavern in a blizzard of flying bottles, crashing chairs, and pommeling fists. Even so, Fornax kept his eyes fixed on the Captain.

Though he was nervously staring about with a wild look of terror in his eyes, Captain Michael remained obediently seated. It was as if he were expecting someone—anyone—to help rescue him from the midst of this mayhem.

Fornax had approached to within perhaps eight meters of where the Captain was seated when he saw it—the glint of an upraised blade! Though the knife appeared to have come out of nowhere, this was definitely no holo-image!

Fornax shouted a warning to his friend, but the place was so loud, the sound of his voice was lost in the din. There was nothing he could do to stop the assassin's attack!

In the next fraction of a second it happened. Silently approaching the seated Captain from behind, the killer grabbed Michael's head, locking it firmly into the crook of one arm. Then, as if he were thoroughly enjoying himself, the assailant snorted out a staccato laugh before moving to brutally slash the Captain's throat.

The cut to the man's neck was so deep, his head flopped to one side like a slab of meat, a blood-stained ear coming to rest on his otherwise untouched shoulder. Then, without making another sound, the killer tossed the murderous knife on the table in front of him and melted into the chaotic throng.

Fornax was horrified! It had all happened so fast, he never even saw the thug's face, nor how he was dressed. All he saw now was blood—lots and lots of blood! And all he smelled was perfume, the same unusual perfume he had smelled before, the perfume worn by the wench who had been working her magic on him only seconds earlier!

Fornax spun to face her, but she too had vanished into the crowd without a trace!

Fornax was sick. A good man now lay dead, and he was at least partially to blame. Like Vishnu before him, the Captain had died right before his very eyes, and he had been powerless to prevent either man's death. How close did he have to be to make a difference?

Positive he would be ill, Fornax stared in disbelief at the drunken faces around him. No one in the pub seemed to care. To them, Michael's murder was unremarkable. In this neighborhood, at this time of day, people were murdered all the time; stabbings and killings were a nightly event. One more or one less, what did it matter?

As Fornax stood there, his stomach doing somersaults, he realized that the BeHolden Day festivities would carry on with scant notice being given to the corpse—or to the widening pool of blood collecting on the creaky wooden floor. Eventually the Jaffna police would be summoned, of course, but it would be more of a courtesy call than anything; the police wouldn't take the time to investigate the death of a lowly DUMPSTER, and certainly not in a place as notorious as the Corkscrew. The authorities would tag the assassination as an "accidental homicide," and it would soon be forgotten.

Smothering the urge to scream, Fornax covered his mouth with his hand and marched stiffly from the saloon. By now he was in a panic. Could there be any doubt that he would be the next to die?

Looking both ways, he stumbled out into the middle of the moonlit street. Though his feet were like clay, his instincts told him to run. He was just about to when, all of a sudden, from out of the darkness, a hand clamped down upon his shoulder.

Figuring this was it, Fornax acted to defend himself. Summoning every last ounce of courage, he grabbed for the man's wrist with one hand, even as he fumbled for his blade with the other. Clamping down hard, Fornax spun to confront his attacker.

He was jolted by the face that stared back at him. It was Lester!

"They killed Michael!" Fornax panted, his face ashen, his body shaking like a leaf. "They slit his throat not three steps from where I stood!"

"There was no other way—it simply had to be done," Lester calmly replied, trying to quiet his jittery friend. "He was working undercover for the British. You and I are working for the Chinese."

Fornax didn't know what to say. He didn't know whether to hug Lester or gouge his eyes out with his blade.

"We need to get outta here before the coppers arrive," Lester said with some urgency. "BC's waiting for us; plus you have an appointment to keep in Hong Kong."

Too numb to argue, Fornax blindly followed Lester towards the tube-station. He had no idea what trouble lay ahead.

14
Overlord

The speaker was a sly Chinaman. Everything about him was evil, beginning with his mustache. It twitched furtively when he spoke.

"Lester has told me a great deal about you," he said, "some good, some bad. He tells me, for instance, that money is about the only thing which seems to interest you. If that assessment is correct—and I hope for your sake that it is—I expect to be able to oblige you handily. You see, I already have all the money I could possibly want; what interests *me* is not more wealth, but more territory."

Fornax squirmed uneasily in the immense chair. Lester and BC had been asked to wait outside in the hallway, leaving him stranded alone in the room with Overlord Ling Tsui. To say that he was petrified would have been generous indeed! Fornax still couldn't get the terrible events of last night out of his head. And now here he was, sitting alone before the man he hated perhaps more than any other in the whole world!

"Emperor," he sputtered, unsure how to properly address the man. "Sir . . . "

The Overlord strutted back and forth across the room as he spoke, his tiny feet making little dimples in the sumptuous carpet of his private study. "Land forces are obsolete, wouldn't you agree? And navies; well, they are even *more* impotent, floating there in the ocean like so many sitting ducks. No, my good friend, the only way for me to enlarge *my* domain is to extend the reach of my weapons through the skies."

As Fornax sat there listening carefully to what the Overlord had to say, he cursed his own unrelenting greed for having landed him in this predicament. He couldn't have been stupider if he'd tried! And now, to avoid suffering Captain Michael's fate, he apparently had no choice but to cooperate with this fiend.

With an evil smirk, the Overlord continued. "It all boils down to this: If I am to seize control of the skies, I will need airships fast enough to outrun even the British suborbs. I will need an orbiting command post so impregnable no one would *dare* attack it, a command post armed with a weapon so lethal my enemies would rather bow down before me than risk unleashing my wrath!"

Fornax swallowed hard. "I know nothing of outposts. Nor of weapons."

"Don't be a fool!" the Overlord roared. "Between the storage capabilities of your Battery and the radioactivity concentrated there at the DUMP, the moon can provide my armies with all the fuel they will ever need! Indeed, what better place to station a fortress than right there on the moon?"

"I am but a scientist," Fornax calmly explained.

"And a good one at that," the deranged monarch agreed. "Surely you can be persuaded to design some big gun for me—an electromagnetic cannon perhaps, or a giant howitzer—anything which I can use, whenever the mood suits me, to thrust shells or missiles or whatever down upon my rivals like so many lightning bolts from Heaven above."

"You're mad as a hatter!" Fornax exclaimed, rising from his chair to look the Overlord squarely in the eye. "I refuse to have any part of this!"

"Angry maybe, but not mad," Ling quietly retorted. "And you *will* do as I ask."

Stepping over to the window and gazing down upon the carefully tended gardens behind the palace, Fornax said, "You have made it abundantly clear what it is *you* want, but I'm still a little bit vague as to what *I* get out of the deal."

"You get to live," the Chinaman rejoined, glaring back at Fornax.

Suddenly, Fornax felt awfully small. Small, and terribly alone. The horrible picture of the Captain slumped facedown on the blood-stained poker table in the Corkscrew Pub stared back at him through the glass.

Still gazing fixedly outside, Fornax swallowed his fear. "I do not respond well to threats," he asserted as boldly as he could.

Impressed by the younger man's cool-headedness under fire, the Overlord softened his attack. "Only jesting, my dear Fornax," he said unconvincingly. "What I meant was, you get to live in *luxury*."

"Go on," Fornax replied stoically. By now he had regained enough of his footing to turn once again and face his adversary.

"For starters, how about your very own personal gcar and driver? Or a luxurious flat on the upper east side? I could even throw in a lifetime membership to the White Zinfandel, the most prestigious club in all of Auckland, a place so expensive, so upper-crust, only a Samuel Matthews could afford its induction fee."

"Such generosity," came the sardonic reply. Though Fornax did his level best not to show it, he couldn't help but be dismayed how easily Ling had brought up Dr. Sam's name. It could only be his not-so-subtle way of telling Fornax that he'd been observed going to Sam's home, just as Sam had feared. Pressing his lips tightly together, Fornax made his gambit.

"And to think, all I have to do is fix it so you can rule the world.

Sorry to disappoint you, Ling, but you'll have to do a whole lot better than a fancy apartment and a club membership if you want to buy *me*."

"Name your price," the dictator barked.

"Afghanistan."

"Afghanistan?" the Overlord asked in a surprised tone, almost choking on the words. "The *country?*"

"All of it," Fornax demanded flatly.

"Such patriotism for a traitor."

Caught completely off-guard, Fornax stammered, "What? . . . Whatever . . . do you mean?"

"Judging by the gray color of your face, I'm confident you know *precisely* what I mean."

"You *are* crazy," Fornax declared.

"Quite," Ling agreed, his dark almond-shaped eyes revealing a pathetic hunger. "Still, wouldn't it be accurate to say that you deserted your beloved country in its very moment of need?"

"That was a long time ago," Fornax admitted, lowering his head in shame. "Anyway, why should you care?"

"Because you killed my son."

Fornax shook his head as if to say no. "You must have me confused with some other soldier," he said respectfully. "I killed neither *your* son, nor anyone else's. In fact," he added proudly, "I fired but a single shot in that whole, bloody, god-awful war."

"My son was an airchop pilot," the Overlord remarked, a note of sadness creeping into his voice.

The truth was so incomprehensible, Fornax couldn't say a word. For an eternity there was complete silence as the two men stared at one another from opposite ends of the room.

Unnerved by the sorrow reflected in the Overlord's eyes, Fornax realized—for perhaps the first time in his life—that there were two sides to every war, that even enemy soldiers had moms and dads who grieved for their dead sons.

"Fornax Nehrengel—that's your *real* name, isn't it? You shot down my son's airchop," the Overlord said in a spiteful, threatening tone. "You murdered my boy, and I assure you, if I don't get your complete cooperation—and I mean now—I will shoot you myself, right where you stand."

Fornax had no doubt that Ling meant what he said, yet he kept quiet, his mind racing to see if there was any way out of this, any way at all.

"As I said before," the Overlord reiterated, "so long as you agree to do my bidding, I will let you live."

"All right," Fornax acceded, preparing to do whatever it would take to stay alive. "I'll do your bidding. Tell me what it is you want."

Delighted to finally have Fornax in his corner, Ling began to talk excitedly, saliva foaming from his mouth like a rabid dog. "Build me a fleet of superfast spaceships. Build me some sort of pulse beam or super gatling gun or anything which I can use to bend the world to my will."

"So long as you're paying the bills, I'll do whatever you tell me to. But aren't you being a bit premature?"

"Whatever do you mean?"

"I've barely had time to analyze our results. If you don't believe me, ask Lester. Surely he's told you by now that we completed the trial run only a few days ago. These things can't be rushed," Fornax said, making a bid to stall for more time. "Not for you; not for anyone!

"And while we're at it," he continued, remembering Dr. Sam's sage advice, "before I can have even a prayer of putting together a vessel capable of doing all the many things you have in mind, I must have an entirely new shuttle built, one designed by me and outfitted to my exact specifications. Not only that, I'll need to replace the pilot you arranged to have murdered, won't I?"

Framing the accusation that way was a daring move on Fornax's part, but he had to know the truth, he had to know whether or not the Overlord would accept responsibility for Captain Michael's death.

Ling's reply was quick and blunt. "I couldn't trust the man any longer, so he had to go," the Overlord sneered, his fu-manchu looking more sinister than ever. "I have always made it a practice to dispose of those who have let me down," he boasted. "I won't have that problem with you, will I?" The implicit threat was not veiled even in the slightest.

"My trustworthiness is beyond reproach," Fornax assured him.

"For your sake, I hope so," Ling declared. "It is agreed then. I will see to it that you get the shuttle you require. But let me remind you, Mister Nehrengel—if you cross me, there is no hole on this planet deep enough for you to hide in."

"You can count on me, sire. I won't let you down."

"Good. That's what I want to hear."

As they ended their exchange and Fornax was dismissed to rejoin Lester and BC still waiting obediently for him out in the hallway, all he could think of was escape. Escape from the Overlord's palace, escape from the mess his ambition had gotten him into, escape from this world!

He vowed that if he ever did get his hands on that new shuttle, it certainly wouldn't be to serve the Overlord's whims, it would be to escape from this evil monster for good!

But even before he could do that, he first had to warn Sam. As the savvy old fellow had correctly surmised, they were *all* in danger, even Carina, his headstrong daughter!

PART II

1
Controversy

University of Auckland
Earlier That Day

Maxwell had been so gentle and considerate in his lovemaking, hastening his rhythm at her prodding, then teasing her madly when he slowed. Delighted by an involuntary tremor, she had made a determined effort to quiet her logical mind and allow a wave of passion to wash away her every fear. Masked by the darkness, the two lovers had labored to crest simultaneously but . . .

"And how would you respond to *that?*" the man asked, his accusing tone jarring Carina from any further recollections of the previous night.

"Oh, dear, I *am* sorry, Dr. Janz. Be a doll, won't you, and repeat the question."

When Carina spoke, she did so with all the politeness a woman in her position could muster. The Board of Inquiry proceedings were barely half an hour old, and already she was bored with them. Her latest book had set off a firestorm of controversy in her department, and now, with Dr. Janz in charge of the witch hunt, this moronic hearing would probably end with her being placed on some sort of academic probation. Carina thought Janz was an idiot, a velcroid to use her father's words. The other four panel members weren't much better, except perhaps Marilyn. She was open-minded, if a bit mousy.

Flustered by the prospect of having to repeat himself, Dr. Janz growled at her. "Just because we haven't found any fossil evidence to support the idea of slow, adaptive change doesn't *prove* that it didn't happen that way. Wouldn't you agree?"

"Don't misquote me," Carina replied, pausing for effect. "I'm not arguing that Darwinian evolution did not occur, only that there have been huge jumps as well as miniscule adaptations. The overwhelming percentage of these huge jumps were poor biological designs, and these grossly-malformed mistakes died before they could even leave behind so much as a *trace* of their brief existence in the fossil record. Every once in a while, though, one of these huge leaps of change produced an organ, or a limb, or even a complete creature which *was* successful."

"Blasphemy!" chanted Professor Franklin.

"Madness!" agreed the double-chinned Dr. Darrell Blanding.

Then Dr. Nodding started in on her. His voice was thick with sarcasm. "Now let me see if I have this straight. Huge jumps in evolution occur, but the fossil record only captures the *good* huge jumps. Is that what you said Dr. Matthews—or may I call you Carina?"

"Really, Dr. Nodding, this is *your* inquisition—you may call me anything you damn well please," she retorted in a poisonous tone. "But since the fossil record clearly supports my notion of occasional bouts of enormous yet relatively quick change, I don't see why I'm on trial here."

Out of the corner of one eye Carina could see Marilyn quietly nodding her head in agreement.

Administrator Janz responded icily. "Don't flatter yourself, Dr. Matthews—it is not you who is on trial here. This university is supported by tax dollars, and the taxpayers do not wish to underwrite heresy. You, my sweet, are controversial."

"Don't *my sweet* me, you bastard! I am many things, but 'your sweet' is certainly not one of them," Carina shot back defiantly. "The taxpayers couldn't give a flying fig about me. It is *you* who is stirring this brew. Your mind is entirely closed to new ideas."

"Listen, you little . . . "

"No, you listen! I have had quite enough of your crap!" Carina shouted angrily, her beautiful brown eyes flashing.

Suddenly rising to her feet, Carina towered over Janz as if she meant to scratch out his eyes right then and there. "This is a damn kangaroo court!" she shrieked.

"Do sit down," Dr. Janz ordered, his voice ricocheting off the walls. "I'm not done with you yet."

Sensing that Carina was about to bolt from the room, Marilyn intervened. Pleading with the taller woman, she said, "You must see this thing through, Carina. If you don't, you're kaputt—done with—they'll expel you for certain. Stay here; finish what you have to say. I promise you, everything will be okay. Your ideas are good, but they're radical. You must stand and defend them."

With a noble bob of the head, Carina flung back a lock of auburn hair from her face. Then, folding her long, lanky legs beneath her, she gathered her pride and sat back down. Even in her moment of distress, the woman was a picture of confident beauty. "I apologize for raising my voice," she said. "It won't happen again. Please continue with your interrogation."

Dr. Janz was well-pleased with himself, and the smug look on his face attested to that fact. Successfully goading this woman into losing her temper was nearly as satisfying as actually getting her tossed off the university research staff.

"Now, where were we?" he asked innocently.

Carina picked up from where she'd left off. "Most researchers would agree that the fossil pattern is one of awesome species stability punctuated by short periods of relatively rapid change."

His jowls rolling madly, Dr. Blanding declared, "But the fossil record is itself exceedingly fragmentary and untrustworthy. Heavens, fossilization is a rare event to begin with!"

"Stipulated," Carina agreed, looking around the room. "But by what means can natural selection act swiftly?"

Answering her own question before anyone else could, she said, "As you well know, it cannot. Other, more cataclysmic . . . "

"Do you mean to *persist* with this sacrilege?" Janz interrupted.

"You really are on a witch hunt, aren't you?" Marilyn objected angrily.

"Watch your mouth, lady, or you'll be next," he cautioned.

Unfazed by the exchange, Carina continued. "As I was saying, the specter of rapid change is a threat to standard theory—and apparently, to you as well, Dr. Janz. Other, more cataclysmic, forces must be at work here. Perhaps an asteroid collision with the Earth, or else an immense radiation burst from the sun, or a strange wobble in the Earth's axis, or some other titanic event, *anything* which would work to interrupt a long period of evolutionary stability and produce a gigantic burst of genetic change. The triggering event, whatever it may be, would be so stressful to existing strands of DNA that it would set off a torrent of mutations, and thus an explosion of new species. Like I said before, the overwhelming proportion of these new species would be duds, unable to survive, but a few *would* survive—and they would truly be masterpieces! It is these precious few who would appear in the fossil record as sudden leaps of evolutionary change.

"So there you have it folks—my heresy. I call it 'Explosive Diversity,' but then you already know that from my book, don't you?"

The room was quiet.

Satisfied that she had put Dr. Janz and the other three simpletons in their place, Carina pressed on. "Gentlemen, if I might be allowed to make an analogy. Imagine, if you will, tying paint brushes to the tails of a dozen barking dogs. Imagine setting them loose upon a canvas, their tails wagging back and forth across the cloth. If you performed this experiment repeatedly, most of the results would be ugly concoctions of color, abhorrent to the eye. Occasionally, though, the results would be pleasant, even beautiful. Once in a great while, they would be every bit as good as the work of an amateur artist. And as farfetched as it may sound, chance dictates that once in perhaps ten million canvasses, the canines will accidentally even paint a portrait of Mona Lisa quality! Go figure."

"I suppose you'll tell us next that an explosion in a linotype factory can produce a copy of the Encyclopedia Commonwealth?" Professor Franklin quipped.

When Carina fired back, she was disparaging in the nth degree. "Dr. Franklin, I have it on good authority from your buddy Darrell Blanding here that if your brains were dynamite, you wouldn't have enough to blow out a birthday candle. What say you to *that?*" she snarled, rising from her chair and twisting her fingers into a disrespectful hand gesture.

Too stunned to respond, Professor Franklin watched silently as Dr. Carina Matthews strode purposefully from the hearing room, her spirited head held high. Like her father, the woman was tall and strong-willed.

As she left, Dr. Janz shouted after her. "The Board will notify you of our final decision, Matthews. Until then, consider yourself on academic probation pending formal dismissal charges. And don't drag your father into this," he warned, "or I swear . . . "

The slammed door masked his threat.

Carina marched briskly down the hall in the direction of the parking lot. Her eyes were brimming with tears. For pride's sake, she was determined to put as much distance between herself and her persecutors as swiftly as she possibly could.

As she zoomed along the sidewalk, the spring sun warming her face, Carina cursed under her breath. "Damn them anyway! You'd think that people calling themselves scientists would be more interested in *promoting* innovative thought than in squelching it! Now I know how Durbin must have felt. And Galileo before him!"

Carina crossed the parking lot at a rapid gait. The words came just as fast!

Even for her, it was impossible to deny the obvious: gradual evolutionary change made much more sense than the explosive variety *she* postulated. That was the orthodoxy, after all, and Carina once thought that way too. But orthodoxies changed, and Carina was proud to be at the forefront of new thinking. What was unconscionable was to now be suddenly threatened with dismissal from the university! And over a theory as simple and straightforward as Explosive Diversity, no less. That was beyond comprehension! How could anyone be so narrow-minded?

Practically beside herself with indignation, Carina fumbled in her purse for the magnetic pad to unlock the door to her gcar. In her haste, she nearly forgot to retract the gcar's charging device before pulling away from the curb.

I'd be curious to hear what 'ole Janz has to say about my *really* controversial stuff, she fumed, barely slowing for the stop sign. Like my newhuman hypothesis, for instance! Now *there's* an idea worth having a cow over! She chuckled irreverently.

Struggling to sort out her feelings as she drove, Carina swung her gcar out into the morning traffic, weaving it carefully through the narrow streets.

Dad tried to warn me, didn't he? The status quo hates to be upset, he always told me. Then there was his lecture about the dangers of shattering the theological calm with my speculations on the future course of human evolution. But I wouldn't listen, would I? And now look at the bind I'm in!

"Damn it!" she exclaimed passionately. Carina couldn't stand it when her father was right. Yet, even in her anger, there was no mistaking the love she harbored for her old man.

Carina rolled down the side window of her sporty gcar. The fresh spring air poured across her forehead, hopelessly twisting her rich brown hair into knots. With each block, her temper cooled.

Pouncing on the accelerator, Carina passed one gcar after another, each time glancing in the rear-view mirror to safely maneuver around the other vehicle, each time airily contemplating her own provocative reflection dancing back at her from off the glass. Carina had inviting features, of that there was little doubt. A nice package, some men would say. Round laughing eyes, unblemished skin, and a world-class figure. It made bedding a man easy, a quality she had turned to her advantage on more than one occasion. Put it all together with a zesty attitude, a first-class mind, and a topnotch wit, and Carina was a desirable catch. Only problem was, she didn't want to be caught!

Not that sex with Max wasn't great, but like Phillipe before him, and Roger before *him*, Max was more of a plaything than a permanent fixture. In fact, she didn't really love any of them. As preoccupied as Carina was with her scientific pursuits, she was unwilling to risk having anything interfere with them—and certainly not for the sake of something as pedestrian as romantic commitment!

As if to make that very point, no sooner had Carina turned into her drive than an idea popped into her head, an idea which had been brewing in there for weeks, an idea which she wanted to be sure and jot down in her diary before it escaped her.

Throwing open the door to her flat, she rushed to her writing desk excited as ever about her latest research project. Dr. Janz and his three-ring circus be damned! This was more important!

2
Newhuman

Carina had her first sexual adventure when she was but a sophomore in high school; and although it didn't culminate in intercourse, the intimacy did proceed far enough for her to uncover no less than two of its several carnal delights. Ultimately, though, her sophomore year was remarkable in another, much more important respect—she became schooled in the value of a daily diary, a habit which stayed with her all the days of her life.

It was there, in Carina's journal, that all her theories found an audience—even the more bizarre ones. And while some of her ideas were brought into the world stillborn, just as many were hatched there alive and kicking, and screaming to be heard. Today's diary entry began, as always, with the date:

"November 26, 2430. Dear Diary: Just as it once was a matter of heresy to declare that the Earth revolved around the sun, so it has also been a deeply ingrained human conceit to assume that the sole purpose behind millions of years of evolution has been to usher *Homo sapiens* into the world.

"And just as some would deny the possibility of evolution out-of-hand, even among those who subscribe to the theory, there are those who still vigorously reject the proposition that Mother Nature is, even today, working unceasingly to improve upon the current human model. Indeed, in a throwback to the earliest days of religious mysticism, most people still cling in desperation to the fiction of an immutable, unchanging Man.

"Two years ago I offered the simple and, to some, the infuriating argument that the present human species was not a finished product, but rather only the latest in a series of experimental versions. Had I known the repercussions, I might have kept my mouth shut.

"Rebuffed by my peers, and lacking any hard proof to support my conjecture, I set out to make a comprehensive comparison of modern day gene-maps with the original gene-map completed nearly four centuries ago. The results astonished me, and I now have unimpeachable evidence which confirms my suspicions: a remarkable genetic variation is working its way through the population from its apparent point of origin somewhere on the Asian continent, most probably the Chinese satrapy of Afghanistan.

"I have given this altered stretch of human DNA a name—signature genes—and I theorize that the presence of these signature genes may correspond to the budding of the latest branch on the human family tree, the *newhuman* branch.

"Because a genetic variation is not in and of itself a sufficient ingredient to endow a new breed, it is premature to consider this fledgling offshoot a distinct race. Yet, given adequate time—and the right conditions—species separation *will* occur.

"As a general proposition, divergence of two related species will result when a geographic barrier or other physical obstruction permits the two lineages to lose contact and evolve unmolested from one other. A mutant toad hops to the next pond, for instance. There, isolated from his former brethren, he successfully populates a fresh niche.

"For plants and simpler animals, effective isolation-barriers might take the form of a mountain range or a fast-flowing stream, the former blocking off one valley from the next, the latter slicing one meadow neatly in two. But among truly intelligent animals, like man, even the distance between two continents would prove insufficient to keep the sub-populations from mixing.

"With geographic impediments thus of limited value in achieving isolation, cultural hurdles like prejudice and racism would come into play. Short of migrating to another world, a nascent tribe of newhumans would have no choice but to blend in with the existing ethnic groups as best they could. It is interesting to speculate how they might fare.

"At the outset, newhumans won't even realize they are genetically different from their neighbors. Reared by oldhumans and indoctrinated to think like them, newhumans will come to believe only that they are weird or perhaps somehow abnormal. Their intelligence will make them outcasts. As children, they will be ridiculed by their peers, and as adults they will be shunned. And unless they are lucky enough to find others of their kind along the way, they will be plagued by terrible loneliness.

"At least in some instances, their abilities and ambition may be so vastly superior to those around them, these newhumans will be tempted to resort to drink or perhaps to drugs in order to nullify their boredom. More often, though, they will be drawn into business or academia and will pursue those disciplines with such fervor and intensity as to become physically addicted to their chosen line of work. Oldhumans will derisively label them as 'workaholics' (or worse), but it won't make any difference—for a newhuman his work would be a narcotic, the only one strong enough to combat his extreme isolation. Which is not to say that oldhumans are as a rule lazy, or that all newhumans will hold hard work in high esteem, only that the great preponderance of newhumans will pursue their careers with such zeal that it might be considered by some an addiction—preferable, of course, to liquor or dope, but an addiction all the same.

"As a consequence of their work ethic, newhumans will enjoy standards of living far above those of their oldhuman cousins. They will have an uncanny knack for correctly gauging the movements of markets, and in this way will come to command resources far out of proportion to their numbers. But more than that, they will come to dominate the old species in a thousand unimaginable ways, a story which has been the drama of evolution since the dawn of life: New replaces old!

"I would speculate that along with that hyperactive, newhuman brain, heightened desires will have evolved as well. Not for *procreation* purposes, mind you, which is a shame seeing as how few of them there are, but rather for *recreation* purposes.

"For these people, sex would be a tonic, a form of entertainment to pacify their hyperactive imaginations. It wouldn't be a perversion, not even in the oldhuman sense of the word, but rather an unquenchable thirst for physical pleasure. Orgasm floods the brain with chemicals which the soul finds addictive. Sex is the ultimate narcotic, and I, its most enthusiastic junkie!

"But, Madame Diary, this is not the only confession I must make to you today; there is one other. Though I say it now in whispers, I admit I am a newhuman. I suspect my brilliant father is one as well. I won't speculate about my mother, God rest her soul.

"Unfortunately, there is no safe way for me to expose myself as a newhuman, or to reveal my research findings on signature genes. Such a disclosure could subject me to relentless persecution—even death. As father always says, 'The status quo hates to be upset.'

"But if staying here in Auckland means persecution, why not leave? Is there no planet in the heavens suitable for migration? Is space really the dead end it is claimed to be?

"I wonder."

3
Space

By the time Carina was done scribbling in her diary, the sun had reached its highest point for the day. But rather than break for lunch, she turned to address the question of why space travel had come to such a dismal end.

Sitting in front of her info-terminal, eyes locked on the screen, Carina pawed at the keyboard. It had taken her only moments to feed the electronic monster her access code and have her status verified by voice-print ID. Her last keystroke had unleashed the search engine on its Boolean journey through the hundred-million-word archives looking for just the right essay to meet her precise needs. Even now, the coaxial tentacles of her info-terminal were reaching out like an octopus to the member country net, locking onto key words and scanning the purple ether for content. Less than a millisecond later it had snatched up its quarry and displayed the article on the video screen for her to read:

"Astronauts began as little more than helpless passengers strapped to ballistic missiles. Although the underlying concept was elementary, building a rocket powerful enough and reliable enough to lift a human into space was a prodigiously complicated business for the technocrats of the twentieth century.

"At the outset, national pride guided America to the moon first. Realization of that goal, however, left the world bored with space, and after that, no one even bothered to revisit the moon for another thirty-five years. In retrospect, it was as if the then President Kennedy realized it was within his grasp to reach into the future, grab a decade of time from the twenty-first century, and slip it neatly into the 1960s. In any event, it was not until the African Smelting and Resource Company discovered a field of meteorite craters containing commercial-grade silver-bearing ore, that space really began to explode with activity.

"Within months of the discovery, ASARCO had landed a skeleton crew on the moon and initiated strip-mining operations. The miners' living conditions were cramped and spartan; nevertheless, within a few years' time a burgeoning *moon-town* had burrowed itself into the protective rock of a nearby crater wall. Luna, as it was called, boasted more than one hundred residents, including a full complement of miners, engineers, cooks, crooks, medics, and bimbookers.

"Unlike the frontier towns of early Earth, life for the citizens of Luna was highly-regimented. Luxuries were at a premium, and if the sheriff of *this* town sent a miscreant packing, it was a death sentence. Beyond the walls of the tiny city there wasn't so much as an ounce of water or a millibar of air. Not only that, lethal radiation and sub-zero temperatures awaited anyone who, even for an instant, ventured outside the cocoon of the colony without wearing a double-density spacesuit. Thus, it was fear, not the law, which kept the residents of Luna in line.

"The strip-mining operations were reminiscent of similar enterprises back on Earth. Giant quarry machines riding atop caterpillar-style tractor treds mashed the rocks into rubble (along with the occasional miner), then cooked the gravel in equally huge kettles until the pure ore oozed out and bubbled to the top. The molten metal was then poured off into cannonball-shaped molds before being cooled and shot back to Earth by railgun. Up to this point, nothing unusual of course, though the next step defied imagination. Suspended in orbit, high above the planet, were a series of enormous steel-mesh 'catcher's mitts.' Each 'mitt' was positioned so as to snag an incoming silver-cannonball and pass it on to a factory on the surface for final processing. Over time the extraction and delivery system became so efficient, and silver so plentiful and cheap, silver foil became the food wrap of choice throughout much of the world.

"Other industrialists followed in ASARCO's footsteps, though the most enduring were the waste handlers. Because of its distance from the Earth's overcrowded population centers and because of its inert surface, the moon quickly emerged as the preferred dumping ground for every manner of toxic human waste, from spent radioactive fuel to an unimaginable array of medical refuse.

"But life on Luna was hard, and seventy years after ASARCO first set up shop there, the moon's inhabitants still numbered under a thousand. It was no migratory haven as some had hoped at the outset, and it certainly offered no new frontier to conquer—at least not in the sense of the American West or the Brazilian Outback. In fact, the moon proved to be such a miserable place to live, it conquered the people who came to settle there in much the same way that North America conquered the hardy Vikings a millenium earlier.

"By the turn of the next century, the mining machines had been totally automated and permanent inhabitation of the moon had ceased. All that remained of man's once energetic presence there were periodic visits to recalibrate the railguns and occasionally repair the robot-driven milling equipment. To this day, the only humans regularly traveling back and forth to the moon are the DUMPSTERS who come to deposit their massive loads of spent nuclear fuel at the designated sites on the far side.

"Unfortunately, in this respect, Mars proved little better. Superficially, at least, the fourth planet was deceptively similar to the third, and it beckoned as the perfect location: Mars's rotation period was nearly the same as the Earth's; its angle of tilt was close to Earth's own; and it had one-third the gravity. But as the colonists quickly learned, it takes more than the length of one's day to make a place livable.

"In the first place, Mars was a dead planet with a frightfully thin atmosphere, no liquid water, and nightmarish temperature extremes. Although it might get all the way up to freezing at noon on the equator in the heat of the summer, at other times, temperatures regularly fell to as low as minus 100 degrees Fahrenheit.

"In the second place, the length of the trip to and from the Red Planet was taxing to even the hardiest of carefully-selected pioneers. It took many, many months in the fastest ships of that era to get there, and the cost per kilogram of goods transported was so high, the early settlers had to endure the most spartan of existences. Some ships that set sail never even made it, as was the case with the ill-fated Mormon expedition of 2187.

"Finally, the atmospheric pressure was so low, a human being couldn't go outside unprotected. And, even if the pressure *had* been higher, the air would still have been lethal because it was ninety-five percent carbon-dioxide!

"Despite all these shortcomings, terraformers had high hopes for Mars. They knew, for instance, that everything needed to make her habitable was right there waiting to be extracted. Not only did she have plenty of water stored there in deep aquifers and frozen into the soil as ice, carbon and nitrogen were present as well, locked away into the rocks as carbonate and nitrate, respectively. The hopeful colonists were told that all it would take to make Mars livable was a plan—and plenty of patience.

"Finding a way to warm up a place as big as Mars was the key to the whole thing. Mars was cold, and thawing her out would require considerable amounts of heat, a feat achievable only with an effective greenhouse gas. Researchers fell upon chlorofluorocarbons, CFC's, as their solution. CFC's were known to be so efficient as greenhouse gases and so stable once in the atmosphere, they were once banned on Earth as pollutants. But one planet's poison was the other planet's wine, and the quantities required for Mars were well within the means of ordinary industrial processes. Hence, terraforming began in earnest.

"The first Mars base, dating to 2097, was built on a sandy patch of ground in the low-lying plains of the northern hemisphere. This site had been decided upon principally because landing an interplanetary transport there was far easier than among the massive cliffs which girdled the planet to the south. The eager settlers had been assured by the scientists back home that if they only planted so and so many tons of a specially-bred lichen, in a mere seventy-five years the planet would be habitable. Alas, nobody took into account dust storms, diarrhea, fatigue, or homesickness, and after two dozen years of living in uncomfortable, tight-fitting spacesuits and working day after backbreaking day planting millions of tiny lichen shoots, the settlers quit in disgust, content to let nature take its course.

"Even so, over the course of the next century the fledgling colony achieved a modicum of success; that is, at least until an errand asteroid struck without warning in 2227. The asteroid punctured the gymnasium roof, rapidly depressurizing the adjacent buildings. Except for a handful of colonists who were doing research in their sealed laboratories, hundreds of pioneers died painful deaths. Even their children weren't spared the horror. The Martian atmosphere was still unbreathable and temperatures still hovered far below the range humans could endure without protective clothing. Some residents simply fell unconscious from lack of oxygen, then froze in their sleep, while others bled to death, their bodies torn asunder by flying shards of glass or razor-sharp chunks of asteroid.

"As the news of the destruction filtered down to Earth—itself being ravaged by yet another one of Rontana's murderous rampages—terran-bound people came to realize just how fragile mankind's hold on space really was. In time, the physical damage was repaired, but the psychological damage never was—humanity had lost its taste for funding space adventures. Though the colony was eventually rebuilt, by the early 2300s Mars had become little more than a small scientific curiosity much like the Antarctic stations have been for centuries; by 2377, the Mars settlement was totally abandoned."

Carina blinked her eyes once and pushed herself back from the screen. She logged-off her terminal, then rose to stretch. She was a tall, lanky woman and her outstretched arms nearly reached to the ceiling. Though she was done reading for the day, the look on Carina's face revealed how unhappy she was with what she'd just learned.

After half a millennium of trying, there seemed to be no practical way for humans to overcome the myriad of problems confronting them in space. Not only did man's comfort zone of between forty and ninety degrees Fahrenheit not exist anywhere else in the solar system, his oxygen needs were so demanding, even a five-percent variation could cause him to pass out or suffer irreparable brain damage.

Moreover, since most of the body's internal systems functioned best with a gravity-assist, weightlessness wreaked havoc with our frail chemistry. The fluids of the inner-ear sent the brain conflicting signals, triggering dizziness and nausea; underworked bones and muscles atrophied; the body's immune systems stopped functioning; faces swelled; even fetuses, confused as to which way was up, aborted spontaneously. Instead of being a utopia, space had turned out to be a bad dream. A nightmare, in fact!

4
Frustration

Though it was only the middle of the afternoon, for Carina this had already been a long and frustrating day. It had begun this morning with Dr. Janz and his infuriating committee, then taken a turn for the worse as she had been forced to come to grips with the devastating truth. Man's failure to colonize the solar system had been utter and complete, and the more she thought about it, the more depressed she became. Outer space was nothing if not a horrible dead end!

There was no "final frontier" as space enthusiasts had hoped for 450 years ago at the dawn of the space age, no fruited plains ripe for cultivation, no offer of a migratory haven safe from the world's tyrants—just a barren, impenetrable brick wall.

But why?

In trying to unravel the conundrum, Carina was reminded of the vexing question her father had put to her more than a decade ago. "What is the reason for persecution?" he had asked, challenging her to grapple with an ugly issue at an age when all the other girls were still in pigtails and bobbysocks. Carina couldn't possibly answer him at the time, of course, and even now, ten years later, was still groping for an explanation. Thus, when she sat back down today with her diary open before her, it was *this* task she intended to address.

"November 26, 2430, 2:00p.m. Madame Diary, once more we will try to answer father's question. I would hypothesize that the reason for persecution is as old as life itself. Over the eons, the phenomenal rise in animal intelligence was driven by the world's predators and their relentless hunting of less capable game. This must have been true not only in the obvious sense of a smarter animal being able to outwit a faster carnivore, but it must also have been true in a more subtle way as well. That is, smarter animals eventually graduated from correctly judging whether a jump *over* a ravine could be managed, to devising an alternate means *around* the ravine.

"As smarter prey more successfully eluded their predators, hungrier predators had to become more cunning as well. Anticipation and second-guessing became an integral part of their survival, and this vicious feedback must have driven the intelligence of the hunter—and the hunted—higher still. These interlocking cycles must have reinforced one another with each round until our species leaped from the jungle, mad as hell and ready to fight. Armed with their big brains, these hairless apes were exceedingly well-equipped to fend off any and all predators. Therefore, it should come as no surprise that Man is a hunter, pure and simple; a territorial beast compelled by instinct to defend, and whenever possible, expand his dominion. Ironically, once Mother Nature ran out of credible predators for Man, he became his own worst enemy. Evolution had simultaneously made him the most aggressive of all hunters and the most resilient of all prey.

"When the human race was young and the Earth sparsely populated, the standard survival-response to cruelty or persecution was to leave one region and settle in another less oppressed land. Interestingly enough, as an unintended consequence of these periodic upheavals, waves of desperate immigrants often catapulted their adopted societies to greatness, unwittingly boosting the living standards of torturer and tortured alike.

"Unfortunately, the reverse has also proved to be the case. Once the Earth got crowded, and there were no longer any places left to hide, the world's most ferocious hunter began hunting *himself* to extinction. As migration increasingly became an impossibility, and as the rallying cries of genocide swept across the globe, brutality and subjugation led, not to escape, but to extermination; not to new and more promising lands, but to gas chambers and other horrors. Rontana and his nightmarish atrocities were but one shadowy reflection of the general malaise, all of which were rooted in the closing of the frontiers.

"Then, as the migratory outlets slammed shut, living standards stagnated. Not everywhere, to be sure, and not all at once, but by the twenty-fourth century, a new Dark Age had descended upon much of the world. Although some—like the Overlord—were grabbing for themselves a bigger slice of the economic pie, the pie itself—for perhaps the first time since the Middle Ages—was no longer growing. The future had become bleak.

"Fruitful and multiplied well beyond the carrying capacity of their little planet, mankind was skidding headlong into a giant bend in the road. Only it wasn't a U-turn, it was a cul-de-sac. Pressed by the confines of a tiny world, overwhelmed by sheer numbers and drowning in an ocean of their own wastes, the oldhumans were consummating their own pitiful version of the lemmings' march to the sea.

"Yet, I am convinced there has to be a way out of this morass. The answer has to be migration. If newhumans are to have a legacy, if my signature genes are to have a future, I must get off this planet!"

But how? she asked herself, numbed by the reality. If space was such a dead end, what hope was there for migration? For newhumans? And to whom could she turn to for help?

Pen still in hand, Carina slid a paper clip onto the page at the start of today's entry. This was a subject she would have to revisit again later on. In the meantime, though, it occurred to her that this was precisely the sort of question her dad might be able to answer. He was smart about such things. If her father couldn't help her, no one could.

Even as Carina got up from her chair and reached for the comm to call him, out of the corner of one eye she caught a glimpse of the holo-snapshot he'd given her last year for her birthday. Still unframed, it stood there next to a vase on a bookcase beside her desk. When she looked at it, a tinge of guilt eroded her lovely smile. The photo was a glum reminder that she hadn't stopped in to see him in some time. With tomorrow being the last night of the university's BeHolden Day break, he would be expecting at least a call from her, if not a visit.

Bracing herself for the inevitable rebuke, Carina cradled the comm in her hand and encoded her father's exchange. After a couple staccato pings, he answered.

"Happy BeHolden Day!" she bubbled, trying to put him in a good mood.

"Who is this?" Sam grumbled indifferently.

"Cute, dad—very cute. You know darn well who it is—Carina, that's who."

"I have a daughter by that name," Sam chided, "but *she* never calls. Come to think of it, she never visits either."

Carina didn't know what to say, so she didn't say anything.

"Is everything okay?" he asked after a long pause. "I haven't heard from you since I don't know when. I was expecting you for dinner the other night, but you never showed."

"I know, Dad, and I'm sorry, but . . . "

"Tell me, little one, how is the Inquisition going?"

"You know about that?" she demanded in a bewildered tone. "Actually, things haven't been going all that well. Janz has been a total pain, and I'd rather not talk about it just now if you don't mind. I apologize for not calling sooner, but between that and everything else, I've been busy."

"Aren't you always?"

"Yes, father, but . . . "

"You have a husband, yes? What about Max? He seems like such a nice boy."

"Come on now, Dad, you know I don't have time to get married. Besides, if you love Max so much, *you* marry him," she said, her sassiness showing through. "Then again, if you loved *me*, you'd let me make my own decisions. Now, it just so happens I'm free tonight, that is if you want me to come up and see you."

"Are we dining out, my busy *single* daughter, or are we dining in?"

"That depends. You know how I hate restaurants," Carina chuckled playfully. "Couldn't we order out from that Italian place just down the road from you?"

"Sure—whatever you want. What time should I expect you?"

"I'll be over at seven," she assured him.

"I won't hold my breath," Sam growled in a tender but scolding tone. "Do I need to call and wake you? I know how you like your afternoon nap."

"Thanks, but that won't be necessary. This time, I'll remember to set my alarm. Only, if I'm going to make it up to your place by seven, I've got to go now. Love ya. Bye."

Leaving her dad no room for argument, Carina clicked off the comm. He was a good man, her father, and if a generation hadn't separated the two of them, they almost certainly would have been the best of friends. As it was, he seemed desperate for companionship up there all alone in his big house on the Cape. At other times, though, he delighted in his solitude. A loner herself, Carina thought she understood.

Eager to close out the day, Carina returned to her desk. Pushing her diary off to one side, she pulled out an e-pad and began scribbling notes. The machine would automatically convert her chickenscratch into binary code, then save it to tape when she was done. Now, while events were still fresh in her mind, it was crucial that she not delay drafting a letter to the university governing board rebutting Dr. Janz and his ridiculous witch hunt. When she sat down to write, though, the words wouldn't come; and for the longest time she just sat there motionless, pen in hand, listening to the e-pad's pathetic hum.

Frustrated by her inability to conjure up the right words for her counterplea, Carina rose to her feet in irritation and went to the window. It opened easily to her touch.

Carina was one of the lucky ones; she had an apartment overlooking the tiny courtyard behind her building. Authentic sunshine and natural moonlight meant the world to her, as did real rain pounding against her window in a thunderstorm.

It was November in Auckland—springtime—and the air tasted fresh. The flowers were blooming and the birds were chirping. And when a butterfly caught her attention, she squealed with delight.

"Tikkidiw!" she sang out merrily, the butterfly stirring innocent memories of childhood. "Tikkidiw!"

Hypnotized by the feathery creature as it bounced from flower to flower seemingly without a care, Carina forgot all about the Inquisition in no time. And in the moments ahead, as the butterfly rode a rising column of air only to later sail completely out of view, she forgot all about her theories and her science as well. The tiny creature's brief visit had made her all warm inside, and she suddenly found herself gripped by an urgent case of spring fever!

Unable to deny her physical need, this woman of passion moaned outloud ever so fervently. What was it her father always used to say? Something about butterflies and little girls. She would have to remember to ask him tonight when they were together.

Shaking her head airily, Carina caught a glimpse of herself reflecting off the windowpane. In the afternoon sun the auburn highlights of her hair shone red—like her passion.

In a bid to finish her work, she stepped back to her desk. But it was useless. Her fingers wouldn't budge, and she couldn't bring herself to pick up that pen. The wonderful magic of the tikkidiw had robbed her of the ability to think, leaving her with nothing more than an unresolved bout of pure animal lust.

Carina was in a bad way. Horny, as they say. Hot to trot. Ruttish.

Steamy recollections of last night's bedroom shenanigans with Max flashed before her eyes. As if a camera, her lewd mind resurrected hedonistic images of every man she'd ever had the pleasure to bed. Though she tried like a wildcat to fight it, she couldn't. What hot-blooded woman could?

All of a sudden, there it was again—the tikkidiw! Riding the light currents of warm air outside her window, the delicate creature danced and turned for her entertainment.

"Tikkidiw," she moaned sensually. "Beautiful little thing of God."

Her soft brown eyes swelled with emotion.

Rather than quenching her appetite, spying that butterfly had only served to whet it!

Now suddenly her heart was pounding!

Her thighs were all aquiver!

Sexual energy coursed through her veins like a juggernaut!

Despite her best efforts to resist, the woman was slowly being consumed by a throbbing internal warmth!

A poet might call it ardent yearning; a fiction writer, red-hot passion.

Carina cursed her insatiability. It wasn't fair! she thought, losing the battle to control her lustful craving. Here she was, alone and needing to be done, and yet, she wasn't even sure what had triggered her carnal urgings to begin with!

A smell, perhaps? The happy sight of that wispy butterfly? Or was it just the hours of bottled-up frustration? Who could say?

Whatever it was, this thing called "need" had grown into a full-blown hunger which had to be dealt with right away!

Desperate for relief, she encoded Max's number on the comm. Time after time it rang, but there was no answer.

Cursing his absence, Carina dropped the receiver to the floor. It wasn't as if she had any *choice* in the matter! Without Max around to service her, she would have to take things into her own hands. Her need could no longer be ignored!

Resigned to the fact that she would have to fly solo this time, Carina left the comm off the hook and reclined full-length on the floor. After a moment, though, she thought better of it, and went upstairs to her bedroom; a noise outside got her to thinking that an inquisitive neighbor might peer through the window of her study and see her performing her ambidextrous remedy right there in her front room.

Upstairs, in the privacy of her room, Carina completed her self-administered therapy. The soothing sound of cack music played in the background. When at long last relief finally pulsated through her being, she set her alarm for six and fell instantly asleep.

5
Dad

When the alarm buzzer went off, Carina stumbled groggily to the bathroom. A sideways glance at the clock told her she had just enough time for a quick shower before heading up the Cape to see her father.

As the tepid water splashed across her face, Carina thanked her lucky stars that she hadn't already depleted her allotment for the month. But what she wouldn't have given for a really *hot* shower!

Carina Matthews, twenty-eight years old, had the pristine, girlish figure of a woman two-thirds her age. Her father, some twenty-five years her senior, still had the rugged good looks of a man who relished his rigorous daily hike. Her mother, however, was another story. Carina knew almost nothing at all about her. It couldn't be helped—she had barely been two when her mother was taken away; not even three when they left the country without her. Nowadays, when Carina looked at her father, *his* eyes still spoke volumes of the memories he harbored for his young, Amerind wife. It was almost too much to bear.

Though Carina might have wished it otherwise, Sam never remarried. It certainly could not have been for want of admiring and available young things, but more likely because he had been content to raise his impressionable young daughter without the interference of another woman. Even so, while growing up, there had been many a day when Carina had hated her father for this. Now, though, as she pulled out of her driveway on the way up to see him, Carina reflected how hard it must have been for him to raise her alone.

Thanks largely to the unbroken string of sunny days this past week, Carina was confident her gcar's batteries were sufficiently charged to make the run up to her dad's estate and back without problem. The trip would take just over fifteen minutes, and as she drove she wondered what it must have been like to live in an era when ground transportation wasn't strictly dependent upon solar energy. She had read somewhere that gcars were once powered by a petroleum distillate they called "gasoline." It was cheap and abundant and made long-distance overland travel commonplace.

As was so often the case, Carina arrived at her father's house late. Though he wasn't angry, he did make a crack about it.

"Girl, you're on Amerind time," he reprimanded, taking her coat and hanging it in the guest closet. "Just like your mother used to be."

"Dare I ask?" she said, unclear what her father was alluding to.

Sam led Carina to an easy chair. He beamed when he spoke. "Many hundreds of years ago, even before the first American revolution, North America was overrun by aboriginal tribes who migrated there from eastern Asia. In fact, your mother's tribe arrived by that very route."

"Migrated?" Carina asked, her ears perking up at the sound of that word. "How?"

"Probably by foot across the land-bridge to what is now the Alaskan province of Canada. It's anybody's guess what drove them. Maybe they were hungry. Or lost. Or perhaps they were hoping to escape some petty tyrant. I don't actually know. Whatever the reason, they migrated. Now, if you don't mind," he snapped with make-believe sternness, "I wish you wouldn't interrupt me when I'm speaking!"

"Yes, daddy dear," she scoffed, crooning like a feisty teenager.

"Some centuries later, when a gang of unenlightened Euro's accidentally bumped into the New World, they thought they had discovered a new route to the Indies. Thus, they labeled the local savages 'Indians.' These aborigines had little technology, and almost certainly no timepieces. To them, a day began when the sun first rose above the horizon; it ended when the sun set. If an Amerind said he would arrive at his destination the next day, that arrival could take place any time between dawn and dusk."

"Am I to assume then that you are critical of my lack of punctuality?" Carina pouted, her pride bruised ever so slightly.

"Land's sakes girl, this is the twenty-fifth century, not the seventeenth!" he yammered, a reckless twinkle in his eye. "Nevertheless," he added tenderly, "it's good to see you, little one. How 'bout a hug for the old man?"

Carina hugged her father affectionately, then said, "Well, what's for dinner? I'm starved!"

"I haven't done anything yet in that regard," Sam declared, moving towards the refrigerator. "Are you still interested in ordering out?"

"Yes, by all means! A poorboy would sure hit the spot about now. You mentioned that Italian place down the road."

"It's agreed, then. I'll call—you pay."

Carina gave Sam a thanks-a-lot-for-nothing look and picked up the comm to dial herself.

The order-out business had changed remarkably little in the past five hundred years. Only now, instead of a foul-smelling, oil-burning wreck driven by a pimpled teenager, the acne-blemished kid was at the wheel of an unreliable, fearsomely-sparking relic of an electric gcar. Like his predecessor from an earlier era, the driver still had scraggly hair, overwrought hormones, and a two-day-old beard. The sandwiches still came wrapped in white glazed paper, they were still inexpensive, and they were still delicious. The bread was warm, the lettuce crisp, and the cheese smooth. Heaven on Earth!

"Tell me, Carina, how is that new book of yours coming along?" Sam asked as he unwrapped his hoagie. "And do explain this Imploding Diversification thing you have cooked up," he said, intentionally botching the proper name of her theory.

"*Explosive Diversity*, Dad! Explosive Diversity," she said, taking a chomp out of her submarine sandwich. "The new book is coming slow, but . . . "

"Slowly, Carina," Sam interrupted. "The new book is coming s-l-o-w-l-y. You must learn to speak it correctly before you can ever hope to write it correctly."

She flashed him an irreverent smile. "The new book is coming s-l-o-w-l-y, but it was the previous one, the one I just finished, which got me into so much damn trouble with Dr. Janz and his asinine committee. Explosive Diversity is the simple notion that external events like a meteor impact, for instance, stresses the environment so severely, existing DNA chains are wrecked, setting off an explosion of new life forms. Then . . . "

"Dear me, that does sound awfully farfetched. But then what do I know? I am just a lowly economist struggling to get by on a professor's salary, living out his last few years all alone, practically abandoned by his children."

"You're so full of it!" Carina exclaimed. "Now eat your hoagie or else I'll eat it for you. Anyway, it isn't *children*—it's child. And you're not struggling to get by—you're stinky rich! As for lonely—that's bull! Mom died twenty-five years ago—you could've remarried."

"Yes, I am full of it, but no, I could never have remarried. I couldn't bear the thought of ever losing another one as fine as your mother. It would . . . kill me," he stammered, looking away.

Sam was silent for a long time thinking of her. Finally, Carina whispered, "Dad, I know you've been trying to protect me, but you never told me how mom died. What exactly happened?"

Sam sighed heavily. "I guess you're old enough now. But I'm warning you, little one—if you're ever to understand the 'why,' you'll first have to understand the 'what'."

"What 'what'?" she entreated.

"The history, my dear, the history. In another time, no one would have cared."

"Cared about *what?*"

"Her genes," Sam asserted sadly. "Her genes."

"I don't understand."

"I know you don't, pumpkin, but let me try to explain. The first part of my story is bound to bore you since it concerns your own field of study, but bear with me a few minutes and let's see if I can't clarify matters somewhat."

Sam cleared his throat and got comfortable, as if he had a very long journey ahead of him. "As you know, the universal gene-map project dates to the early twenty-first century. Though I don't pretend to understand the technology involved, this mammoth undertaking enabled scientists to locate every one of the hundred thousand or so genes which make up a human being, while simultaneously copying each gene to identify its chemical makeup and determine its function."

"Is this really necessary?" Carina asked in an exasperated tone. "You know very well that I'm familiar with the universal gene-map."

"Are you going to let me finish or not?" Sam growled. "The techniques developed for the mapping project have long since been used to develop an archival storage facility complete with a detailed gene-map for every domesticated animal and every food-grain of commercial importance. By the way, though they never got around to using it, a copy of this gene-store was even deposited on Mars by the early terraformers. I suppose it's still up there somewhere."

"What exactly is your point?" a frustrated Carina grumbled.

"To make you understand what happened to Nasha—my wife, your mother. As I was saying, the gene-mapping project almost never got off the ground. Public criticism ran rampant. So did profitable self-dealing. Although some of the arguments advanced by its foes were valid, just as many were pure nonsense," Sam explained, ticking off the pros and cons one by one.

"The criticism began—as so many anti-science campaigns have—with the Fundamentalists asserting that trying to learn every letter of the human genetic alphabet was tantamount to reaching for the forbidden fruit; that the knowledge sought was too powerful for human beings to know; that the knowledge itself belonged in the *Lord*'s realm!

"Then came the civil-libertarians with *their* words of wisdom. Fearing Nazi-like eugenic measures, they claimed that the ability to know which genes predisposed a person to a specific disease or contributed to his intelligence was an invasion of one's privacy, an invasion which was bound to cause discrimination against select gene carriers."

"And I suppose," Carina broke in, "the do-gooders countered *them* with a promise something along the lines of, 'Yes, but mastering the chemical formula of life will usher in a utopian era, an era in which diseases can easily be cured and where genetically-altered plants and animals will feed a starving world.'"

"If I didn't know better, I'd say you were catching on, little one," Sam exclaimed. "Fearing that funding for the project's huge cost would siphon financial support away from their own, much more worthy research, a collection of self-serving scientists labeling themselves Saganites, advanced one of the strangest arguments of all."

"Oh? And what was that?"

"Since about ninety-five percent of the human genome was reputed to have no function whatsoever, these misguided scientists labeled the supposedly nonfunctioning genes as 'junk-genes' in a desperate effort to arouse public opinion against the large and expensive effort. Under the able leadership of the charlatan who was their namesake, the Saganites were eventually successful in derailing the entire gene-mapping project before it could ever be completed."

Suddenly interested, Carina remarked, "Gosh, I never knew that."

"So it lay dormant and unfinished for years until Dow Chemical and DuPont Plastics joined forces. Together they lobbied the United States Congress for a patent law variance in which they agreed to complete the gene-map in return for being granted perpetual patents for any pharmaceutical discoveries they made while doing the work. Though this was a dumb idea . . . "

"Why was it so dumb?" a perplexed Carina asked. "Seems like a fair enough trade to me," she said in her typically naive way.

"Well, honey," Sam replied in his standard father-knows-best tone, "drug research is not conducted out of altruism on the part of the chemist. Like all us other mortals, chemists want to make money; they want to be rich. And if you don't believe me, just try talking one of them out of their Nobel prize money."

"Sure Dad, well and good, but what does that have to do with perpetual patents?"

"Just this. Since the financial rewards stemming from drug research depend on the life of a new remedy, and since patent protection lengthens the life of a drug's monopoly in the marketplace, the shield afforded by a patent simultaneously *raises* the profit potential of a new product while *stymying* research on competing products. Although perpetual patents assured huge returns for the new pharmaceuticals put out by Dow and DuPont, it was a barrier to the research efforts of all the other companies. Like I said—a pretty dumb idea."

"But the map *did* get done," Carina countered.

"Oh, yes, your precious map did finally get done," Sam snapped irritably. "But the damn thing's what killed your mother!"

"What the hell?" Carina cursed, visibly shaken and suddenly at the edge of tears. "How could something that happened four hundred years ago have killed my mother?"

6
Designer Genes

The stunned look on her face said it all. It seemed incomprehensible that something which had happened so very long ago could have had such devastating consequences for the present. Carina blinked back the tears as her father continued with his explanation.

"Once man could identify specific genes, he sought to manipulate them. By early in the twenty-first century, biologists had developed diagnostic screening tests for a whole host of common genetic diseases including diabetes, Alzheimer's syndrome, and cystic fibrosis. The actual cures for these diseases came later, of course; in some cases, much later."

"That's all well and good," Carina said, "but by discovering which genes regulated what functions, the DNA mappers set the stage for repairing legions of dysfunctional genes."

"Quite so," Sam agreed. "Eventually, genetic engineering made possible the elimination, not only of genetic diseases, but even allowed for the correction of hundreds and hundreds of genetic *mistakes*."

"Now that's something I know about," Carina blurted out proudly. "Early on, it was shown that there were no biological barriers preventing the transfer of animal or plant genes into diseased people to help them do some things better, like producing insulin or metabolizing fat. Scientists even learned how to construct synthetic genes, and—using transplantable skin cells as a delivery system—they found a way to cure all sorts of ailments."

"You're right, of course," Sam granted, "but that isn't the half of it. Whereas a cure for diabetes couldn't possibly arouse much of a controversy, the same didn't hold true for a cure for, say, brown eyes."

"Brown *eyes?*" Carina declared emphatically.

"Yes, pumpkin, brown eyes. That's what the battle for genetic purity ultimately came down to. As soon as the biologists learned how to manipulate genes for desirable physical characteristics like wavy hair or big breasts, the battle against genetic choice erupted. There were protest marches, political candidacies, terrorist bombings, leaflets, lawsuits, even religious fanatics. They all lined up on one side of the issue or the other."

"I hate to admit it, Dad, but I'm not terribly clear even what exactly the issue *was*. What was so damn controversial about genetic choice anyway?"

Sam nodded his head knowingly as he answered. "It seems commonplace to us now, but back then, the issue was whether or not one had the right to manipulate the genetic traits of his offspring. Radical groups like the Randomists insisted that the luck of the draw was God's way, while more moderate thinkers of that age agreed that selecting the right genes for one's children was as vital as selecting the right schools for them.

"Once genetic choice was legalized, couples could readily obtain prescription-genes from nearly any corner pharmacy. Each vial was filled with a soft gel that had been laced with strands of laboratory-engineered DNA. Prospective parents could choose from a long list of synthetic genes, each designed to annihilate the natural gene and ensure that their infant would be endowed with a specific physical trait more to the parents' liking. Just prior to ovulation, the gel was inserted high into the woman's vaginal tract; then, over the ensuing thirty-six hours, the hopeful users were to engage in frequent love-making. Unless they got carried away and neglected to follow the label instructions precisely, odds were quite good that the preferred gene would 'take' and the undesirable one would be sloughed off. And even if the parents failed to dislodge the offending gene, the couple could always just simply abort the distasteful fetus, buy another vial, and try again."

"The ultimate vanity," Carina said, turning up her nose.

"A very curious chapter in our history, to be sure," Sam nodded. "The brand manufactured by the DuPont/Dow consortium I told you about earlier was called *Designer Genes*. And because of that patent-law variance they slipped by Congress, their brand had a commanding market share right from the start. *Designer Genes* were especially popular with the newlyweds, no doubt because of their slick marketing strategy—bright-pink vials for the most popular female traits, soft-blue ones for the most highly regarded male traits."

"Like what?"

"Oh, I don't know. Things like broad shoulders for boys and narrow waists for girls."

"But what about *non*physical characteristics? Like excellent vision? Or exceptional creativity? Wasn't anyone concerned with *those* things?"

"It's interesting that you should raise that question, little one, because amazingly few parents opted for brighter, more imaginative kids. In my Ph.D. dissertation I studied the demise of the Bright Gene Company which marketed IQ-stimulant genes. It went out of business circa 2137."

"My, my, but isn't that strange!" Carina responded, never ceasing to be amazed by how much her father knew. "Are most parents afraid to raise bright children?"

"Bright children *are* tougher to rear," Sam admitted. "But then you wouldn't know anything about that, would you, my sweet but single daughter?"

"Can we forget about my personal life already and get on with your story? Surely *Designer Genes* weren't the only brand."

"Quite right. Someone else marketed a *Gene-Bits* brand and someone even started a chain of specialty stores called, if I remember correctly, Genes-R-Us. They stocked all competing brands, and aspiring parents could even view a computer-enhanced hologram of their child-to-be depending on whether they chose this vial or that one. It was all the rage at the time."

"I suppose they had to enforce a no-refund, no-return policy," Carina quipped irreverently.

Sam smiled but ignored the crack and went on. "Once people began to think in terms of 'good' and 'bad' genes, leaders began to think in terms of 'good' and 'bad' races. And when economic times got desperate, people rallied around whichever leader offered them the most convenient scapegoat for their misery. Rontana was the first—and the worst—of those leaders. *He* was the one responsible for killing your mom," Sam muttered with finality.

7

Ali Salaam Rontana

"But where did he *come* from?" Carina exclaimed.

"Actually, his precise origins are unknown," Sam answered pointedly. "But a little over two centuries ago, this lunatic we've come to know as Rontana appeared on the world stage leading an army of Moslem bandits from his mountain hideaway deep inside Persia.

"All the crazies of the world have had a manifesto and Ali Salaam Rontana was no exception. Directing his followers with a call of, 'Kill their genes; kill their ideas,' Rontana's maniacal cry was just the latest in a long string of excuses for slaughtering one's neighbor.

"Rontana's manifesto—*Deicide, Infanticide, & Ecocide*, or simply D.I.E. for short—was pure unadulterated lunacy. Yet, in a seemingly flawless, almost clinically logical way, Rontana led the readers of his book step by step through the compelling case for murdering millions of children in order to spare the environment."

"Oh, God, that's sick!" Carina declared, hiding her face in her hands.

"There's more," Sam said.

"I don't want to hear it!"

"Damn it, little one!" Sam roared, fire in his eyes. "No single person alive on this earth today means more to me than you do. But for the life of me, you have lived a sheltered existence long enough! It is about time you heard the truth! Goodness, child, haven't you ever wondered how we came to live here? I wasn't born in Zealand, you know."

"I suppose you're going to tell me about Rontana one way or the other," Carina grumbled, resigning herself to the inevitable.

"Count on it," Sam said. "If I remember my history right, Rontana cited five reasons for infanticide in his manifesto. First, there was the exploitation of infants as a food source."

"Cannibalism?" she gulped, her voice cracking. Just the thought of it made her want to retch, and for the next few seconds she feared that her recently-downed poorboy wasn't going to *stay* down. "They . . . ate . . . babies?"

Sam nodded grimly and went on. "Next, there was the competition for resources. By starving or murdering—but not actually *eating* the infant—the killer increased the availability of resources for himself—and for his kin.

"The competition between males for access to breeding-age females was the third reason given for promoting infanticide. By murdering another man's offspring, the killer gained the opportunity to utilize that man's female to produce more of *his* own offspring. This 'murder and rape' approach was Rontana's personal favorite."

"My goodness, Dad, how can you possibly remember all this stuff?" Carina quizzed.

"My grandfather was a pretty sharp fellow in his day, and he made damn sure I memorized it all when I was a young man."

"For God's sakes, why?"

"I'll tell you why in just a minute, but let me finish this before I lose track. Now where was I? Oh, yes, number four. This one Rontana labeled 'compassionate infanticide.' Where it was practiced in the past, it has typically been carried out by a mother—and with remorse—right after the birth of a newborn. The circumstances are almost always the same. The mother already has a thriving four-year-old; however, she lacks the resources to raise both children at once. To ensure the survival of the older child, she has no choice but to put the newborn to death.

"And then there's number five. This one is pathological in every sense of the word. For the killer there is no gain whatsoever; except, of course, the sheer joy of killing.

"As you can see," Sam closed, "Rontana was a complete nutball. Nevertheless, he was passionately worshiped by millions."

"I just don't see how normal people could have lined up behind such a man," Carina said earnestly. "Were times really that awful?"

"Fanatics require a personality cult to be successful. This means they must debunk God and science and any other conventionally held 'truth.' Remember, the 'D' in D.I.E. stood for deicide, the act of killing a deity. It was central to Rontana's plan. Only by debasing society's current crutches could he substitute his own personality cult for the heroes he dethroned.

"Although several hundred million people died at his hand, Rontana wasn't the only psychopath of that era, and it wasn't until the next century—*my* century—that the bloodshed reached truly staggering proportions."

"Your childhood must have been miserable!" Carina exclaimed sympathetically.

"Oh, not really. I was born in Missouri in the year 2377, the same year, by the way, that the Mars colony was abandoned. I was just a boy when the early wars of attrition got underway in a serious fashion. I knew precious little about them, however, because I grew up in a serene location far from the cares of the world, right smack in the center of the

American heartland. Farmington was surrounded by clean air, tall corn, humid summers, and the echoes of Mark Twain. I was not especially well-liked as a boy, nor was I particularly good-looking, but I *was* a good student, and I *was* honest, and my inquisitive nature tried the patience of nearly every teacher who crossed my path. I was a hard worker and very ambitious," Sam boasted proudly.

"At my grandfather's urging, I left Farmington when I was eighteen and moved into the Canadian Rockies west of Calgary to attend college. Not only did Alberta's School of Economics beckon to me for admission, there was a darker side to my decision as well."

"Darker? Whatever do you mean?" Carina asked, suddenly troubled.

"Like I said, my grandpa was a pretty smart guy, and the reason he made me learn so much about Rontana was because *his* father had led the commando team which finally assassinated the kook."

"Your great-grandfather murdered *Rontana!?*"

Sam nodded in the affirmative. "They called him Tiger. But that is a story for another day. My grandpa was a U.S. Senator, and he sat on some committee which made him privy to all manner of military secrets. He came to me one day, and he was real sad. He said, 'Sam, war is coming, and if any of the Matthews are to survive the destruction, you must leave the country right away!' Then he sat me down and told me how the world was ganging up on America and how he believed she would be defeated if hostilities erupted. He said he had arranged for my safekeeping in Canada.

"Though I didn't like it at first, I went, and two years later, war *did* break out. The results proved out Grandpa Nate's worst fears. When it was over, the Great War had cost the world that shining beacon of freedom called America."

Sam's voice trailed off, and Carina imagined that a tear came to her father's eye.

"What a waste!" he declared. "What had once been the United States of America is now mostly desert and deformed scrub brush, its billion and a half citizens either dead or scattered to the winds like myself. The rich soils of the American heartland once fed the world; now they are heavily contaminated and completely unproductive."

"Well, what became of *you?*"

"Throughout the war I was relatively safe because it was not fought on Canadian soil. I was just a nondescript college student hidden away on the campus of a nondescript university nestled in a nondescript suburb of Calgary. I graduated from college the month after hostilities ended in North America; only by then I had acquired a lovely, nondescript wife."

Sam smiled widely as he thought back.

"Nasha was a local girl. Like yourself, she was slim of waist and sharp of mind. While I worked on my advanced degree and taught part-time, Nasha clerked in the provincial offices where we first met. In 2402, when I was twenty-five, we added a baby girl to the family. Life was looking real sweet! Hooray for Samuel Matthews, newly-minted Ph.D. from the Alberta School of Economics and his common-law wife, Nasha. In keeping with the tradition of your mother's tribe, we named you after a prominent star, just as Nasha had been named before you."

"A star? What a wonderful tradition!"

"Nasha's people *were* wonderful. I was given an Amerind name and inducted as an honorary member of her tribe. We were both given best wishes for a long and prosperous future. Unfortunately, our life of bliss was fleeting," Sam explained, his face drawn.

"This is the part where my mother dies, isn't it?" Carina asked, her face pale.

"Yes, pumpkin, I'm afraid so. Not even two years after reveling in the joy of your birth, Nasha was taken to that godless torture camp where she died. A terrible sadness descended down upon my life."

"What exactly did she do *wrong?*" Carina wailed, trembling uncontrollably.

Sam smiled narrowly. It wasn't a joyful smile, but rather the kind of smile that slips out when a person wants desperately not to cry.

He said, "Even though the Great War ended in '99, the search for scapegoats continued for quite a long time afterward. And the Canadians, despite being victorious, blamed their non-white aborigines for having dragged their country into the murderous war with America. Your mother was part Aleutian which, by definition, made her one of the guilty."

"I don't understand! What the hell was she guilty *of?*" Carina exclaimed, her voice almost a scream.

"The ruling French Canadians decreed that Canada's genetic stock be cleansed, that is, made more Caucasian, more white. Nasha didn't fit their purist specifications. Like I said earlier, once people began to think in terms of good and bad genes, leaders . . . well, what I mean is, Rontana-type thinking still rocketed through the social fabric. She just never came home that day," Sam confessed calmly. "Pumpkin, you have *got* to believe me—there was nothing I could do to save her."

"But *Daddy!*" she cried out, imagining Nasha slowly dying in that Alaskan gene-extinction camp. "They robbed me of my mother! And all because she had the wrong goddamned *genes?* And now what? I discover these stupid signature genes and convince myself that I'm *special?* What a jerk I've been! How did the purist bastards know who to round up and where to find them?" she blurted out, the tears welling up in her eyes.

"Nasha was a clerk in the provincial offices, a position sensitive enough to demand a background check, including, among other things, a set of gene-prints, a recent photograph, and a disclosure of one's genetic stock. Proud of her heritage, she boldly wore the identicard which categorized her as an 'A'. The 'A' stood for Amerind or maybe aborigine—I'm not sure which anymore—but it doesn't really matter. Once her identity as a native was in the computer, she and others like her were easy prey when the purge began."

"But how did *you* avoid the concentration camp? Hell, how did *I?*"

"Fortunately, the genetic authorities knew nothing of your birth because Nasha and I had a common-law marriage, and, as was the custom of her tribe, you were born at home. That is what saved your life.

"Dark Eagle—Nasha's older brother—booked the two of us safe passage to the coast and onto a freighter bound for the Hawaii Free State. From there we sailed for Auckland where I have secluded myself ever since."

While Carina tried to digest everything that her father had told her, Sam was quiet for a long, long time. Finally he broke the silence with a sigh.

"Now you know how I feel about your precious gene-map," he remarked bitterly. "*Death* is the only known cure for brown eyes!"

Before Carina could even open her mouth to reply, there was an urgent knock at the door. Though she didn't know it yet, the man impatiently waiting outside was about to change *everything!*

PART III

1
The Red Planet

In Orbit Above Earth
Two Weeks Later

Depending on the position of the two planets in their respective orbits, the distance from the Earth to Mars could be as little as eighty million kilometers or up to several times that amount. As the nav-computer churned out its calculations for the jump, Fornax used his pocket slide rule to double-check the numbers. At Drive speeds approaching 140 thousand kilometers per second, even a small error could have disastrous results. He estimated the 100-million-kilometer trip at a bit under twelve minutes.

Weeks ago, with the late Captain Michael at the helm, the prototype had performed admirably in its test run to the moon; today, Fornax had a much more ambitious goal in mind—something grand enough to not only prove out the new equipment, but also impressive enough to dazzle his special guest.

When Lester had first broached the idea of inviting Carina and her father along for today's maiden flight, Fornax couldn't see the sense of it, thinking it was some sort of trap the Overlord had set. But once she stepped onboard, Fornax forgot all his fears. Even in her ill-fitting dee-dee, the woman was uncommonly attractive; indeed, he scolded himself for not having paid more attention to her earlier.

Then there had been all this business about christening the ship. It had seemed so silly to him at the time, but now, in retrospect, Fornax was glad for having agreed to let her do it. While it was true that the word she used was new to him, somehow—once its meaning was clear—"Tikkidiw" sounded vaguely appropriate. "Beautiful little thing of God," she explained in that brassy voice of hers, "an ancient Cornish term used to describe a butterfly." It made perfect sense, Fornax agreed. Much as a butterfly might flit from flower to flower in search of nectar, this new ship of theirs might flit from planet to planet in search of freedom.

Then, to make her happy, Fornax had ordered a likeness of a blue butterfly emblazoned on the ship's hull. When he told her what he intended, Carina's approving smile led him to believe he was on the right track with her. Who would have thought it, but there was almost nothing he wouldn't do now to gain her favor. Come to think of it, the jump to Mars had been her idea too! After his meeting with Overlord Ling in Hong Kong, Fornax had gone straightaway to Sam's place to warn him of the danger. Carina had answered the door.

Her eyes were swollen, as if she'd been crying. Sam and her had obviously been engaged in a serious discussion, and Fornax could tell from their strained expressions that the dialogue had been intense enough to leave the two of them at odds.

Figuring it was none of his business, Fornax didn't ask what they had been arguing about. Instead, he jumped right in and proceeded to tell them both of his audience with Overlord Ling. He didn't get far, though, before Sam—incessant matchmaker that he was—had led the three of them into his sumptuous living room and seated Fornax next to Carina on the couch.

Thinking nothing of it at the time, Fornax concentrated on telling them his story. He told them how he thought Ling was consumed by his thirst for power and would likely stop at nothing to achieve his goal of world domination; how Lester was one of his henchmen and couldn't be trusted; and how the Overlord had promised to provide Fornax with a shuttle for his experiments so long as he was left with a battle-ready warship when Fornax was through.

That wasn't the end of it, though. Fornax also related how, in a moment of desperation, he had agreed to Ling's terms. It had been a hasty decision, he knew that now, and the thing uppermost on his mind presently was running away and finding a place to hide from this jackal. It was at *that* point that totally out of the blue she had brought up the subject of Mars.

Fornax was totally unprepared for this, as was her father. Nevertheless, he couldn't help himself. Sitting next to her that evening, listening to her explain why they should take Ling's ship and go to Mars, the man was mesmerized! He imagined their bodies locked together in an unending embrace—like steel to a magnet, like a planet to its sun.

At that moment in time, with Carina sitting there barely inches from his shoulder, she had seemed so accessible, even eager. But today, everything was different! Today, Fornax wasn't so sure anymore where he stood with her. Today, as she ambled before him gracing the bridge of the *Tikkidiw* and eyeing the ruggedly-built BC for the first time, Fornax felt as if he'd been betrayed. It was bad enough that she wasn't paying any attention to *him*, but to have her quietly looking BC over as if he were a piece of freshly-hung meat, well, *that* was aggravating in the extreme! And then to have BC looking hungrily back at her was almost too much to bear. Fornax was confused and hurt.

Carina, though, knew *exactly* what she was up to! Having two suitors competing for her ample affections rather amused her. Indeed, having two admirers vying for her attention was a whole lot more interesting than just having one—or as things stood presently—none. On the heels of refusing yet another marriage proposal from Maxwell, the two of them had just called it quits.

Then, to complicate her life even further, Dr. Janz had baited her with a proposition. He would agree to drop the Board's proceedings if only she would go to bed with him. Although Carina flatly spurned the distasteful offer, it never came to that. The Board's vote went against him three to two and he was forced to call off the inquiry anyway. When push came to shove, Professor Franklin, Dr. Blanding, and Marilyn had all voted to retain her.

Even so, the lecherous bastard looked to be an unending source of trouble. In Janz's final report summarizing the Board's narrow decision, he had made a point of suggesting that since Carina's mother had been of Amerind stock, Carina's inherent "cultural bias" might taint her scientific objectivity, thus disqualifying her from any further research grants. Even now, a week later, the man's gall nearly brought her to tears.

Tired of having been repeatedly hassled by Dr. Janz, tired of having been without a man for so long, tired of having to take sexual matters into her own two hands night after night, Carina was more than happy to set aside her current troubles for a moment as she debated which of these two fine young men standing before her in the forward cabin of the *Tikkidiw* could better satisfy her needs.

On the one hand, there was Fornax. Here was a man of obvious intelligence and above average good-looks, but what worried her about him was that his work might be his life. Driven by an inner fire to succeed, his brooding eyes seemed devoid of the seething animal lust she craved so badly.

On the other hand, there was BC. Here was a man blessed with fair skin, cold-blue eyes, and a powerful build. Not terribly bright perhaps, but with exceptionally nice buns and a firm, flat stomach.

Could any woman faced with such an awesome decision make up her mind?

Hesitant to make contact with BC's steely gaze, Carina held back, patiently waiting until he again looked up, his muscular hands still manipulating some dial or other on the nav-console. When he finally acknowledged her presence with a nod, she was instantly throbbing with desire.

Though she said nothing, her eyes were alive with words. "Take me, you fool! Make mad love to me! Right here! Right now!"

Witnessing this quiet exchange firsthand, Fornax seethed with anger. He addressed BC brusquely, hoping to draw her attention back to him. "Are you ready to start earning your pay, bub?"

Unsure what he had done wrong to earn such insolence, BC stared hard at Fornax before nodding his head, "Yes."

"Well then, Mister, engage the Drive," Fornax ordered, asserting himself as captain of the ship. "I have laid in a course for the Red Planet," he said, glancing over his shoulder to check Carina's reaction.

True to her character, Carina didn't flinch. But, had Fornax been looking over at Lester instead, he might have noticed a dab of sweat bead up on the scrawny man's forehead. It was all Lester could do not to think of yesterday morning's call from Overlord Ling.

In the ensuing minutes, as the gleaming ship sped across the solar system towards Mars at half the speed of light and the Earth became a tiny, blue speck in the night sky, Lester replayed that conversation through his head:

Ling had begun by inquiring whether or not Lester had installed the locator as Ling had instructed.

"Of course, boss," Lester replied. "I put it in while Fornax was off retrieving a set of strips we'd left on the moon for re-charging. You know me—I always do what I'm told."

"I'm glad to hear it," the Overlord answered, "because your next assignment is apt to be a little more challenging than simply hiding a locator-beacon onboard a shuttle."

"What do you have in mind?" Lester asked, his voice weary. The man was growing tired of constantly being at the Overlord's beck and call.

"I may need your brother and niece as bargaining chips later on," he said, leering ominously into the comm.

"I don't understand."

"I may need you to hold them for me as hostages."

"Hostages? Even Carina?" Lester questioned, his voice quivering. "What is the meaning of this? She knows nothing . . . "

"Look, Lester," the Overlord retorted sternly, "you have sold out your country for me, you have sold out your best friend Captain Michael for me; surely you're not squeamish about selling out your *brother?"*

"Well . . . of course not . . . " Lester stammered bravely.

"Good! Then it's settled. Now when do I get my warship?"

"Soon," Lester replied, doing his best to remain evasive.

"What kind of answer is *soon?"* Ling exploded, his mustache twitching nervously. "Are you holding back on me, boy? I have ways of finding out, you know. And in case you've forgotten—punishment always awaits those who have crossed me."

Lester bristled at being called "boy." But remembering Captain Michael's demise in the Corkscrew Pub the week before last, he swallowed hard before answering.

"I give you my word, sire: I'm not holding out on you. The new shuttle was assembled in orbit a few days ago and since then we've been hard at work ferreting out the bugs."

"Bugs? What bugs?"

"The glitches. The defects. The problem areas."

"I see," the Overlord answered. "And are the *bugs* out yet?"

"We'll know for sure after tomorrow's flight. If everything checks out, then we'll turn the ship over to you as promised. That is what you want, isn't it?" Lester asked meekly. He knew Overlord Ling was particularly unforgiving to those who made him wait.

"Of course that's what I want, you fool! And don't crack wise with me, Lester, or try anything stupid. I'll be tracking your every move! Now good day to you."

Abruptly dismissed, the conversation was ended. The short jump to Mars was over as well, and as the *Tikkidiw* shuddered to a halt, Lester forgot all about Ling and yesterday's talk. Glancing out the viewport now, he could see the glass-domed buildings of the long-ago abandoned colony some two hundred meters away in the distance.

Afraid that his guilt-ridden face might reveal his duplicity, Lester cast his eyes lower as the five of them suited-up in their dee-dees and scrambled excitedly to the Martian surface, the first humans to do so in over half a century!

Despite several previous trips to the moon, Fornax had never really grown accustomed to the disquieting confinement of being stuffed inside a spacesuit. But, as the others stumbled frantically about in the gathering dusk trying to gain their footing on the uneven Martian surface, he kept his discomfort to himself. Something else had caught his attention.

"Now isn't that strange?" he said, mentally comparing the ground beneath his feet to the compact, graveled terrain he was used to on the moon. He could feel the difference, even through the lining of his padded boots. "The ground here is springy. You know, like a mattress. Or a bed of moss."

When he got no reply, Fornax tapped his headset to be sure the others had heard him. They had, but were too stunned to reply. While the afternoon shadows prevented them from closely examining the dimly-lit turf beneath their feet, what they saw in *front* of them was mind-blowing!

The sunset revealed an austere planet of rusty, rugged beauty. An unimaginable variety of landforms—canyons, craters, volcanoes, ice-fields, and flat plains—combined to make Mars a world of great visual drama. Sweeping the horizon with their eyes, they recognized that many of the geologic processes known so well to Earth, like volcanism and erosion, had also once been active here on Mars, sculpting out her terrain in a highly unusual fashion.

Ancient tectonic movement had disfigured the planet, leaving behind two remarkably different hemispheres. To the south lay heavily-cratered highlands, while to the north, smoother plains dominated the landscape. Incredible as it might sound, the northern steppe was a full three kilometers *lower* in average elevation than the southern plateau. Immense canyonlands and giant extinct volcanoes were among the spectacular features which straddled the demarcation line between the two hemispheres. The terraformers' colony was established just north of these massive bluffs in a low-lying area of ancient lava flows spotted with silent volcanic cones.

Stunned by the thrilling panorama, Fornax lingered there on the Martian mesa staring breathlessly out across the pitted ravines. Only then did he realize how dangerous and stupid a game he had been playing by brazenly ignoring Sam's advice.

"The status quo hates to be upset," Sam had said. But Fornax wouldn't listen! At the time, he was blind to the consequences. Only now was he beginning to grasp the full power of the forces his discovery might unleash!

My God, what have I done? he asked himself, Sam's words reeling ominously through his head. How could I have been so stupid? And all in the name of money! Sam was right: the reopening of Mars for settlement *will* destabilize dictatorships around the globe. Just think of it! With my Fornax Drive, Mars is now only half an hour's ride away! Whereas centuries ago only a few hundred people could make the trip here, now thousands, perhaps *millions*, might do so!

Even as he stood there contemplating the possibilities, Carina was doing likewise. Her mind was crowded with thoughts of migration. Ever curious, she stooped to touch the ground with her gloved hand. The realization struck her like a bolt of lightning!

The lichen! She had forgotten all about the lichen! *That*'s what was underfoot! *That*'s what had made the ground so springy!

The terraformers had said it would take seventy-five years for the lichen to blanket the planet making the atmosphere breathable, but it had now been over three *hundred!* Left undisturbed for so long, the lichen had spread everywhere!

Seized by impulse, she scanned the enviro-scope built into the visor of her suit. The voice-activated counters displayed the outside conditions—barometric pressure, temperature, oxygen content. Much to her satisfaction, the oxygen reading, though low, was in the safe range. Considering how, when terraforming first began in earnest centuries ago, Mars's atmosphere was completely *devoid* of oxygen, this was a truly phenomenal development!

The special lichen worked! she bubbled excitedly to herself. It worked!

Yet, oxygen or not, it wasn't as if she could just rip off her spacesuit and roll around in the grass—it was still pretty damn cold out there, plus the background radiation levels were still uncomfortably high. Even so, her scope measured a balmy fifteen degrees above zero, a temperature appreciably warmer than before the lichen was planted. It seemed as if the chlorofluorocarbon treatments had done some good after all!

Mars might just be habitable, she told herself, imagining a sanctuary here for newhumans. If so, the Fornax Drive would have to be kept under wraps or else the whole planet would be quickly overrun by fortune hunters and gold diggers.

If only she could convince the others! But how? Even her father had doubts about this whole business of signature genes and newhumans.

For a long moment Carina thought about the thick mat of lichen and about the more than adequate oxygen level registering on her enviro-scope.

Then, she made up her mind.

Breaking the seal on her helmet with a deft flick of the wrist, Carina jerked the dome off her head.

Dumbfounded, Sam stared at his daughter in disbelief.

Carina returned his look with a tight inquisitive smile. Then, as the frigid air of Mars struck her face, she drew a deep breath!

2
Plate Tectonics

Suddenly the situation was wildly out of control!

From out of the corner of one eye, Fornax had seen Carina fumbling with her helmet, but it never occurred to him that she would be fool enough to take it off. Boy, was he wrong!

When he glanced over in Sam's direction to point out an interesting rock formation, Fornax knew instantly. The old fellow's face was painted gray, his time-worn features consumed by a nervous look of horror.

Following Sam's disbelieving eyes with his own, Fornax spun around just in time to see Carina pull her protective headgear up and over her head. He shouted frantically into his headset for her to stop, but it was too late—she had already yanked the damn thing off her head and was holding it in her hand!

Too stunned for words, Fornax just stood there watching. When the cold air hit Carina's face, she shivered. Then, before he knew it, she had drawn a deep breath!

Acting on impulse, Fornax bounded towards her as swiftly as his clumsy suit would allow. BC did the same. A quick reflex glance at his scope confirmed that there was indeed sufficient oxygen out there, but it was anybody's guess what *other* gases might be mixed in. Even minor amounts of an airborne toxin might be enough to kill, no matter *what* the oxygen level was!

The thin air made Carina lightheaded and she promptly sank to the ground, dropping her helmet at her feet. Arriving there just ahead of BC, Fornax scooped up the headpiece and started to force it back down over her head. Her lips were quivering from the cold and yet she protested.

"I'm okay," she snorted, though by this time her lips had turned a lovely shade of blue. "I was unprepared for the thin air, but I can breathe I tell you! It was a shock, like if I'd jumped instantly from sea level up to the peak of a tall mountain—but I'm okay now."

Fornax ignored her recital as he strained to re-tighten the pressure-bolts lining the neckpiece of her suit, thus reestablishing the seal around her helmet. At the same time, BC checked her pulse and respiration.

"Are you all right?" her father asked in a terrified tone as he arrived at a slow trot. Behind him, sauntering over at a leisurely pace, was his brother Lester. Derision filled his words.

"Damn fool woman!"

"For God's sake, man, show a little compassion!" Sam exclaimed testily. "She's your niece! Must you always be such a jerk?"

While the two of them were busy exchanging words, BC helped Carina to her feet. She could feel the strength of his grip even through the thickness of her suit.

"I apologize for scaring you," she said, "but I had to try. You have got to believe me, BC—except for the cold, this air is breathable! It's like . . . like . . . standing up on top of a mountain. Given some time to adjust, I . . . we . . . could *live* here! The lichen worked, don't you see?"

BC was tempted to tell her that she was one gutsy broad, but thought better of it. Why encourage the lady? It could only lead to more trouble!

"I don't know anything about your damn lichen!" he boomed sternly. "But I want no more theatricals. From you, or from anyone else! Is that understood?"

When all four heads had nodded their compliance, he continued. "Later, when we get indoors—and if we have the time—we'll conduct an air toxin test to verify what you're saying, Carina. But for now, everyone please leave your suits on. Can you walk?" he asked. She stood flanked by Fornax and her father.

"Yes, boss," she answered, batting her eyes at him.

"Okay then, let's go," he said, pointing in the direction of the colony buildings a couple hundred meters away.

As they trudged towards the abandoned structures, Fornax stared in bewilderment across the surface of Mars. It was no longer the stark, red planet he had seen in books and through his telescope as a boy. Now it was carpeted by a tangled, thick lichen mat, four to five centimeters in depth and covering the ground in all directions, even partway up the base of the enormous bluffs he saw in the distance. In fact, about the only surface *free* of lichen were the glacine globes covering the colony habitats just ahead. Apparently, the glass skin of the habitat domes was so hard and smooth, the encroaching lichen had never been able to gain a foothold there. Otherwise, the entire planet was blanketed with the stuff!

Fornax speculated about it outloud. "What I don't get is this: If simple plants could be *seeded* here so successfully, why didn't they germinate on their own millions of years ago just like they did back on Earth?"

"Actually, they may have," Carina advised in that petulant know-it-all voice of hers.

Hearing her tone, Fornax narrowed his eyes and gave her a queer sort of look. His question had been strictly rhetorical, and he never expected anything beyond "ho-hum" for an answer. It was anything but.

Clearing her throat to speak, she said, "I have it on good authority that on the second rover-mission to Mars, stromatolite-like microorganisms were discovered along the shoreline of an ancient Martian lake."

"Stromato-*what?*" BC barked into his headset.

"Stro-mat-o-lites," she repeated slowly. "Unfortunately, despite several hundred years of searching, those were the *only* Martian fossils ever recovered. In fact, those scientists were later accused of 'discovering' the specimens in Utah, not here on Mars, so the issue of primitive life is still unresolved."

"That's not much of an answer," BC said, struggling not to be left out of the conversation. "Even if there was life here at one time, where did it go?"

"Perhaps I can shed some light on that," Carina offered. "At a time in Mars's past when a more benign climate prevailed, liquid water collected on the surface. The large channels which resemble dry riverbeds are a testimony to that era. Back even before the dawn of the space-age, scientists reasoned that where there once was liquid water, there was at least the *possibility* of life. Since then, studies have shown that liquid-water habitats persisted on Mars for at least as long as it took for life to evolve on Earth. Thus, in searching for fossil remains here on Mars, the most obvious places to look were locations where there had previously been a standing body of water."

"Like the dry lake beds?" BC guessed.

"Yes, indeed," Carina nodded. "Not only were lakes a good place for life to flourish, but as a bonus, when an organism died, its remains had a good chance of being preserved in the sediments of the lake bottom."

"That makes sense," Fornax said, "but where did it *go?* What caused life to die out here?"

"It goes without saying that there have been drastic changes in the climate of this planet. The fundamental problem with Mars is not its distance from the sun, but rather its lack of plate-tectonics," Carina answered with apparent confidence.

"That's just plain silly!" BC remarked, still trying to keep up with the discussion. "What in the world does plate-tectonics have to do with the preservation of life?"

"Do be quiet and pay attention," Carina scolded, her face warming up after its brief exposure to the elements. "Atmospheric carbon-dioxide is depleted in the presence of standing water. On Mars, without plate-tectonics to recycle the carbon, the atmosphere would have been rapidly leeched of its CO_2. With the greenhouse effect lost, the planet would have quickly become too cold to sustain life."

"You may be on to something there," Fornax agreed, drawing on his limited knowledge of chemistry.

"Of course I am," she exclaimed indignantly. "It is possible that primitive life endured for a few hundred million years, but after that, sub-zero temperatures would have meant the end for life on Mars."

"But if that were true, how does the *lichen* survive the terrible cold?" BC asked.

"Good question," Fornax paralleled, wishing he had thought of it himself.

"Some species of Earth-lichen weather the cold by converting the water in their vascular systems from a liquid to a glassy solid without permitting any cell-bursting ice-crystals to form in the interim. The Martian-bound lichen were a genetically-engineered descendant of those strains. Over the years, tons-upon-tons of the special lichen were shipped by unmanned shuttles . . . "

The feisty woman's explanation careened on, but as the sun's rays faded into gray dusk, Fornax's mind strayed. Had he suspected the complexity of Carina's answer, he might never have asked her the question to begin with! As it was, he wondered whether she would ever shut up long enough for him to get to know her better. Surely there were other things she could do with that beautiful mouth of hers besides talk!

" . . . built in the lowlands, hoping to eventually release some of the frozen water for use in irrigating the various . . . "

BC's thoughts ran along a somewhat different line. He was more concerned with what the next twenty-four hours might bring. What unknown dangers lurked in the shadows just ahead? Would Ling send Whitey and Marona to hunt them all down? Would J hang him out to dry as he had Captain Michael? And what *about* Carina? The girl was definitely a turn-on, but maybe she was just a little bit too smart for an ordinary fellow like himself. If only she would shut up, then perhaps . . .

BC was sorely tempted to silence the drone of her monologue by switching off his headset. It never came to that, though, because moments later her lecture abruptly ended of its own accord when she stumbled on a loose boulder and fell to the ground.

Camouflaged beneath the thick lichen carpet were stones and rocks of all sizes, and as dark as it already was, even the intense lumina-beams of their lanterns were of little help in negotiating the uneven surface. Fortunately, they were now no more than a dozen meters away from the closest of the glass-domed structures.

• • •

"I thought I might be hearing from you before long," the gunman said, hissing like a snake into the comm. "Were you satisfied with our work at the Corkscrew the other night?"

"By all means!" Overlord Ling replied. "I couldn't be more pleased. As always, you and Marona did a splendid job for me. I hope you found the payoff to your satisfaction. Luscious red-heads are hard to come by these days. How long did she last anyway? My people tell me she put up quite a fight."

"Don't they all?" the assassin lamented, a sick smirk swallowing his face. "Regrettably, she lasted only four days. Hardly worth the effort, if you ask me. Still, it was a delightful, even blissful, ninety-six hours. Marona, especially, enjoyed tormenting the pretty young thing. I don't know what it is about red-heads, but they're a breed apart, wouldn't you agree? But then that's not why you called, is it? With Captain Michael out of the way, you must have something pretty important on your mind to be calling so early in the day."

"I need you to go to the moon for me. To the DUMP, actually."

"The moon, eh? That'll cost you," Whitey explained, flexing his arm muscles and stroking the bulge of his biceps as if they were the object of intense passion. "Space jobs are always more treacherous, plus you'll have to provide me with a ship, weapons, and a full complement of dee-dees. The crew's my responsibility—I only use my own people."

"I can appreciate the wisdom in that. Would double your standard rate cover it?"

"Triple," came the curt reply.

"In that case, you have yourself a deal," Ling said, relieved that he didn't have to go higher.

"It's a shame, but I'll have to do this one without Marona. She's not fond of spacesuits, you know. Too confining."

"Father knows best."

"Tell me, Ling, what exactly *is* the job?" Whitey cross-examined in a businesslike fashion.

"Not long ago, I had a new shuttle commissioned, one equipped with an experimental, but very costly propulsion system. For the very reason that it *was* so expensive, I had Lester Matthews affix a locator onto the hull so I could keep track of her at all times. But before I knew it—poof—the ship was gone!"

"Gone? Gone how?" the assassin asked, puzzled. "As in Lester *stole* it?"

"That's always a possibility—Lester is, after all, untrustworthy in the extreme—but stealing something this big doesn't fit his penny ante style. Whatever the explanation, the ship vanished without a trace. One minute it was there; the next, it jumped completely off our screens to I don't know where. I haven't heard from Lester—or the ship—since. I'm beginning to become, shall we say, perturbed."

"You said it was an experimental craft. Maybe it just blew up."

"Perhaps. But since locator-beacons are themselves nearly impervious to destruction, the shuttle couldn't have exploded without leaving behind *some* trace."

"So where do you think it is?" Whitey probed in a frustrated tone.

"I don't really know. All I *do* know is this: before long the shuttle will have to return to the moon DUMP to refuel. And when it does, I want you there to commandeer the ship and bring it back to me."

"And its crew?" Whitey questioned, worried that he might not get to kill anyone on this mission.

"Do as you will," the Overlord granted. "Cut all their throats for all I care, though I should point out that there is likely to be a sweet-looking girl onboard. A tall one, at that. You might wish to have your way with her first."

"Girl? What girl?" Whitey quizzed, suddenly interested.

His cruel mustache twitching madly, Ling laughed. "Sam's only daughter; Lester's niece."

"You've known me long enough to appreciate that I have no qualms about who I murder, but let me understand you correctly. You want Lester eliminated along with all the others? I thought he was one of your most loyal henchmen?"

"Yes, you're right, of course, but I fear he has outlived his usefulness. Lester has changed a lot over the years, you know. I recruited him as an informant before the Great War because his grandfather—Senator Nate Matthews—had access to sensitive military secrets. As a Navy lieutenant, young Lester helped us to pinpoint and sink the U.S. fleet stationed off the coast in the East China Sea. Thousands of American lives were lost in the attack. To cover his rotten deed, he even sabotaged and sunk his own frigate. The *Intrepid* I believe it was called."

"Sounds like my kinda man," Whitey interjected enthusiastically.

"Lester was well paid for his treachery, but the man was greedy. And he was stupid. He squandered his blood money in short order, then, nearly destitute, joined our merchant marines before eventually striking out on his own. Since then, I have used him on occasion to run guns to revolutionaries we support around the world. Even today, most of the business conducted by Matthews Transportation is in moving goods I have requisitioned."

"So why kill him?"

"That's the difference between being an elected head-of-state and a dictator—a dictator doesn't need a reason! Still, if you must know, it's because Lester's organization has been infiltrated by one of J's men, a fellow you've met before, a fellow code-named BC. Now, are you up to this or not? Will you go to the moon for me and get my shuttle back, or do I have to call in someone else to handle it?"

"Consider it done."

"Good."

3
Abandoned

The threaded handle on the airlock yielded slowly to their efforts. But after a few minutes of concerted effort, the pads finally released and the exterior door sluggishly disengaged.

Stepping ever so cautiously across the newly-opened threshold, the five suited figures were welcomed by the tepid glow of a yellow ceiling lamp. An eerie mechanical voice droned out a prerecorded instruction. "To pressurize the chamber," it said, "press the flashing green button on the far wall."

Without flinching, Sam crossed the entryway to where the light was flashing, depressed the button as per the instructions, then stepped back to see what would happen. As they all studiously watched, the outer door swung shut. Within moments, they could hear the reassuring swish of rushing air as the atmosphere in the chamber was normalized.

When the swishing sound ceased, the inner door swung open and the mechanical voice spoke again. "Please remove your suits as you enter the colony. A storage closet is ahead and to your left."

Moving swiftly to countermand the machine's invitation to disrobe, BC declared, "Do not—I repeat—do *not* remove your suits! Let's risk just one life at a time, shall we? Now, do I have any volunteers?"

BC was not surprised to see Carina's hand shoot up, but he waved her off, preferring to remove his own helmet instead.

Though he found the air chilly, it was not particularly cold. While the others looked on, he drew several breaths. Experiencing no unusual discomfort, he said, "Everything seems okay here. Even so, keep your helmets with you just in case we experience a sudden loss of pressure. And let's skip the heroics, shall we? Heroes are nothing more than well-meaning people who managed to die a stupid death."

Everyone nodded their agreement as they removed their headgear and began to scrutinize the abandoned facility. Unlike some timeworn video where—to the sounds of creepy music—the star of the show bursts into the deserted building only to discover gruesome death and destruction, the scene here was pathetically serene and tranquil. There were no goblins, and there certainly wasn't any death. As far as today's visitors could tell, the former residents had simply packed up their bags and gone home.

The five were standing in what once must have been a community mess-hall. It was a large, hexagonally-shaped room at least twenty-five meters across. In each of the six walls was a doorway, the first one leading to the airlock they had just entered through, and the others presumably leading to the corridors which radiated out from the central hub. The entire complex was of a modular design so that it could be taken apart, unit by unit, and moved elsewhere if the circumstances dictated. Giant bolts punctuated the junctions where the connecting pieces met.

Metal doors separated the corridors from the mess-hall proper, and each door, save one, had a glass panel in it which afforded them a view partway up the darkened corridors beyond. Moving clockwise around the room, Sam tried two of the doors to see if they would open, but they were sealed shut from the inside.

Noting a numbered keypad on the wall next to one of the doors, BC hazarded a guess. "The door probably won't budge unless you enter the right combination. Security doors like this would have helped guard the residents against unwanted invasions of their privacy."

"And against unexpected pressure losses," Carina said. She shuddered as she thought grimly of the asteroid collision 200 years ago.

"That makes sense," Lester agreed. "Like an apartment building where a tenant can unlock the downstairs door from the safety of his upstairs flat."

Deciding he must be right, the five turned their attention back to the community room.

In the center were several long tables, some of which were flanked by benches, others by folding chairs. Ideally, the arrangement accommodated the room's dual function as both an eating area and a meeting place.

Affixed to one wall were cabinets and pantries brimming with medical supplies, paper goods, cooking and eating utensils, seasonings, detergents, even toiletries. And on the long beige counters underneath, stood an assortment of appliances and mixing bowls. Off to one side, there was another set of cabinets housing keyboards and video monitors, some of which were designed to keep track of such pedestrian things as interior temperature, air pressure, and waste treatment.

Spying a canister of lemonade mix on the shelf, Carina was reminded of an essential bodily function which badly needed attending to. It had been some time since her last visit to a bathroom, and her bladder was urgently telling her that something simply had to be done about the oversight.

To divert the men's attention away from her nervous squirming,

Carina pointed to the expansive glass dome overhead. "It must have been truly lovely to eat breakfast here," she said, "what with the sunshine streaming through and all."

But even as she spoke, the woman silently reasoned it through. The residents wouldn't have run all the way back up to their rooms to take a pee—there must be one here!

But where?

Running her eyes along the perimeter of the room, Carina found what she was looking for. There, a dozen meters away, the door without a glass panel. Had to be!

Crossing her fingers that it wasn't locked, Carina edged over in that direction to test the door handle. When it gave way without protest, she let out a sigh of relief. Thank God!

As Carina had guessed, the door led, not to a corridor, but to a toilet. Inside the lavatory were several private stalls. It made her think that perhaps it was a community bathroom shared by both sexes.

Shutting the outside door, the anxious woman rapidly peeled off her flightsuit. After the cramped, metallic facility onboard the *Tikkidiw*, the enormous size of the stall and its cool porcelain fixtures were a welcome relief. Then too, the gentle gravitational tug of the fourth planet made the experience that much more pleasurable as compared with using the ship's urinary suction-device. This was what going to the bathroom was *supposed* to be like!

Her heart sank, though, when she realized there was no toilet paper. It couldn't be helped, she thought, reaching for the flush lever—she'd have to air-dry.

Immediately upon exiting the toilet Carina rolled up her suit into a ball and threw it onto one of the long tables. Then she sat down contentedly, folded her arms, and smiled. "It looks as if the colonists just packed up all their stuff and went home," she said as if nothing had happened.

"Transporting all this stuff back to Earth would have been too expensive fuel-wise," Fornax explained. "So they basically just left everything behind. Everything, that is, except for disposable provisions like . . . "

"Like toilet paper?" Carina interrupted, a mischievous grin on her face.

"Yeah, like toilet paper," Fornax replied, slowly catching her meaning. "You found a *bath*room?"

"Sure did!" she bubbled, pointing in that direction. "Right over there. But watch out, fellas, there's no T.P."

The four men promptly hustled that way, emerging a few minutes later a much happier lot. All the dee-dees were then piled in a heap on the table and they shortly got down to business.

Carina was the first to speak. "So what do we do now?" she asked.

"I think we should collect up as much durbinium as we can get our hands on, zoom back to the DUMP to charge it, then sell the damn Batteries to the highest bidder." That was Lester's greed talking.

"Then again," he continued, more brash than before, "we could start auctioning off plots of land right here on Mars. With the *Tikkidiw* being the absolute only means of getting here, we'd clean up!" Fantasizing outloud, Lester parodied an imaginary advertisement. "Matthews Space Lines—Our Destinations Are Out Of This World!"

"Aren't you forgetting something?" Fornax challenged.

"Nothing I can think of," Lester claimed, feigning innocence.

"How 'bout me, for one," Fornax snapped. "Your fuehrer, for another."

"My *what?*" Lester blurted.

"Your fuehrer," Sam explained. "Your boss. Your Overlord."

"Oh, him. Forget about him," Lester sneered. "There's no way Ling can touch us out here."

"Maybe not," Fornax admitted, "but what about me? This is *my* invention, you know."

"What *about* you?" Lester laughed haughtily. "I'm not afraid of you!"

"Hold it right there, you two!" Sam exclaimed, moving to defuse the situation. "Ahead of doing anything else, we need to do that air toxin test BC told us about. Hell, we don't even know for certain if the air out there is actually safe to breath! So, before you start breaking ground for a subdivision, Lester, let's first get that out of the way, shall we?"

"Sounds sensible enough to me," Lester acknowledged.

"Me too," Fornax said, glancing across the room. "Let's check out these cabinets—the testing equipment we need might be in one of them."

Retreating from the racket of Sam arguing with Lester arguing with Fornax, BC grabbed hold of one of the locked door handles and made as if he were trying to jimmy the lock. All this talk about getting rich off the Fornax Drive would just not do. BC had his orders. J had been quite specific. Bring Fornax and his discovery back to England intact. Nothing more. Nothing less.

Intelligence work was always that way. Interesting job if you didn't care where you slept, what you ate, or how long you lived. J was used to giving orders, regardless of the consequences. "Boys," he might say, "we need to fertilize this tree. Jump in that hole I've dug for you there at the base, and I'll cover you up."

BC would have done it, no questions asked. So would have Captain Michael along with each and every other person in their Section. And J would have buried them alive too, if he thought there was so much as a 53% chance that it was the Tree of Liberty they were nourishing.

As was his way, J did not bother agents with detailed instructions. "Give a man a mission," he would say. "Let him sink or swim."

There was a time once when BC worked up the nerve to question him about this; said his method must use up a lot of agents.

"Some," he admitted, "but not as many as the other way. I have confidence in the individual, and I try to pick people who are survivor types."

"And how in the hell do you pick a 'survivor' type?" BC asked.

J grinned wickedly. "A survivor type is one who comes back!"

BC swallowed hard. It had seemed funny at the time; it hardly seemed so now. He was about to find out which type *he* was. There would be no calling home for instructions, no checking in for updates.

BC was on his own, and it was a good thing too. By this time, Ling had almost certainly dispatched one of his henchmen to the moon to learn what had become of the *Tikkidiw*. It was a sure bet he would send Whitey or someone of his ilk to hunt the five of them down.

All was not lost, though. If BC moved quickly, and without hesitation, he ought to be able to reach the moon ahead of any of Ling's people. The *Tikkidiw* was, after all, the fastest ship in the solar system, and even from a distance of 110 million kilometers away, he still ought to be able to get to the moon, deposit the spent strips for recharging, and get underway again with time to spare. All it would take now for them to come out of this thing alive was a little bit of luck, plus the smarts to turn the *Tikkidiw*'s great speed to their advantage.

Though only a fraction of a second passed while BC stood there trying to work out a strategy, he had continued to fumble with the locked doorlatch the whole time. From across the community room Carina had seen him standing there fiddling with the knob, and with the other three men still busy jabbering away and looking through cabinets, she had wandered over to be by his side.

Thus far, it had taken every bit of her willpower to keep quiet about her lustful feelings, but there was no way she could contain herself any longer! Here was an opportunity to have her itch scratched, and Carina wasn't about to pass it up!

Cornering BC safely out of earshot of the others, she said, "Haven't you figured out what it takes to open her up yet?"

At first, BC was too stunned for words. His perplexed look was met by a lecherous grin.

"I want you," she said, pressing her leg against his.

"So I gathered," he replied, caressing her hand with his own. "But what about Fornax? I think he's got the hots for you."

"There's more than enough to go around," she cooed, returning his caress. "Besides, I can always do him later. You, I want now!"

"That . . . sounds . . . good," he stammered, nearly choking on the words. "But I'm afraid it'll have to wait. We have got to get out of here. And I mean right away!" he emphasized, dashing her hopes for an early liaison.

Putting on a face of resolve, BC marched to the center of the room and gathered everyone's attention beneath the canopy of the immense glass dome.

"Listen up, everyone," he said. "I have an announcement to make. We have to return home posthaste. Our lives may be in danger."

Just as BC was about to reveal that his mission here was for Queen and flag, the sky above his head went white with a horrendous flash of lightning.

"Oh, my God!" Carina gasped. But her words were drowned out by the exploding sound of thunder.

Then, as the sky lit up for a second time, they all dropped to the floor praying it wasn't true!

4
Storm

Without an atmosphere, without water vapor, without even wind, clouds and rain and thunderstorms and lightning simply could not exist on Mars. And so it had remained for countless millennia.

The arrival of the terraformers changed everything, however. The lichen they brought with them from Earth and then planted so meticulously here on Mars had taken hold to such an extent, it had permanently altered the face of the planet, thickening the atmosphere and warming the continents as it spread.

Even the lichen's tenacious roots had played a role, breaking down the surface rocks, releasing the gases bound up within them, and hurrying the "thickening" process along.

Then too, there was the water vapor given off by the lichen as it grew. Water vapor was the classical greenhouse gas, and while not nearly as potent as carbon-dioxide in this role, it nevertheless did its part in helping to trap more of the sun's warmth near the surface.

The planet-molders didn't stop there, though; they conspired to do the lichen one better! Knowing how chlorofluorocarbons were notorious greenhouse gases, the terraformers set their sights on pumping tons of CFC's into the frigid atmosphere. Though this ambitious program carried with it the risk of inhibiting the development of a protective ozone layer, it nonetheless succeeded in warming the planet immeasurably, thus nudging the ecosystem even further in the direction the terraformers wanted it to go.

Seeded with these gases, the adolescent atmosphere gradually began to mature. And as it did, the prevailing temperature extremes steadily diminished. More moderate temperatures spurred more lichen growth; more lichen growth meant more carbon-dioxide, more water vapor, and a heightened greenhouse effect. With each passing day conditions improved, and as the lichen blanketed the planet, its color darkening the surface, even more of the sun's warmth was retained.

The tempering process was classic CHAOS at work. Each turn of the screw tightened the spring further, and once the critical stage was reached, the self-reinforcing cycle took but a geologic instant to run its course. In a chaotic cascade of events that would have made even Dr. Sam proud, Mars once again prepared herself to harbor life.

Of no less importance to this development, however, was one other: now that all the necessary ingredients had been assembled in one place, the witch's brew of weather was finally brought to a boil. By the time Fornax & Company arrived on Mars, the newly-warmed planet had rudimentary atmospheric mixing plus a budding global weather system.

And with heat had come humidity. And with lightning had come thunder. And with nightfall had come rain—tons upon tons of it—all falling in a torrential downpour of Biblical proportions!

The storm which now descended upon them was an explosively-loud howling squall. Tearing out of the highlands to the south, the tempest rocketed through their valley like a juggernaut. Propelled by powerful hurricane-force winds and accompanied by blazing pyrotechnics, the onslaught of wind and rain struck the Mars base like a level-one tidal wave!

Terrified that the glass dome would suddenly collapse and come crashing down upon their heads, the five hastily re-suited and scrambled into the bathroom. It was the one place nearby where a solid metal door might stand as a shield between them and all that glass.

There was no escaping the cavalcade of thunderclaps, however. Like a fleet of heavy trucks rumbling across an old wooden bridge, they rolled by overhead one right after the next. Insulated walls or not, down below where *they* were, the din was almost too much to bear. Muted and scared, they sat there huddled in the bathroom like children, waiting out the storm. They could not even talk to one another over the noise, and by the time it was over more than two hours later, the five of them had gained a new respect for the Martian gods of weather.

When the typhoon finally receded into the distance and they crawled cautiously out of their hole, they looked outside only to make a horrible discovery! Not a hundred meters away was the shoreline of a rapidly forming lake!

Fed by the run-off pouring out of the mountains to the south, the developing lake was quickly inundating the very lowlands where they were camped. And with each passing moment the shoreline drew closer, the rust-colored water swirling up in the direction of the *Tikkidiw* and the Mars base beyond.

Sam spoke first, his ears still ringing from the colossal thunderstorm. "BC, when you said earlier that our lives might be in danger, I had no idea."

"Nor did I," BC replied, shaking his head.

"Danger?!" Carina exclaimed. "What are you two talking about? This is downright exhilarating! Can't you see? Mars has rain! It has air!

We can live here!"

Bubbling with excitement, Carina removed her dee-dee for the second time that day and hung it over the back of a chair. Uppermost on her mind was coming up with a way to convince a small band of fellow newhumans to join her in migrating to the Red Planet.

At the suggestion that anyone could possibly want to live here, BC lost his temper. "Of all the harebrained schemes! This is no place for us! I'm telling you—we have to get the hell out of here!"

"Are you looney?" Lester exclaimed, directing his remarks to BC. "In case you missed it, we've just made two amazing discoveries. First, the Fornax Battery; now this. If Mars can support life, if people can actually live here, we'll clean up! The *Tikkidiw* is our ticket to untold wealth! Before we leave here to go *any*where, we have got to come up with the best way to turn this thing to our advantage."

Fornax was as surprised as anyone to find himself agreeing with Lester, of all people, but it had never been his intention to turn over the *Tikkidiw* to Ling to begin with. Now with Lester unexpectedly lining up behind him, he just might be able to avoid doing that after all. Funny how necessity sometimes makes for strange bedfellows!

"Now see here," BC started to argue.

"No, *you* see here!" Lester barked, his mousy face contorted with emotion. "Who the hell put you in charge anyway? In case you've forgotten, bub, this is *my* operation. I run things around here. You're just the hired help."

"Hired help?" BC roared. "Why you bastard! Maybe it's slipped your mind, Lester, but *you* put me in charge, remember? Back in Melbourne. And now I'm *taking* charge," the fair-skinned man declared with authority. "I'm not who you think I am. I'm not who *anyone* thinks I am. I'm undercover. Here on assignment. My mission is to bring Fornax and his invention back in one piece. What happens to the rest of you is officially none of my concern!"

"Commonwealth Secret Service?" Lester stammered, nearly devastated by the horrible truth. If C.S.S. had learned of his association with Overlord Ling, then it only stood to reason that Ling might have become aware of BC's true identity as well. That would explain several things, beginning with why Ling had insisted he install a locator onboard the ship, as well as why he had insisted Lester bring everybody along on the trip, Carina included.

White-faced and trembling, Lester just stood there mouth agape. Things were about to get dicey. He wasn't safe now from either man, J *or* Ling. J would have him pegged as a conduit for illegal DUMPING; Ling, as a double-agent under J's control. Considering what had happened to Captain Michael under similar circumstances, Lester could very well be the next one marked for death!

The indignant tone of Sam's voice snapped Lester out of his deliberations.

Sam was vehemently objecting to BC's assertion that he would now be taking charge.

"And to whom were you supposed to give Fornax's discovery?" Sam asked, his eyes narrowing. "I must tell you, Mister BC or whoever you are, I am not amused by all this spy stuff, not one little bit. What is Lester talking about anyway? How does your secret service figure into this?"

Even before BC could answer, Fornax spoke up. "How could I have been so stupid? Damnit, BC, I trusted you!"

"And well that you had, or you would surely not be alive today," BC said, everyone's attention riveted on his cold blue eyes. "And to ensure your *continued* safety, it is my job to deliver you to a Commonwealth safe house upon our return. Once you're safely tucked away in protective custody, I'll undoubtedly be assigned to take out the Chinese agents who have been after you and your gadget practically since the beginning. These are the same people who murdered Captain Michael that night in the Corkscrew. Now, for the last time, let's do that air test thing you've been talking about and then get the hell out of here!"

"Now wait just a goddamned minute!" Dr. Sam angrily challenged. "We are not subject to Commonwealth law, and I, for one, am not going *any*where against my will! I may be twice your age, hot shot, but there are four of us here and just one of you, so if you give me any more static, you'll be returning home to your boss holding your bloody arse! And while we're at it, *curse* the Chinese—we have no quarrel with them!"

Carina's jaw hung open. Not only was she surprised to hear her father raise his voice and use foul language, her reaction to BC's revelations was radically different from that of the others. All this intrigue warmed her bosom like no fire ever could. This man, BC, excited her!

Again Fornax spoke up. "Look, even if we wanted to go straight home, we couldn't! We need more fuel, and the only place I know of where we can recharge the power strips is on the moon. That may take several days. Then, to keep my invention from being copied without my permission, we need to go straightaway to the World Court in SKANDIA to file for patent protection in each of the member countries. After that, we can sell the patent rights to whomever we please."

BC laughed outloud. "Forget it, Fornax. You'd be dead long before the ink dried on your first patent. The people pursuing you don't care one little twit about such formalities. Out-of-date capitalistic notions like copyrights and licensing agreements and rules of property mean *nothing* to them. Take it from me, partner, we've been battling the Overlords off and on for nearly a century now. They have no Christian frailties like you and me, and above all else, they're *mean*. I assure you the Chinese are desperate for this technology; they will stop at nothing to get it. They will kill you, and me, and Carina, and whomever else is standing in their way."

Fornax was not deterred. "Listen, I know all about fighting the

Overlord. Maybe you don't realize this, but I am an Afghan by birth. I fought in the war, for God's sake. Ling even blames me for killing his son. Claims I shot him down in a battle five years ago. So don't presume to tell *me!*"

All it took to perk up Carina's ears were the words, "Afghan by birth." From her genetic studies she was well aware of the high incidence of signature genes among the nomadic tribes of Afghanistan. It suddenly occurred to her that maybe she had been too hasty in concentrating all her affections on BC.

For his part, Sam was still shaking his head in disbelief. "How could I have been so gullible?" he grumbled, staring hard at BC. "How long have you known about all this?"

"Almost from the start."

Even in that moment of stunned silence, BC rushed to evaluate his options. At the beginning of a forest fire or an epidemic there is a short period of time when a minimum amount of corrective action will contain and destroy it; after that, it becomes an all-out war to stop it. That's where BC was now—on the brink. He had to decide on a course of action, one that would keep all these nice folks from getting killed!

For starters, he couldn't very well leave the four of them here on Mars intending to pick them up later. If anything went wrong while he was gone, there would *be* no later; Carina and the others would be stranded here with no way of getting home.

At the same time, BC was equally uncomfortable with taking them all along with him to the moon. As Fornax said, the strip recharging would take several days, only BC wasn't sure he could control the four of them that long. Though he definitely needed to keep Fornax at his side, the other three were like so many kilos of extra baggage.

To begin with, Lester was inherently untrustworthy. Now that he knew BC was on to him, he was apt to be downright dangerous as well.

Sam, while clearly a loose cannon, was probably unwilling to risk his daughter's life just to make a point.

And Carina? Well, she was a handful in her own right. Still, he couldn't very easily ignore the offer she had made him earlier; here was a woman he would have to arrange to spend some time with!

BC didn't believe in luck. Luck was a tag given by the mediocre to account for the accomplishments of genius. Yet, if things didn't start going his way—and soon—they would shortly all be out of luck. There could be no more delays—it was time to suit-up and get on their way! BC said as much; this time he got no objections.

They left the colony by the route they had come: out through the airlock and up the small, muddy rise to where the *Tikkidiw* was parked. Lightning flashed in the distance. It was completely dark now, and after the rain they had to pick their way carefully across the wet and slippery surface, their lumina-beams lighting the trail. There was no comm-chatter or lecture hall speeches on the return-trek as there had been on the hike in.

Back in the shuttle, BC and Fornax went over the ship's diagnostics to be certain the storm hadn't damaged anything. It wasn't long, though, before Sam had wandered over to where they were working, with Carina following close behind. He was in an apologetic mood.

"Agent BC, I called you a hot shot before. In all probability, my assessment of you was correct. Still and all, I'm confident that between *your* bravery and *Fornax*'s intelligence, we'll get through this thing alive. But before you go and do something rash, may I remind you of something a fine young man once told me. Something about heroes being well-meaning people who had managed to die a stupid death. That's good advice, wouldn't you agree?"

BC hardly had time to acknowledge Sam's observation when Fornax engaged the Drive for their jump to the moon.

Afraid of what lay ahead, the band of sweat widened on Lester's brow.

5
Above The Horizon

If Mars could properly be likened to a newborn—mortal, yet far too fragile to survive on her own—the moon could only be characterized as a corpse—cold, lifeless, and beyond help. One was alive, the other dead; one had a bright future, the other only a bleak past. The contrast startled them all, although none more than Carina.

"This place gives me the creeps," she confessed, surveying the collection of low-slung buildings which dotted the landscape. Between where she stood alongside the ship and the DUMP craters beyond, Carina counted no less than five buildings. The drab-colored structures were little more than metal pup-tents, yet they housed the DUMPSTER sleeping quarters as well as an old-fashioned machine shop, a tiny armory, a small but efficient atomic power plant, and an antiquated comm-link. Set against the gray, radiation-bleached terrain, the gleaming *Tikkidiw* seemed downright hospitable.

"Can we get on with it?" Lester asked, clearly chilled by the desolation. "I don't want to spend any more time here than I have to."

"I don't blame you," Sam chided as they passed through the airlock on their way into the main building. "If my boss made a sport of killing other people, I'd be worried too!"

"No one's going to get killed," Carina protested as she popped off her helmet revealing a full head of flowing brown hair. "BC'll take care of us," she said, sending a smile off in his direction.

"We'll see," Lester replied, kicking on a second row of halogen lamps. "The night is still young."

BC's eyes combed the room, taking in every detail. To complete their work in the allotted time they'd have to begin without delay and move swiftly. All at once businesslike, the man from Commonwealth Intelligence began handing out assignments with military efficiency.

Motioning first to Fornax, he said, "If you still think it'll do you any good, feel free to use that terminal over there to type up a description of your invention. If you're going to file a patent application, you'll need to first prepare an abstract. When you're done, enter this code and press the SEND button. A copy of your file will be automatically uploaded via comm-link to the *Tikkidiw*'s onboard computer for later retrieval. You can even encrypt it if you like. Just press ALT CTRL F3 before hitting SEND."

Fornax grunted noncommittally. Ever since their argument back on Mars, he had been thinking. BC had given him much the same advice that Sam had given him earlier, which is to say, not to put anything concrete down on paper. By now the conclusion was inescapable: in order for Fornax to stay among the living, he had to see to it that the secret of his device never became public. So long as the critical elements of his Battery remained forever tucked away safely inside his head, odds were he'd come out of this thing alive.

Still, there was something eminently appealing about making BC and the others think that he *hadn't* changed his mind. By doing nothing more than going through the motions of committing his notes to diskette, Fornax could, in one fell swoop, both placate Lester and irritate BC—two worthwhile endeavors in their own right! But rather than being stupid about it and revealing anything of consequence, Fornax had a better idea. What he would keypunch into the computer would be complete gibberish. Technical sounding gibberish perhaps, but gibberish nonetheless. It was about time he regained control over his own destiny—and this was precisely the way to do it!

BC continued giving orders. "Lester, I want you to remove all the strips from their casings and drop them into the nearest crater for recharging. Sam, I want you to go next door and collect up some weapons from the armory."

"What do we need weapons for?" Lester exclaimed.

"Just a precaution," BC said. "You don't actually believe that Overlord Ling is going to let us just waltz in here, do our business, and leave without a fight, do you?"

"Well . . . I . . . " he gasped weakly.

"I thought you were going to turn us over to Commonwealth Intelligence for safekeeping?" Sam protested.

"In due course, Sam, but for the moment my boss doesn't even know I'm out here with you. In fact, while you and Lester are busy taking care of things down here, Carina and I will be taking the *Tikkidiw* upstairs, above the horizon. As soon as England spins into view, I'll radio headquarters for instructions."

"That takes the both of you?" Sam questioned, his eyes narrowing. Though he sometimes took a dim view of Carina and her men, he had learned long ago not to interfere. Even so, this hardly seemed the time for such shenanigans.

"Well," BC stammered, trying to come up with a good excuse. "The radio's line-of-sight telemetry requires that we have the receiving station in view. Now, to line up the antenna . . . "

"Land's sakes, boy!" Sam exclaimed. "Spare me the bloody details! Just be quick about it, will you? Do what you have to, then get back down here as soon as possible. In case you've forgotten, there's important work to be done!"

At that, BC and Carina did an about-face and headed back out through the airlock in the direction of the *Tikkidiw*. Fornax stared after them with a mournful look. How he wished she would pay *him* that kind of attention!

• • •

"He means well, you know," Carina volunteered once they reached orbit.

"Who? Your dad? The man absolutely dotes on you!"

"You think?" she giggled.

"Believe me, I've seen all kinds, and they don't come much finer than that one."

Even as he spoke, BC took a peek out the viewport. They were orbiting high above the moon, and he was staring down upon the distant Earth to see which hemisphere was visible.

"Is that the Pacific?" he asked, squinting out at the expanse of blue.

"Yes, I suppose," she replied haltingly.

"It seems we'll be stuck here waiting awhile," he said, carefully eyeing her reaction. "Perhaps we can find something to talk about in the meantime."

Clearly disappointed, Carina pouted. "What I can't figure out is, why you would ask me to tag along with you up here if all you were going to do was *talk*."

BC was evasive. "Life's funny that way," he said, making every effort not to appear overly anxious. "But we do need something to pass the time until the telemetry is right. Remember what we were talking about before?"

"Refresh my memory."

"On the question of life. Something still bothers me. So far as I know, except for the Earth and now Mars, there is no evidence of life anywhere in the galaxy. And yet, my intuition tells me that the universe should be literally *brimming* with life. How can that be?"

"Can't we just forget about all that and make love instead?" she proposed, reaching out to him with her hand.

"Look, I'm serious!" he said, fending off her advance. "I'm no scientist, but I know for a fact that our sun is a common star. Not only that, there are billions more like her in our galaxy alone. It seems to me that life should have arisen wherever the conditions were roughly right, and even if that probability were low, there should still be tens of thousands of living planets. I'd have to conclude that the chances for intelligent life originating elsewhere are really quite good."

"BC, your logic is impeccable," she replied, frustrated at having been turned down, "and I can't fault your reasoning. But the facts suggest otherwise. Despite a careful search of the heavens, a search conducted over several centuries with everything from telescopes to robot-probes to rockets carrying meticulously-calibrated instruments, the galaxy has not yielded so much as a single sign of non-terran life."

"Carina, I know that is true, but what of it? For a thousand years the best minds believed the Earth was flat! Couldn't they be wrong about this one too?"

"Fair enough," Carina allowed, a tone of exasperation creeping into her voice. "But consider this: For an intelligent civilization only slightly more advanced than our own, interstellar travel should be simple and cheap. Just see how fast we ourselves can now go using the Fornax Drive. Granting only curiosity on the part of an alien civilization, I would argue that eventually they would send out a series of 'smart' probes to explore the galaxy and report back on locations meriting further study. These autonomous probes would have been specifically designed by their masters to use materials they found en route to refuel and to replicate.

"Allowing a hundred thousand years per interstellar flight and an additional thousand years for each probe to construct a copy, a single replicating probe would take—let me see—only 300 million years to send out a descendant to *every single* star system in the galaxy! Allowing six billion years from the initial formation of a planet until the time an intelligent species first begins sending out probes, we should have heard by now from anyone whose star system was more than six point three billion years old. That, by the way, is the age of nearly *half* the stars in the galaxy. If a civilization at approximately our level of advancement had ever existed, their spaceships would already be here by now. Since they're not, that means they don't exist!"

There was a slight quiver in her voice as she concluded. "We are alone."

Those last words left a sad, awkward silence in the ship. By all appearances, it did not please her to think that mankind stood alone in the galaxy.

For his part, BC wasn't totally convinced. A species capable of sending out the sophisticated probes Carina had described would also have had the good sense to camouflage their emissaries so that we humans could not readily recognize their presence. Not only that, why should they even *care* to communicate with us? What could our backward civilization possibly have to offer *them?*

But rather than voice his reservations, BC let her final words hang in the air. "Yes," he echoed, "we *are* alone. Finally."

Understanding his meaning, she smiled and reached across to touch his hand. This time, he didn't pull away.

"I want you," she panted. "Make love to me. Now."

Hoping to hurry things along, Carina undid the top two buttons of her blouse. The crests of her proud firm breasts greeted his ravenous eyes.

"Do you want this body?" she asked.

"Yes," he answered, swallowing hard. "Yes, I do."

By now BC was blushing. He was unaccustomed to such a direct woman, and it put him off his game. Unsure of himself, he leaned across and gave her a tentative kiss.

There was no hesitation in Carina's response. She kissed him hard, her red-hot tongue searching feverishly for his.

BC broke out in a sweat. Swamped by a tremor of hot craving, it was everything he could do not to lose control.

Her passion ignited, Carina would no longer take "no" for an answer. She pressed herself forward against him. Her nipples were hard like polished stones, etching out an unmistakable message of love on his heaving chest.

She reached down. The burning heat of his lust was hard against her leg. At its touch, her heart began to gallop. Her breath came in gulps.

Locked now in a tight embrace, they slid from his chair. Like autumn leaves they settled to the floor in slow motion. Weightlessness cushioned their impact.

"This'll never work here," he panted breathlessly, his strong hands caressing her bosom. "There's no *gravity!* Every thrust of mine will push you farther and farther away!"

"What can we do?" she quizzed, begging him to hurry.

"What if we go to my bunk and use the sleeping tethers?"

"Ooh, that sounds downright pagan! No one's tied me up in a long time!"

Gleefully tearing off her clothes, Carina stripped bare and sailed down the corridor towards BC's berth. He followed her in hot pursuit.

Leaping spread-eagle onto the bed, she said, "Okay, bub, I'm all yours!"

Each bunk on the ship was equipped with elastic tethers designed to prevent a sleeping occupant from floating out of bed during the night. By strapping one tether across her tummy well below her breasts, he fixed it so she couldn't float away yet would still have full range of motion with her legs. It couldn't have worked better if he'd planned it!

They went at it enthusiastically, like newlyweds. Only, the coupling didn't last long; they were both in such a bad way, they came almost immediately.

When BC finally rolled off her, it was with a businesslike air that he spoke. "Now tighten your love muscles and keep your knees pressed together," he said. "Or else we'll be combing it out of our hair for weeks. Remember—*every*thing floats in zero-g!"

"Oh, shut up and hand me that blanket," she instructed playfully. "You fill me up pretty good, flyboy," she cooed, admiring the tattoo on his arm. It was of the one animal she could relate to, a butterfly.

Shortly, though, she closed her eyes and fell fast asleep, a satisfied smile painted across her moistened lips.

For a long time afterward, BC just lay there at the edge of wakefulness, his dreams running together in a jumbled procession of thoughts. He dwelled first on the awesome task which still lay ahead of him, then on the pleasant one just completed. Though he knew better than to get emotionally involved with a woman, his last thought before dropping off to sleep was that, when it came to sex, he much preferred one with gusto!

• • •

Carina was still horny when she awoke three-quarters of an hour later, and though he initially spurned her offer, she was insistent.

This time, their love-making was not nearly so feverish or rabid as it had been before.

This time, they moved more slowly and with greater deliberation, enjoying the positional advantages afforded them by the ship's microgravity. They soon discovered that there were certain wonderful things lovers could do for one another when they weren't burdened by the evil forces of "up" and "down."

This time, his thrusts were much less rapid, but no less ardent. As if to compensate, her gratifying moans were just that much more prolific.

This time, it took longer for their passion to crest, but when her being finally quivered and a pounding orgasm rocked them both, they collapsed, exhausted, their thirst quenched.

In due course they uncoupled and lay apart, their heart rates gradually returning to normal. Although life seemed awfully sweet at that moment in time, it was all about to turn sour.

Occupied as they'd been, BC had failed to notice the menacing blip on the radar screen. By the time he swung the ship around to take a closer look, it was already too late!

6

Treachery On The Dark Side

When the warning shot whined through the darkness, crashing harmlessly into a nearby crater wall, the three men were caught completely unaware. Lester was well away from the main building ambling aimlessly about with nothing to do, Fornax was inside putting the finishing touches on his notes, and Sam was busy shuttling back and forth with weapons, taking them from the armory up to the crew's sleeping barracks. Sam's search of the armory had been fruitful, producing a couple of harpoon guns along with several blades, two auto-load machine-guns, and a dozen or more medium-range force guns. But the most lethal weapon in the arsenal by far was the antiquated grenade launcher. In the hands of a trained professional, this nasty little contraption was capable of hurling an explosive projectile nearly eight klicks with deadly accuracy. Including a satchel of shells, it had taken him and Lester the better part of fifteen minutes to haul everything the hundred or so meters across the compound.

Of the three men, only Fornax was out of his dee-dee at the time of the attack. Perched on a stool in front of the computer, he was merrily clicking away on the keyboard, ostensibly drafting a description of his Battery for an eventual patent application. But when he saw the flash of light outside his window and heard Lester's exclamation over the comm, Fornax knew he had to move with alacrity. Hastily grabbing up his suit and helmet, the frightened man barely had time to punch the SEND button before scrambling for the door. Encryption wasn't an option!

The explosion and flash of light served to rivet everyone's attention on the newly-arrived enemy craft, not just Fornax's. Even BC, high in orbit overhead, was thrown into a panic. His stomach muscles drew taut as the tactical situation revealed itself. Sam and the others had no protection whatsoever against an air-to-surface missile attack. Nor did they have any way of fighting back. They were sitting ducks!

A raspy voice boomed over the comm. BC recognized its owner immediately. It was none other than Whitey himself!

As the killer spoke, his ambitions became clear. He sneered viciously into the comm, his black eyes aglow with evil. "My orders are to commandeer the shuttle you've stolen and return it to its rightful owner. Failing that, I'm to assassinate all persons connected with this project. Which—except for the little lady—I much prefer doing in any case. I'm told she's a nice piece of . . . "

"Listen, you slime mold!" BC shouted, nearly crushing the comm in his anger. "If you even look cross-eyed at her, I swear I'll . . . "

"Ah, the skirt has a suitor! How quaint. But no matter. Either way the result's the same, loverboy—I win. Now I'm only going to say this once: Land your craft immediately and surrender!"

"And if I refuse?"

BC had his answer all too quickly. Without uttering even so much as another syllable, Whitey sent a second missile hurtling down from his orbiting command post towards the mottled surface below.

The flash of ignition sent Sam and the others scurrying for cover. They had all been listening to the heated exchange and had at least an inkling of what to expect.

Like its predecessor, the second missile narrowly missed the compound. And like its predecessor, it slammed harmlessly into a nearby crater wall, kicking up a swirling plume of moondust.

The raspy voice sounded again. "Last chance, BC. Land and surrender your ship. Now! If you refuse, the next torpedo will be the last thing your friends'll ever see."

"Murdering my people won't help you get what you want," BC said quietly. He figured he had nothing to lose taking a more diplomatic approach. His charges were vulnerable, and he knew it. "If you'll just agree to back off, I'll set 'er down wherever you . . . "

BC's offer of surrender was cutoff mid-sentence as yet another self-propelled shell plunged towards the surface. Unlike the previous ones, this one was squarely on target!

It struck the main building dead center. A blinding flash of light erupted where it hit. It was as if a small nuclear device had been set off at the point of impact.

For several long moments BC and Carina watched in absolute horror as the crew quarters disintegrated before their very eyes. Bits and chunks of metal and glass vaulted skyward as the titanic concussion leveled the building and everything around it. The devastation was so complete, no one near the epicenter could have possibly survived the murderous rain of shrapnel!

The initial explosion was followed by a drumroll of smaller explosions as a battery of propane tanks stored on the premises detonated.

Next came a series of blasts which BC guessed might be the hoard of grenades Sam had found earlier, along with the launcher. Then, with a sense of finality, the armory blew.

BC's cold blue eyes flashed red with anger. The mission had gone off-the-wire and he was to blame! He alone had provoked the attack. He alone could have prevented it!

Finding her voice, Carina screamed. "Oh, my God! The bastard's killed my father!"

By now the tears were streaming down her pretty face. "The bastard murdered every single one of them!" she blubbered, wiping her nose with the back of her hand. "Let's get the son-of-a-bitch!"

"We will, Carina, I promise. But the man's not stupid. And we're nearly defenseless. I doubt if we have enough fuel for a jump back to Mars and I *know* we don't have the weapons to put up a proper fight. All we have is this stupid harpoon gun and a knapsack full of grenades! What I wouldn't give for an argon force gun right about now! How could I have been so stupid! If only we hadn't . . . I mean, if only we'd kept our eyes on the radar instead of . . . "

Again the comm came alive with the crackle of sound. It was almost as if Whitey knew their every thought, heard their every word. "I have some business to attend to down on the surface. Then I'm coming for you. And don't try anything funny, BC—I'm tracking your every move. If I see you drop out of orbit or if you try to follow me, I swear I'll blow you from the sky! Ling be damned: I'd just as soon kill you as return his ship!"

Rather than risk calling the man's bluff, BC watched with helpless fascination as Whitey's shuttle descended and touched down in a flat spot a few hundred meters from the twisted remains of the moon station. Carina stood behind him, her hand on his shoulder. Within minutes they witnessed seven figures emerge from the spacecraft and begin making their way cross-country towards the wrecked base. The newcomers moved with awkward clumsiness as if this were their first time in a dee-dee, the first time they'd experienced low-g. Their lumina-beams cut the darkness before them, tracing out a path BC and Carina could track easily from the air.

Though the comm was silent throughout, Carina was still urging BC to action. By the time the marauders had covered about half the distance to the base, she became insistent.

"Is it your intention to just sit there?" she exclaimed, her face red with impatience. "Isn't it about god-damned time you *did* something?"

"Patience, woman! As soon as they get a little bit further away from their ship, I'm going to land and try and cut off their escape."

Even as he spoke, BC was busy laying in a course which would put the *Tikkidiw* down at close quarters to Whitey's already-parked shuttle. It was then that, out of the corner of one eye, he witnessed a remarkable event.

From behind a cluster of rocks not fifty meters from where the assortment of buildings had stood only five minutes earlier, came a volley of machine-gun fire. Moments later, there was another!

BC's heart started thumping madly. The unexpected barrage of gunfire had taken out no less than two of the interlopers! And to avoid being strafed, the others had been forced to make a hasty and awkward retreat! Obviously, one of their friends had survived the attack and was fighting back!

"Yes!" Carina hollered with uncharacteristic glee. "Take that, you bastards!"

"I'd hate to meet you in a dark alley!" BC exclaimed, though he shared her sense of "hurrah."

"Then just don't ever rub me the wrong way," she said, arrogant as ever.

"I'll try to remember that," BC replied, recalculating the odds. His hand had been strengthened immeasurably by this turn of events and he'd had just enough time to devise a plan—sketchy, tentative, and subject to change without notice as they say, but a plan nonetheless. It could be summarized in four simple words—Go On The Offensive!

A quick headcount of the number of lumina-beams remaining on the field of battle clinched his decision. BC grabbed for his kevlar tee-shirt and got suited-up, talking each step of the way.

"There's two on the bluff over there," he said. "Plus three more who made it back to their ship. It's high time I got down there and finished this—*my* way!"

But when he swung the *Tikkidiw* around to bring her in for a landing, he was suddenly greeted by another new development.

"Did you see that?" Carina said, extending her hand and pointing excitedly to a spot on the opposite side of the shattered compound. In the space of the last moment a grenade had been launched against Whitey's ship from that very location. Thing was, the spot was too far away from where the machine-gun fire had emanated for the same person to have managed both shots. That could mean only one thing—at least *two* of their friends must still be alive!

"You think Dad's okay?" she whispered, crossing her fingers as she fought back the tears.

"We'll know in a minute," BC said as he set the *Tikkidiw* down with a jolt. "Now take hold of this joystick, and as soon as I'm clear of the ship, back 'er outta here."

Then, executing a military-style salute, the handsome man exited the *Tikkidiw* at a bound. He had with him a harpoon gun and a satchel full of explosives.

Actually, in the bulky dee-dee it was less of a bound and more of a clumsy, cumbersome stroll. Yet, despite the handicap, he swiftly closed in on the enemy shuttle.

Like a cat on the prowl, BC stalked his prey. Harpoon gun in hand, he advanced with quiet dispatch. The three guards who had earlier beat a hasty retreat were now milling restlessly around the outside of their craft.

Staying in the shadows, BC crept closer. He knew what he had to do. Once he was within range he would kneel, take careful aim on his quarry, and squeeze off a couple of rounds. It would all be over in a matter of seconds!

In the meantime, Carina had withdrawn the *Tikkidiw* a safe distance away as instructed. She was still close enough, however, to observe what was happening. And what was happening nearly made her ill.

In rapid succession BC took out two of the three guards with his harpoon. The third one got away before he could stop him, but by then Carina had seen enough.

Nothing in her experience could prepare her for the gut-wrenching trauma! Watching someone in a pressurized dee-dee get skewered with a harpoon was in a class all by itself. The wound itself needn't be lethal to produce devastating results. All it took was a scratch in the suit's fabric and the difference in pressure would do all the rest! Driven by rapid decompression, the victim's blood and guts would spew forth through the puncture hole like a fountain. It was an ugly scene to behold, and Carina was forced to view it twice in under fifteen seconds!

Then, before she knew it, the whole thing was over. BC had killed the two men and moved on.

In the space of another step he reached the front of Whitey's shuttle. There he stopped and unslung his satchel of explosives. Here was a craft whose hull was so durable and tough, it was, for all practical purposes, impervious to every space hazard known to man, from gamma ray radiation on up to good-sized meteors. So far as he knew there was only way to crack open the skin of a shuttle like an egg, and that was to strike at the one place where the hull was perforated by a manmade opening—at one of the exhaust ports.

Though BC had it squarely in mind what he must do, events conspired to stop him. Before he could act, the ground at his feet shook with the concussion of another incoming grenade. Like its predecessor, this one's point of origin was several hundred meters away at the moon base. And like its predecessor, it was wide of the mark, missing Whitey's shuttle, though by not nearly as large a margin as the first. One thing was for certain, though: at the rate things were going, the very next one might hit home!

BC was out of time!

7
Grenades

Although BC didn't know it at the time, Lester was the one responsible for lobbing grenades in his direction. And as difficult as it was for BC to believe later on, at the time, Lester didn't realize how his gradually improving aim was endangering BC's life. Afterwards, all Lester claimed to have seen through his scope was Whitey's shuttle. That, plus a few suited figures moving around in the shadows nearby.

Not even Sam was wise to BC's predicament. He had been badly injured in the blast. Yet, despite his injuries, he was vigorously attending to some unfinished business. Which is to say, putting his machine-gun to good use in finishing off the two scoundrels who had taken refuge on the bluff across from him.

Fornax wasn't of much help to BC either. In fact, he was nowhere to be found! Judging by the extensive damage to the base, it was an even bet he was dead, his brains undoubtedly splattered all over the walls of the building he had been working in when the missile hit.

As for BC himself, he was gingerly edging his way along the smooth skin of Whitey's shuttle. Feeling the pressure of time swiftly ticking away, he was making every effort to hurry, but not so fast as to make a mistake. That third man, the one who had gotten away earlier, might be lurking anywhere! Though BC couldn't be certain, he thought he'd heard the sound of an airlock opening and then shutting again. The man may have gone back inside. Then again, another man might have come out to join him!

All his senses on red-alert, BC crept stealthily along the outside of the shuttle's length. Just aft of the radar array he made an interesting discovery. A special port had been cut into the ship's hull. Despite his many years of flying, BC had never seen anything like it on a spaceship before.

Stopping briefly to examine the blast-scarred paint around the aperture, he decided it could only have been designed with one purpose in mind—as a torpedo tube to launch deadly missiles from orbit! So far as he knew, no other DUMP shuttle was similarly equipped.

Making mental note of the vent's size and location for his eventual report to J, BC kept on going until he'd located the exhaust nozzles of the main thruster at the tail of the shuttle. If he'd done his homework properly, this was the most vulnerable spot on the entire ship.

Working quickly now, he plucked a handful of grenades from his satchel and jammed them all up inside the nozzle as far as his arm would reach. Then, taking a deep breath, he pulled the pin on one last grenade, shoved the live round into the exhaust port along with the others, and began running in the opposite direction as rapidly as his suit would allow. He had twelve seconds to live!

They say nothing focuses the mind quite like a noose around one's neck, and as BC scrambled away he tried to convince himself that death did not scare him like it would an ordinary man, that he was prepared to die, if necessary, in the service of his country.

But it was all a lie! Death *did* scare him! A hero should make the *other* silly bastard die for *his* country!

Stumbling over loose rocks, BC counted aloud as he sought to outrun death in a mad, twelve-second dash to safety.

On Earth, a twelve-second fuse was plenty long enough—and for two very good reasons. For starters, an Earth-soldier would begin by throwing the confound grenade as far *away* from himself as humanly possible. Then too, the Earth's gravity in conjunction with her air friction would prevent the shrapnel from flying very far.

But on the moon the situation was different. The explosive power of a half-dozen grenades could propel a sliver of metal eight or nine kilometers! And even the tiniest tear in a man's suit would be lethal.

BC counted out the seconds as he ran.

"One-one-thousand. Two-one-thousand."

Surprised to hear his voice over the comm, Carina turned to see what was afoot.

"Three-one-thousand," he declared humbly.

From where the *Tikkidiw* was parked, all she could see was BC clambering hastily away from Whitey's ship. It didn't make any sense to her at first, and another instant had elapsed before she guessed the reason why.

His breath came in gulps now.

"Four-one-thousand . . . Damn! I'm not going to make it . . . Five-one-thousand . . . Not enough time!"

Hearing the desperation in her man's voice, Carina acted out of instinct to shield him from harm. This one was special: she wasn't about to let him die—no way!!

Burying that thought deep down, Carina did what any self-respecting starry-eyed lover might—she disobeyed orders!

Figuring that in an explosion the titanium hull of the *Tikkidiw* could withstand the flying debris better than BC's flightsuit could, Carina ignited the ship's maneuvering rockets, swung the vessel around, and, as if she'd practiced it a hundred times before, stationed it like a pro between him and the grenade-rigged shuttle.

At almost the same instant, hundreds of meters away, Lester again took slow and deliberate aim on Whitey's craft, adjusting the sights to compensate for his two previous misses. He seemed quite intent this time.

"Six-one-thousand."

"Seven-one-thousand."

Though BC was still hurrying away at top speed, he hadn't gotten far. Hampered by the moon's craggy surface—and by his own spacesuit—his progress was distressingly slow.

At the count of, "Eight-one-thousand," there was a hiccup in time. And in the space of the next moment, a ground-shaking concussion catapulted him through the air like a circus clown shot from a cannon. In pathetic slow-motion BC flew head over heels, coming to rest on the ground a dozen meters away.

Dazed and disoriented, he struggled to right himself, to get back to his feet. But no sooner had he made it to his knees than he was slammed back down again by another horrendous detonation, more powerful than the first. This time, a huge fireball leapt skyward behind him. And like a clay pot locked in a kiln, he was baked hard by the heat.

None of it made any sense! There had been two separate and distinct explosions instead of one. But how could that be? Had he counted wrong? Had the grenade gone off *early?* Had the fuses been tampered with? Just what the hell was going on?

Though BC didn't know it at the time, the first explosion, the one which had sent him flying through the air, was Lester's doing. He had finally managed to strike the front of Whitey's shuttle with a grenade. The second, much larger blast, was the detonation BC himself had set off by stuffing grenades up inside the nozzle of the main engine. The ensuing fireball was the ignition of the chem-fuel canisters stored alongside the booster engines.

Still agitated by the whole sequence of events, BC couldn't understand why he hadn't been cut to ribbons by shards of flying metal. The exploding grenades should have strewn razor-sharp bits of metal and glass everywhere! He should be dead by now!

Rolling first to one side, then to the other, BC checked to see whether he'd fallen behind a huge boulder. He hadn't.

What then? he wondered, propping himself up on one knee.

Then it all started to come together. Carina! He should've guessed it—here was a woman who would never do what she'd been told!

Visibly shaken, BC staggered forward towards the *Tikkidiw.* It had absorbed the brunt of the wreckage from the blast and was now silhouetted against the black sky by the glowing derelict behind it.

He shouted Carina's name into the comm. But his desperate cry went unanswered!

A lump formed in the man's throat as he imagined the worst. Had she died trying to save him? God, say it wasn't true!

Working himself into a panic, BC stumbled around to the far side of the *Tikkidiw* and began pounding on the hull with both his fists like a madman.

"Carina!" he shouted, banging on it with all his might.

But with no air to carry the sound, the effort seemed to be getting him nowhere. Then, all of a sudden, the airlock opened and out stepped a grinning Carina.

"Heh, flyboy, what's all the racket about?" she teased seductively. "Can't you see I'm okay?"

Doing his best to swallow the emotion in his voice, BC stuttered. "Carina, I . . . I . . . "

"Makes perfect sense. I was worried about you too. And, oh, by the way, you're welcome!"

"Yeah, thanks," BC said with a smile. "But for both our sakes, I hope you didn't total this bird in the process."

"My, my, but aren't we the testy one!"

The words were barely out of her mouth when another grenade screamed into a nearby outcropping.

"What the hell is he still shooting at us for?" BC shouted, a perplexed look on his face. "I've got to get us the hell outta here. And I mean right away!"

Hustling Carina back into the *Tikkidiw,* BC slammed the airlock door shut and ignited the maneuvering rockets. The shuttle responded obediently to the controls.

"Thank God it wasn't damaged!" he sighed, flying the *Tikkidiw* out beyond the range of the grenade launcher.

"Just what the hell do you think you're *doing?"* Carina demanded to know, her face crimson. "You're flying the wrong way! You've got to go back and rescue my dad! And Fornax too! They both may be hurt! You told me you were a medic—you're their only hope!"

When BC didn't answer immediately, she continued. "Goddamnit, BC, I saved your *life!* Now you must save theirs!"

"Listen to me, woman—why would someone fire on us *after* I blew up Whitey's shuttle? That's damn peculiar, wouldn't you agree?"

"What's your point?"

"My point is, I would very much like to know who had his hands on that grenade launcher. Even in the dark, there's almost no way the gunner could have confused the two shuttles."

"What are you saying?"

"Maybe someone other than Whitey wanted us dead."

"My uncle?"

"That's a strong possibility."

"Well then, let's zoom over there and find out," Carina urged. "The others may be in danger!"

BC acted as if he hadn't heard her. "The worst of it is, I'm not even sure if I got 'em all. I'm almost certain one of the guards got away. And for all I know Whitey may still be running around loose down there too."

"And just where is he gonna go?" she pointed out sensibly. "You blew his ship to smithereens, remember? It's kaputt! Finished! Gone!"

"Good point," he said as he fired up the engines. "Very good point!"

8
Damages

The unprovoked attack had leveled the entire place!

But with no wind to carry the sounds or smells of battle to them, the scene on the moon could not convey the same sense of destruction as it might have back on Earth. BC and Carina could not smell the burnt rubber; they could not hear the crackling of burning timbers; they could not touch the scorched metal; they could not taste the stench of death.

No sooner had they landed, than Lester met them, pointing to where Sam lay hurt. There was no sign of Fornax, however.

From the way Sam lay on the ground, his face in agony, his body in a twisted heap, BC knew the old fellow was in bad shape. But short of removing the man's dee-dee and doing a physical examination, it was nearly impossible for him to judge the full extent of Sam's injuries. That he needed to be taken to a hospital Earthside, and right away, was self-evident.

BC made quick work of unloading a low-g stretcher from the ship. When he returned with it to where Sam lay, the stretcher floating beside him on a thin cushion of air, he cornered Lester, congratulating him on his prowess with the grenade launcher.

"You handled that thing like a pro," he said.

"Thanks," Lester replied, unable to resist having his ego stroked. "I guess my aim improved once I got the hang of it."

"Just exactly what happened here?" BC asked, surveying the situation as he carefully positioned the low-g gurney next to Sam. "Was Fornax still inside when it blew?"

"Must have been," Lester rejoined coldly. "All I know is, Sam and I were working outside when the missile hit—and I haven't seen Fornax since. The blast must have loosened a huge boulder which rolled over Sam's leg, crushing it. It was a miracle the rock didn't tear his suit. But Sam, even though he was hurt, just sat there, picking off as many of them as he could."

"It's a wonder you weren't hurt by the same blast!" BC remarked.

"I was too far away at the time," Lester replied, though not very convincingly.

"Very fortunate indeed," BC mumbled. "Now help me with this gurney. If Sam doesn't get professional help soon, he won't make it, and I don't have the tools to treat him here."

Lester nodded, but said nothing.

BC was furious with himself! Everything that could have gone wrong, had. And *he* was to blame!

• • •

As soon as they got back to the *Tikkidiw* and back above the horizon, BC radioed in to headquarters. J was fit to be tied! With Fornax dead, the moon base destroyed, and Sam seriously wounded, who could blame him? But in typical British stiff upperlip fashion, J held his choicest words for another occasion. Though he didn't say much, what he did say hurt.

"There is one thing no head of the Bureau can know, and that is how good his intelligence system is. He finds out only by having it fail him—something you weren't supposed to let happen!"

They were hurtful words, for which BC had no ready answer. Still, unless Sam actually died, all was not lost. Sam, more than anyone else, held the key to understanding the Fornax Battery. At any rate, that's what BC told his boss. And J bought it, or at least enough of it to agree that it was in both their self-interests to ensure that Sam was promptly treated. The *Tikkidiw* would be met in docking orbit by Commonwealth medical personnel; they would attend to Sam and Carina, thus allowing BC to return with Lester to the moon for a more thorough search of the wreckage.

By the time BC had engaged the Fornax Drive for the jump to Earth, Sam had passed out, his face ashen, his breathing labored. Tears were trickling from Carina's eyes as she stroked her father's clammy forehead.

The medical team that met them in orbit performed triage on Sam right there in the hospital-ship. His leg was set easily enough, but there had been internal injuries as well, injuries that would require the attention of a specialist Earthside. The decision was made to transport him for micro-surgery right away. Once the repairs to his body could be made, the miracle drug Acceleron would be administered to hasten the healing.

From where he sat in the cockpit of the *Tikkidiw*, BC watched them leave. Sam and Carina would ride home with the medicos onboard the suborb, landing within the hour in Manchester, England. From there, Sam would be transported to a topflight government facility for observation and further treatment.

It was the right thing to do—under the circumstances. But BC didn't like it, not one little bit! Carina was unlike any woman he had ever met, or was likely to. Oh, she'd be safe enough there in Manchester under J's watchful eye, but BC didn't like the idea of letting her out of his sight, not even for the short time until he returned. J wanted him to go back to the moon with Lester to sift through the rubble of the wrecked moon base, and he didn't want Carina around distracting BC while he worked. J had always been quick that way, picking up on his agents' weaknesses.

The theory behind the trip was that some of Fornax's papers might have survived the blast. After all, the man had been hard at work typing up his notes at the time of the explosion. Though improbable, there might still be some printouts or drawings which could be recovered from the scene. No one had yet stopped to consider the possibility that Fornax might have had sufficient time to transmit his work to the *Tikkidiw* before he died, least of all BC. Doing J's bidding, and without argument, was the absolute only way for him to redeem himself and perhaps salvage something from his failed mission.

The main building was a grotesque mass of twisted metal and shattered glass. That Fornax must have been killed by the missile's impact was inescapable. Neither inside nor out were there any signs of his remains. Whitey's missile attack had ignited the oxygen tanks stored in a shed next to the building and the resulting firestorm had incinerated every scrap of paper, melted every computer disk, and scorched every document in the place. After fifteen minutes of searching, it was clear there was nothing left to be found.

"Fornax must've been incinerated," Lester remarked unsympathetically.

"What a terrible way to die," BC said, shaking his head bitterly. "How many good men have already perished because of this damn thing? First, Captain Michael. Now, Fornax?"

Lester shrugged his shoulders as if he didn't care. His presence was required elsewhere, or so it seemed. He began acting as if he'd been suddenly summoned away to a meeting. "My oxygen's getting low," he explained as he started to back away. "If it's all the same to you, I'll be heading back to the ship now."

"Yeah, okay. I'll follow in about five. I still need to turn over a few more rocks."

"Suit yourself," Lester said as he shuffled off towards the ship, "but there's nothing here."

"Just the same, I'm going to give it a few more minutes. When you get onboard, switch on the radio and listen for any word from J. He should be contacting us soon with an update on Sam's condition."

"Roger that."

BC's suspicious eyes followed the man as he left. Lester was nothing if not nefarious. Now there seemed to be something sinister about him as well. BC had an antenna for such things, and it told him to beware!

Doing his best to put Lester out of his mind, BC tried to concentrate instead on the troublesome matter at hand. Something definitely didn't add up here! Short of a nuclear bomb, it was almost impossible to incinerate a man in a heat-resistant double-density spacesuit! So where was the body?

Squatting down on his haunches, BC studied the chaotic scene more closely. An unoccupied dee-dee lay in a disheveled heap upon the floor. The gloves, the boots, and the helmet were all there.

Thinking to himself that the blast must have knocked the spacesuit out of its storage cabinet and onto the floor, he took his time examining it. Just as he expected, the outer skin wasn't charred even in the slightest. Not surprising given its legendary durability, although the visor on the helmet did have a single hairline crack running diagonally across its face. Obviously, it had been struck with great force.

As BC examined the composite surface of the cracked visor, its mirror-like finish echoing his own image back at him, he caught the reflection of something moving in the background behind him!

The hair on his neck stiffened!

His heart started pumping faster!

Without giving himself away, BC tilted the visor ever so slightly, hoping to gain himself a better view. At the very limit of his peripheral vision, he detected the glint of an upraised, steel-hardened blade!

Too tall to be Lester, too brawny to be Fornax, the aggressor had to be none other than the guard BC had lost track of earlier!

Unsure what to do, he froze. Like a rank amateur BC had violated the most basic rule of good spy-manship—*never venture out unarmed!*

Figuring this errand would be a walk in the park and all he'd be doing was kicking through the rubble undisturbed, it had never occurred to him to come out here packing a sidearm. Now he was about to pay for that arrogance with his life!

Or was he?

Twisting his head ever so slightly, BC caught sight of something he hadn't noticed before. Lying there on the floor, just to his right, was a force gun! Along with knocking a spacesuit to the floor, the blast must have spilled over a weapons crate as well!

Emboldened by his good luck, BC steeled his muscles for action—and not a moment too soon! Even as he rolled onto his side in the direction of the gun, the figure behind him lunged forward. Though BC spun out of his assailant's reach, the killer pressed his attack without faltering.

Catching the man's right wrist with his own left hand, BC gasped audibly as he stopped the advance of the razor-sharp blade just centimeters from his suit! One nick and he'd be dead!

Struggling for his life now, the adrenaline started pumping through his veins like a juggernaut!

Calling on every last bit of strength, BC reached up with his free hand and tried to loosen the seal on the man's helmet. But he was outmatched. His opponent just batted his hand away as if it were nothing! And, when BC tried a second time, the man butted him in the head with his helmet!

BC recoiled, falling backwards to the concrete, his right hand behind him, desperately searching the floor for the gun. Yet, even as he went down, he dutifully noted the chalky white hue of his adversary's hair!

The blade surged forward again, this time striking BC across the visor. By now, though, his hand had closed in on the stock of the force gun.

Gripping the weapon with fierce intensity, BC spun his arm around and shoved the barrel into Whitey's gut. His heart racing, he pulled back hard on the trigger and fired a single round into his opponent at pointblank range. But what happened next astonished him!

Seemingly unfazed, Whitey lunged at him again, the blade *still* clenched in his gloved hand!

BC fired again.

And again.

And again.

Finally, after what seemed like an eternity, Whitey fell heavily against him, knocking them both to the floor and sending the blade spinning slowly out of his twitching grasp. The evil man was dead!

Exhausted, BC took a deep breath and crawled out from under the lifeless corpse. Here was a snake the world could easily do without! J would be happy at the outcome, and BC's reputation would be at least partially restored. It didn't quite square the ledger, but it was a start!

A buzzer sounded in his ear warning him that he was low on oxygen.

BC started back towards the *Tikkidiw* with a look of grim determination on his face. The more he contemplated Lester's role in this whole grisly affair, the more worrisome the thoughts that ricocheted through his brain.

9

The Skunk

When BC scrambled back onboard the *Tikkidiw* he could tell from the surprised look on Lester's face that he hadn't been expected. Somehow that made sense, but before he could interrogate the man about his role in BC's close encounter with Whitey, the beeper sounded, signaling that there was an incoming message from London. Grabbing a pencil and a pad of paper, BC took it down:

SAMMY HUNGRY
COOKIES IN CUPBOARD
MARY MARY QUITE CONTRARY

Mindful of Lester's watchful stare, BC didn't decode the dispatch outloud. Since London was transmitting in Seussarian code, that could only mean one thing—the agency's channel had been compromised!

The cable had good news and bad news. **SAMMY HUNGRY** was J's way of telling him that Carina's father was expected to make it. On the other hand, **MARY MARY QUITE CONTRARY** could only be translated to mean that Carina herself was now in some sort of danger, reason unclear. More ominously, **COOKIES IN CUPBOARD** meant that the *Tikkidiw*'s radio had been used in his absence, probably to contact Overlord Ling.

The conclusion was inescapable. While BC had been out grappling with Whitey, Lester must have called home asking for orders. The little weasel must have divulged Sam and Carina's whereabouts to his cohorts. That's why Carina was now suddenly in trouble!

As if things weren't already complicated enough, all BC had to do now was rush back to Earth, rescue Carina, then get them both the hell out of the Overlord's reach! But life was never really that simple, was it? Just where were they supposed to go to anyway? Mars?

It was at just about that moment that Lester spoke up, interrupting BC's thoughts. "It sounds like a nursery rhyme. What does the damn thing mean?"

"Well obviously it's encoded, but I make it out this way: **SAMMY HUNGRY** means that Sam is alive; **COOKIES IN CUPBOARD** means that we are to return to Manchester in two hours' time; and **MARY MARY QUITE CONTRARY** means that we are being tracked by hostile enemy forces."

It was a lie, of course, but it couldn't be helped: Lester was the enemy, after all, and couldn't be trusted with the truth. He was responsible, at least in part, for everything that had gone wrong—including the tragic loss of Fornax! The expiration of such an amazing intellect was truly a waste, a needless sacrifice for which Lester must ultimately be held accountable. With Fornax out of the picture, with all his records lost, even building a new Battery had become an impossibility!

"If we're being tracked, shouldn't we return home right away?" Lester asked, eager to get off the moon and on his way back to Earth.

"My orders are two hours," BC replied. "Anyhow, our mobility is limited. The power-strips you put in the crater are at least half a day away from being fully recharged. If only we could reach the Mars station, that would be the perfect place for the lot of us to lie low for awhile."

"Listen, bub, forget it!" Lester exclaimed. "I have no interest in escaping to Mars, and I sincerely doubt whether my brother does either. I'm sure he wants nothing more than to live out his remaining years happily tucked away there in Auckland. Plus, I have a prosperous business to attend to back in Melbourne."

BC chuckled. "Thanks for the input, Lester, but I have to put Carina and Sam's welfare before yours. And while we're at it," BC continued in a condescending tone, "you haven't the foggiest idea what's best for your brother. In fact, you think he's a lazy s.o.b. and you're insanely jealous of his success."

"Don't flatter yourself!" Lester barked nastily back. "My relationship with my brother is really none of your concern!"

BC spoke with a fierce look in his eye. "Au contraire, mon ami. It is every bit my concern! In fact, every little detail becomes my concern when the success or failure of my mission hangs in the balance! Now sit your butt down and shut up so I can figure out a way for us to get from here to Manchester undetected!"

"Okay, already!" Lester relented sullenly, taking a chair.

BC continued. "I figure your buddy Overlord Ling won't risk sending another team to the moon to get us. And since it's too hard for his people to hit us in orbit, or even onboard a suborb, they'll wait until we make Earthfall. Then they'll strike. I imagine they'll hope to get all four of us at once—you, me, Sam, and Carina."

As he said her name, a faraway look welled-up in his eyes.

"You really have the hots for her, don't you?" Lester remarked, a dirty smirk plastered across his greasy face.

"No, not really," BC stammered, caught off-guard by the question.

"Tell me the two of you went up there all alone and the only thing you did was talk," Lester snickered.

"You really are a lowlife aren't you?"

"Takes one to know one."

"Which reminds me. What do you think convinced Whitey to attack us almost as soon as he arrived on the scene? It was almost as if he had no fear of reprisal; as if he already knew we were defenseless. How do you suppose he knew?"

"I dunno," Lester replied dumbly. "But I don't like your tone, not one little bit! What are you insinuating?"

"Look, don't play games with me, you moron! You're already facing a prison term for shipping illegal wastes to the moon, so just answer my questions and perhaps the judge will go easy on you. As I was saying, Whitey was a complete pro, so don't you think . . . "

"What d'ya mean 'was'?" Lester asked, surprised. "I thought you said he got away?"

BC smiled as if to say, "gotcha." Picking his words carefully now, he answered. "No, what I said was, a *guard* got away. And I told *Carina* that, not you."

"She must've told me," Lester answered unconvincingly, "and I naturally assumed it was *Whitey* who escaped."

"Naturally," BC replied in a disbelieving tone. "But like I was saying, Whitey was a pro, and a pro would normally have stopped to analyze his opponent's defenses before striking—reconnoiter, as it were. That is, unless of course, he already *knew* the precise location of his target and already *knew* we couldn't retaliate! I ask you again: How do you suppose he knew?"

Lester moved uneasily in his seat, but said nothing.

"And there's something else that bothers me," BC continued. "Whitey didn't even take the time to threaten the *Tikkidiw.* He didn't seem to care even in the slightest about her whereabouts! How do you explain *that?"*

"I take it you're somehow disappointed by the lack of attention?" Lester snapped flippantly back.

"No. Just surprised. And you wanna know why?" BC asked, not intending to wait for a reply. "I think the reason he ignored the *Tikkidiw* was because he already knew exactly where she was! Plus, he must have known *ahead* of time that we lacked the necessary weapons to hurt him. And how, pray tell, did he know all this? Because even before we took the *Tikkidiw* up on her maiden voyage, someone must have planted a locator onboard the ship."

"That's ridiculous!" Lester declared defensively. "There was 'round-the-clock security at the shed in Sri Lanka."

"True enough," BC admitted, "but there were certain people—yourself included—who could come and go as they pleased."

"*Me?*" Lester squawked, gasping for air. "Don't be silly! I worked for the Overlord, sure, but why would I have targeted my own ship?"

"Maybe you're right. Maybe I am being silly. But answer me this: After I blew up Whitey's shuttle, why did you still go ahead and launch a grenade at the *Tikkidiw?*"

Again, BC didn't wait for an answer before plunging ahead. He had smelled the proverbial rat, and it was time to flush him out!

"There's no way you could have confused the two ships—not if you were looking through the aiming sights anyway. It had to be deliberate!"

"Idle speculation, BC; nothing more. You can't prove a thing! All you are—and all you'll ever be—is an underpaid British agent with an overactive imagination. I demand you put a stop to this charade at once!"

"In the first place, Lester, this is not a court of law—I don't have to *prove* anything. And in the second place, my immediate concern is for Carina, not you. I intend to rescue her, with you or without you. What'll it be?"

"I'm with you, of course," Lester sighed, believing his life would be spared. "But your people *assured* us she would be safe with them."

"Yeah, I know," BC replied, "but things have changed. We may have to fight our way in."

Stepping over to the ship's weapon cabinet, BC undid the latch and swung open the outer door. "You have your choice of weapons," he said. "Is there any you prefer? Any you can handle especially well?"

"I frequently hunt great-whites off the coast," Lester announced, "so I suppose a harpoon gun would suit me fine."

"Sharks, eh? Why do I find that poetic?" BC said as he felt inside to release the safety latch. Pushing the inner door aside, he removed a harpoon gun from the rack along with a handful of steel-tipped arrows. The points were extremely sharp, making them lethal at distances up to several hundred meters.

Looking up for a moment, he said, "Lester, old friend, you stink like day-old dirty diapers. And frankly, I'm sick of your lying mouth. Jail is much too good for the likes of you."

Then, in the course of the next instant, BC armed his weapon and swung around to face the man. His range was no more than one-and-a-half meters. Without saying a word, he let the arrow rip into the man's chest!

There was an explosion of blood as the gleaming shaft sliced through Lester's rib cage and tore open a gaping hole in his aorta. Bone was pushed aside by metal as the harpoon completed its murderous trip through his body.

Run through like a shish kabob, Lester lurched backward, his torso twitching involuntarily. The steel barb jutted bloodily from his back. As he went down, death-spasm after death-spasm convulsed his living corpse. With each twitch, the steel tip could be heard scratching against the metal floor of the ship.

A few guttural sounds emanated from the dead man's throat.

Then the ship was quiet.

10
Rescue

The silence onboard the ship was deafening. BC did not enjoy killing, and yet in the past half-hour he had had to commit murder twice, both times at close range. It sickened him.

Emotionally and physically drained, this all-too-human mortal buried his head in his hands and began to sob cathartically. His primeval male instincts wasted no time reasserting themselves, however, and he quickly wiped his eyes dry, embarrassed to have even succumbed to such a juvenile wash of emotion. Drawing a deep cleansing breath, he flushed the adrenaline from his system and sank into a nearby chair, struggling to rationalize his actions.

Surely, if he hadn't acted first, Lester would have tried to kill him sooner or later. The man was inherently evil! By guiding Whitey straight to them to begin with, Lester had thrown all their lives into jeopardy. Not only had he a hand in Captain Michael's murder, he'd directly contributed to Fornax's demise as well. And he very nearly succeeded in having Sam killed too! The man had to die, of that there was little doubt!

But enough was enough! It was time for the killing to end! BC had come to a monumental decision—he had to get out of this bloody business and on with his life!

By now the corpse was white and cold. There was blood everywhere, along with urine and excrement. The sphincter muscles relaxed soon after death, and the body discharged its waste products where it lay—sort of nature's own fertilizer on the road to decay. It was an awful mess, but BC cleaned it up the best he could, discarding Lester's body out through the airlock along with the rest of the trash. Turning away, he left it piled in a heap on the moon's pocked surface.

BC had made up his mind, and he said so, outloud, as if he were still trying to convince himself.

"No more killing!"

The words echoed grimly back at him from the walls of the empty ship. "No more killing!"

Then, exploding with fury, he roared, "You fool! You stupid bloody fool! This isn't over *yet!* Not by a long shot! You still have to go down there and rescue her! And that won't be easy! Now get your Brit-shit together and do what needs to be done!"

BC was not a deeply religious man; but he did have a conscience, and right now it was bothering him. Fornax had been an honorable man; he deserved better than Lester, better than being tossed irreverently out on the ground like a broken sack of so many potatoes. But without a corpse, how to afford the man a decent burial? It was all but impossible.

At that particular moment in time, the only thing BC could think of was the helmet which had helped save his life. If it hadn't been for that cracked visor, he might never have seen Whitey coming! As a symbolic gesture to Fornax's memory, it would just have to do.

Retrieving the busted helmet from the fractured ruins of the smashed moon base, BC carried it under his arm to the nearest DUMP crater. The crater was a fiery pot of boiling radioactivity, a cauldron of spent fuel rods. Mesmerized by the eerie glow, he held the helmet high above his head as if he meant to offer it up as a sacrifice to the gods, a sacrifice meant to assuage his guilt. The words came hard.

"Fornax Nehrengel, wherever you are, I know this isn't much of a funeral pyre, but it's the best I can do under the circumstances. Forgive me, my friend, and accept my apology. Your death was my fault, and I will have to live with that for the rest of my life. May you rest in peace and may we meet again aboard that big spaceship in the sky. Ashes to ashes, dust to dust."

And with that, BC solemnly tossed the helmet atop the radioactive pile.

He stood for a moment watching as it melted into nothingness. Then his faculty for problem-solving again took over.

Ever since they landed, a thought had been nagging at him, crystalizing in his head. What if Fornax had managed to transmit his data-tape after all?

Up until now, BC had been operating under the assumption that Fornax had died before being able to upload his file to the ship. But what if he were wrong? What if BC had again underestimated the man?

Confident that he might suddenly be onto something, BC sat down at the ship's computer to find out for sure. Fornax's terminal had been comm-linked to the ship before this all began and it didn't take BC long before he fell upon a masterfile bearing the heading FORNAX. The directory listed six subsidiary files, one of which was entitled PATENT.APP

BC was ecstatic! He practically shouted with enthusiasm! He had hit pay dirt! Somehow or other, at the last moment, Fornax had managed to save his work!

Had BC known that what Fornax *actually* left behind was little more than a bland recital of well-known physics, he might not have been so elated by his find. But not being a scientist, and not being able to wholly comprehend the material, BC was totally unaware of Fornax's brilliant subterfuge.

Eagerly, he read the summary: "A single, eight-strip Battery has enough power to propel a modest-sized ship from here to the other side of the galaxy so long as one doesn't stop too many times along the way. But understand this: the big burst of energy consumption is not in the going, it's in the stopping and the starting. Once you engage the Drive, you'll keep right on sailing until you hit the brakes. It's pure Newton's Law—an object in motion tends to stay in motion until an outside force acts upon it."

Skipping further on down, BC read some more: "Heisenberg said that the obvious way to measure the position and the velocity of a particle is to shine light upon it. Although some of the light-waves will be scattered by the particle, revealing its position, the energy of the light will disturb the particle, altering its velocity in an unpredictable manner. As a consequence, the more accurately one tries to measure the *position* of a particle, the less accurately one can measure its *speed*. And vice versa. This dilemma is referred to as Heisenberg's Uncertainty Principle, and it led to a reformulation of physics into something we now call Quantum Mechanics. What Durbin did was to add the element of CHAOS into particle motion . . . "

After skimming down through a couple of more paragraphs, BC was convinced he had exactly what his bosses at Commonwealth Intelligence were after. Copying the entire document to a mini-diskette, he got on the comm to tell London he was bringing in the files J wanted.

The channel wasn't secure, and that was a problem. As J always said: Control the communications of a country and you control the country. Here was a perfect example!

The liaison officer BC talked to was circumspect in the extreme. An assault on the Manchester facility was expected within the hour, thus their conversation had a certain sense of urgency to it. Sam couldn't be moved yet on account of his guarded condition, but they would send up a suborbital-taxi to meet BC anyway, once he reached docking orbit.

Without need for further provocation, BC's warrior instincts took control. Carina was in imminent danger and perhaps he alone could save her!

Working rapidly now, BC punched in the coordinates for the jump to Earth. But as his hand lay urgently poised on the POWER button, an alarming thought suddenly occurred to him: If he didn't find and disconnect the locator-beacon which Lester had hidden onboard the ship somewhere, the Chinese would still be able to track his every move!

With the seconds ticking rapidly away now, BC raced to his berth. In the pocket of his therma-vest was a pencil-thin device called a directional finder. It had been designed by the Agency expressly for this purpose.

Jerking the finder from its holder, and clicking it on, BC kicked himself for not thinking to use the damn thing earlier. Had he done so, Fornax might still be alive this very instant!

In much the same way that the needle of a compass will align itself with magnetic north, a directional finder could ferret out a locator-beacon by homing in on its telltale radio signal.

Pointing the slender electronic gizmo this way and that, BC wove his way through the ship, following the flashing indicator to its source. Sure enough, inside of two minutes, he found the troublesome metal cylinder hugging the bulkhead inside a tiny recess next to the airlock. The device was perhaps ten centimeters long and five in diameter, surprisingly large considering how some of the newer models were compact enough to be inserted in an aspirin tablet and swallowed!

Shaking his head, BC switched the thing off. Then, returning with it to the galley, he flushed it out the garbage chute.

Since BC and the liaison officer had been talking on an unsecure channel and since their comm traffic had almost certainly been monitored by Ling's people, everyone—J included—would be expecting him to arrive by suborbital-taxi. Only, that just wouldn't do! If BC was to gain the upper hand and take them all by surprise, he would have to forego the trip by suborb to the surface and take the *Tikkidiw* directly down through the atmosphere instead.

This was a very risky stunt, one which had never been attempted by a pilot before. But with Chinese soldiers on the way, Carina might soon be dead if he didn't hurry. If his stunt failed and the ship blew up, or if afterwards he couldn't lift off again due to the Earth's gravity, Carina would be no worse off than she already was. Either way, he had to try!

The descent was incredibly hot and bumpy, nothing at all like the usual smooth ride onboard a suborb. Even though the *Tikkidiw* was equipped with a laser-guided landing array which did an admirable job of automatically piloting the ship to the ground, BC was ill-prepared for the buffeting during reentry. As soon as the shuttle lurched to a halt on the grounds of the hospital, he did what he had been trying *not* to do since before he harpooned Lester—throw up! The giddy rocking of the ship, combined with the stress of the moment, had finally gotten the better of him. And once it began, it came in a tumultuous explosion, splashing on him, his shoes, and the deck of the ship.

Undaunted, BC got shakily to his feet. Wiping the filthy residue from his mouth, he slipped the mini-diskette he'd made into his pocket, grabbed a force gun and his trusty harpoon, then staggered to the door. When the airlock snapped open, he took off across the hospital's broad lawn wearing a look of frazzled determination.

Always well-guarded, the Manchester facility had a reputation for being a high-security compound. With the threat of an attack by Chinese commandoes expected at any moment, tensions were running high, especially among those whose duty it was to protect the many prominent business and government leaders who were the private hospital's only clients.

The sudden appearance of the *Tikkidiw* on the hospital lawn set the stage for a dangerous confrontation, and BC was promptly met by a platoon of gun-toting guards. Firing a couple of warning shots over his head, they promptly leveled their automatic weapons on his midsection.

"I'm only going to give you one opportunity to identify yourself!" one of the armed sentries brusquely ordered, though he knew BC by face.

"Smithers, don't be a cad!" BC retorted breathlessly.

"Orders, sir. Now kindly identify yourself," Smithers repeated.

"Lieutenant Bart Collins."

"You weren't expected for hours, sir. And then by suborb, not by whatever *that* is," Smithers exclaimed, pointing to the battle-weary *Tikkidiw*. "Before I can let you pass, you must . . . "

"Listen Smithers, cut the crap!" BC barked as he handed him the copy he'd made of Fornax's file. "This diskette needs to be given to J immediately. See to it, will you?"

Mumbling something into his comm, Smithers nodded his head before instructing a pair of guards to escort BC inside. They accompanied him to a waiting room on the second floor. It was across the hall from the intensive care unit where Sam was still under observation.

Carina was there. Upon seeing his face, she ran to his arms.

"How is he?" BC asked.

"The doctors saved his leg, but just barely. And how are *you?*" Carina questioned, screwing up her nose. "Phew! You look and smell like you've been through a war!"

"Yes, two wars actually," he replied without elaboration. "Look, I don't have time to explain. We've got to get out of here! Your uncle tipped off Ling's people as to your whereabouts and they'll be here at any minute!"

As if to provide emphasis to his statement, a battery of yellow lights suddenly started flashing in the corridor and a warning message blasted across the P.A.

"Yellow alert! Yellow alert! Security breach! North wall! Yellow alert! All men to their posts!"

The guards who had escorted BC up to Sam's room left at a run, powering up their force guns as they went.

"We have to leave *now!*" BC shouted, grabbing for Carina's arm.

"Not without my dad, we're not!" she exclaimed, pulling away from him.

"We have no choice, damn it! Even with the Acceleron shots, he won't be healed for at least another two days. We can't wait that long. Believe me: he'll be okay. But you and I simply *have* to go!"

BC again grabbed for Carina's arm, this time dragging her from the building and towards the *Tikkidiw*. The air around them was filled with the smell of spent powder and the electrostatic crackle of discharged force guns.

Within moments, BC was at the ship's nav-console, typing in the jump coordinates. He punched the POWER button enabling the Fornax Drive and . . . and . . . and . . . nothing!

Dumbfounded, BC stood there in frozen silence. Again he punched the button, and again, nothing! Nothing at all!

"Damn!" he erupted, his own worst fears realized. "I was afraid of something like this! We're trapped! How could've I been so stupid! I've already handed over the diskette—we have nothing to bargain with for our lives!"

"Don't be silly! You forgot to first turn on the ship's main power," Carina pointed out, her meekness approaching audacity. "That's what Fornax always did before flicking on the bloody thing."

Thinking to himself that the little wench was probably right, BC gritted his teeth and looked at her cross-eyed.

She smiled wickedly back.

Instantly, the Drive kicked in—and they were off!

11
Bagel

The several Lagrange points in the Earth-moon system are patches of space where the gravitational tug of the two bodies precisely balance one another. An object parked at any one of these five points falls neither towards the Earth nor towards the moon. BC chose Lagrange Point Number Five—L5 in pilot lingo—as the destination for their first jump.

It all happened so fast, they hardly exchanged a word until the ship came to a rest at L5. Then Carina broke the ice.

"You can't leave him there, you know."

"Who? Who can't I leave *where?*"

"My father, silly. I'm very fond of him you see."

"Gee, I never would've guessed," BC said, beginning to grasp just how much of a handful this woman really was.

"Now you're making fun of me!" Carina carped. "Isn't it about time you took me serious? I have no mother, you see, so I couldn't bear to lose Sam."

"Nor will I allow you to. I promise."

"You are a good and honorable man," Carina declared, her voice cracking. Then the tears came. And they came hard!

The sudden deluge caught BC off-guard. This woman was a confusing creature, at once soft and cuddly, then vehement and wild. Explaining her was beyond his ability. What had brought on the river of tears, and what he could do to stop them, were questions he could not answer. All BC knew for certain was that this woman needed comforting—and that's what he did.

Reaching out to her, BC wrapped his arm around Carina's shoulder and tried to hug the tears away. It was little more than a gentle embrace of warm companionship, something meant to cheer her up.

Sniffing back a few whimpers, she abruptly pushed him aside, as if he had somehow insulted her.

"Whew!" she blurted outloud. "You need a shower!"

BC was taken aback. "Well, I guess I've had a rough day," he sheepishly admitted, taking a good whiff of himself. In the past several hours he had harpooned one man, shot another, sweated up a river coming down through the atmosphere, and thrown up his lunch all over himself. To say that he looked and smelled like a mess was a bit of an understatement!

"Rough day?" Carina growled. "I'll give you rough day! I've been shot at, nearly blown up, practically had my father killed, and almost left for dead! And it ain't even half over yet! So don't talk to me about a rough day! And while we're at it, bub, let's get one thing straight—I'm not crawling into the sack with any fellow who smells the way you do! So either get yourself cleaned up or else take me home!"

BC's jaw fell open. But before he could say anything, she pointed down the corridor and said, "Shower's thataway, bub." Then she stood in front of him with her arms crossed, one over the other, like a determined housemother.

BC grinned, stripped off his putrid garments and headed for the shower stall. At the sight of his nakedness, Carina licked her lips with the tip of her tongue and patted his firm behind as he went by.

A shower in space was always a real treat, and not just because the supply of clean water was at a premium. Micro-gravity was the *real* culprit.

The narrow shower stall was enclosed from floor to ceiling with a plastic curtain. Zipping the curtain all the way shut was an absolute necessity because, in the absence of gravity, the soapy water would form bubble-like globules. And if not contained, these globules would spread like wildfire throughout the ship. Every wall, every floor, every countertop, would wind up a slippery mess!

With the shower nozzle only centimeters above his head, and plastic all around him, BC felt like a prisoner inside a tubular cell. Attached to the metallic floor at his feet were two cloth-like toe-straps to hold him in place while he showered. Beneath the floor, a tungsten fan gave off a high-pitched whine as it drew the tepid water and soap-filled air down over his body and out through the drain. BC had barely started to lather up when the water automatically shut off and a special heat lamp clicked on, drying both him and the shower cabinet in moments.

When he stepped from the plastic cocoon, newly-cleaned and dry, she was there, waiting for him and looking very edible. Her nipples were erect, and her body was scented with the natural perfume only an aroused woman could generate.

Mouth wet with desire, she came to him, her dark eyes ogling his physique. Bending her knees, she squatted before him and pressed her lips against his muscular abdomen just below his belly-button. This made him twitch amorously.

Wiggling her nose like a rabbit might, she then bounded to her feet and said, "You smell much better now."

"You're a damn tease!" he cursed, taking a deep breath to cool his ardor.

"Yes, I know. But now it's *my* turn in the shower. Oh, and do something about that growth, will you?" she remarked, pointing towards his manhood.

Before BC could reply, she had zipped the curtain shut and flicked on the water.

Her belly kissing trick had fired up his passion. But BC did his best to talk it back down again while he searched for a change of clothes. By the time she was finished bathing, he had dressed. She was ripe and eager for sex; he was in a somber mood.

"Not now, Carina," he pleaded, rejecting her advances. "There are some things we need to get straight."

"I can't believe my ears!" she declared indignantly. "Well if you won't do me, I'll just have to do myself!" she exclaimed, pressing her fingers against her most private of parts.

"Knock it off!" he ordered, tossing her a robe. "Hear me out."

Pretending to pout, she reluctantly put on the gown. "What's a girl to do? If you won't make love to me, at least you could *feed* me. What's there to eat on this tub?"

"My, but aren't we a handful," BC said as he opened the pantry.

Without stopping to ask what she wanted, he took out the first thing he found. It turned out to be the twenty-fifth century's version of a bagel and cream cheese sandwich wrapped in perma-foil. He handed her one and said, "You're a nice girl, Carina, but I really can't get involved. There's no room in my life for a steady woman. An agent's married to his work. I've undertaken a solemn duty, you see. To crown and to country."

"Hah! And here I thought chivalry was dead! I couldn't care less about any of that crap! For heaven's sake, BC, I'm not looking for a husband—I'm looking for *sex!* You can do *that*, can't you?"

"Well, yes . . . of course . . . but we hardly know one another."

"What's to know?" she shot back.

"Well, for starters, tell me about your mother. Your dossier is silent as to her whereabouts."

Carina stopped munching on her bagel and grew quiet. "Why should you care anything about my mother?"

"You brought her up yourself," he reminded her. "Earlier, just before the tears."

"Yes, so I did," she replied, swallowing hard. "If you must know, my mother was executed in one of those Alaskan gene-extinction camps."

"Oh my God, I'm sorry I asked!" BC apologized. "What a jerk I am."

"You're not a jerk. And don't be sorry. Truth is, I hardly knew the woman. But now that you know, I hope you're not afraid to be tainted by one of my kind."

"Your *kind?* Whatever do you mean by that?"

"I'm not a hundred percent white; that's what I mean. My mother was not Caucasian, she was Amerind."

"You know something, Carina, you really do surprise me," he said, the pitch in his voice rising. "And you wanna know something else? You were right about me. I'm not the jerk, *you* are! For you to sit there all so smugly and think that even for one minute I'm that narrow-minded is downright insulting! What makes you think I could even give a *hoot* about your genetic stock?"

Pushing back from the table in an explosion of anger, BC slammed his half-eaten bagel down on the edge of his plate and stormed off in the direction of his berth. Kicking and swearing as he went, the man was oblivious to the mess he'd left in his wake. Let it only serve as a warning to others that slamming anything down onboard a spaceship is not a particularly good idea, much less a bagel thick with cream cheese! The culprit once again? Micro-gravity.

Like a frisbee, BC's plate careened left, striking a full cylinder of orange juice. Knocked into the air, the cylinder splashed ruinously across the room, its contents spilling everywhere!

Observing the opposite but equal dictates of Newton, the bagel bounced to the right with far more serious consequences. After a short flight it landed cream cheese side down on the flight deck. Carina rode it like a skateboard when she chased after him, eventually slipping off and falling against the bulkhead with a groan.

"I'm sorry!" she cried, rubbing her sore head and begging for forgiveness. "I'm terribly self-conscious about my heritage; I had to be certain you weren't one of those purist types."

"Get to the point," he snapped without offering to help her back to her feet.

"Sam attended college in Alberta. That's where he met my mother, a local Amerind girl named Nasha. After the War, the French Canadian purists decided Canada's gene-pool needed cleansing. People like my mother were rounded up and sent to the gene-extinction camps. Because I was born at home, the authorities had no record of me, so I was spared. It was too much for Sam, though, so we fled Canada and settled in Auckland. The rest, as they say, . . . "

" . . . is history." Finishing Carina's sentence, BC's face lost some of its sternness.

"When I was a kid, my father once asked me to explain to him the reason for persecution. At the time, the answer eluded me. It still does. How 'bout it, BC? Can you explain it?"

"No, not really, but one of my tutors had a philosophy on this. I was raised in an orphanage, you see, and Mother Theresa always said that words like Amerind and Caucasian were little more than unfortunate labels. But she also said that if you were to then superimpose attributes like laziness or tightfistedness upon those labels, you would create a basis first, for distinction, and later on, for hatred. Finally, if you were to add in *cultural* differences like religion or dress, voilà, you have the makings for persecution and war. It's the labels that create the Hitlers and the Rontanas."

Fascinated by his explanation, Carina said, "You're more of a poet than you can possibly know."

"Oh, not really. We're all brothers under the skin, as it were. Despite some superficial differences, all the so-called human races are but separate 'tribes' comprising a single species."

"But BC, evolution isn't stagnant!" Carina exclaimed. "Somewhere, somehow, someday, one of those *tribes*, as you so eloquently call them, will diverge completely from the others. And when *that* happens, humans will no longer be all of one species."

"Well, I don't know . . . " BC started.

"These *newhumans* would have a slightly altered gene-map," Carina patiently explained. "A woman with the new gene-map would be the Lucy—the mother, if you will—of the new species."

"Well, I don't know . . . " BC tried again. "What I mean is . . . well, how could you tell the difference? Would these . . . newhumans . . . be *freaks?*"

"Am I a freak?" Carina asked, trembling.

BC's face went white as he struggled to comprehend her meaning.

12
Eden, Part II

Though it seemed like a month had passed since they last stood inside the community mess-hall, it had in fact been only a matter of a day and a half. It didn't take them long to get reacquainted with the place.

The main room was in the shape of a hexagon twenty-five meters across. Sprouting from its abdomen like so many legs on an insect, were several unexplored dark corridors which presumably led to the base's sleeping quarters.

Along one edge of the community room, closets and shelves lined the wall from floor to ceiling. These pantries were filled to overflowing with an extensive assortment of sundries; items which, while essential to the operation of the colony, had been too bulky to take back to Earth when the settlement was abandoned. The shelves were stocked not only with necessities like toilet paper, cleaning detergents, medical supplies, kitchen utensils, and cooking spices, but also with an abundance of trivialities like playing cards, poker chips, chess pieces, and dominoes.

A second set of cabinets housed all manner of electronic equipment. Together with keyboards, data-entry ports, and video monitors, this was the command center for the entire complex, the "brains" for the entire place. Located here were the instruments needed to monitor and adjust a wide variety of environmental concerns including temperature, air pressure, and waste treatment. Then too, security, communications, and even food preparation were centralized here, making this spot perhaps the single most important two square meters on the planet.

As BC pulled up a chair to sit at the nearest keyboard, he spoke to Carina for the first time since they made the jump to Mars.

"So what you're trying to tell me is that you're like what, another Eve? Is that it?"

"Actually, I prefer Lucy, not Eve," she corrected in that tone of hers, "but, yes, that's it."

"I've met some mighty strange women in my day, but you, lady, take the cake. I don't have the slightest idea what you mean by *Lucy*."

"Let me explain," she offered, eager for an audience. "After diverging from the great African apes some 5 million years ago, as many as five different hominid, or prehuman, species may have cropped up at one time or another in our history. Hundreds of years ago, on a hillside in Ethiopia, anthropologists discovered the skeletal remains of a female hominid dating from just 40,000 years earlier. The team was so excited by their find, they worked through the night digging her out, cack music blaring from a portable audio-player the whole night long. Their favorite song, 'Lucy in the Sky with Diamonds,' was played over and over again, and by morning, the precious fossil had acquired the nickname of *Lucy*."

"You expect me to believe that a fossil discovery was named after a *song?*" BC asked, unable to hide his skepticism in the cold air of the mess-hall.

"Scientists are an eccentric lot, there's no getting around that. But the remarkably well-preserved bones were carefully studied and it was concluded that they constituted the oldest skeleton of a distinctly modern human being ever found. Lucy was declared to be the first of her kind—the mother of the race—and all *Homo sapiens* are thought to be her descendants."

"So if *she* was Lucy, how can *you* also be Lucy?" BC asked as he tried to decipher the multitude of dials and switches laid out on the console before him.

"I am the mother of the *newest* primate line," she proudly asserted, "the *newhuman* line."

When BC didn't immediately reply, she continued. "Don't you think it's rather conceited of us to assume that primate evolution conveniently ceased with *our* species?"

This time, BC wasted no time replying. "Don't you think it's rather conceited of you to assume that *you* are the matriarch of a new race? And even if you were the mother, who—my misguided friend—is the father?"

"I haven't found him yet," she conceded. "What about you?"

"Are you out of your mind?!" BC exploded. "I want no part of fathering a new race! I'll fulfill my obligation to the Crown as an officer in Her Majesty's secret service, I'll even fulfill my obligation to serve as your protector until this is over, but believe me, Carina, I seek no place with the gods. Leave me out of this newhuman stuff!"

Carina's lower lip jutted forth in a pout. "I'm disappointed, of course, but maybe you're right. All things considered, you're probably not suitable anyway. It would be a shame to sully my newhuman genes with your . . . your . . . "

"Look, I think I've had just about enough of your egocentric crap, so why don't you just leave me the hell alone!" BC shouted angrily. "I have a lot of work to do here if we're going to get this place powered-up, and you've been doing nothing but irritating me since we first landed!"

"So let me help," she said, sliding over next to him in front of the console.

Angry to the point of confusion, BC didn't object. Irritating as she was, Carina wasn't his biggest problem; getting more electrical power out of the system was.

To his left was a multi-axis remote-joystick which controlled the orientation of the rooftop solar panels. Like the rest of the colony, the command center required electricity to operate, and in the fifty-odd years since the settlement was abandoned, the alignment of the solar collectors had deteriorated. He was trying to remedy that problem by repeated trial and error.

Crude though his adjustments were, once BC had the panels repositioned, the voltammeter readings soared and the electric furnace kicked in. Before long he was able to turn on the rest of the station's internal systems.

Still grumbling about Carina and her crazy ideas, he tapped into the base computer and started reviewing the online files. Beginning with the quartermaster's manifest, he discovered that in the underground storage-bins there was ample dehydrated food to sustain a colony of seventy for up to six months. Some quick division told him this was enough dried provisions to last the two of them for up to twenty *years,* if necessary. All they had to do was add water!

Scanning further, BC uncovered the construction engineer's blueprints for the entire complex. The facility had been conceived and laid out in a modular fashion; thus, if the colony ever had to be relocated, the various units could be separated from the main node and reattached later on someplace else. Each of the sleeping wings were actually enormous cargo bays that had been flown in here from Earth, soft-landed, then fitted to the mess-hall like so many spokes on a giant wheel.

After fiddling awhile with another of the many knobs on the command console, BC hit upon a way to override the security system, thereby gaining access to the web of corridors beyond. Using a copy of the blueprints as a guide, he and Carina set out to learn more about this unusual place.

At the end of the first long hallway was a library. Much to Carina's amazement, many of the books catalogued there were actually printed on paper! No big deal on Earth, of course, where printbooks were still very much in vogue, but considering how a single fiche weighed only the smallest part of an ounce yet could hold as much information as several full-length printbooks, it didn't make any sense. Why would the colonists have lugged so many of the bulky printbooks along with them from Earth when they came here?

Carina could only speculate, of course, but there was something so very tactile about holding a book in one's hand and turning its parchment-like pages, something very sensual about inserting that bookmark at the end of a particularly good chapter and slowly closing the cover, something very arousing about peeking ahead when you weren't supposed to and reading the ending. Ah, the joys of making love to a book! Was it any wonder, then, that in addition to the thousands upon thousands of fiche covering every subject imaginable, there were at least eight or nine hundred threadbare printbooks as well? Of course not! Though mostly lowbrow, they had obviously seen plenty of use.

Though Carina was fascinated by the extent of the collection, before long the two of them moved on, continuing their canvass of the premises. At the end of an adjoining hallway, they came across something even more amazing than the library—a cavernous climate-controlled storeroom jammed full with case after case of ungerminated seeds, all meticulously preserved and sealed for future planting. Although the terraformers didn't stick around long enough to get the job done, apparently they had much more than just lichen in mind when they set out to remake Mars. In a quick census, Carina counted eighty-two varieties in all—turnips, corn, peas, tomatoes, grapes, hickory nuts, walnuts, potatoes, tulips, white-pine, pin-oak, petunias. The list just went on and on!

While Carina was busy inventorying the cache of plants, BC uncovered something even more incredible. In fact, it made him gasp! There, in the next room, suspended in cryogenic freeze, were animal embryos for several dozen species of farm animals—chicken, hog, rabbit, 'roo, Holstein, bio-canine, earthworm, butterfly, llama, honey-bee, carp, and catfish, just to name a few. As near as he could tell, though, there were no representatives from the Arachnid or the Insecta families, a discovery which set his mind at ease. Tough guy that he was, BC hated spiders and bugs!

"It's a veritable gene-store!" she exclaimed, coming over to stand next to him. "Just like Dad said!"

"You must be thrilled," BC remarked, his voice overflowing with sarcasm. "Eve in her garden of Eden. Only I'm no Adam—and I'm certainly no farmer! But then, it's all academic anyway because we're not going to be staying around here long enough to worry about running out of food."

"But what if we lose power and everything goes bad?" Carina whined. "Or what if that lake out there fills up with enough rainwater and we get flooded out of these buildings? This stuff wasn't left here to be *ignored*, this stuff was left here to be *used*. It's up to you and me to . . . "

"Whoa, slow down there, little lady," BC exclaimed. "In the first place, you told me I was unsuitable, remember? And in the second place, we don't know the first thing about terrafarming. This *stuff*, as you call it, is way over our heads."

"Not terra*farm*ing, you fool—terra*form*ing. And so what if it *is* over our heads? You simply have to go get my dad—he'll know what to do."

"Indeed, I plan on getting him one way or the other. But not for the reason you think. The Overlord believes Sam knows everything there is to know about the Fornax Drive, and now that I know you'll be safe here awhile, I'm going to see whether or not he can be moved yet. By this time the Acceleron should've kicked in."

Carina's eyes lit up. But before she could ask, he stopped her. "I'm going alone; you'll only be in the way. Besides, I have to make a stop on the moon beforehand."

"Why risk it?"

"We need more fuel; those strips ought to be recharged by now."

"Take me with you."

"Out of the question!"

"I don't wish to be left here alone," she declared. "What if something goes wrong and you don't return? I'd be stranded here forever!"

"For goodness sake, what could possibly go wrong? I'll be back before you know it. An hour at the most."

"And if you're not?"

"There's enough food in the storeroom to last you a lifetime."

"But I'll be lonely!"

"You? I seriously doubt that," BC objected, slipping on his kevlar tee-shirt. "In the first place, you like being alone; I could tell that about you from the very beginning. Then too, if you really do get lonely, you can always put yourself to work down here in the gene-store. I imagine you'll be able to cook up *something* to keep you company. A puppy, perhaps."

"You'll be back in an hour?" she confirmed.

"Hour and a half, tops."

"Promise?"

"Cross my heart and hope to die."

13
Prisoner Of War

The jump back to the moon was uneventful. But being a cautious man, BC was taking the utmost care to avoid being observed by a DUMPSTER crew when he landed. Nuclear fuel disposal was much too important a business to be slowed down for long, especially by a trifling like a blown-up moon base; if not there already, a DUMPSTER crew would be on the scene soon enough to rebuild the tiny facility. BC had no wish to make their acquaintance.

As a precaution in case he got caught, BC disconnected the Battery from the main power coupling. Then, before suiting-up again to go outside, he slipped the O-ring into his shorts. It was a little uncomfortable at first, especially since he had such a long way to hike.

BC had hidden the *Tikkidiw* behind a nearby escarpment and was thus several hundred meters away from the craters when he started out. As he lumbered past the wreckage of Whitey's shuttle, he kept telling himself that Carina would be okay, that all he had to do was use his head and be careful.

Still bothered by the fact that he hadn't found any trace of Fornax's body after the blast, BC wandered off in the direction of the battered moon base. As soon as he got there, he knew he was in trouble. *Whitey's body wasn't where he'd left it after the fight!*

Suddenly realizing he wasn't alone, BC turned abruptly on his heels and started to go. But it was already too late! Within moments he was confronted by a squad of six men, all clad in gray dee-dees.

"So, who do we 'ave here?" one of the men asked in a voice familiar to BC.

"Is that you, Red?" BC exclaimed in a friendly tone, extending his hand.

"Drop the 'good buddy' act," Red hollered in his booming voice. "You're a wanted man, a man with a bloody price on 'is head. A man we were all lucky enough to run into."

Red smiled an evil smile. In his hand was a shock-gun, a weapon riot-police used to bring down a man without killing him.

Angling for a way out of this, BC said, "So why split the reward six ways? Kill these other blokes and take me in on your own."

Red chuckled. "Don't push your luck, mate. The reward's the same whether you be dead or alive."

"In that case, kill me now 'cause I have absolutely no intention of being cooperative."

"All in good time," Red assured him. "But first: why don't you tell me what you're doing 'ere?"

"I might ask you the same thing!" BC shot back.

"Yes, you might," the big man agreed. "Truth is, me an' me buddies were sent here at the request of a close family member to reclaim Whitey's body. Now it's your turn, mate. What are *you* doing 'ere?"

"Kiss my . . . "

BC's indignant words were left hanging in the air as the contact closed and Red's shock-gun emitted its frightful charge. The electric surge penetrated BC's suit and he collapsed to the ground in a spasm of unspeakable pain.

• • •

"Well, if it isn't the mettlesome underpaid agent from Commonwealth Intelligence," Overlord Ling sneered, much amused. "It was about time we officially met. I've heard so much about you. Welcome to my humble abode," he said with a bow and a delicate sweep of the hand.

BC nodded his head politely.

"And Red," the Overlord continued, "I do thank you for bringing me this scoundrel. Pity about the rest of your crew. I understand they all perished in a freak accident of some sort."

"Yes, such a shame," the big, dense man declared. "The reward kinda makes up for it though. This fella put up quite a fight."

"Do tell," the Overlord grinned, his fu-manchu all atwitter. Giving BC the once-over, he said, "You, my friend, have caused me a great deal of grief."

"Truly sorry, milord," BC said, gazing around the room for a way out. The chamber they were in was more like an enormous hall than a room; the building, more like a palace than a house. There were probably guards everywhere, and if he ran, he'd almost certainly be shot on sight!

"You have cost me not only several perfectly good men, but the Fornax Battery as well. By all measures you deserve to die. However, letting Red here just blow out your brains would be much too easy. Besides, I may have a need for you yet!"

"I aim to please," BC replied coolly.

"Why were you on the moon?" Ling questioned.

"I was buying groceries," BC taunted.

"Insolent slug!" Overlord Ling shouted, his face crimson.

"Let me wring 'is bloody neck," Red interjected.

"I'll bet you were there to refuel," the Overlord said, brushing Red aside. "Only you got caught first, didn't you?"

Turning to Red again, Ling said, "When you got there, were there any durbinium strips recharging in the craters?"

"Honestly, boss, we didn't even think to check."

"No matter, I can get all the durbinium I want if the need arises, but tell me this: Was he on foot when you found him?"

"He was walkin' kinda funny, but yeah, he was on foot."

"So his ship couldn't have been parked very far away then," Ling reasoned. "It must still be there! When you go back, Red, I want you to look for it. Do a Level One search. The ship must be stashed within a kilometer or so of the base."

"Don't waste your time!" BC exclaimed. "The ship's not there. I flew it in, yes, but Carina dropped me off and she won't be returning again until I transmit her the all-clear signal."

"You're a liar!" the Overlord exploded. "That story is as bogus as the Battery plans you duped Lester with. You know very well Carina's not qualified to fly that ship. And even if she were, you were searched when Red brought you in. You weren't carrying a transmitter. You had no way of signaling her when you were done. No, Mister Smart-Aleck Secret Agent, I think you're lying. I think the ship you and Fornax stole from me is still parked right there on the moon," the crafty Overlord concluded.

"You'll never find it," BC maintained.

"Perhaps not, but in the meantime—until I *do* track her down—I'm going to hand you over to Chou Kim, my fat little henchman in Sri Lanka. He'll beat you every night, but otherwise your stay there will be most unremarkable."

"You only have yourself to blame," BC retorted bravely. "If you hadn't hired that animal Whitey to kill us, we would never be having this conversation—and Fornax would still be alive!"

"You wouldn't want to save us all a whole lot of trouble and tell me where you hid my ship, now would you?" Overlord Ling asked.

Unmoved, BC did not answer.

"I thought not. Tell me, Mister Loyal British Agent Man, where is the honor in dying for your country? *They* don't care, you know."

BC shrugged his shoulders. It was senseless to argue. J wouldn't lift a finger to help him, and BC knew it. Give a man a mission, J would say; let him sink or swim. BC could only imagine an exchange between J and Overlord Ling on the subject. It might go something like this:

"You have BC?" J would say. "How did you get him?"

"That's not important," the Overlord would reply. "What *is* important is, do you want him back?"

"Even if you have him—which I doubt—that's BC's problem, not mine. Agency policy is: we never trade. Do what you will, but you'll get no satisfaction from me!"

"We'll mail him back to you one piece at a time," the Overlord would threaten.

"Then we'll be forced to *bury* him one piece at a time," the iron-man would stoically reply. "A survivor type is one who comes back!"

BC gritted his teeth in painful submission as he returned to the here and now. Mustering all his courage, he said, "I'm sorry, Ling, but I can't help you."

"Pity. Well good riddance to you then. Red, dump this limey bastard in Sri Lanka. I'll tell Mister Kim to be expecting him. Then get a new team together and return to Luna. When the ship is found, I want it towed to Sri Lanka as well; but no one is to touch her without my express permission. I will see to it personally."

Red nodded his head as he led his prisoner away. BC had good reason to be scared, though that wasn't what was troubling him. It was the feisty woman he had left stranded on Mars.

By now it was a foregone conclusion he wasn't going to make it back in an hour like he'd promised. With Sam in the hospital, Fornax dead, Carina stranded on Mars, and he himself a prisoner of Overlord Ling, who could possibly save them all now? Who?

PART IV

1
Reincarnation

Manchester, England
Four Days Earlier

Completely bewildered, the dark-eyed man was unsure where he was, or even how he got there. Confused, he crawled clumsily out from the immense cargo bay, only to be greeted by a ferocious exchange of gunfire.

As if mired in a strange dream, he saw—but did not actually hear—the battle. Though the soldiers weren't actually shooting *at* him, he was nevertheless dangerously close to the fight. Somehow, despite having been stunned by an earlier blow to the skull, he still had the presence of mind to press himself flat against the ground.

Lying there in the grass, surrounded by a handful of giant oaks, and safe from the tracers buzzing menacingly overhead, the man tried to fathom who he was and why he was dressed in such an odd outfit. None of it made any sense! All he knew for certain was that his head was pounding!

The suit was an inflexible, tight-fitting, gray-colored garment, equipped with a securely-fastened headpiece, contoured gloves, and a pair of custom-molded boots. It vaguely resembled a heavy-duty wet suit, though rigid. He fumbled to remove the helmet, but could not. The man, though agile, had no better luck with the visor; it too was stuck shut.

He realized by its salty taste that blood was running down his cheek and into his mouth. There was no way for him to wipe it away, though, and he began to feel hopelessly trapped inside the stifling gear.

The confused man shivered involuntarily as a wave of claustrophobia swept over him. Afraid now that he might pass out, he struggled to stay focused.

How did I get hurt? he asked himself groggily. Who am I, damnit? *Where* am I?

Rolling over to study the craft he had crawled out of, a look of astonishment crept across his face. The vehicle lay gleaming in the midday sun. As he stared at the rectangular-shaped service hatch he had exited from, then at the strange, butterfly-like insignia on its hull, recognition slowly dawned.

It's a spaceship! he thought excitedly. A bloody spaceship!

Looking down at himself, the man suddenly realized that the rigid scuba-like thing he was wearing was actually a spacesuit! A dee-dee! But how could that be? Had he been to *space*?

No, that was just plain silly! Only DUMPSTERS went into space. And they certainly didn't land here—wherever *here* was!

Drawn more by instinct than by reason, the befuddled man crept away from the parked shuttle on all fours. Cumbersome spacesuit and all, he wormed his way across the lawn towards an enormous oak.

From his vantage point beneath the giant tree he observed a squad of elite commandoes vaulting into the compound from over the far wall. Brandishing automatic weapons and force guns, they advanced with grim determination. But as quickly as they pressed their assault, the marauders were being cut down by a platoon of tough-looking soldiers crouched along the foundation of the main building. Though brave men were clearly dying at every turn, the man couldn't hear their anguished cries, trapped as he was inside the soundproof spacesuit.

On the verge of hyperventilating, the man propped himself up against the trunk of the big oak. Feverishly he struggled to escape the confinement of the suit. Finally, just short of total panic, he found the clasp which held the headgear in place. Prying it open, he threw the helmet to the ground with a great sigh of relief, delighting in the rush of fresh air across his sweaty blood-caked face.

No longer cooped up inside the helmet, his breathing slowly returned to normal. Yet, within moments of getting it off, he again started to feel queasy. The now unmuffled roar of battle poked at his sensibilities, bringing back sharp memories of another war in another place. Alarmed by the everpresent danger, the man promptly moved to strip the rest of the dee-dee from his body. Then, propelled by fear, he ran unsteadily for the farthest point of the walled compound.

The man had covered no more than half the distance to the wall when a colossal explosion rocked the complex. The ground beneath him began to roll. Startled by the deafening sound, he slowed his pace just enough to glance over his shoulder at its source. Turning his head, he caught a glimpse of the spacecraft eclipsing the sun as it leapt skyward atop a huge column of dust and debris blown aside by the ignition of its drive.

Bewildered, the man couldn't imagine what form of propulsion could possibly power a ship of that size straight up into the atmosphere at such a velocity. A short-lived grin spread across his dirty face, however, as he absentmindedly pondered the dimensions of the crater it must have left behind in its wake!

Distracted by this spectacle, the man neglected to pay much attention to where he was going. His foot struck a protruding root with devastating results!

Flying headlong into a sturdy, rustic oak, the last thing the man saw that afternoon was the tiny speck of the spaceship as it accelerated out of sight.

• • •

When he finally came to after having lain unconscious on the ground for several hours, it was dark. Only *this* time he knew where he was. More importantly, he knew *who* he was!

Determined to be on his way despite a throbbing headache, the man dragged himself to his feet and limped slowly towards the edge of the fortress-like facility.

In an instant, he was over the wall and into the city, his keen mind focused on what he must do next!

2
Identity

The shabby building had galvanized-aluminum walls, a roof littered with broken shingles, and a gravel parking lot rutted with potholes. Despite its run-down appearance, the place was shut up tightly, as if it held some deep dark secret. The giant padlock on the warehouse door was caked with rust and would not budge. Fornax's attempt to jimmy the lock with his blade left it unimpressed.

Searching for another way in, he inched his way along the corrugated metal wall of the structure until his tiny flashlight revealed a window large enough for him to crawl through. With the butt of his blade he broke the glass, then wormed his way carefully over the sill and into the darkened machine shop. Although this wasn't the first time he'd been inside Lester's freight terminal, the glow from his penlight was so dim, he stumbled around clumsily for several minutes until he came across a light switch.

Flickering fluorescent bulbs hung along the cobweb-embroidered centerbeam of the ceiling. They hummed with an annoying buzz, popping every once in awhile then briefly going out. The flickering bulbs made the place look even more surreal than it was. Even when they were all on at the same time, they generated barely enough light to penetrate the dark bowels of the cavernous warehouse. Fornax used what little light he had to scrutinize his surroundings.

Strewn haphazardly about the aircraft-hangar-sized room was every piece of equipment Lester must have thought essential to the running of his transport business—end loaders, flatbed trucks, engine blocks, tires, empty oil cans, dollies, and so forth. It was a jumble of broken-down machinery, and seeing it, Fornax was reminded how, on his first visit here, he'd had the impression of Lester's unseen tie-in to organized crime. Only now, as he stood there shivering in the damp, poorly-lit freight terminal, did Fornax begin to digest just how close he had come to *not* being there at all!

Picking his way through the chaos, Fornax moved towards the opposite end of the warehouse. The events of the past day and a half rocketed through his mind: the missile attack which had knocked him out cold; the subsequent discovery that, not only was he low on oxygen, but that the *Tikkidiw* had left the moon without him; the jubilation upon witnessing her return; the relief at finding fresh oxygen tanks in the cargo hold; the terror of riding back to Earth as an unintended stowaway in that same cargo hold; and finally, before catching the overnight tube to Melbourne, the elation at being a firsthand observer as the ship he himself had built vaulted back into orbit riding the thrust of his very own invention!

Newscasts had carried the report of a terrorist bombing at the moon base, and although unidentified British officials had ascribed the incident to distraught Rontanians seeking a homeland, Fornax knew better. He knew, for instance, that the mercenary named Whitey—the same man who had killed Captain Michael that night in the Corkscrew Pub—had been responsible for the attack. He knew, or strongly suspected, that Whitey had been thwarted in that attack. But what he did *not* know, and what he kept asking himself over and over again was why Whitey had been ordered to kill him in the first place? Then too, what had become of Sam and the others?

In Fornax's own, nondescript obituary the local paper had reported that both he and Lester had perished in a freakish gcar accident. The accompanying press release stated that Sam, despite having been badly injured in that same wreck, had survived the crash and was now supposedly confined to a bed at the Auckland provincial hospital where he remained in guarded condition.

Fornax was confident that this information was as false as the reports of his *own* death! It only stood to reason that if Sam was hospitalized *any*where, he was hospitalized back in Manchester, not in Auckland. Otherwise, why would BC have landed there to begin with? Saving Sam had to be the only possible reason!

Which left BC and Carina. Where had *they* disappeared to? Fornax wondered, suppressing a tinge of jealousy. Since the newspapers hadn't disclosed anything as to their whereabouts, it was a foregone conclusion that the two of them must have been onboard the ship when it leapt skyward from the hospital lawn.

All this, and more, occupied Fornax's mind as he combed carefully through Lester's dingy office looking not only for some pocket money, but also for a weapon to defend himself with. Considering what had happened already, and considering what he was up against now, Fornax needed something more lethal than his trusty blade.

While he searched the premises, Fornax pondered the practical ramifications of his own recent "death." If it hadn't been done already, his bank account would soon be frozen. Then too, his position at the university would shortly be forfeited, his apartment re-let, and his certified passport permanently revoked. Taken together, a rather frightening state of affairs! Fornax would have to move fast now if he was going to stay one step ahead of these devastating events!

Contemplating the imminent loss of his possessions and his identity, Fornax intensified his search, rummaging methodically through one file cabinet after another. Most of what he found were unimportant trifles like expired bills-of-lading and angry dunning notices, but finally, after a frustrating half-hour of hunting, he struck pay dirt—a drawer full of money! A second discovery was of even greater importance—a cache of identicards along with matching certified passports!

Sifting through the box of fake I.D.'s, his eyes soon fell upon a set he could profitably employ. Except for the color of the man's hair (something Fornax could remedy with a sinkful of peroxide and a cupful of toner), the counterfeit papers for a fellow by the name of Sven Rutland matched Fornax Nehrengel rather closely. He was definitely of the right build and correct age.

Envisioning himself as a typical blue-eyed blond-haired SKANDIAN, Fornax grinned. He had visited SKANDIA once, years ago, and figured that with the right complexion, he should have no problem blending right in with the locals.

No sooner had Fornax stuffed the fake I.D. into his pocket than he heard the creaking of the warehouse door. The grating sound terrified him, and for a brief instant he froze. But suddenly appreciating how vulnerable he was with only a blade for protection, Fornax sprang into action, flipping off the light and hiding in the chairwell of Lester's massive wooden desk.

The intruder carried a flashlight. As he drew closer and closer, eerie shadows danced off the far wall. Judging by the way the prowler moved, Fornax decided that he either had to be a man of small build—or else a woman. One thing was for certain though: the unwelcome guest was not one of the hefty goons Fornax had met on his first visit here.

When the trespasser paused to examine the shattered windowpane which Fornax himself had knocked in, Fornax distinctly heard the newcomer's boot grind bits of broken glass into the concrete floor. Then the thug came closer, cocking his gun as he approached.

Anticipating the worst, Fornax crouched with his knees bent and his back pressed flat against the underside of the desk. The heavy wooden desk would not only double as body armor, if Fornax had to, he could easily lift the desk with his back and slam it against the intruder like a battering ram!

Firmly planting his feet for just that course of action, Fornax tensed his muscles and waited. From the shifting shadows thrown by the snooper's flashlight, he figured the man was standing at the doorway, slowly scanning the office Fornax himself was hiding in. Fornax held his breath, but the wait wasn't long. Apparently satisfied that the room was empty, the flashlight moved on to the next room, and then the next.

Fornax trembled, afraid that the unwelcome guest would return for a more thorough search. But his fears were unfounded. Indeed, before long, the footfalls retreated as the prowler worked his way judiciously around and between the silent machinery which filled the warehouse.

Hoping to catch a glimpse of the intruder, Fornax relaxed his taut muscles and cocked his head out from beneath the desk. Stunned by what he smelled, he nearly exclaimed his shock outloud: *lingering in the air beside him was the faint scent of a woman's expensive perfume!*

Carina? he silently exclaimed, his heart jumping wildly. Could it possibly be?

Sinking to the floor, Fornax tried to reason it through. Before long, though, a frown had furrowed his face. Carina's presence there was simply not a logical possibility. In the first instance, she would never have come to such a dangerous place alone; BC would have seen to that. Then too, Fornax doubted whether she knew how to operate a flashlight, much less a force gun. No, it had to be someone else. But who?

Then it came to him. The woman in the Corkscrew Pub! The one who was there the day Captain Michael was killed!

He had never seen her face, but he *had* remembered her unusual perfume. It had left an indelible imprint on his mind, an imprint which was now quickly resurrected. This was one and the same perfume!

Still crouching behind the giant desk, Fornax listened intently for the sound of the warehouse door creaking shut. Although he let out a sigh of relief, he didn't budge. And, despite a terrible cramp in his calf, he patiently remained out of sight for another half an hour, just to be sure the coast was clear. Then, exercising extreme caution, he silently abandoned his hiding place, exiting the premises by the way he'd come in.

Sensing that he was in more danger now than ever before, and convinced that this murderous woman now had him under surveillance, Fornax decided he had to adopt his new identity as soon as possible.

With a growing sense of urgency, he sped across the gravel parking lot in the direction of the tube-station. He simply had to reach his flat in Auckland before it was too late!

3
Dead

The blue sky over Auckland made Fornax feel so young and alive, by the time he reached his apartment the following day, he had forgotten that he was in fact dead. Not dead as in "dead and buried," but rather, dead as in "no longer alive." In the cold eyes of the law, Fornax Engels had expired.

As Fornax had foreseen, the publication of his obituary had triggered a flood of events, perhaps the most devastating of which was that his landlord had wasted no time exercising his rights under the Housing Shortage Act to re-let his flat.

Taking advantage of his legal prerogative, the building's owner had acted swiftly in Fornax's absence, removing his personal belongings from his tenement and depositing them in municipal storage. There they would remain for five days before being sold at public auction. After that, anything not claimed by an heir would be given over to Provincial Social Services for distribution to the needy.

Once Fornax digested what had become of everything in the world that he held dear, the man realized he was truly dead. A persona non grata. A man without a country. A soul deprived of an identity.

Afraid that another tenant from his building might recognize him, Fornax didn't wait around the apartment complex very long. He was terrified, not knowing where to turn or what to do next. He needed a place of safe refuge, a place to sleep, a place to think.

It occurred to him that since Carina had not yet been declared dead, presumably her apartment had not suffered the same fate as his own. So, after stopping off at the pharmacy for a bottle of bleach to makeover his skin and hair, Fornax went to Carina's place.

Her flat was a drab, two-story affair in the middle of a long row of similarly drab, two-story townhouses. As he expected, she wasn't home. So he did the only sensible thing—broke in!

Having just committed a jailable offense, Fornax wasted no time getting to work. Coloring his hair was the first order of business. He found an empty flask in her bathroom cabinet. Observing the directions printed on the outside of the bottle, he used the peroxide to bleach his scalp, his eyebrows, even the hairs on his chest. Voilà, Sven Rutland was born!

While he waited for the tint to take, Fornax hydrated himself a burgwich from her pantry and sat down to eat. Scanning the top of Carina's desk as he munched the foul-tasting meal, his eyes fell upon a folio bound in expensive red leather. From the letters embossed on its cover, he recognized it as Carina's diary. Understandably curious, he flipped through the pages until his eyes caught upon a paperclip marking the entry dated November 26, 2430.

Fornax read her notions in wide amazement. It was rare indeed that he took the time to think of much beyond his own narrow self-interests, and rarer still that he contemplated matters as esoteric as evolution. Yet he was stunned by what the woman had written. Her ideas concerning newhumans were novel, even explosive!

Fornax was moved by what he read. He saw in Carina's words a different woman than the one he had met onboard the *Tikkidiw*. Deciding it would be a shame if her work were lost forever, and figuring that her belongings might soon be treated just as callously as his own, he pocketed her diary for further study.

Once he had finished eating, Fornax bounded up the stairs to view his bleach-blond SKANDIAN hair in the bathroom mirror. As he passed the upstairs window on the way to the toilet, he noticed a commotion in the parking lot outside her flat.

A rather large, black gcar had just pulled into the lot and several tenants were milling excitedly about as if they had never seen such a vehicle before. From where he stood at the window, Fornax studied the machine, trying to figure out what made it so unusual.

A chill ran down his spine as he found the answer: *exhaust fumes were pouring from its tailpipe!*

That could only mean one thing—the sedan was gasoline powered!

In his experience, only Overlord Ling possessed such a vehicle; therefore, it went without saying that the beefy-looking henchmen jumping out of it could only be looking for him!

Swallowing hard at the realization, Sven Rutland bolted for the door!

4
Leverage

London
Two Days Later

The head of Commonwealth Intelligence sat facing Samuel Matthews from across his swimmingly huge desk. Outside, a cold rain was falling on the bureaucratic maze of red-stone buildings.

"Quite frankly, I'm just a little bit disappointed by your attitude," J remarked, stern-faced. His jowls quivering, he gave Sam the once-over. J was amazed how good the man looked considering how it had been only a week since he was injured in the attack at the moon base.

For his part, Sam twitched uncomfortably in the tall straight-backed chair. Though the Acceleron had done its job admirably, healing his wounds in a tenth of the time his body would have taken otherwise, he still had plenty of pain. And because of an allergic reaction to the prescribed painkillers, he had resorted to guzzling tortan to ease his suffering, an otherwise pleasurable alcoholic beverage, but a devilish habit to break once begun.

"Are you listening to me?" the hefty gray-haired gentleman demanded, his heavy British accent coloring his words.

"Well," Sam mumbled, struggling to throw off the dilatory effects of the tortan, "actually, I'm not."

"Now see here, Matthews—we saved your bloody life! We nursed your sorry butt back to health. The least you could do is lend us a hand!" J bellowed, his meaty hands raised in anger. The man was hunkered behind an enormous wooden desk which sprawled halfway across the middle of his otherwise elegant office. A vintage Victorian lamp hung over his head.

"I would if I could, but I can't," Sam retorted, his uncombed hair giving him a roguish look.

"Or *won't*?" J shot back, his grizzled face looking peeved.

"Can't," Sam repeated earnestly. "I understand your dilemma, I really do. Fornax is dead and BC has disappeared. He's absconded with your precious ship, *and* my precious daughter, I might add. Plus, the diskette he gave you, the one which purportedly contained the sum total of Fornax's work, in fact contained nothing more than a bunch of high-tech gibberish. You, my friend, have been had!" Sam chuckled.

"You may find it amusing, Matthews, but I do not!" J exploded, pounding his powerful fist on the desk top. "Nor does Overlord Ling. The only working model of that Battery is onboard the *Tikkidiw*. Once the ship is located, BC and your precious daughter become expendable. For all I know, BC's *already* working for the other side."

"Don't be silly!" Sam interjected. "He's true-blue if ever there was one."

"He duped us with that bogus tape, didn't he?" J snapped back.

"That was Fornax's doing, not BC's," Sam pointed out.

"No matter," J replied, his chiseled face turning gray. "Frankly, at this point, I don't care *what* happens to BC. On the other hand, *you* may care what happens to your daughter. Not only that, you may care what happens to *you*," J noted somberly. "You yourself are apt to be targeted."

"Land's sakes!" Sam trembled. "Why me?"

"If the Overlord thinks he can use you as leverage, or if he thinks you can lead him to Carina, then that's reason enough."

"You're just trying to scare me," Sam retorted bravely.

"Honestly, Matthews, I don't know *what* will come to pass. Hell, they may even blame you for the loss of Lester. They may decide to kill you just for sport!

Shivering involuntarily, Sam nodded his head in assent. He reminded himself of a lesson he'd learned long ago—Never To Count The British Short. For the moment anyway, this fellow named J held all the cards; nothing would be gained by further obstinance.

"Okay, you win," Sam relented. "What can I do to help?"

"That's more like it," J said, clearly satisfied with himself. "Now, let's get down to business. First of all, I'm going to ask you to sit down with one of our engineers and tell him everything you saw, and everything you heard Fornax say, about this Battery of his. We have a preliminary sketch of the thing, and I want you to help our people understand how the damn thing works. Next: I want to station some of my people around your estate in Auckland to keep a watch over you."

"I'm to be a prisoner in my own house?"

"Don't think of yourself as a prisoner. Think of yourself as a celebrity," J said, rising to his feet. The man looked tough, like an ex-marine might, with tree trunks for legs. A dense mat of thick hair gripped his arms, the back of his compact neck, even his fat knuckles.

"A celebrity?" Sam grumbled, a dubious look on his face.

Ignoring him, J continued. "Lastly, I want you to take these." He pushed a bottle filled with little red pills across the desk towards Sam.

"What are they?" Sam asked, grabbing the vial before it rolled to the floor.

"Vitamins," J answered, wandering over to peer out through the bulletproof glass window. A gardener was busy at work in the courtyard below.

"I've got my own brand, thank you," Sam retorted, setting them back on the desk as if he wasn't interested.

"Not like *these*, you don't!" J boomed from across the room.

"What's in them?"

"Locators."

"So you can *track* me?"

"Precisely!" J answered, faintly amused. "The tiny encapsulated locators will pass harmlessly through your body and be expelled in the normal fashion. So you must be sure to take one each and every day."

J's demanding tone rankled Sam. "I won't do it!" he stated flatly.

Turning from the window, J came towards him with fire in his eyes. "If you refuse, I'll be forced to place a bodyguard on you 'round the clock! On the other hand, if you cooperate, then you'll be free to go wherever you choose. By swallowing these vitamins, we'll always be able to locate you. The men I post on your grounds will not only be armed, they'll be carrying directional finders as well."

"It seems you've thought of everything," Sam declared irritably.

"That's my job."

"You Brits sure do love the cloak-and-dagger shtick, don't you?"

J snarled, his body taking on the look of a fierce bulldog.

"Are you going to tell me where my daughter is or not?"

"I honestly have no idea," J asserted in what Sam took to be his sincerest answer yet.

"But you'll tell me when you find her?" he asked, ever hopeful.

"Of course!" the stout man responded without conviction. "Now take these with you," he said, again handing Sam the vitamins, "and go see our engineering people. Smithers is waiting outside my office; he'll escort you downstairs. When you're done there, he'll put you on a suborb back to Auckland."

"Oh, one more thing before I leave."

"What's that?" J demanded impatiently.

"What does the 'J' stand for?"

"Jupiter. As in the supreme god of the Romans," the tough-looking man replied haughtily.

"You're so modest," Sam returned, stomping indignantly from J's office. "I would have thought jackal, perhaps, or jerk, or jackass, or . . . "

Sam's unkind words were lost when J slammed the door shut behind him.

5
SKANDIA

SKANDIA
Two Weeks Later

The star-studded sky was clear and crisp. Indeed, nearly every night lately had been cut from the same cloth. Even so, the newcomer still wasn't accustomed to the penetrating cold. Though he had done his best to blend in with the locals, this man without a country remained a stranger in a strange land. Fitting in required a good deal more than just changing the color of one's hair!

Fornax had been to SKANDIA before, that much was true, and he had recently befriended an elfin man named Viscount Nordman, yet he still knew practically nothing of their language—and even less of their customs and traditions. In an attempt to draw as little attention to himself as possible, this man named Sven Rutland had settled in a remote fishing village perched on a striking fjord far to the north. It was a lonely existence, one which had been randomly dealt to him by virtue of accidentally discovering a forged identicard which happened to resemble his former self.

Yet, in spite of all the hardships he had had to endure lately, there was one consolation to a setting so far removed from civilization. With the dark nights being especially long at this season, and with the few village lights being especially dim at this hour, the perfect moment had finally arrived for him to unpack the wooden crate which sat poised on the floor beside him. His telescope lay waiting patiently within.

From an early age, Fornax had been an avid stargazer. Indeed, it was this pastime which had started him thinking about the spent nuclear fuel accumulating at the moon DUMP in the first place. So enamored was he to this hobby that he wasn't about to leave his telescope behind when he left Auckland. Thus, after successfully escaping from Carina's flat only moments ahead of the Overlord's goons, Sven Rutland surfaced next at Fornax Engels' estate sale.

There he purchased not only his trusty telescope, but something else which he could not bear to be without—his graduate level physics text. There was no sense in having one without the other: the chapters concerning the properties of durbinium had been as instrumental in formulating the design for his Battery as his telescope had been in pointing him in the right direction to begin with.

The boards forming the lid of the crate yielded easily to his screwdriver. As he pried them loose to reveal the personal treasure packed within, it was hard to suppress his excitement. For the past two weeks now, the telescope had remained safely stowed away in this box; tonight he intended to focus it once again on the magnificence of the beckoning solar system.

With nervous anticipation, Sven bundled himself in a heavy coat, threw open the balcony door, and secured the telescope's tripod to a heavy, rough-hewn pine table. Ignoring the cold, he began his survey of the heavens by bringing the moon's mottled surface into sharp relief.

It was like meeting an old friend on the street after a long separation. Seeing luna's white face again reminded him of all that had happened in the months since he first set out as a lowly DUMPSTER in search of riches. Even after all this time, Fornax had very little to show for his trouble, yet somehow, the money didn't seem as important now as it had at the start. The sea change was disquieting. Fornax was like a powerful ship sailing under full steam but without benefit of a rudder. Thus far anyway, no other driving force had asserted itself to take the place of money in his life.

After studying the moon for awhile, the next celestial body to demand his attention was Saturn along with her company of magical rings. Like a siren, she summoned him to her breast. Only, her endless icy squall was far too cold to hold his interest for long. Soon Fornax turned elsewhere in search of something warmer.

The only lady friend he had in the sky was the strumpet Mars. With her, it was personal.

"By God!" he exclaimed, querying his telescope. "Have I actually been there? Or was it all a dream?"

An involuntary shiver resurrected the memory of Carina popping off her helmet and drawing that first, daring breath of frigid Martian air. Oh, how he envied her impetuous nature! Oh, how he missed Sam's eminently practical essence!

By God! It *wasn't* a dream! I *have* been there! We *all* were there! And that's precisely where Carina and BC must have gone when they left here. Where else but Mars?

According to her diary, these newhumans could only "hatch" in isolation. What better incubator than Mars herself? he thought as he fiddled with the control knobs on his telescope trying to bring the Red Planet into focus. Try as he might, he simply couldn't get a clear view!

Time after time Fornax made a slight adjustment, then again

observed Mars through the eyepiece. Yet each time the results were the same—she was obscured from sight by an envelope of haze, and nothing he could do seemed to remedy the situation.

Fornax was growing more irritated with each passing minute.

"Damn!" he swore, thinking that the focusing mirror must have been bumped out of alignment when his landlord cleaned out his flat or else during the long trip up here.

A disappointed Fornax gave up viewing for the evening, determined to disassemble, clean, and reassemble his telescope the following day. Unfortunately, before he had a chance to refocus his newly-aligned instrument on Mars, a North Atlantic storm system swept in, enveloping the fjord in pea soup for nearly a week.

When the next clear night finally arrived, he once again trained his cylindrical apparatus on the fourth planet, only to discover that she was *still* mired in a cloudy film!

Can't be! he told himself angrily.

Fornax had recalibrated his instrument with the utmost care—it was in perfect working order. The fault had to lie elsewhere!

Swinging his telescope around to take a cursory peek at Saturn low in the winter sky, he found her image to be crisp and clear. The same was true of the moon—her face was sharp and unblemished.

But how could that be? If the problem wasn't his telescope, it had to be Mars! Only that didn't make any sense *either!* How could a planet as big as Mars be entirely cloaked in fog? It wasn't possible! Her atmosphere was far too thin to support a cloud-deck of that magnitude.

Or was it?

Confused, Fornax slumped in his chair and closed his eyes. His forehead creased in puzzlement. It was all so damn peculiar! he thought. Then, suddenly, he burst from his seat! There was one way to know for sure!

Bristling with curiosity, Fornax mounted his retrograde tracking engine to the base of the telescope stand. He then clipped his video camera over the eyepiece. Finally, he set the timer for six hours and fell into bed for a night of restless sleep.

Fornax had a hypothesis, and this was the most practical way for him to test it. While he slept, the retrograde tracker would keep the telescope trained on Mars. Every ten seconds or so, the video camera would click its shutter and by morning he would have a time-lapse record of the changes in the Martian shroud.

Shortly after sun-up, Fornax had his answer. Wiping the sleep from his eyes, he replayed the videotape for a stunned audience of one. At its conclusion, he no longer considered his telescope the culprit in this mystery. Something much more powerful was at work here!

The time-lapse photography had brought the Martian veil into stark perspective. By adding in the element of motion, the camera had transformed the haze from a static blob into a flowing, swirling tempest.

Fornax beheld a surging boiling storm. Like so many jagged ribbons of light, violent eruptions of lightning repeatedly slashed the whirling layer of clouds. Vortices of energy dominated the upper elevations. Large rolling eddies continually broke down into smaller ones. And every so often, one of them would pop open to reveal a tantalizing glimpse of the rain-soaked surface below. Fornax could only imagine the sounds that must have accompanied this awesome display, the titanic claps of thunder which must have been bellowing out from those massive rainclouds, the low mean rumbles as they lumbered slowly across the lichen-choked valleys.

Fornax was spellbound, scarcely able to believe his own eyes. Mars had weather! Only, this was no localized thunderstorm like they had encountered on his first visit to Mars, *this* was a planet-enveloping deluge!

He played the tape back three more times, studying it intently with each replay, but there was no way for him to escape his initial interpretation—Mars had weather!

Like the primeval Earth before her, Mars was giving birth to a global ocean, an ocean which, while making it possible for Mars to be impregnated with life, would also drown anything or anybody caught in its fury.

As he stood there mouth agape, a sixth sense told him Carina was in trouble, and that it was up to him to save her. He would have to go find Sam, and together they would have to figure out a way to reach her.

This time, though, he'd need something more than just a blade in his pocket for protection. This time, he would need a gun! It had occurred to him that if a durbinium battery could be made tiny enough, it could power a pocket-sized blaster. Not only that, if he was to have even a prayer of pulling this thing off, he'd have to brush up on his SKANDIA. "Vo is me?" he practiced with some hesitation.

The wheels of his intellect churning again, Fornax plotted his return to Mars. Chivalry, not greed, was the driving force pushing him forward this time!

6
Tortan

Auckland
The Next Afternoon

When his knock at the front door went unanswered, Agent Nicholas Cornwall worked his way judiciously around the enormous residence, parting the shrubbery as he went. He had been told by the guards posted out at the main gate that Sam was somewhere on the grounds, and it worried him that Sam hadn't answered the door.

Several other buildings dotted the manor, and before returning to the front porch of the mammoth white mansion, Agent Cornwall methodically checked each one, knocking on doors and peering in through the windows.

With a butterfly flitting silently around his shoulder, the good-looking stranger removed a small tool from his breast pocket. Quietly employing it to gain entrance to the main house, Cornwall passed, first through the foyer and then into the living room. Beyond that was what he supposed was a library or a study. There he found Dr. Sam collapsed on the floor, cold-stone drunk.

Grasping Sam's limp wrist, Cornwall automatically checked for a pulse. Though it was weak, Sam was alive.

Checking further, Cornwall found no obvious injuries. He was struck, however, by the telltale stench of alcohol. This was not completely unexpected. J had briefed him on Sam's accident—and on Sam's developing penchant for using tortan as a surrogate painkiller. Agent Cornwall had come prepared with a medic-kit and three De-Tox syringes.

Staring now at the drunken man sprawled out lifelessly on the plush red carpet, the newcomer groaned with irritation. It had already been a long day, one which had begun in darkness with a flight from London by suborb, and one which was apt to continue a good deal longer while he waited for his comatose patient to sober up.

Hours earlier, while it was still the middle of the night in England,

Agent Cornwall had boarded J's specially-outfitted suborbital transport for Auckland. It was a heavily-armored craft stocked full with sophisticated electronic equipment, mostly tracking and comm. But air travel was always the same, and on the advice of the pilot that they'd probably hit some chop crossing through the cloud-cover coming out of England today, he snugged up on his shoulder-harness accordingly.

Cornwall had never quite gotten used to being tightly strapped into a rigid chair before being accelerated to four-g's, this despite dozens of transits by suborb. He was still white-knuckled ninety minutes later when he off-loaded in Auckland with orders to talk to Sam.

Only, Sam was in no condition to talk!

Expecting that the inevitable mess would be far easier to clean up in the john, Cornwall dragged Sam across the study floor, dumping him unceremoniously in an adjoining bathroom. As was customary for a man as wealthy as Dr. Samuel Matthews, the bathrooms in his home were self-cleaning, an amenity Cornwall was glad for under the circumstances.

All he need do was seal the bathroom door shut and manipulate a few dials to engage the clean-cycle. From the ceiling of the lavatory, and from each of two adjoining walls, nozzles would open and high-powered jets of soapy water would let loose. A few moments later, all the water would be flushed out through a drain in the floor and a blast of hot air would bake the ceramic surfaces to a shine.

Mentally preparing himself for the worst, Cornwall rolled up Sam's sleeve, found a good vein, and injected him with the first shot of De-Tox. A second would come an hour later, and a third an hour after that. These inoculations would not only sober Sam up, they would make the thought of imbibing more tortan so repulsive his habit should be broken for good!

When Sam vomited between shots two and three, Cornwall knew he had made the right decision moving him into the toilet.

By 3 p.m. some of the color had returned to Sam's face. A short while later, he had made it back into the study from the bathroom sink. Propping himself up against the wall, Sam squinted his eyes as if he were unable to focus.

The clean-cut visitor was the first to speak. He had to raise his voice to be heard over the sound of the toilet's cleaning mechanism. "Dr. Matthews, my name is Agent Nicholas Cornwall of the Commonwealth Secret Service. I have been . . . "

"By what right do you break into my house and inject me with foreign fluids?" the older man objected confusedly.

"I am a duly authorized . . . "

"Answer me, boy! By what right?" Dr. Sam shouted. "And what the hell did you do with my tortan-whiskey? Land's sakes, boy, can't you see I'm in *pain*?"

Disappointed that Sam was being so contrary, Cornwall again tried to explain. "Sir, I am a duly authorized agent of Her Majesty and . . . "

"Her Majesty?" Sam exclaimed. "What in tarnation does the *Queen* have to do with it? This is Zealand, not Britain! We haven't been part of the Commonwealth for two hundred years! Now listen, you limey bastard, get out of my house, and I mean now!"

Sam moved as if to forcibly eject Agent Cornwall from the premises. But it was a laughable impossibility. Unless, of course, one took Sam's atrociously bad breath into account. But even then, there was no way he could force Cornwall to leave. Sam was more than twice the man's age, and in a weakened condition to boot!

Patiently pushing the older man aside, Cornwall said, "I'm not going anywhere! I'm here about your daughter."

At that, the color ran from Sam's face. He sat down heavily, took a deep breath, then asked the hardest question of his life. "Is she . . . dead?"

"Well, sir, we don't actually know."

"Then what's this all about?"

"It's about one of our best agents," Cornwall explained, picking his words carefully.

"And who might that be? BC?"

"Yes, sir, one and the same. Dr. Matthews . . . "

"Call me Sam," he said, a friendly tone coming into his voice.

"Sam, I am Agent Nicholas Cornwall of Commonwealth Intelligence. We have been informed that BC has been taken prisoner by Overlord Ling and that his ship, the *Tikkidiw*, has been found and towed to Sri Lanka. We believe . . . "

"And my daughter?" Sam interrupted. "What has become of my daughter?"

Cornwall didn't answer.

"Damnit, man, *what?*"

Lowering his eyes, Cornwall asserted, "Honestly, Sam, we don't know."

"Then why the hell are you here?"

"J wants to move you to a safe house," Cornwall said, his sandy-colored hair falling across his forehead.

Annoyed, the older man ambled down the hallway in the direction of his grand sitting room. Cornwall followed close behind.

"I'm sick and tired of hearing what J wants!" an exasperated Sam murmured, taking a chair. "What about what *Sam* wants?"

On a table next to him was a portrait of his daughter. He looked at it, but did not see. Even now, his head was still swimming from the ill-effects of the tortan stupor; only two hours ago he could have passed for dead in the study of his manor.

"It's not that easy," Cornwall answered. "They have BC. They have the ship. J doesn't want you captured as well."

"I thought those tiny red vitamin pills were supposed to keep me safe," Sam said, surveying his wonderful collection of statues and the like. It was an eclectic mixture of antiquities and objets d'art including a mummy case, a thousand-year-old suit of jousting armor, and his favorite, an erotic bronze sculpture of a naked woman consumed by passion.

"The pills would help us pinpoint your location, but only I can keep you safe. Now, if you'll just direct me to your dresser, I'll pack a few of your things. We'll leave after first light in the morning."

"This is bribery!" Sam complained. "Blackmail!"

"London thought you might see it that way. Nevertheless, they felt you still would come without putting up too much of a fuss."

"And they are correct," Sam agreed. "Only I need a shower first."

"Quite right, sir, and may I recommend some mouthwash as well?"

7
Aftermath

Distressed by the news that BC had been taken prisoner, Sam had trouble falling asleep that night. It wasn't so much that he cared about BC's welfare, it was that his daughter had seemingly vanished into thin air.

And it wasn't as if Sam were ungrateful for BC's efforts, or even that he was unmindful of the risks BC had taken on Carina's behalf, it was only that she was now nowhere to be found!

According to Cornwall, after BC's daring rescue, Commonwealth Intelligence had tracked the shuttle on radar to L5. A short while later, they lost all contact with the ship.

Beyond that, the only thing Cornwall had been able to tell him was that some days after the *Tikkidiw* disappeared, Overlord Ling had contacted J offering to ransom BC, a proposition J respectfully declined. No mention was ever made as to Carina's whereabouts, and as far as J was officially concerned, she was now either dead or else a prisoner of war along with BC. Apparently, it had not occurred to anyone except Sam that there was another, less catastrophic possibility—*perhaps she was holed up on Mars!*

Still, he couldn't help but worry about what had become of her. Sam had been without a wife for a good many years now, and Carina was the only family he had left.

As Sam lay there in bed that night unable to sleep, he tortured himself over more than just Carina's disappearance. He had never yet quite been able to come to grips with the death of Fornax. The truth be known, Sam blamed himself! He, after all, had been the one who had sent Fornax to see Lester in the first place. And though Sam couldn't possibly have known it at the time, by then Lester was already in bed with the Devil, a horrifying circumstance which had ultimately cost Fornax his life!

For hours, Sam lay awake, agonizing over that grim turn of events. Thinking back upon Lester's first "death" as a supposed casualty of the Great War, Sam wished that his nefarious brother had *stayed* dead, that he had never resurfaced in Auckland that rainy afternoon carrying

Carina's dresser along with him.

Sam sighed with remorse, cursing Fornax's premature death. What a waste of a brilliant intellect! And to think, he'd never had the chance to tell young Fornax how much he had grown to like him! Hell, there might have even been a chance for Fornax and Carina to have gotten together! Now it would never happen!

As the night wore on, Sam began to dwell more and more on his daughter. Though he had often cautioned her to speak her radical ideas in whispers, he had always found it hard to muffle her enthusiasm for science, or to stifle her zeal for discovery.

"Ideas are more powerful than things," he would say, afraid that Carina would attract naysayers like the troublesome Dr. Janz.

"The status quo hates to be upset," he had warned, afraid that she would be branded as a heretic.

But she wouldn't have any of it!

Carina's controversial newhuman theory pitted a handful of "breakthrough" humans against billions-upon-billions of deeply entrenched "status quo" people who weren't apt to surrender their planet without a fight.

Sam recognized that, for a lucky few, escape to another world was the only sensible course of action. But how to decide who to take and who to leave behind? How to decide who was worthy and who was not? Playing God distressed Sam to no end.

When Noah loaded his famous ark, he surely faced an equally tough dilemma. Since cows always traveled in herds, surely more than two showed up to board his ark. As a consequence, he was compelled to select the "best" two from among them.

But on what basis is a cow "best"? The fattest? The smartest? The one with the longest tail? The biggest teats? The one most eager to *go?*

How did Noah decide?

Sam debated the paradox with himself. Wasn't Nasha the victim of some sick pervert's ideas as to what constituted a "good" or a "bad" gene?

Weren't Carina's notions about signature genes *equally* reprehensible?

Weren't her ideas little more than a high-tech version of those damnable six-pointed stars the Nazis had sewn to the garments of twentieth century Jews?

Sam considered this last question for a moment, then exclaimed his answer out loud.

"No!"

There *was* a difference, and an important one! The Jews in their time—and Nasha in hers—were butchered by xenophobes invoking their own particular brand of genetics as an excuse for slaughtering others. Migration, on the other hand, no matter *how* selective, would be invoking genetics as an excuse for *promoting* life, offering the immigrants not death, but a new lease on existence.

Sam thought of his own native land, America. In *her* time she had been great because she openly accepted wave after wave of immigrants, people who had been persecuted in their own countries for having been too smart or too dumb or too pious or too swarthy or too something, yet people determined to be free. These alleged misfits jealously guarded their newfound freedoms and zealously defended their freshly-earned right to unabashedly practice capitalism. The resulting prosperity lasted for half a millennium! It was only after a well-organized bunch of bigots came to power in the middle of the twenty-fourth century—choking off immigration in the name of genetic purity—that the American dream finally came to an end! After that it was all downhill.

Realizing that in his present state sleep would never come, Sam switched on his bedside lamp, swung his legs out over the side of the bed, and sat up, still wrestling with what to make of his daughter.

Maybe Carina was on the right track after all, he thought, keeping quiet so as not to wake Cornwall. Maybe migration *was* the right solution.

And what of Carina? Where had she gone? What had become of her? Surely, if she were still alive, she would have tried to contact him by now!

A tear came to his eye. He choked it back.

God, how he missed her! If only she hadn't looked so much like her mother. If only . . .

His eyes misted and Sam started to cry. But the painful rush of memories wouldn't stop!

"French Canadian bastards!" he bellowed to the empty room between sobs. "Purist misfits! Why did you take her from me? Oh, Nasha, sweet Nasha, you were such a gentle spirit. Is my daughter lost to me as well?"

Getting a grip on himself, Sam made up his mind. He couldn't go back with Cornwall in the morning—*he had to find his daughter!*

Sam tiptoed downstairs so as not to disturb his house guest. The sun was just peeking above the horizon. Though he couldn't know it yet, events were about to spin totally out of control!

8
Hostage

Tired eyes notwithstanding, it felt good to be up at dawn. The day's humidity still hugged the ground. Then too, the traditional insects of the season had not yet had a chance to begin harassing the good citizens of North Cape. In other words, it was a perfect day for Samuel Matthews to make a run for it!

The man hadn't felt this alive in weeks, and for the first time in a long while Sam took a moment's pleasure in the red and orange tulips which bordered the front of his house by the hundreds. Loitering aimlessly about on the veranda of his estate, Sam drank in the cool morning air while he plotted how to slip unnoticed past the guards posted just outside his main gate. Good men predict, he reminded himself confidently, but great ones act!

Sam's unruly hair and wide smile gave him an air of youthful rebelliousness, this despite his bloodshot eyes from a fitful night without sleep. Performing his morning ritual, he poured himself a measure of juice, and, without even thinking, downed his daily red vitamin pill, courtesy of J.

But no sooner had he done so than he realized his mistake. *He couldn't very well make a clean escape with a locator-beacon chirping merrily away in his belly!*

Cursing his stupidity, Sam racked his brain for a quick way to bring it back up. But before he could, something out of the ordinary caught his attention. A coverall-clad gardener was hard at work near the entrance to his manor. In his hands was a pair of pruning shears. The man was occupied trimming a row of shrubs.

Donning his eyeglasses for a better look, Sam thought it curious, curious indeed!

It wasn't that the presence of a gardener on his grounds was unusual in and of itself, only that Sam didn't *have* a gardener, at least not for the moment. Last week, in the midst of a drunken fit during his most recent bout with tortan, he had fired the landcare company over some piddling thing. He was certain he'd never taken the time to replace the one he dismissed.

Warily keeping his eye on the light-haired fellow busily pruning bushes, Sam stepped off the veranda and started across the immense lawn in that direction. The freshly-cut grass was still damp with morning dew.

Perhaps one of J's men got bored playing lookout and took it upon himself to tidy up the place a bit, Sam speculated as he meandered slowly in that direction. On second thought, that was absurd! J's people had been nothing if not freeloaders since they first arrived!

From where he was standing, halfway across the lawn, Sam could not see the hedge-trimmer's face. The stranger clearly had the blonde hair of a SKANDIAN, though just as clearly, he was *not* wearing the standard uniform of a British sentry.

Curiouser and curiouser, Sam reflected, considering the possibilities. He was starting to get a bad feeling about this. J's people had been instructed to stay *outside* the gate at all times. Not only that, he had never seen a one of them out of uniform before! Who could this be? he wondered, thinking that perhaps he should return at once to the house and wake Cornwall.

Unfortunately, Sam never got the chance.

He had advanced only a few more steps when all mayhem broke loose!

Suddenly, and without warning, an enormous gcar pounded through the front gate at high speed, sending sections of wrought-iron flying in every direction!

As the automobile sped through the gateway, the two Brits standing guard outside the fence opened fire. Their shells bounced off the gcar's ponderous, armored frame as if they were made of rubber!

Then, moments later, their impotent offense was answered. Bullets spewed out at them from an automatic weapon mounted on the tail of the gcar. Unprotected, the two men didn't stand a chance!

The gasoline-powered sedan sped up the driveway, skidding across the wet lawn to where Sam stood, paralyzed. By then, the gardener had dropped to the ground in an attempt to avoid being struck by ricochetting cartridges.

A pair of beefy men with mean-looking haircuts jumped from the vehicle. As they approached Sam, he got a whiff of the gcar's exhaust fumes. He didn't need an introduction to know that these two gangsters were in the Overlord's employ!

Sam never had a chance to yell for help. One of the two goons grabbed him from behind while the other sprayed a dose of knockout gas into his bewildered face. Collapsing instantly into the first man's arms, Sam found himself being tossed into the back seat of the big sedan. He was now the prisoner of Overlord Ling!

As the gcar whisked Sam away, the stunned groundskeeper got up, brushed himself off, and ran over to where the two guards lay dead. Rifling through their pockets, he found a palm-sized directional finder on each man. There could be only one explanation: *If the sentries were carrying finders, Sam had to have been tagged with a locator!*

Taking one of the finders in hand, the man extended the antenna, clicked on the finder, and listened for the telltale signal. It promptly commenced pinging-out distance and direction readings.

Satisfied that the directional finder was in working order, the SKANDIAN strapped it to a harness on the handlebars of his moped. He then smashed the second finder with his boot, hurriedly mounted his moped, and took up the pursuit as fast as the motorbike's little solar-powered engine would carry him. It never occurred to him to bother picking up either of the guards' weapons. In his saddlebag was a blaster of his own design, one with a lot more stopping power.

Having been finally woken up by all the commotion, Cornwall bounced out of bed and chased down the stairs in his skivvies. Arriving on the veranda too late to be of much good, he stood there helpless, trying to re-create what had happened.

Now that the Overlord had both Sam and BC, *everyone's* future looked rather dim! The worst part was, how was he going to explain it all to J?

• • •

She lay prone on the padded bench, her ankles hooked under a restraining bar.

Straining against the burden of a heavy barbell, the muscles of her washboard stomach rippled as she extended her arms yet one more time. Her lithe body glistened with the sweat of an extended workout.

When the comm buzzed, she had been at her calisthenics for nearly an hour—first the pushups, then the weights, then the situps, then the weights once more. Not willing to break her routine, she didn't stop to answer it, pausing instead to hear the caller's message between reps.

"Honestly, Marona," the Overlord complained into the machine, "this is the third time I've called. Surely, you've gotten my messages by now. For God's sake, why won't you answer my calls? How many times must I apologize for your father's death? Look, I'm sorry, but now I have someone—actually, two someones—who should interest you. If you'll just do me this one favor, I'll *give* you the man who murdered Whitey. Please call me at your first . . . "

Flicking the heavy barbell into its V-shaped cradle like it was nothing, Marona flew to the comm with the speed and agility of a panther.

"*Who,* damnit?" she yelled into the receiver before Ling could hang up. "Who killed my father? I want to tear the man's eyes out!"

"Not so fast, little one," he teased, knowing he had her exactly where he wanted her. "You will get what you want; but I will get what I want first."

"Listen, ding-a-Ling," she said, knowing how angry that made him. "Don't toy with me! My father and I are . . . were . . . very close. I *want* the man who killed him." There was determination in her voice.

"All in good time," he retorted craftily, his yellow skin looking more sinister than ever. "But first . . . "

"I know, I know," she interrupted impatiently, "but first, you have a job for me." Wiping the sweat from her forehead with the back of her hand, she asked, "Well, what is it already?"

"You've worked undercover for me in Afghanistan before; I need your expertise there again."

"Dreadful country," she mumbled, shivering ever so slightly.

"Yes," he agreed, his voice fading to a whisper. "My son died there, you know."

"How sad," she declared in an uncaring voice. "But what do you need me for? I thought you squashed the rebellion?"

"No, I'm afraid not—the Afghans don't squash that easily," Ling admitted. "But this isn't about the war, this is about the Fornax Battery."

Marona laughed. "Don't you have that *yet?* Dad always said you were a dufus." Chuckling again, she said, "And you expect *me* to find this Battery for you? In Afghanistan of all places?"

"No, you impertinent witch!" the Overlord exploded, finally at his wit's end. "I *have* the damn thing!"

"Then what do you need *me* for?"

"It won't work!" he exclaimed. "A piece is missing, a coupling of some sort, and we have no way of knowing its thickness or its span. I need you to seduce one Samuel Matthews and see if he can't be persuaded to help us fix the damn thing."

"And I suppose this Matthews is a young strapping stud, eager for nonstop sex with a hot bimbooker like me," she sneered viciously.

"Not hardly. But the man is rich!"

"And where am I to meet up with this burnt-out ole geezer?"

"In prison. I'm having him sent to my cousin's dungeon."

"I have to seduce this bloke behind bars?" she questioned, strands of shiny hair falling across her fine-looking shoulders. "Sounds kinky!" she delighted, warming to the idea. "I *love* it!"

"No, that's not what I meant! You'll be incarcerated along with a bunch of authentic real-live rebels. A short while later, Sam'll be dumped into the prison cell along with you and the others. I have already been in contact with the cagemaster in Farah, and he is expecting you."

"Then what?" she asked, intrigued by this cat-and-mouse game.

"Then you wait."

"Wait? Wait for what?"

"Our friend J doesn't want me to have Sam. I expect he'll send a team to rescue the man, and by the time he does, Matthews—as you call him—will insist on keeping you at his side."

"And if the Brits don't show?"

The Overlord didn't have an answer.

"Listen, Ling, the only reason I'm even considering doing this is so I can get my hands on the bastard who killed my daddy. Don't think for a *moment* I won't come after you if you cross me!"

"Marona, I have no intention of crossing you," he promised. "None whatsoever."

• • •

Cornwall was leaning across the counter in Sam's kitchen as he spoke into the comm. He had a frown on his face. "The damndest thing is, I came down here to *rescue* the man. Now look what's happened!"

"A darn shame," J conceded without conviction.

"Well what are we going to do about it?" Agent Nicholas Cornwall demanded, frustrated by his boss's nonchalant attitude.

"Not a thing," J replied with cold disdain. He was more than a little irritated to have an underling question his motives.

"I don't understand how you can say that," Cornwall barked, angry with himself for having ever let Sam out of his sight. "It's one thing to throw BC to the wolves—he's one of us, he knows the risks—but Matthews is a civilian, damnit! I could never forgive myself if he were tortured."

"I'll not bargain with terrorists, or be held hostage to Overlord demands," J said. "It's a moot point in any event—we don't have anything to offer up to the Chinese in trade."

"But if they already have the ship, what do they want Sam for?" Even as he spoke, Agent Cornwall let his eyes roam around the kitchen looking for the bottle of red vitamin pills. If Sam had taken one before being kidnapped, it might still be possible to track him. Cornwall kept that possibility to himself.

"Frankly, I don't know why they snatched him," J admitted, his box-like frame preempting the entire office. "My guess is the Battery doesn't work, perhaps never did. BC must have disconnected something or other and they haven't been able to beat the truth out of him yet. Perhaps. . . "

"But, sir, Sam can't possibly help them fix it. He's an economist, for Christ sake! He doesn't even know which end of a hammer is up!"

"Don't you think I'm aware of that?" J sighed, praying that this conversation would end so he could get back to more pressing work.

"But, *sir*, they'll kill him!" Cornwall said, not backing down. It was beginning to dawn on him that J wasn't about to lift a finger to help save the man. If Sam was to come out of this thing alive, Cornwall would have to get the job done himself.

"I can't help it if they kill him," J replied dispassionately. "It's a matter of longstanding policy never to bargain with . . . "

"But, *sir!*" Cornwall insisted, raising his voice this time. "We saved the man's life! It hardly seems appropriate to abandon him *now*. Couldn't we bend policy just this once?"

"Damnit, man, no!" J shot back even before the younger man could finish. "Look, Nicholas, I admire your loyalty. And I understand your guilt, I really do—he was, after all, snatched right out from under your very own nose—but the answer is still no!"

"Sam is expendable then?" Cornwall trembled, though the answer was frightfully obvious.

"Indeed," came the calm reply.

As Cornwall hung up the comm, he calculated the odds. Should he dare risk it? He had worked once before with an airchop pilot who was active in the Afghan underground, a fellow who, while not actually in the employ of the British, was sympathetic to their cause. The man's name was Harsha Gandu.

9
Abbargan

His mind enveloped in a dense fog, his brain hammered by a punishing headache, Sam courageously squinted his eyes trying to fathom where he was and how he got there.

Studying his surroundings, he realized that he was in a prison—or more accurately, a dungeon—complete with dank air, nasty-looking spiders, and a mean-looking guard seated out front. Hemmed in by smelly, unshaven men with husky builds and angry dispositions, Sam decided against introducing himself.

Very much out of his element, he quietly listened as the other prisoners argued amongst themselves. It wasn't long, however, before he recognized that several of the men were in fact women, albeit tough-looking women, but females nevertheless. Like the men, they had powerful legs and well-developed arms; and like the men, they were eyeing him warily.

After awhile, one of the swarthy men came over to confront him. "My name is Harsha Gandu," the robust man began tersely. "I am an Afghan freedom fighter. Who are you, and why are you here?"

Before Sam could even answer, the man who had introduced himself continued his interrogation. He wore that look peculiar to men who were used to being obeyed without question. It was not the same as anger, it was more like a thundercloud just before a storm.

"Are you a spy?" he asked, his eyes narrowing. "Did the Overlord put you in here with us so you could spy for him?"

"No," Sam chuckled as he extended his hand, "I'm not a spy. My name is Samuel Matthews. I'm a Zealander, and I'm not even sure why I was brought here—wherever *here* is. I suppose they intend to hold me for ransom."

"Ransom?" one of the other rebels exclaimed doubtfully. "You expect us to believe that you've been *kidnapped?*"

His head still pounding from the knockout gas, Sam angrily replied. "Do I look like a freedom fighter, you dolt?"

Growling as if he might strike Sam, the second prisoner addressed the first. "He's nothing but a lousy spy, Harsha. Let's kill the bastard!"

"Just a minute, Lotha!" Harsha intervened. "We can kill him later if you please, but let's first hear what the old man has to say." Then, turning his attention back to Sam, he said, "If you're being held for ransom, old man, you had better hope your friends pay up soon. According to the cagemaster, we're all due to be shot the day after tomorrow."

"And what crime merits such punishment?" Sam queried, astonished that in this day and age someone should be put up before a firing squad.

"We're fighting to drive the Chinese out of our country once and for all!" one of the women asserted as she stepped forward into the light.

Sam studied her face. He quickly decided that beneath the thin layer of dirt and grime she was rather attractive. When he spoke, his tone was friendly. "Well then, I guess we *both* have problems with Overlord Ling."

"What possible problem could a soft-bred Zealander like yourself have with Overlord Ling?" Harsha snapped indignantly, his shoulder-length hair bouncing from side to side as he spoke.

"Actually, I'm an American by birth," Sam explained, his face curling into a frown. "My problem is, I've been caught in the middle of a property dispute. I've got Great Britain on one side and Ling on the other. It has become a bit of a tug-of-war with each side believing I have a piece of property in my possession which rightfully belongs to them. But the truth of the matter is . . . I don't have it."

"He's lying!" Lotha bellowed out from across the cell, his loud threatening voice echoing against the stone walls. Lotha was a big, scary man with frightening features. His speech was slurred and nasal, probably the result of his misshapen skull.

Ignoring the cretinous outburst, Harsha addressed Sam. "So just how do the British fit in with all this?"

In his typically professorial manner, Sam explained. "The history of hatred between China and Britain stretches back nearly a thousand years to a time when the first English ships visited Chinese ports. The subsequent traffic in illegal opium eventually led to open warfare between the two nations. When the Chinese destroyed the opium stored in British warehouses, the English responded by seizing Hong Kong, and later, advancing against Peking. The ensuing 'Opium War' sealed their fate.

"In the twentieth century, with the rise of communism in China, and with the continuing decline of the British empire, England was no longer able to project her power half a world away. Stymied, Britain reluctantly agreed to cede control of Hong Kong back to China so long as the Chinese agreed to guarantee the civil liberties of the Hong Kongers.

"It wasn't long afterwards, however, that China reneged on her earlier promise and burnt the city to the ground, slaughtering millions of former Commonwealth citizens in the process. And if that weren't enough to make them bitter enemies, during Rontana's time, the Royal British Air Command leveled Shanghai with saturation bombing, ostensibly to snuff out armies sympathetic to Rontana's cause.

"And more recently," Sam concluded, "during the Great War, China sank a major part of the American fleet, striking a lethal blow against a key British ally."

"So the British hate the Chinese," Harsha retorted sarcastically. "What else is new? And what the hell does that have to do with *you?*"

"You sound bitter," Sam noted, seeing the distant look in Harsha's eye.

"I *am* bitter! We've been at war with the Overlords since before I can remember . . . And you *still* haven't answered my question!"

"I knew an Afghan once," Sam recalled, "and he had the same fire in his belly as you do. Ravi Gandu was his name. I suppose he was no relation of yours, though. Gandu's a rather common name in your land, is it not?"

"My father, perhaps. How did you know him?"

"We met at the university," Sam replied, testing out this Harsha by being intentionally vague.

"In Canada?" Harsha volunteered, hoping to pass the test. "Before his death my father often spoke of an American who befriended him. Maybe you were that man."

Thinking that Harsha's claim to be Ravi's son was coincidental almost to the point of absurd, Sam said, "Ravi's dead?"

Harsha nodded his head but added no details.

"My condolences. Ravi and I were once friends."

Though he didn't believe a word Harsha said, Sam thought back to his college days in Calgary and to his classmate, Ravi Gandu. Although the Canadians had been more than happy to accept Ravi's money for tuition, they thought of Afghanistan as "that mongrel nation." Their repugnant Purist-Opportunity Laws had prevented Ravi from remaining in Alberta upon graduation as Sam had, so Ravi was compelled to return to his home country. Except for exchanging a few polite letters after his deportation, Sam never saw or heard from him again.

Returning to the present before other, more painful memories could resurface, Sam inquired, "Tell me, who are all these other nice people?" As he spoke, his eyes darted around the room-sized cell trying to find at least one other friendly face.

"Don't answer this old man's questions!" Lotha shouted. "He's a plant, I tell you! A spy!"

"Really, Lotha, he's practically family," Harsha countered. "Sam, those you see around you are like yourself—prisoners of war. We don't all know one another; you see, many of us were captured in different skirmishes. Even so, I assure you, we're all fighting for the same cause."

"Is that so?" Sam wondered aloud.

"We are a proud people," Harsha continued, "but if you knew my father, you already know this to be true. An Afghan male admits his inferiority to no one; nor does he call any man 'lord'."

"As in *Overlord?*"

10
Badal

"Yes, Sam, as in *Overlord.*"

Harsha had searched the faces of his fellow prisoners before answering. There was an undeniable sadness there, one that couldn't be quantified. "The Chinese have tried to emasculate us by outlawing our Code of Honor."

"Which is what?"

"It's just macho idiocy!" the attractive but grimy-faced girl said.

"And what is *your* name?" Sam asked, flirting. "I see a pretty face under that layer of dirt."

Smiling, she reached out her hand to shake his. "Marona is what they call me—Marona Savitar. Glad to make your acquaintance."

The ice broken, the others introduced themselves in rapid succession: Lotha, Saron, Navi, Buddha, and Ratna, all with last names Sam could not hope to remember, or pronounce.

Except for the long hair, Harsha vaguely reminded Sam of Fornax—bright and energetic. Lotha was a large man of few words, and apparently, fewer thoughts. Navi seemed a bit undersized for a soldier, though he lacked nothing in the conviction department. Marona was an articulate woman blessed with an extraordinary physical presence, yet possessing the most graceful, gentle demeanor Sam had encountered in a good many years. She reminded him of Nasha, and had he not been thirty years her senior, he would have been tempted to make a play for her. Instead, he tried to put her out of his mind.

"So, tell me about this macho Code of Honor the Overlord wants to suppress so badly," Sam said, averting his eyes from hers.

"It's a three-part code, really," Harsha explained. "The first element is hospitality—what we call 'milmastia' in our language. It is the obligation to protect, with one's life if necessary, the person and property of your guest. If your guest takes refuge with you, it is your milmastia obligation to take up his cause as well."

Navi continued from where Harsha stopped. "The second element of our code is the 'badal'—the obligation to avenge the spilling of blood.

A badal is not just a matter of a death-for-a-death, but rather the more singular tooth-for-a-tooth."

"These revenge-quarrels can last for generations!" Lotha enthusiastically added. "We take our inspiration from men like the brave unknown soldier who, despite overwhelming odds, downed an Overlord airchop with a single shot before being killed himself. These are *our* heroes!"

"Yes, boys, that's all the macho stuff," Marona interjected, enchanting Sam with her eyes, "but the *third* element—the one which the men sometimes forget—is the obligation to be merciful."

Picking up from where Navi left off, Marona elaborated. "Except for adulteresses, one does not kill women, nor small children, nor poets, nor Hindus, nor priests, nor men who have taken sanctuary in a mosque. And except where a blood feud is involved—and here only blood money will discharge the debt—mercy is to be granted at the intercession of a woman, or a priest, or one's opponent in battle if he begs for it."

Sam had a confession to make. "Despite my love of history and despite my friendship with Ravi, I never took the time to learn much about his culture. To be honest, except for a few words introduced into English, like kebab and khaki and khan, I guess I didn't even know Afghanistan *had* a culture. For that, I sincerely apologize."

Harsha nodded his head knowingly as Sam went on. "Even so, I respect your Code. The Chinese, on the other hand, do not. Nevertheless, they cannot conquer your land unless they first conquer the ideas which bind your people together. Ideas have always been more powerful than things, and *that* is why they wish to ban your Code."

"No one will conquer *us!*" Lotha exclaimed defiantly. "The Greeks tried, the Persians tried, the Huns, the Muslims, the Russians, the British tried *twice!* No one succeeded. Our Code has seen us through the hard times. Our vices are revenge and obstinance! Our virtues are frugality, hard work, and bravery!"

"None of which will protect us from the bullets of the firing squad," Navi reminded him.

Sam was impressed by what he heard. Though many had sought to, no one had been able to wipe out the resilient Afghans. And despite much hardship, there had been no Diaspora as there had been with the Jews, no thousand-year imprisonment on the barren reservations as had been the fate of the Amerinds, no long march to the sea as there had been with the Koreans. To the contrary, the tenacious Afghans had held their ground time and time again, repulsing scores of would-be invaders at every turn. It occurred to him that that resilience, that toughness of spirit, might make them perfect candidates to tackle the colonization of Mars.

Taking a deep breath, Sam gambled whether or not it was the right time to broach the subject. He decided that it was.

"If all that remains of your future is a firing squad, you might consider what I have to tell you. I know of a place where you would be free to practice your way of life without fear or persecution. In fact, I was headed there myself before I was kidnapped."

"The old man is nuts!" Lotha declared rudely. "He's dreaming! There *is* no such place on Earth."

"Actually, I'm *not* dreaming. But you are right in one respect: there is no such place on Earth."

And then Sam proceeded to tell them about Fornax and Lester and BC and Carina. And about Mars, especially Mars.

They all listened enthusiastically, but none more closely than Marona.

And yet, with no way out of that terrible prison, it was all so much idle talk. Like BC before him, Sam was on his own. In this game, he was just a pawn; the Brits were not about to rescue him. They were not explorers, these British, they were inventors; they were not adventurers, they were conquerors. But above all else, they were administrators. They had no deep abiding interest in space. From here on out, Sam would have to fend for himself!

11

People Come Crashing Through Open Doors

The word "Afghan" came to English from the Sanskrit "Avagana" which itself was derived from the Sumerian "Ab-bar-Gan" meaning "High Country." As he drove the torturous mountain roads, one eye on the guardrail and the other on the directional finder strapped to the handlebars of his moped, Sven Rutland, the blond-headed gardener, decided that his native land was aptly named. It had been so long since he deserted her, it all seemed strangely new.

First by moped, then by tube, then by moped again, Sven had followed the ping of Sam's locator to the city of Farah deep in the Afghan heartland and eventually to an ivy-covered, stone-walled citadel at the edge of town. He drove past it and parked behind a nearby clump of trees.

Dis is vhere day 'ave Sam, Sven told himself, silently practicing his SKANDIAN.

Stashed away in the saddlebag of his motorbike was a special weapon, a blaster of his own design. It could only be described as a handheld gatling gun powered by a sliver of super-charged durbinium. With Jenny, as he had come to call her, Sven could defeat a small army!

For hours he just sat there watching the fortification. A few uniformed guards came and went, but all in all, the area was uncommonly quiet.

Tank za lord! he sighed as he patiently waited for darkness.

When nightfall finally yielded a nearly moonless sky, Sven slipped across the road, stealthily approaching the prison with Jenny gripped firmly in the palm of one hand. Though this man had no formal training in espionage or other such matters, he was a sensible fellow accustomed to using his head.

Entering the stone dungeon by the same door he had seen a pair of guards use earlier in the evening, Sven steeled his muscles for a confrontation. He expected to find a sentry posted just inside, and was immediately suspicious when there was none. He had no way of knowing, of course, that the cagemaster had been instructed by Overlord Ling to keep the guard light, this to serve the Overlord's own sinister purposes.

Beyond the door was a single passageway. Pressing himself flat against the cold stone wall of the dimly-lit corridor, Sven crept down the hallway until it opened up into a cavernous room some seventy meters across and at least ten from floor to ceiling.

Stationed at the opposite wall of the mammoth chamber a lone night-watchman dozed sleepily behind a disfigured old desk. In the shadows beyond, Sven could make out the rusted iron bars of a huge prison cell. Several persons were milling about inside the great metal cage, but the lighting was so poor, he couldn't tell if Sam was among them.

Doubting whether his aim was good enough to hit the cagemaster at this range, Sven swallowed hard and boldly started across the immense hall towards the seated guard. He didn't get more than a few steps before a voice behind him ordered, "Halt! Who goes there?"

Freezing in his tracks, his right hand clasped tightly around the unusual-looking gun, Sven cursed his recklessness. Meanwhile, across the room in front of him, the man at the desk rose groggily to his feet, embarrassed to have been caught off-guard. Sven prayed that it was too dark in the dungeon for the guard to see the blaster he was holding in his hand.

Again the stern voice behind him sounded. "Who goes there?"

Sven heard the hesitant footfalls of the newcomer approaching him from behind; in front of him, the watchman at the desk drew his piece. Suddenly, Sven was out of options—*he had to act!*

Dropping to a crouch, he spun around and discharged his weapon at the man to his rear. The short, focused burst of high-energy neutrons hit the guard, blasting his very molecules into a fine mist of blood and guts!

Sven was mortified by the results! This was the first time he'd ever had to use his gun on a human!

Rolling over onto his belly, Sven took careful aim now on the stunned sentry standing motionless next to his desk. He didn't fire, though, figuring that if he missed his quarry, he could easily hit one of the prisoners in the cell beyond. Rather than run that risk, Sven decided to bluff. And, to avoid being misunderstood, he temporarily dispensed with his fake SKANDIAN accent.

"Throw down your weapon!" he ordered, getting to his feet. "Let go of it, damn it, or I'll blow your head clean off!"

The other man didn't flinch.

"I mean it!" Sven yelled as he took a few tentative steps toward the cagemaster. "Throw down your weapon or you are *history!*"

Still the night-watchman ignored the order.

By this time, Sven had approached close enough to see the determination in his opponent's face. A sixth sense told him he was about to be fired upon. With sad reluctance, Sven fired first.

Though the energy-pulse did not strike the guard squarely, the stream of neutrons blew him to vapor nevertheless. And, as the man melted into nothingness, a disquieting cheer erupted from the caged warriors.

Sven didn't feel much like a hero. In fact, it suddenly dawned on him that he had a completely *new* problem on his hands. Not only did he have absolutely no idea who these other people were, he had no way of rescuing them all. His moped was large enough to carry only him and Sam, not a horde of a dozen or more!

Though the rebels were impatient to be released from their cell, Sven wasn't about to let them loose until he was sure he had what he'd come for. Interrogating the darkness, he again slipped into his fractured SKANDIAN.

"Sam, vhere are you?"

Sam answered from the shadows. "I'm back here! Is Cornwall with you? Is Carina okay?"

"Cornball? Vho is Cornball?"

"Aren't you from Commonwealth Intelligence?" Sam asked, confused.

"Hell no!" Sven declared emphatically. "Shtand back! I 'ave to blast za door."

As soon as the prisoners moved away, Sven leveled his remarkable gun on the giant lock, vaporizing it, plus most of the metal around it. Even the nearby bars glowed red for seconds afterward.

"We're free!" Lotha shouted as he bounded from the cell. "We're free!"

"Free to do *what?*" Harsha challenged in a less than enthusiastic, but levelheaded tone.

"Free to return to our base camp," Lotha replied indignantly. "Free to kill more *Chinese!*"

"And lead these strangers to our hideaway?" Harsha asked, remaining cautious. "Doesn't it strike you as odd that one man was able to waltz in here single-handedly and set us free? Don't be a fool, Lotha! This SKANDIA with the dark eyes is *dangerous!* Didn't you see what he did to the cagemaster with his incredible gun? He could turn it on *us* at any moment!"

Losing his accent altogether, Sven declared, "You dullards do as you please—I'm here only for Matthews." Turning to Sam, he said, "Let's get outta here!"

"Who the hell *are* you?" an exasperated Sam asked. "And where did your strange accent go?"

12
Rebirth

"Sam, don't you *recognize* me?" Sven exclaimed. "The blonde hair and accent are just a ruse! It's me! Fornax!"

"You're a liar! Fornax is dead, God rest his soul. And it's repulsive—nay, *outrageous*—that you should just sit there and try to trick me that way."

"Sam! Listen to me. Listen to my *voice!* Look at my *eyes!* Can't you see that it's true?"

Caught between reality and hope, between fact and fiction, Sam's usually keen mind stalled. "No, Fornax was killed by the same blast which nearly did me in."

Turning to the brutish Lotha, Sam declared, "I do not know this man. He's an imposter. You'd be well advised to take him as your prisoner."

A big grin descended upon Lotha's face, but before the big Afghan could move against him, Sven spoke up to defend himself. "Butterflies cause tornadoes."

Dredged from the past like that, his words stunned Sam with their clarity.

"The status quo hates to be upset," Sven quoted, seeing that these private expressions were having their intended effect.

Sam couldn't believe his ears. "It *is* true!" he said, squinting his eyes as if it would help him to see better.

"Good men predict, but great men . . . ah . . . perform," Fornax exclaimed as Lotha approached, a menacing look in his eyes.

Sam chuckled and warmly extended his hand to the other man. "*Act,* Fornax—not perform. Great men *act!*"

Waving Lotha off before he could do any damage, Sam smiled. "Friends, this is Fornax Engels, the brilliant man I was telling you about. I don't know how he got here, or even where he's planning on taking us, but I'm confident he has an interesting story to tell."

"You won't be disappointed," Fornax assured him, cradling Jenny in his arms.

"Okay, then, let's hear it," Sam ordered.

"Remember that dreadful night on the moon? The night Whitey attacked us?"

"How could I forget?"

"Well, when he . . . "

Harsha interrupted. "I thought you told us this guy was dead? And what's all this crap about butterflies and tornadoes?"

"Oh, shut up and let the man speak!" Marona demanded, bracing herself for the truth regarding her father's death.

"Thank you," Sam nodded affectionately. "Please continue, Fornax."

"I was at my keyboard working when the bastard first fired at us. The damn thing scared me nearly half to death, so I headed for a locker to get my dee-dee."

"Understandably," Sam cut in. "By the way, the Brits are pretty upset about the file you left them. Your Battery doesn't work."

"Is that so?" Fornax laughed. "Imagine that. The truth of the matter is, I figured I'd stay alive a lot longer if I didn't give away my secret."

"You mean you purposely falsified the diskette?" Sam asked.

Fornax nodded.

"Good thinking!" Sam exclaimed, slapping his knee with delight. "I always knew you were a brilliant S.O.B.!" he added, suddenly tickled that Fornax had come to his rescue. "I congratulate you on your deception, young fellow. Now, back to your story. You got scared, so then what?"

"Figuring the main building would be hit sooner or later, I donned a suit and headed for the door. I made it outside okay, but the concussion from the next missile must've knocked me cold. Apparently, I rolled down an embankment and must've come to rest behind a big boulder. When I regained consciousness, everyone was gone! I guess you must have assumed I'd been blown to bits along with everything else.

"Abandoned and alone, I thought I was destined to die as soon as my oxygen ran out. That's when the miracle occurred. BC came *back!* He was searching for something, I guess it was me. By the way, where is he?"

"Finish your story," Sam urged.

Fornax continued. "Like I said, I saw him land. But by the time I'd come up the rise to greet him, he was engaged in a terrible fight with another man."

"That must have been Whitey," Sam interjected as Marona hung on his every word. "Why didn't you stop to help him?"

"It wasn't so much that I was afraid to—I couldn't. My oxygen was red-line by then. But I knew where the spare tanks of O_2 were stored in the cargo hold of the *Tikkidiw*, so I headed there straightaway. My head was pounding and I was slow; by the time I'd switched tanks and gotten myself back together, BC had lifted off. I myself became an unintended stowaway in the hold of the ship. It was a helluva bumpy ride back to Earth."

"Ouch!"

"And then some," Fornax agreed, rubbing his head. "After BC jumped out of the ship to retrieve Carina, and during the confusion while the place was under attack, I snuck away. Later, I scrounged up a fake ID, then made my way to SKANDIA. Armed with my new identity, I took a flat up north and settled in. I figured the Chinese—and perhaps the British as well—would murder or imprison poor Fornax if *he* ever surfaced again, so I've kept him under wraps ever since."

"Okay, Sven, it sounds to me like you've been using your head," Sam admitted. "But what brings you all the way out here to rescue *me?*"

Stopping a moment to gather his thoughts, Fornax smiled. "One evening, while I was on the run, I focused my telescope on Mars. I could hardly believe my eyes! She was enveloped in a sea of clouds!

"That's when I knew I had to move, and move fast. If *I* could see she had weather with *my* little telescope, anybody could. Sooner or later, someone would decide to investigate; better us than them. I figured you'd want to be in on it.

"When I arrived at your estate, there were guards posted outside your gate; I had to find another way in. That's when I hit on the idea of masquerading as your gardener. And it's a good thing too, because when the guards were shot down by the Overlord's men, I found *this* on one of them."

Fornax reached into his pocket to produce the directional finder still blinking out Sam's location.

"Of *course!*" Sam exclaimed, slapping his palm against his forehead. "The vitamins!"

"Is that where it was hidden?" Fornax exclaimed. "In your gut?"

"Well actually, I'd say it was down the hall in the head just now, but yes, that's where it was. It's like I always told you, Fornax—if you want to achieve the gift of long life, take a vitamin every day! Land's sakes, boy, what a story!"

"Yeah, what a story," Lotha agreed sarcastically.

"So what do we do now?" Sam asked.

"Yes, what's next?" Marona chimed in, delighted to finally know the name of her father's killer.

"The first order of business is to get our butts out of here!" Fornax answered.

"The *Tikkidiw*'s parked not awfully far from here," Sam volunteered.

"Really? Where?" Fornax asked, surprised. "I thought BC had the ship?"

"So far as I understand it, the ship's at the spaceport in Sri Lanka," Sam replied.

"In that case, that's where you and I are going. Is Carina there too?"

Sam shook his head as if to say, "No."

"Hold on there," Harsha interrupted, his long hair falling into his eyes. "I have no future here; I'm going with you. To Sri Lanka, and then to Mars." He spoke with conviction, mindful of the deal he had struck with Cornwall not to let Sam out of his sight.

"I'm coming too," Marona said, flashing Sam a provocative smile.

"I have no means of getting the lot of you to Sri Lanka," Fornax said, motioning for Sam to follow him. "Nor do I care to."

"It's all or none," Sam said. "If you won't take them, then leave me as well. The Afghan Code of milmastia demands it."

"What do you know of our Code?" Fornax challenged, practically revealing his nationality in the process.

"Not much, but enough to insist that we all escape together."

"I don't have papers for everyone," Fornax argued. "Plus, traveling as a group, we're bound to stick out like sore thumbs."

"That problem's easy enough to solve," Harsha interjected. "We can disguise ourselves as Chinese soldiers."

"You can't be serious?" Fornax exclaimed.

"Oh, but I am! Back at base camp we have uniforms and identification papers from Chinese prisoners we've captured in the war. Plus, we all know enough Mandarin to help us slip through enemy territory to the coast. From there it's a short trip across the bay to Sri Lanka."

Not convinced Harsha's plan would work, Fornax objected. "Making-up you swarthy types to look Oriental may be simple, but us *white* boys will not pass so easily!"

Though said in jest, the racial slur lit a fire under the Afghans. This was all the more ironic because hidden beneath Sven's guise of being a SKANDIA beat the heart of a true Afghan!

"In that case, you *white* boys will have to travel as our prisoners for the duration of the trip!" Lotha declared vehemently.

"Never!" Fornax angrily protested, leveling his weapon on Lotha's midsection. "This is getting out of hand, Sam. Let's vamoose!"

"No, Fornax!" Sam intervened. "The big baboon's right! It's the only way. Besides, with that gun of yours, you'll never be *any* man's prisoner."

Reluctantly nodding his head, Fornax lowered his blaster then led them all quietly out of the dungeon by the same route he had entered. He found it curious that they should encounter no resistance as they escaped.

• • •

"Marona, darling, I didn't expect to hear from you so soon. You must have something terribly important to report."

Speaking crisply into her wireless fieldcomm, she said, "As you predicted, oh intelligent one, a man did come to break Sam out of the donjon you stuck both of us in."

"Did you say, *a* man?" Ling asked dumbfounded. "As in, just *one* man?"

"Yes, just one man," Marona said, cupping her hand over the mouthpiece to muffle her voice. She was crouching in the shadows behind a row of bushes well away from the rebel camp.

"But that's impossible!" the Overlord exploded. "The Brits always operate in teams of two or four."

"Lord Ding-a-Ling, keep your voice down!" she snapped, afraid she'd be overheard. "I don't think this was a Commonwealth operation."

"Who, then?" he croaked, struggling not to lose his temper.

"He was a SKANDIA by the name of Sven Rutland," Marona reported. "And he carried an incredible weapon, a force gun of a make and calibre I've never encountered before."

"Sven Rutland? That name means nothing to me. But I'll have my people check the files."

"Don't bother," she said, flexing her muscles. "I'm certain it's an alias."

By intentionally pausing and volunteering nothing more, Marona succeeded in infuriating Overlord Ling even further.

"Well, woman," he exploded again, "what was the man's *real* name?"

When she didn't immediately answer, he snarled. "Out with it already!"

"He called himself Fornax," she replied indifferently.

For the first time, there was silence at the other end of the line. Marona had underestimated the impact Fornax's name would have on the man.

"Sir?" she whispered into the fieldcomm. "Did you hear me? I said his name was Fornax."

"I . . . heard . . . you," he stammered, his narrow eyes slanting even further. "But it's just . . . not possible . . . "

"Like it or not, it *was* him," she declared confidently. "I'd recognize that schnoz anywhere. Do you want him taken out?"

"To the contrary!" the Overlord said, regaining his footing. "I want him brought in undamaged! You'd better forget about avenging your father for now and bring me this Fornax instead. If you succeed, I'll make you richer than the avarice of Midas."

"And Sam?"

"Kill him. Kill 'em all!"

"But he's so cute," she cooed wantonly into the fieldcomm.

"I'm warning you, woman!" Ling began in a threatening tone.

"No, I'm warning *you!*" she blurted, fed up with his petty despotism. "You're good at giving orders, your majesty, but not so good at making up your mind. First, you want Matthews, then you want Fornax. First, I'm to *rescue* Matthews, then I'm to kill him. Frankly, I'm tired of your bullshit! From here on out, *I* decide who lives and who dies."

Furious, Marona broke the contact without ever hearing Ling's warning: "Don't underestimate him like your father did!"

13
Assault

The collection of escapees huddled together in the jungle awaiting nightfall. It had been an arduous odyssey, and Sam particularly was grateful for the break.

On the outskirts of the once-prosperous town where they had been held captive, Harsha commandeered a gtruck and drove them to the rebel camp. From there they made the torturous journey by road to Kabul where they proceeded by coal-burner, first to Bombay, and then on to the slum-city of Pondicherry on the eastern coast of Indiastan. From Pondicherry they ventured by trawler across the short stretch of ocean to the port of Talaimannar, south of Jaffna, before finally traversing the remaining distance down to the launch facility on foot. Biding their time until sunset, they now rested in the lush green forest waiting.

Fornax had a frown on his face. He had been to the launch compound several times before, and he knew that if the *Tikkidiw* was indeed there as Sam said it would be, there was only one building large enough for it to be hidden in.

"I don't like this," Fornax whispered as he, Sam, and Harsha lay prone on the grass peering through the bushes into the compound.

"What's not to like?" Sam asked, unsure what Fornax was getting at.

"The place is empty. Not a guard in sight. Normally, there would be at least two sentries in front, plus two to four more inside."

"Maybe they're on dinner break," Sam suggested, half-kidding.

Fornax glared at him. "Get serious, will you? I've met the Chinaman who runs this place, and I can tell you, Mister Kim is a stickler for detail. I smell trouble!"

"You're just tired," Sam replied. "Hell, it's been a long day for all of us. How could your Mister Kim possibly have known we were coming? And even if someone tipped him off, why would he dismiss all his guards? It would be much too easy for someone like us to happen along and steal the ship, not to mention just about everything else around here."

"Maybe it's not even here," Fornax reasoned. "Maybe it's all an elaborate trap!"

"Let me see if I have this straight. You think the Chinese cooked up this elaborate scheme just to recapture a bunch of escaped POW's?" Harsha asked.

"Don't flatter yourself," Fornax said. "They don't want *you*. They want Sam . . . or perhaps *me*."

"Now who's flattering himself?" Harsha rejoined testily. "Except for us, no one even knows you're alive!"

"Exactly," Fornax grunted, ratcheting his thumb in the direction of the other escapees. "And just how well do you know the rest of these thieves?"

"Like I told Sam back in Farah, this is the first time I've met some of these people. Lotha, Saron, and I were captured together, Navi and Marona were taken somewhere else, Inda and Ratna somewhere else yet."

"So there you have it," Fornax summarized. "Any one of them could be a mole and you might not even suspect a thing."

Finding Fornax's keen mind a welcome change from the slow-wittedness of his friend Lotha, Harsha nodded his head. "I guess so . . . but what would you have me do? Go home, turn the lot of us in, and ask them to politely line up before a firing squad?"

Warming appreciably to Harsha's sense of humor, Fornax smiled as he got up off the ground and brushed himself off. He liked the man, even on the basis of their short acquaintance. Harsha was the sort of big ugly-handsome galoot that women went for and men took orders from. "I see your point," he said. "I hope to God you see mine."

"I do," Harsha acknowledged. "And now I see some guards as well."

Sure enough, even as he spoke, two men leisurely strolled up to assume their posts outside the building which presumably housed the *Tikkidiw*. Clamped tightly beneath their arms were what looked like automatic machine guns.

Undeterred, Fornax & Company slipped past the perimeter fence and onto the grounds, edging stealthily in the direction of the sentries. No one had to remind them that in the hands of an expert, an automatic weapon was an astonishingly effective means for separating one's enemy from his life!

Fornax and Jenny bravely led the way. Once they were in close enough, it took him only seconds to vaporize the two guards. Because the blaster was silent, it made all the difference in the world. The two guards melted into nothingness without so much as a whimper!

Bolstered by the fact that they had gotten this far without an alarm being sounded, the would-be hijackers hurried to the barnlike shed. But even before Fornax flung open the hangar's doors to reveal the *Tikkidiw* smiling back at him like an old friend, he shivered with apprehension.

This had been too easy! he thought. Just like back at the prison! They *let* me get away with this!

Glancing nervously over his shoulder, Fornax cursed his stupidity. Why did he ever agree to let these thieves tag along with him? If any one of them proved now to be a rotten apple, *everyone's* life would be forfeited! How could've he been so gullible?

It couldn't be helped, he told himself. In for a dime, in for a dollar. It was time to get on with it!

Putting aside his fears as best he could, Fornax set his mind to firing-up the shuttle for takeoff. According to Sam, the ship had been brought to Sri Lanka after BC was captured, but to date, Mister Kim's engineers had been unable to figure out how to make the thing run.

While it was indeed possible for the ship to have suffered a serious malfunction somewhere along the line, the more likely scenario was that BC himself had purposefully sabotaged her, but in a simple yet easy-to-remedy way. What was hard to understand was this: If BC had in fact removed a critical part from the Battery and stuck it in his pocket—intending to reinsert it later on—the missing component would have been found on his person when he was captured. In that case, the Chinese could have easily reconnected it without any further ado. But since that's *not* what happened, there had to be another explanation!

What if BC had removed the power coupling, then hid it *onboard* the ship? Considering its small size, the coupling could've easily been overlooked. Chou Kim's men wouldn't have known what they were searching for—nor where to find it!

But Fornax knew, or at least thought he did.

Along with everything else, BC was a medic. And what better place to hide something so tiny, yet so vital, but in his kit? That was the first place Fornax thought to check.

A power coupling was nothing more than a metal O-ring. On cursory examination it looked much like a thick wedding band, only it was threaded with tiny grooves on the inner wall. Like a bolt, it could be screwed in to join two cables of different capacity. Dropped inside a medic kit, next to tweezers, scalpels, searing irons and the like, it wasn't apt to draw much attention. At least that's what Fornax thought as he searched frantically through BC's gear. But it wasn't there!

"Someone's coming!" Harsha warned as Fornax tried to figure out where to look next. "I need your blaster to hold them off!"

Just as Fornax was about to hand Jenny over to Harsha, the solution to his O-ring problem presented itself. "I can't give her to you," he answered, though he knew that decision might cost lives.

"You *what?*" Harsha shouted, the color running from his face.

"If I'm going to get the ship aloft, I'm going to have to yank a part out of her."

Seeing Harsha's distressed look, Fornax got belligerent. "Damn it, man, we'll *all* die if I can't fly us out of here. I need five minutes. Do what you have to, but give me FIVE minutes."

With that, Fornax scooped up his blaster and scrambled to the back of the ship, there to dissect Jenny and attempt reconstructive surgery on the Battery. He heard the sound of automatic weapons fire erupt in the background. Pained screams followed closely on their heels.

Fornax's pulse quickened. With Jenny in pieces on the floor, the only way he could help save the lives of his new friends was to get the Battery online—and soon!

As he twisted the O-ring coupling out of Jenny and onto the separated Battery cables, minutes rushed by like seconds. Though he couldn't see what was going on inside the shuttle hangar, it sounded as if a full-scale war was in progress. In rapid succession, one burst of fire was answered by another. Then came a mortal scream. Then, a pained thud.

His stomach knotted. The Afghans were in full retreat, the intruders close behind! The Afghans were racing for the safety of the ship; their pursuers, moving to cut them off.

"Close the hatch!" Fornax screamed, tightening the O-ring the last half-turn. "Get everyone in, and close the damn hatch!" he shrieked as the power readings soared. The Battery was back online!

Slamming the Battery compartment door shut, he turned, only to be confronted by the gaunt blood-soaked face of one of the less fortunate members of his group. Most of the soldier's cheek was missing.

"Is everyone here?" Fornax croaked, nearly gagging at the sight. "Is Sam here?"

"I'm okay!" Sam yelled from across the cabin. "Which is more than I can say for some of these poor bastards!"

"We've got to get outta here *now!*" Harsha exclaimed. "Does this thing work or not?"

"We're about to find out," Fornax replied as he coded in the coordinates for the jump to orbit.

"What about the roof?" Marona yelped as Fornax smacked the POWER button.

By then they were already fifty kilometers up! The flimsy tin roof had made no difference to the *Tikkidiw*; the ship merely shuddered as she punched a hole in the sky.

Judging by his passengers' gray expressions, Fornax was certain none of them had ever been catapulted into space before. Even tough-guy Lotha was white-knuckled! Seeing their ashen faces Fornax couldn't help but be reminded of his own inner terror on the occasion of *his* first ascent.

Those who hadn't gotten ill coming across the channel from Pondicherry earlier in the day, looked as if they might do so now. While Fornax explained the untidyness of heaving in zero-g, Sam directed the neediest to the shuttle's toilet.

Then came the unpleasant task of jettisoning the most seriously wounded soldiers into space. For all Fornax knew, two of them might have been dead already.

With little more than a first-aid kit onboard the *Tikkidiw*, and without a single medic among them, the casualties didn't stand a chance if they continued on to Mars. The shuttle's escape pod was their only hope.

If the miniature ship could be maneuvered into docking orbit, it might be seen by someone and the wounded eventually rescued. Otherwise, the tiny escape pod would be little more than a fancy coffin for its three occupants. The air friction—scarce as it was at this altitude—would conspire with the Earth's gravitational field to draw the orbiting pod into a descending spiral. Eventually, the fiery, man-made meteorite would burn to a cinder upon reentry.

Perhaps less out of reverence than out of a concerted effort to regain their composure, silence descended upon the group as the casualties were laid to rest in the escape pod and it was cut loose. Tears welled up in Marona's eyes as she hugged Sam. Harsha and Lotha were fixed with stoney gazes even as Saron and Navi drew into themselves.

More than anyone else, Sam felt responsible for their deaths. Saddened by the loss of these young people, he quietly eulogized. "I would like to offer a moment of silence for our fallen comrades."

Lashing out at Sam, Lotha spoke with defiance. "This is all *your* fault! It is honorable to die for one's country, but to end *this* way is . . . is . . . inexcusable!"

The other man's words ignited passions Fornax didn't realize he still harbored. He grabbed Lotha and threw the big man up against the bulkhead, an impressive feat considering how Lotha was at least a head taller than he was.

"Listen, you bastard!" Fornax spat, surprised by his own strength. "I was shooting down Chinese airchops while you were still in grade school! And while we're at it, let me clear something up for you: there *is* no honor in dying for your country. None whatsoever! The honor is in making the other poor son-of-a-bitch die for *his* country. The honor is in the living, in the keeping of your country free, in the seeing that your ideals survive.

"And one more thing, you big dolt: Don't you *ever* blame Sam for anything ever again! He stood up for you when I was content to leave your sorry ass behind. Now, back off or you'll be joining your friends in the escape pod shortly!"

His eyes on fire, Fornax showed no sign of compromise. He turned to address the nav-console. The first jump would be to the moon to pick up more fuel. Then it would be on to Mars!

PART V

1
Out of the Garden

That night, as Carina lay awake, her mind reeling, her internal thermostat completely out of whack, she attempted to convince herself that everything would turn out okay, that her dad was still alive, that BC hadn't been killed, that someone—*anyone*—would come looking for her before it was too late!

Lying spread eagle on the bed, her hands wet with effort, her eyes fixed on the cold, white ceiling, she wondered how long it would be until the end came. Unless loneliness killed her first, she would almost certainly be killed soon by the rising floodwaters.

It seemed such a pity that she should have to die this way, that she should be denied the chance to pass on her newhuman genes, that she would never get the opportunity to prove that she truly was the next Lucy, and not the radical crackpot like Dr. Janz had claimed.

When the torrent of thoughts wouldn't stop, Carina climbed wearily from her bed, intent on walking laps down in the mess-hall until exhaustion set in. Round and round she went, her arms pumping viciously, her inability to concentrate transporting her from one subject to the next.

Racing around the mess-hall almost at a run, she spoke aloud as if someone were there to listen to her, to answer her.

"I'll be back in an hour, he told me, hour and a half tops! And still I wait. What has it been now? A week? A *month?"*

Carina hadn't even bothered keeping track after the third day.

"Oh, Carina, you *like* being alone, he told me before he left. Oh, and if you do get lonely, you can always put yourself to work down in the old gene-store. Cook up something to keep you company. A puppy perhaps."

Carina spoke in an unhinged, sing-song voice. Her eyes were puffy as if she hadn't slept in days; her hair, grimy as if it hadn't been washed in a week.

"I'll be back in an hour, he said, but he never even took the time to call and tell me he'd be home late for dinner. The nerve of the man!

You'd think he'd at least have the decency to call and say he was gonna be late! Where is he, damnit?" she screamed as if the walls could answer. "Am I to dine alone forever?"

The incoherent debate continued through yet another lap. Carina had never been without a man this long and even hour after hour of masturbation hadn't helped pacify her. Clearly, the woman was at her wit's end!

Had she been blessed with a stronger constitution, it might not have mattered so much that she was stranded alone a million kilometers from nowhere. But as it stood, it was amazing she had managed to hold on *this* long!

Yet, as the overcast days had rolled by in an endless procession of gloom, Carina began to unwind. Lonely and dejected, her frustration had turned, first to anger, then to fear. And still later, when the rains came, the fear quickly disintegrated into terror as one explosive storm after another ripped through the region, inundating the very valley where the Mars base had been built. Before she knew it, the shores of the burgeoning sea had swelled literally up to her doorstep as the awesome, nonstop downpour threatened to totally swamp the buildings and drown her where she stood.

Concentrated in the highlands to the south, the deluge fed frothy streams into small rivers which soon overflowed their banks only to sweep urgently across giant waterfalls into greater rivers and even greater lakes, all of which eventually emptied into the ocean just outside her door. Soon she would have to make a choice, a bleak choice: *Either abandon the colony for higher ground or else stay where she was and face imminent death!*

Realizing this, Carina had tried frantically for days to reach Earth by comm, but to no avail. With the constant cloud cover, she didn't have the slightest idea in which direction to point the antenna, much less how to operate the radio.

And to make matters even worse, not enough sunlight had been filtering through the everpresent film of dense clouds to properly recharge the solar cells. Power levels were running low throughout the complex, and with each passing day Carina had had to shut down more and more of the base's systems. Only the most essential enviro-operations still remained online.

Unfortunately, her difficulties didn't end there—not by a long shot! An even bigger crisis had recently revealed itself—the airlock would no longer shut properly!

Though Carina had no real way of knowing whether the problem was electrical or mechanical, rust or just the weakened power cells, the results were the same—she couldn't get the heavy metal door to budge! And now, with each passing hour, more and more seawater was seeping into the supposedly watertight facility. Once it got deep enough, everything electrical would begin to short out and she would be forced into the wilderness whether she liked it or not. The problem wasn't so much that she couldn't breath the outside air, it was more a question of shelter.

The air, though not quite up to Earth standards, was perfectly satisfactory. Like a remote Andean village, the air here was cold and thin, yet pristine—the kind of air which would not permit much physical exertion before exhaustion set in. Still, given time, one could adjust. But where to live? That was the big question!

Not that the woman was a carpenter or ever hoped to be, but Carina wondered how she could go about constructing a house without lumber, without concrete, without bricks, without masonry, or copper pipe, or porcelain, or any of a thousand other materials common to Earth, but unavailable here. How would the terraformers have approached the problem? How had the Brazilian outbackers done it?

Wielding their axes and their shovels and their knives with the expertise of the natural woodsmen that they were, the pioneers who had conquered Earth's untamed stretches in the past not only had the good sense to site their wilderness cabins where game was plentiful and where giant oaks towered overhead, they also had the presence of mind to avoid setting off into the wilds alone. Carina enjoyed neither luxury.

Mars had no trees, of course, and thus no lumber, but that wasn't the only thing a house could be built from. There was concrete, for instance.

From a printbook Carina found in the library, she learned that to stir up a batch of concrete required four things—clay, limestone, sand, and gravel. Unfortunately, while the Martian soil almost certainly contained substantial quantities of clay, finding any limestone would be a bit more problematic. Limestone was an artifact of earlier life, only Mars had always been a dead planet. No life, no limestone. No limestone, no concrete. It was just that simple!

Yet, Mars did have one resource, and in great abundance—lichen!

It occurred to her that just as primitive tribes had once fashioned huts from bricks of grass and mud, perhaps she might do the same, only using blocks of lichen-sod. The thickness of the lichen-block walls would make them excellent insulators against the cold and the wet, and, as an added bonus, the lichen-blocks would continue to "grow" until all the gaps between them had grown shut, thus sealing off any drafts.

Of course, there would be more to it than that. What could she make a roof from, for instance? How could she heat and cool the place? How could she cut the blocks and boost them into position?

So many questions; so few answers!

2
Bell Curve

Round and round she went, her mind playing the nastiest of tricks on her. Unable to communicate with her home world, unable to remain where she was, unable to survive on her own outside for very long, Carina's future seemed awfully dim. A lesser person would surely have cracked before now.

"There's enough food here to last you a lifetime. Isn't that what he said?" she cackled at the edge of incoherence. "And if you really do get lonely, you could always make yourself something to keep you company . . . a puppy, perhaps . . . a puppy, perhaps."

On and on she droned, just this side of sanity. It had gone on like this for days until finally, this morning, as much out of loneliness as out of scientific curiosity, Carina had found herself standing at the entrance to the gene-store.

The mammoth chamber was jammed full with bins of carefully preserved seeds and cases of frozen animal embryos. As she stood in the doorway looking around the climate-controlled storeroom, she tried to digest what the settlers must have had in mind when they left behind this awesome legacy.

Initially, when she and BC first discovered the gene-store, Carina's earliest inclination had been to complete the terraformers' original plans by unleashing all the plants and animals they had marooned here, thus giving birth to the new Eden as they evidently intended. Although it had undoubtedly been their goal to achieve a balanced food chain with sufficient green plants to support grazing animals, plus enough predators to keep the number of grazers in check, her present plans were much more modest.

Whereas several hundred colonists might have been able to keep all those animals in check, *one* colonist certainly could not. Carina was afraid of being overwhelmed by sheer numbers, and with good reason! A couple of harmless dogs could quickly swell into a pack of hungry wolves; a few meandering cows could grow into a crushing stampede; a pair of cute bunny rabbits could multiply into a pestilence capable of raping the countryside.

And while it was certainly true that, in time, Mars would develop its own delicate balance of hunter and hunted, meat-eater and grazer, tyrant and weakling, ecological equilibrium would just have to wait awhile. Homesick and desperate for companionship, all Carina wanted was someone to talk to before she cracked.

"Defrosting" a puppy and incubating it in a warm bath of Acceleron, proved far easier than she could possibly have imagined. Within the hour, she was bottle-feeding a precious little collie, suitably named Sandy. His presence did more to mollify her depression than any wonder drug could have, and though she still paced restlessly around the complex talking to herself, at least now she had company.

It had always troubled her how much of a complete lottery evolution had been, how chaotic and unpredictable its results. Evolution had not been survival of the fittest, as some had claimed, it had been survival of the *luckiest!* And if God were to rewind the tape of life back into time now, and let it play out again, He would get a totally different set of survivors. Perhaps, humans wouldn't even be among them!

But that wasn't the only thing that was troubling her. It was disturbing to realize how, in the past few hundred years, the best and brightest females had been substantially curtailing their reproductive activities, while at the same time, the tramps of the world had been indiscriminately screwing their brains out and keeping their dim-witted results to boot!

This was a circumstance markedly different from what had taken place in the previous millennium. In those pre-industrial days, women of high status had had appreciably *higher* fertility rates than women of low status. Not only could they afford to marry earlier than their lower-class counterparts, they also enjoyed better health standards.

After industrialization, however, the fertility situation reversed itself. This was due, in no small part, to the career opportunities which suddenly opened up to women of high status. Ironically, the very members of the working class who displayed the enterprise and ability to improve their lot were the ones who limited their baby output the most; those who did *not* advance economically continued to breed well beyond their capacity for taking good care of their own offspring. And contributing to that trend was a new development—brighter women began using the technology of birth control and of abortion more regularly. As industrialization tipped the economic scales towards smaller families, it did so with a vengeance at higher socioeconomic levels. What was once another pair of hands to help on the farm became another mouth to feed and another college tuition to pay.

The unintended consequence of repeatedly discouraging relatively-high intelligence women from breeding was to reduce the overall intellect of the progeny, thus shifting the bell curve of I.Q.'s to the left and haplessly driving the oldhuman race into an evolutionary cul-de-sac.

But, as in all such things, the women were not the only ones culpable—their bright husbands also had to shoulder some of the blame for springing the evolutionary trap which eventually snared the species.

From the outset, humans had been inquisitive, territorial beasts who objected to being caged, and yet, the post-industrial world had presented them with cages at every turn, cages which withered mankind's spirit and sapped his strength.

Not only had the physical frontiers like the American West and the Brazilian Outback been closed, the intellectual frontiers had for the most part been closed as well, as millions of Dr. Janzes around the globe waylaid innovative thinkers in their webs of bureaucratic hurdles and stifling politically-correct dogmas.

Those who were the most ambitious and the best educated saw the most clearly how the borders of exploration had been slammed shut in their faces. And not wanting to introduce children into a world no longer able to cope with nonconforming overachievers, they began to postpone parenthood—or to avoid it altogether—always being sure to abort any accidental indiscretions along the way.

Without any new lands to conquer, without any migratory havens to escape to, without any isolated places for the geniuses of the world to take refuge in, the defining human characteristic atrophied. The species had reached an impasse, a virtual *plateau* in its intellectual development!

Again she spoke aloud, this time as if Sandy could answer her. "Can you point to even a single sign that, as a species, we are getting smarter? Was Albert Einstein a better scientist than Isaac Newton, or Archimedes? Was Durbin? Has any playwright in recent years topped William Shakespeare or Euripedes? We have learned a lot these past 3000 years, yet much of the ancient wisdom still seems sound today. Which makes me think that we haven't been making much progress. We still don't know how to resolve the inherent conflict between individual goals and global interests. And we are so bad at making important decisions that whenever we can, we leave to chance—or to someone else—what we are unsure about. I ask you, does that sound like progress to you?"

Sandy flashed her a knowing smile, but didn't answer. He was a dog, after all, with cares no more distant than his next dish of water. Still and all, it seemed incongruous to her that Mother Nature should allow herself to be boxed in this way, that the human race should end with a whimper instead of a bang, that she herself should have to die such a meaningless death!

Exhausted, finally, after another hour of pacing, Carina collapsed into a chair to rest. But as she sat there petting Sandy, it hit her—*she* was the solution to mankind's dilemma!

It was a wonder it hadn't occurred to her before, but applying the very same theory which had caused her so much grief back on Earth, the answer was clear: Nature's route out of the cul-de-sac man had slipped into, was a giant leap *over* the impasse, a genetic megajump *around* the blockade. And where would mankind land? On the untested new path marked out by the signature genes she herself had discovered. Newhumans were evolving in response to the insurmountable problems oldhumans had created for themselves. And for her to die without being able to share this knowledge with the world would be a shame of Biblical proportions!

Believing now that more was at stake here than just her own death, Carina decided she was not going to give in to the Martian gods of rain without first putting up a fight. Not only would she take the landrover and make a run for it, hoping to find a dry cave somewhere, she refused to pull up stakes without first leaving her mark.

It had occurred to her that a future generation of settlers might truly appreciate having the nutrition only a living sea could provide. And while she had no reliable way of judging the water's depth or even its salinity, defrosting Sandy had been so easy, she decided it only made good sense to seed the ocean with all the fish and crustaceans the gene-store had to offer.

Though it took her several hours, afterwards, when she stood at the water's edge shivering and contemplating the animals she had just sent on their merry way, Carina realized her job wasn't done. Without trees there could be no wood, and without wood there could be no fishing boats, nor paper, nor any of a thousand other things the future would require.

So, with her hormones running amuck and Sandy lapping at her feet, she returned one last time to the gene-store to perform her magic before abandoning the colony in the landrover. If death were to come now, she could at least die comforted by the fact that the next generation of colonists might sit under the shade of one of her trees and wonder how it all came to be.

Her work complete, Carina slung the last box of dried provisions into the all-terrain vehicle. On her last pass through the mess-hall she had watched as the spray from yet another wave crashed through the open doorway of the airlock and into the room. To conserve power, she had long ago silenced the mechanical voice which had been chanting out meaningless instructions to close the door. Now it didn't matter; now, nothing mattered!

Briefly wondering whether or not the terraformers would approve, whether they had had any idea of the climactic changes they would be unleashing when they first set up shop here so many years ago, Carina climbed into the landrover, propped Sandy on the seat beside her, fired up the engine, and drove off into the storm.

It was anybody's guess what the future might hold!

3
Gone

"I just don't understand it," Fornax said in an angry, confused tone. "No one is here!"

The others with him were peering down the dimly-lit corridor into the mess-hall. They were equally baffled.

"As dark as it is down there, and with all that water sloshing around, it's mighty hard to tell whether or not anyone's been through here since we left," Sam remarked, his tired face showing his age. "Land's sakes, it's like a damn swimming pool down there!" he said, the glow from his lumina-beam reflecting off the murky surface.

"You mean we came all this way for nothing!" Lotha barked, his misshapen skull taking on a macabre look. The big man was still upset over the long hike Fornax insisted they make from out where he'd landed the ship. Shocked by the encroaching ocean, Fornax had set the *Tikkidiw* down well away from the water's edge, just in case the shoreline was unstable and gave way.

"I thought you told us this would be like a haven for outcasts . . . for runaways?" Saron said, her eyes filling with tears.

"Don't cry," Harsha implored. Putting his arm around Saron's shoulder, he turned to address Sam. "Seriously, old man, what went wrong here? There's no power, no lights, no heat. If your daughter *was* here, she's gone now. Or else dead."

"You must be right," Sam admitted, the color draining from his face. "The rains came, the water rose, she left the airlock open, then she panicked. God, I can't believe I've lost her!"

As the crash of another giant wave shook the foundation, Marona rushed to Sam's side, pressing her hand into his and doing her best to console him.

"Don't be so quick to jump to conclusions," Fornax said. "She may be holed up in one of the storage areas. For all we know, BC and Carina never even *made* it here. If someone as inexperienced as I was able to go underground disguised as Sven Rutland, surely BC was able to disguise Carina and stick her someplace safe before he was captured.

"Then again, if she *was* here all this time, she almost certainly would have left behind something to reveal her presence—an unmade bed, perhaps, or a garbage can filled with trash. We passed some rooms on the way down here. Let's start in the library, then check the sleeping quarters, then the storage areas. We'll keep on going until we hopefully find some sign of her."

The superstructure groaned as yet another massive wave hit the exposed side of the base.

"This place gives me the creeps," Saron trembled.

"It's all rather spooky, I'll give you that much," Harsha agreed. "I suggest we stay together."

"Good idea," Sam nodded. "I don't want anyone getting hurt in the dark."

"Okay then, let's get moving before the charge on our lumina-beams runs down," Fornax advised.

Though he did what he could to hide his fear, as Fornax led the way back up the corridor towards the first bank of residence quarters, he swallowed hard. Up until this very moment, it had never occurred to him that Carina might be dead. All along he had assumed that the story would have a happy ending, that he would arrive on the scene like a knight in shining armor to save his would-be damsel from distress, that with BC safely tucked away now in the hands of the Overlord, he would finally be able to make a play for her.

"Cap'n," Harsha addressed Fornax respectfully, "I think I've found something."

He was pointing to an unmade bed and a room strewn with women's clothing.

"It's hard to say whether this stuff's been laying here for an hour or for the past fifty years," Sam declared sensibly. "But judging by the mess, I'd have to say this is my daughter's room."

"That's not all," Fornax noted. "Take a look at these."

He held up a sheath of papers on which Carina had scribbled some notes. "This is her handwriting—I recognize it from her diary."

"Then it *is* true!" Sam bubbled ecstatically. "She *was* here after all."

"So where is she now?" Marona questioned, brushing up against Sam. "She couldn't have just vanished into thin air!"

"No, of course not. Let's go check the storerooms."

In rapid succession, they traipsed through the library, the maintenance shed, the storage-locker, the food pantry, and the gene-store. Though they found plenty of evidence that someone had been there recently, there was no sign whatsoever of Carina herself.

"Sam, I don't know what to say," Fornax remarked as another groan washed over the building. "But if she's still here now, I can't imagine where she's hiding."

"Must've got washed out to sea," Sam muttered as he stared

unseeingly down the long aisles of the food pantry. "You know how impetuous she was."

"If we don't get out of here ourselves—and soon—we'll *all* be washed out to sea," Harsha urgently pointed out. "This place is breaking up. Let's load what we want to save in the landrover, and get back to the ship before the roof caves in!"

As if to add emphasis to his words, the walls shuddered under the force of yet another wave pounding against the submerged portion of the building.

"Landrover?" Fornax yelped. *"What* landrover?"

"Well, I didn't actually *see* one," Harsha confessed, surprised by Fornax's reaction. "I just assumed that in a big colony like this one, they would've had *some* sort of caterpillar-style truck stored either in a maintenance shed or else . . . "

"You're a genius!" Fornax exclaimed, grabbing hold of Harsha's arm mid-sentence. "And the only room big enough and with a large enough door leading to the outside, is the equipment garage!" he boomed even as he chased up the gangway in that direction.

In a matter of moments, he had his answer.

"Had to have been," he assured the others as they tried to catch up with him.

Pointing to a truck-sized empty spot in the center of the concrete floor, he declared, "The ATV must've been parked right here in front of the door. Because of the flooding she probably decided that escaping to higher ground was her only hope. So she took it and left!"

"Left?!" an astonished Sam blurted out loud. "Why would she leave? Where the hell would she *go?"*

Again Marona moved to console him. Though only Fornax seemed to notice, with each passing moment Marona had tried to endear herself further and further with Sam.

"All I have to do is follow the treadmarks," Fornax replied, beginning to become concerned by how much Marona was fawning over the old guy.

"How will you do *that?"* Lotha asked, the concept beyond his comprehension.

"Raise the garage door," Fornax ordered, "and I'll track her on foot. It should be fairly simple to follow something *that* big. The landrover should've left a trail of broken rocks and smashed lichen even a *fool* could trace!"

"You're the fool!" Lotha taunted defiantly.

"I've just about had enough of your mouth!" Fornax shouted back.

"Oh? And what d'ya think you're gonna do about it?" Lotha dared him as he cocked his fist. "You're not so tough without your fancy blaster, now are you?"

"Okay, boys," Sam intervened. "Break it up! My daughter's *life* is at stake here, for heaven's sake! We have no time for your foolish games! Fornax, I think it's a good idea if you go after Carina. But I think it's a bad idea for you to go out there all alone. Take Harsha along with you. The rest of us will stay here and see if we can't seal off this wing from the rest of the complex. Maybe we can use the ship's towbar to lift part of the base to higher ground."

4
Cute

Despite the fact that the manufacturer had designed the landrover to be virtually untippable, Carina hadn't gotten more than a kilometer before driving the machine down a steep embankment and flipping it over on its side. Fortunately, she had had the good sense to knock herself out in the process, or else she might have wandered off before they arrived. As it was, her face was pale and her breathing shallow when they found her.

"Is she dead?" Harsha asked, surprised at how raw the weather had become in the short time since they set out from the base on foot.

"No, she's definitely alive," Fornax said, issuing a sigh of relief. "But she's out cold."

Even as he spoke, Fornax leaned across the seat to check her pulse. Unzipping the front of her flightsuit to check for broken bones or gashes, he suddenly recoiled in horror.

"My God, Harsha!" he yelped, his face white with fear. "There's something . . . something . . . furry . . . "

"Move aside!" Harsha ordered, pushing his way in front of the other man. "Let me see."

Without flinching, Harsha reached inside Carina's jacket where Fornax had indicated, then exploded with laughter as he pulled the ball of fur out with one hand.

"It's a puppy!" Harsha chortled sunnily. "A cute little puppy!"

"Where did *he* come from?" Fornax wondered aloud.

"Maybe your friend BC left it behind to keep her company."

"He hardly seems the sort," Fornax snapped.

"She's awfully cute, if I don't say so myself," Harsha commented, studying the lines of Carina's delicate face.

"Maybe too cute. Now let's see if we can't wake her," Fornax said, searching the cab for a swatch of cloth. "Here, take this rag outside and get it wet."

Harsha did as he was told, and as Fornax slapped the wet washrag to her forehead, Carina shivered.

"Wake up, girl!" Fornax urged as the puppy gently licked her face. "Wake up!"

After a few moments, some of the color came back into her cheeks. "Sandy, is that you?" she whispered. Her words were garbled as if she was still in a daze.

"Who's Sandy?" Harsha asked, a perplexed look on his face.

"I dunno," Fornax answered, shrugging his shoulders. "The pooch, maybe?"

"Is that you, Sandy?" she repeated, rubbing the welt on the side of her head.

"No, Carina, it's me. Fornax."

Her eyes blinked wide as if she couldn't see. "Fornax? No, it can't be. He's dead! Who *are* you?"

Quickly tiring of this game, Fornax grabbed her roughly by the shoulders and shook her awake. "Damnit, Carina, snap out of it! It *is* me! We have come to rescue you. Your father is here as well."

That got her attention.

"Dad's here?" she asked, trying to get her bearings. "Where *am* I?" she said, obviously still out of it. Then squinting her eyes, she declared, "Fornax, it *is* you! How did you get here? I thought you were killed! And who in blazes is that behind you?"

Laughing, he exclaimed, "Whoa, slow down! All your questions will be . . . "

"I'm so glad you're not dead," she confessed, suddenly throwing her arms around him. "We never had a chance to . . . I mean, we never . . . what I'm trying to say is . . . "

"I think I understand," Fornax said, blushing. "Now shut up and let's get you back to the base."

"We can't go back!" she argued, appalled by the suggestion. "The whole place is filling with *water!*"

Remaining calm, Fornax explained. "The colony is modular, with airlocks at each joint. Your father believes we can detach a couple of sections and move them to higher ground, away from the water. By the way, what in the world were you doing out here? And where did this mutt come from?"

"Oh, you're so *cute* when you're mad," she teased, wantonly squeezing his thigh with a gloved hand.

Embarrassed by her forwardness, Fornax cleared his throat. "We should get started."

"Yes," Harsha agreed, "maybe we can use the landrover's own winch and chain to flip this thing rightside up again."

Fornax nodded his assent and pointed to a big rock a dozen meters away that they could tie onto. Inside, he was all aglow with anticipation—at long last he was about to have a chance with this lovely girl!

• • •

The junior operative stood at attention before the elder man's desk. As was required by his station, he addressed his superior with respect. "Boss, one of our listening posts recently intercepted an interesting message."

J did not invite the younger man to sit. "Nicholas, I have highly-trained specialists to handle this sort of radio chatter. Why are you bothering me with such details? For that matter, why are *you* even involved? Surveillance is not your area," he boomed, his chubby face getting red. "Didn't I give you specific orders . . . "

"I know, I know, but BC was my friend. Plus, I felt like I'd let Sam down. So I asked operations to code me in on any inbound traffic containing any of a dozen or so key words. You can hardly call that disobeying a direct order," Cornwall declared, maintaining an even tone. Though he wasn't about to lie, he carefully avoided mentioning the fact that he had *already* gone outside the agency to hire Harsha Gandu following Sam's kidnapping. The two of them had worked together once before, when Captain Michael wanted Fornax's gene-prints destroyed on short notice.

"Yes, yes, do get on with it!" J demanded in an unfriendly tone.

"Well, one of the key words I told them to watch out for was 'Mars,' and in a garbled transmission received just yesterday, a variant of that word showed up," Cornwall reported excitedly.

"A variant?" J inquired in utter disbelief. "You're disturbing me over a fragment of a word which is itself only four letters long? How *stupid* of you!" he exploded. "Let me see that damn printout!" he screamed, impatiently grabbing the message from Cornwall's trembling hand. "And do sit down already!"

J studied the transcript. It read as follows:

" . . . under control . . . contact with car . . . sha gan . . . soon mar . . . "

"This is *it?*" he exploded again. "This is the entire message? What the hell good is *this?*" he cursed, crumbling up the communiqué and tossing it across the desk at Cornwall. "What in the world's a 'sha gan' anyhow?"

"Hear me out," Cornwall insisted with unexpected firmness. "Although it was the three letters M-A-R which caused the computer to flag this wire, that word fragment could just as easily have stood for 'marooned' or perhaps 'mariner,' as for Mars. In fact, excluding capitalized words like proper names—people, places, and such—there are 127 words in the English language alone which begin with the letters M-A-R."

"Didn't it ever occur to you that perhaps your three magic letters were buried *inside* of a word instead of being placed conveniently at the start?"

"I'm not grotesquely stupid!" Cornwall responded angrily.

"No, of course not," J replied in a soothing tone. "You were saying?"

"I had operations run a cross-sectional analysis on those one hundred and twenty seven words, and it turns out that eight of them have connotations which are space-related. Consider the word 'mariner,' for instance. In the twentieth century, the Americans launched a series of unmanned probes to study Venus and Mars. They were called the Mariner missions."

"Unmanned probes?" J asked perplexed. "No, that can't possibly be right. Sometimes I worry about you, Cornwall," he said, unexpectedly switching gears. "Do you really know what the spy business is all about? I mean, what it's *really* all about?"

"Perhaps not, sir," he confessed. "Sometimes I wonder. I mean, if only we'd done more to help Sam."

"True enough, but this is all a game, and just because you lose a hand doesn't mean the game is lost," J summarized coolly.

"I understand, but . . . "

"Think of it this way," J continued. "In the French card game called *piquet*, the players are scored by accumulating tricks and various combinations of cards. If one player wins all of the tricks, he is said to *faire capot*, the French word 'capot' meaning a cover, or a hood, or a cape. By taking all the tricks, the winner defeats his opponent so thoroughly that the loser is covered over, as in the sense of being buried, or in the sense of having had a hood thrown over his head."

"Where are you going with this?" Cornwall groped.

"Over eight hundred years ago—during the Thirty Years' War—the Germans borrowed the term 'capot' and gave us 'kaputt.' From the sense of having lost a game, kaputt came to mean finished or broken. Then, around 1900, the British adopted the term from the Germans and kaputt came to mean broken, or ruined, or destroyed. Finally, the Americans grabbed it from us, giving it its modern meaning of useless or utterly finished. But, it is in the oldest sense of the word that I use it today."

"Finished?" Cornwall volunteered.

"No, not that meaning. Hoodwinked!" J barked, his grizzled face twisting into a mean-spirited grin. "As in you have been hoodwinked! Now get the *hell* out of my office, and leave me alone!"

Dejected, Cornwall went on his way. Perhaps he'd never really understood, until now, just how the man he worked for actually thought. To J, *everyone* was expendable! That he had refused to lift a finger to save Captain Michael or BC was bad enough, that he had been willing to throw Sam to the wolves was repulsive, but to suggest that this was all a game bordered on the criminal!

Their little talk had helped in one way, though. It had helped Nicholas Cornwall make up his mind. He had to do two things: First, he had to find out where they were holding BC; second, he had to find out just what the devil this message meant. Until then, he wasn't going to get a good night's sleep!

5
lekhaim

It was an exhausting effort made doubly so by the inclement weather, yet by the end of the next day, one bank of sleeping cubicles—plus the garage and a host of storage areas—had been detached from the rest of the complex and hoisted to higher ground.

In the hours that elapsed while Fornax and the rest of the men disassembled, moved, and reassembled the modular building units, the three girls hatched a plan to host Mars's first BeHolden Day dinner that evening. That it wasn't the fourth Thursday of November was of no consequence; they had plenty to be thankful for, not the least of which was being safely away from the still-rising waters.

Since the mess-hall was already submerged and had to be left behind, there was no table large enough to accommodate everyone. In fact, there were no tables period—even floor space was at a premium!

So, with the landrover parked just outside in the pouring rain, they sat cross-legged on the concrete floor, an odd assortment of pillows cushioning their various bottoms. Amazingly, despite all the commotion, the women had somehow found the time to change and freshen-up. They all looked stunning, but none less than the beautiful, dark-eyed Saron. Much to Carina's chagrin, she had seated herself next to Fornax, her low-cut blouse revealing a set of wonderfully well-developed breasts.

The men ate hungrily as if it had been days, and as Fornax gulped down yet another bite of the aromatic entree, it dawned on him that not since Sven Rutland had dropped his pruning shears down on Sam's wet lawn, had he eaten a decent meal. Precisely *what* he was eating remained a mystery until Saron assured him that it was turkey—or at least a reasonable facsimile thereof. Fortunately for all of them, Saron was a bit more domesticated than Carina, the one woman in the group who had proudly claimed to have no culinary talents whatsoever.

Indeed, Saron had *several* rather endearing qualities—two to be precise—and even as Carina glared at Fornax from across the room, he couldn't help himself. His eyes were glued to those dandies, and with good reason—the last time he'd been with a woman was an even more distant memory than his last good meal!

Like the others seated around the floor of the garage, the dark-haired Afghan temptress to Fornax's left sat in the fashion of an Amerind—knees bent, legs spread open wide, her heightened skirt revealing just a hint of delicate pink thighs.

"Saron's an interesting name," he observed as her right knee brushed up against his, sending an involuntary shiver charging up his leg.

Enjoying his reaction, Saron smiled, "Yes, very interesting. Actually, though, Saron's not my given name. Some people find it a bit too long."

"I'd love to hear it," Fornax begged sophomorically.

"Yes, do tell," Carina urged watchfully from the other side of the room.

"Surasundari," she answered, carefully enunciating each syllable. "Sur . . . a . . . sun . . . dar . . . i . . . It means 'darling of the Gods'."

"Indeed," Fornax said, struggling to suppress his most primal of instincts.

"And what is *your* background, Fornax?" Marona asked as she got up to pour a glass of wine for everyone. Clearly favoring Sam, she served him first.

From the fiery look in Carina's eye, it was difficult to tell which woman made her angrier—Saron as she cuddled up next to her Fornax, or Marona as she fawned all over her father. That neither man saw through their affections angered her even further!

The more Saron's breasts played peek-a-boo with Fornax, the more Carina fumed. For his part, Fornax found it curiously refreshing to see the usually unflappable Carina jealous. After having been so resentful of the attention she had paid BC, he was delighted to have the tables turned, if only for a while.

"What's my background?" Fornax repeated, caught a little off-guard by Marona's question. "Well, most recently, I lived in SKANDIA, and before that, in Auckland."

"You don't look like a Zealander to me," Marona persisted as she circled the room pouring the white Zinfandel. With Fornax's eyes fixed on Saron, and Carina's riveted on Fornax, no one noticed Marona slip a tiny white grain into Navi's goblet before filling it with wine.

"Actually, I'm not a Zealander by birth," Fornax admitted, "but enough about me. Now that we have the wine, it's time for a toast."

Unfolding his stiff legs, Fornax stood up. As the others followed suit, he raised his cup and spoke.

"To my old friends, Sam and Carina, let me only say this: If I hadn't been blinded by greed, I might never have gotten you two mixed up in this. For that, I am truly sorry. But despite the setbacks, the future holds great promise.

"And to my new friends of the Afghan resistance, consider this: For those of you who would tame her, Mars offers a great opportunity. Though there is no Overlord here, make no mistake about it, this land will be harsh and unforgiving. It will require every bit of your resolve to carve out a future here, plus incredibly hard work. But it can be done. Lekhaim!"

"To life!" came the age-old reply. "To life!"

Then they tipped their glasses and drank.

Soon the dinner conversation turned lighter and laughter erupted. Before long though, Navi excused himself, complaining of a sour stomach. Not long afterwards, the party broke up, the dishes left to the morning.

As Fornax escorted Carina back to her room, she remarked, "I couldn't help but notice how you were staring at that . . . that . . . Saron."

"Forgive me," Fornax exhorted, "but that dress was more becoming than the army fatigues she was wearing when I first met her."

"I'm not sure that's a good enough answer," she fired back, her beautiful eyes flashing.

"It'll have to do," he retorted valiantly as they reached her door, "because I have no other."

"It couldn't have been that you had sex on your mind, and she was just handy?"

"You *are* forward, aren't you?"

"I'm a difficult woman to satisfy," she cooed tenderly, "but would you like to come in and try?"

"Right now?" he asked, nearly choking on the words. "With your father right next door?"

"It's not as if he'll be *watching*," she teased, drawing him close.

"I know," he agreed sheepishly. "But . . . "

"I'll not ask again," she warned.

"You don't have to. Just lead the way."

And she did.

• • •

To describe what they did as making love would be too refined, too cultured, too tame.

Their first time was probably more savage, more wild, more unrestrained, than either of them had intended. And to watch the two of them writhe around there on the floor, one had to wonder whether either of them had ever been housebroken!

It all began innocently enough in the shower. With the hot water pounding against her throbbing skin, he coated her body with soapsuds. In no time at all, he had worked her into a steaming lather. Massaging her body with the scented fragrance, his hands explored her nakedness.

She groped for his manhood.

Impatient to consummate their passion, they dried hurriedly and jumped into bed. She squealed with delight as he entered her, but they were both in such a bad way that before they knew it, it was over!

• • •

No sooner had Nicholas Cornwall arrived back in his dingy office than he pulled the crumbled message from his pocket, placing it on his desk for further study. In his opinion, J had been too quick to dismiss it.

Over and over again, he read it, hoping to eke out its meaning. Over and over again, he struggled to fill in the missing gaps:

" . . . under control . . . contact with car . . . sha gan . . . soon mar . . . "

Could he have been wrong? Cornwall asked himself, nervously tapping his pencil on the desk. What if M-A-R was a proper name, after all? What if it were a person, or maybe even a place?

Cornwall knew he could solve his riddle quickly enough if only he chanced running it through the computer. The main drawback was, J would get wind of what he was doing even before he was done! And yet, deciphering the mystery by hand seemed like such a gargantuan task.

Then too, he'd have to run those word fragments as well. What was a 'sha gan' anyway? It had to mean *some*thing! he thought as he got up and began pacing back and forth across his mere closet of an office. Was he dreaming or was that Har*sha Gan*du's name buried in there?

And what about 'car'? That wasn't a very common word anymore; nowadays, most people said 'gcar.' Maybe the 'g' was lost in the transmission . . . or maybe, c-a-r was short for something else. Perhaps it was the first syllable of a *longer* word.

Deciding he needed a dictionary, Cornwall bounded down the oak-paneled corridor towards the agency's library.

Thumbing through the giant, leather-bound book spread eagle upon the lectern, he ticked off word after word:

" . . . carat . . . carbine . . . carbon . . . cardiac . . . cargo . . . carousel . . . cartridge . . . "

And that's when it hit him! "Carina!" He nearly knocked over the bookstand as he shouted her name, "Carina!"

Swallowing his excitement under the threatening glare of the head librarian, Cornwall returned to his office, his mind racing. Whoever sent this message had made contact with Carina!

Then the pace of his step slowed as a dark frown creased up on his forehead. The "whoever" could only be an Overlord agent.

Now all Nicholas Cornwall needed to do was figure out the agent's name!

6
Of Shape & Form

"*That* was great!" she exclaimed, propping herself up on one elbow, her ample breasts wantonly displayed for his viewing pleasure.

Seeing his fascination with them, she remarked in a scholarly tone, "Above-average breast size is highly correlated with above-average intelligence, you know."

"You're making that up," Fornax laughed, checking her expression to see if she was serious.

"They have to be good for something, don't they?" she cooed, cupping one of them with her free hand. "I mean, larger breasts don't produce more baby's milk, nor do they make it any easier to get pregnant, so what function could they possibly serve?"

"Attracting mates?" Fornax offered, a thoughtful look on his face.

"Well, there *is* that," she agreed, jiggling them indecently.

"Come to think of it, maybe it's not so much their *size* as their *shape* which is so alluring."

Carina rolled over on her back to tease him, but he ignored her and sat abruptly up in bed. Waxing philosophic, he said, "What is the *why* of shape?"

"Excuse me?"

"What I mean is, a wheel is round by *design*—humans learned that that shape made transportation possible. The Earth, on the other hand, is round by physical *law*—a spinning fluid is drawn by the force of gravity into the shape of a sphere."

"Oh, but the distinction is not always an obvious one," she said, covering herself up as the discussion grew more technical. "Is a drinking glass round because that is the most comfortable shape to hold, or is it round because that is the shape assumed by spun pottery or blown glass?"

"But what about boobs?" he wondered openly. "Does gravity dictate their shape in a spun-pottery sort of way or . . . "

"Or does that particular shape perhaps turn men on, thus assuring the continuation of the species?"

When she spoke, it was with a devilish twinkle in her eye. Pumping up her chest with a deep breath to exaggerate their size, she said, "Aren't these what attracted you to me in the first place?"

"Well, not exactly," he answered flustered. "To be perfectly honest, it had more to do with your enthusiasm for the sport than anything else. Your sex drive seems so wonderfully high. How would you account for *that?*"

"Intelligence. And frustration."

He answered her with a blank stare.

Naked, she slipped out of bed to brush her teeth. His pulse quickened at the sight. The woman was tall, all legs, and round in all the right places.

"Horniness and intelligence go hand in hand," she explained. "But evolution has played a nasty trick on us females. As compared with you men, it's relatively difficult for us to have an orgasm. So, we're frequently left unsatiated."

"I'll try harder next time," he promised. "The purpose of the male orgasm is evident—women couldn't get pregnant without it—but besides making you feel good, what is the purpose of the *female* orgasm?"

"Ah, the 64,000 dollar question. Female orgasm enhances sperm retention. So does masturbation. In my view, the struggle to achieve a satisfying orgasm has been one of the key strengths of our species, perhaps even the number one reason for its success."

"Has space completely warped your brain?" Fornax asked incredulously.

"Hear me out," she admonished. "Raising children takes an awful lot of effort, and most women are simply not up to the task of doing it alone—they need the help of a man. Traditionally, however, male primates have banded together in small groups to hunt and to make territorial conquests. These male-only hunting parties could sustain themselves over long periods of time, leaving the females alone to fend for themselves in their absence. I ask you: what incentive did the men have to return home?"

"They missed playing with their children?" Fornax volunteered meekly.

"Not likely," Carina responded as she gathered the covers and straightened the bed. "Most men would just as soon not be bothered with children. No, I would argue that once humans had evolved enough intelligence, the pleasure of sex became a factor in drawing the men home from the hunt. Not only would his mate's nearly insatiable need massage his ego—thereby assuring that he would come back for more—but his regular presence at home would have had the added benefit of shielding both her and her offspring from harm.

"Her problem was, she would never know *when* he would return—or for how long. Her 'solution,' if you will, was to be continually in heat, or at the very least, continually receptive. The evolutionary trick to perfecting continuous receptivity was delaying, or in some cases preventing, sexual satiation."

"Wow!" Fornax exclaimed, her analysis blowing his mind. "Receptivity? Isn't that just a fancy word for horny?"

"And how!" she agreed enthusiastically. "The itch that can't ever be scratched."

"You are bawdy, aren't you?" Fornax responded with a grin upon his face. "Yet, this *is* an intriguing theory. Let me see if I have this straight: a woman's sexual frustration helps cement the bond between her and her man, and as an accidental side benefit, his continued presence around the hut helps protect the weaker family members from harm. I have to admit, it never would've occurred to me to look at sex quite that way. But answer me this: wouldn't that kind of insatiability also promote a distressing amount of promiscuity?"

"And then some! But that too would have had an evolutionary advantage."

"*What?!*" Fornax blurted out. "This I gotta hear."

Carina continued. "The threat of female promiscuity—that particularly human emotion we call jealousy—was yet another reason for the male to stay close to home. In order to ensure the paternity of the offspring he was responsible for, the men had to control the sexuality of their women."

"And that jealousy, as you called it, has a darker side, doesn't it?" Fornax questioned suspiciously. "I can almost see it coming."

Carina nodded. "Because he couldn't possibly be there every minute of the day to watch over her, the male response to the threat of female promiscuity was to restrict her domain."

"I *knew* it!" Fornax exclaimed, clearly unhappy with the direction she was going.

But without so much as missing a beat, she charged on. "First, by indoctrinating the women with puritanical moral codes to help ensure their fidelity, then by designing and enforcing rules of property and education which limited their freedom, every woman of childbearing age was bound tightly to a particular male."

Fornax was fuming. "For God's sake, Carina, you know damn well that a woman's lot has been steadily improving over the centuries! As societies have modernized, women have become *less* dependent on their men. And less threatened by them. I'd have to argue that we have evolved *out* of our violent, male-dominated past."

"You sound like a freaking politician!" she bellowed. "Woman's lot has improved, yes, but only in a handful of countries. And it has not been an unmitigated blessing. As women became more independent, men rebelled: divorce rates rose, childbearing declined, and the frequency of forcible rape became an abomination."

"Isn't it strange, though, that it is the women, not the men, who are the fiercer adherents to those restrictive moral codes supposedly written by us jealous, insecure men?"

"My very point," Carina fired back. "Look, poor Moses probably wouldn't have been kept wandering around the desert for forty years trying to think up the Ten Commandments if it hadn't been for all those horny bedouins . . . "

"Let's leave poor Moses out of this, shall we?"

Gathering her thoughts, Carina pressed on. "Despite what men have done to tame female sexuality, perhaps the most insidious, most compelling form of indoctrination has been accomplished by the mothers. They are the ones who have encouraged their daughters to identify with their families, and their husbands, and their children, rather than to develop their *own* abilities."

"You sound bitter."

"Actually, I'm not. In fact, in one sense, I've been fortunate. Because my mother died before the brainwashing could begin in earnest, I missed the standard indoctrination. Maybe *that*'s why I'm so bawdy—I don't know any better."

An unpleasant silence followed. Finally, Fornax asked, "You miss her, don't you?"

"I was just two," she answered bravely, a note of sadness creeping into her voice. "I didn't know her well enough to miss her."

Then, without warning, Carina abruptly shifted gears. "Listen, you must go back and find BC."

"*What?*" he declared, scarcely believing his ears. "I'll do nothing of the kind."

"You *must*," she implored.

"Do you love him?" Fornax asked, almost afraid of the answer.

"Not at all."

"Then why?"

"He's your friend—you owe the man your life."

"Keeping track of me was his *job*. I'm sure that rather than worrying about me, he would've been much happier out killing someone so as to advance his rather vague notion of duty to the Crown."

"Vague notion?" she asked in shocked disbelief.

Like stones dropped into a very deep well, Fornax's cruel words echoed back at him. A distant look gushed into Carina's eyes and her face reddened. She turned away.

"Vague notion?" she repeated, almost choking on the words. "BC is not a stone-cold killer. To the contrary," she said, turning to face him again, "he is a kind and gentle man."

"Woman, you're so . . . so . . . damn exasperating!" Fornax exclaimed. "First, you accuse us men of only coming home for sex, then you accuse us of enslaving our women, then you accuse *me* of abandoning my best friend! How can you be so goddamned arrogant?"

"Then you'll do it?" she confirmed excitedly.

"Of course, I will! I'm not sure how yet, but, yes, after a good night's rest, I'll do it!"

• • •

Growling like a bulldog, J bared his teeth at Agent Cornwall. "You just couldn't leave well enough alone, could you?"

Fearing the retribution now that he had been caught, Cornwall trembled. "Whatever do you mean?"

"Don't play dumb with me, you traitor!" J exploded in an accusing tone.

"Traitor?" Cornwall said, coughing out the word. "I've been the most loyal man you've recruited since . . . since . . . before Captain Michael. How can you call me a traitor?"

"May I remind you, young Nicholas, that the Captain was *himself* a double agent! And he died a most horrible death."

"You're out of your head!" Cornwall snapped back, trying to defend his good name. "I am *not* a double agent and you know it! Okay, I admit I hired Harsha Gandu to help me keep track of Sam, but unlike yourself, I couldn't just let the man twist in the wind."

"You simpleton!" J yelped. "The Overlord would *never* have killed Matthews! Ling was intending to use him as bait, as leverage to force BC to reveal how he'd sabotaged the ship. I should imagine you have now sealed *both* of their fates!"

"Whatever do you mean?" Cornwall gulped, the blood slowly draining from his face. "With Sam out of the way, they no longer *have* any leverage over BC," he stammered, suddenly afraid he'd made a big mistake. "BC would never have told them anything anyhow."

"According to our intelligence reports, within days after Sam escaped the *Tikkidiw* was stolen from a warehouse on Sri Lanka. We're not sure exactly how he did it or who helped him, but we are certain of one thing—*he* snatched it. Now, without Sam *or* the ship, Ling doesn't have much of a reason for keeping BC alive, does he? You've killed him."

Suddenly nauseous, Cornwall slumped into a chair, gasping for air. "Where is BC now?" he asked meekly. "Couldn't we just go in there and pull him out?"

"At last report, Chou Kim was holding him at the spaceport. Frankly, with all these developments, it would be a miracle if he were still alive."

Realizing what he had done to his friend, Cornwall reached for a garbage can to throw up into.

Not letting up, J gave him an ultimatum. "Unless you cooperate with me fully, you'll be tried and hung for treason. Do you understand what I'm telling you?"

Cornwall answered him with a blank stare.

Continuing to display his arrogance, J declared, "The agent's name you have been searching so unprofitably for—the one with the M-A-R in her name—is one Marona Savitar, a.k.a. Marona Fumoro, a.k.a. Marona Baru."

Cornwall shook his head, not recognizing any of the aliases. "Sorry, boss, but I've never heard of her."

"That's too bad," J smirked, "because Marona is Whitey's daughter."

His shocking words hung like a thick film in the air.

"And, according to my information, along with Sam and your buddy Harsha, she too was in that Afghan prison cell. Not only have you signed *BC*'s death warrant, you have killed Dr. Samuel Matthews as well. *And*, if I understand that garbled message correctly, you've more than likely fingered Carina for elimination also. A fine day's work, wouldn't you say?"

Cornwall threw up.

It didn't seem to faze J, though; he was unrelenting. Even before Cornwall had wiped the wet residue from his mouth, J started in on him again.

"On the off-chance that BC is still alive, I have devised a plan to keep him that way. In order to convince Overlord Ling that BC knows something we don't want *him* to know, I propose to launch a commando raid against Sri Lanka in an attempt to assassinate him."

"Him who?" Cornwall asked, dumbfounded. "You want to send in a team to shoot BC?"

"I don't want him shot dead, you fool—only winged. If we make it look convincing enough, the Overlord will have a reason to keep BC alive."

"If you're willing to go to the trouble to stage an assassination attempt, why not just rescue the man?" Cornwall objected, gathering his wits about him.

"If the Overlord possesses something he thinks I want, then the game becomes much more interesting."

"Storming the Sri Lanka compound could turn into a suicide mission!"

"That's why *you* are going to lead it," J remarked proudly.

"How can you stand yourself?" Nicholas scoffed, wiping his chin.

"You are insubordinate, aren't you?" J shot back haughtily.

"Has living the way you have, been worth it?" Cornwall sneered, the disdain oozing from all his pores.

Waxing philosophic, J answered. "Sometimes it requires intense perseverance to achieve success. And since the rewards for one's persistence are rarely known until after it's too late, unremitting dedication to an idea or a goal is a hard way to live. Those of us who have been steadfast, and who have been triumphant as a result, will counsel patience to those who would ask the secret of our success. On the other hand, history is replete with stories of dedication and of patience gone berserk. Upon *their* deathbeds, these unfulfilled, frustrated people will bitterly counsel frivolity to anyone standing near. Unfortunately," J grinned, "neither truth is altogether true."

7
Murder

At the sound of the thunderous pounding on his door, Fornax shook the sleep groggily from his eyes and sat up in bed. Recalling what a pleasure last night had been he briefly glanced over at his bedmate and smiled.

"Okay, already!" he shouted as the frantic pounding continued.

"What can they possibly want at this hour?" Carina protested, fumbling for her watch.

"I'll see," Fornax said, slipping on his trousers.

"You have nice buns," she teased as he started for the door.

He took a bow, and by the time he'd flung open the door, his anger had subsided.

Lotha literally burst into the room, his face white with fear. "Navi's dead!" he clamored, his bulk filling the doorway. "When I went to wake him for breakfast this morning there wasn't any answer. I went in anyway and found him slumped over the desk. And I found *this* in his hand," Lotha reported as he handed Fornax a piece of writing paper.

"This is a suicide note!" Fornax exclaimed, reading it aloud:

It was a mistake for me to come to Mars. Life here is just too brutal; too lonely. I want to go home, but I'm stuck here with these dullards for the rest of my life. Forgive me God, but I just can't face this. Goodbye.

"I can't believe what I'm reading," Fornax asserted as he reached for his shirt, deftly holstering his blade in the process. "Take me to Navi's room right away."

As the two of them hurried down the corridor with Carina following close behind, Fornax interviewed Lotha. "Did you touch anything?" he asked.

"Except for the note, I left everything as it was," Lotha answered.

"Good. Who else knows of this?"

"So far, just you and me. And Carina."

Navi's cold and lifeless body was just as Lotha had described—head down upon the desk, arms sprawled out to either side.

Although the faint scent of an unusual perfume hung in the air, there were no signs of a struggle. The door hadn't been forced, nor was there an obvious murder weapon in sight. On the desk next to the body was one curious item, though—a tiny glass vial containing grains of a mysterious-looking white powder. Judging by the half-empty cup of water on the dresser, they were apparently supposed to assume that Navi had poisoned himself.

Sniffing the air, Fornax trembled as it dawned on him what he smelled. He had gotten a whiff of this deadly perfume twice before—once in the Corkscrew Pub the day Captain Michael was murdered and once again in Lester's warehouse the day Sven Rutland was born. Each time, death had been associated with that smell. Encountering it here could mean only one thing!

Momentarily shelving his fears, Fornax held the strange vial up to the light. "What do you make of this?" he inquired, his voice cracking.

"I have no idea," the big Afghan confessed as Fornax carefully wrapped the vial in a tissue and dropped it into his pocket.

"Go fetch Sam and Harsha for me," Fornax directed. "Have them both meet me here right away."

Once he and Carina were alone, Fornax said, "I'd like you to do me a big favor. Last night at dinner Navi complained of a stomachache. Find his wine glass and bring it to me right away. I want to have the contents tested. I'll bet we find the stuff in his glass to be just as vile as the stuff in this little white bottle. This was no suicide," he asserted confidently. "This was murder."

"Are you serious?" she questioned incredulously.

Fornax nodded. By now Lotha had returned with the two other men. "Go get the wine glass," he whispered. "And be careful not to spill it."

"Lotha, why don't you wait in the hall while I interrogate these two."

As he shut the door behind him, Fornax turned on Harsha. "Listen, you bastard!" he yelled, grabbing the long-haired Harsha brusquely by the shoulders. "What the hell is going on around here? Why did you murder this man, for God's sake?"

"Murder?" Harsha gulped innocently. "Lotha told me it was suicide."

"Suicide, my ass!" Fornax swore. "This man was poisoned, and you were sitting right next to him at dinner last night. It would've been a simple matter for you to have slipped something into his drink."

"Only I didn't," Harsha contended. "I swear it. What possible motive would I have?"

"Really, Fornax," Sam interrupted. "On what do you base your accusation?"

"Wasn't this the same bloke you were suspicious of from the start? Didn't you tell me he claimed to be the son of an Afghan fellow you befriended in college? And wasn't that just a *little* too convenient even for you, Sam?"

"Well, yes," Sam admitted, scrutinizing Harsha as he spoke, "I did think it was a bit of a stretch, but he's been a model citizen ever since."

"Model *citizen?* Damnit, Sam, he's a *spy!* I say we waste the man right where he stands!"

Even as he spoke, Fornax skillfully popped his blade from its holster and pressed the steel tip up against Harsha's chin.

"Whoa, slow down," Harsha pleaded, jerking his head back a notch. "I haven't been quite honest with you—that much is true—but Navi's killer, I'm not."

"Out with it, then!" Fornax insisted, keeping the blade tucked tightly beneath the man's chin.

"Okay, already, let me explain," Harsha said, clearing his throat. "I am a free-lance operative. I do undercover work for the Brits from time to time . . . "

"Them *again?*" an exasperated Fornax sighed, withdrawing his blade a few centimeters. "Every time I turn around . . . "

Harsha cut back in. "A few months ago I got this frantic call from an agent Nicholas Cornwall of Her Majesty's . . . "

"I know Cornwall," Sam interjected.

"So do I," Fornax concurred in a less confrontational tone, reholstering his blade as Harsha continued his explanation.

"Like I said, I got this call. Cornwall asked me to help him ditch a set of gene-prints from an armory up north. It was supposed to save some guy's butt from being captured by the Overlord. Well, I didn't mind doing the job because the gene-prints belonged to a fellow-Afghan named Fornax Nehrengel," Harsha explained, nodding his head in admiration. "This Nehrengel was a bit of a folk hero to us, what with him having blown away the Overlord's kid and all.

"Then, more recently, when Sam was snatched, Nicholas asked me to keep track of him. Apparently on this one, Cornwall went outside the normal channels and his agency is unaware that I've been brought into it. I've been nothing more than a passive observer since you broke us all out of jail."

"And the story about Ravi, your supposed father?" Sam asked.

"Just a ruse to gain your confidence," Harsha admitted. "I never met the man."

Sam might have expressed his disappointment, but by this time Carina had returned to the room empty-handed.

"No wine glass?" Fornax quizzed, his forehead creasing.

"Sorry," she answered, knowing that he would be upset. "Marona and Saron had already cleaned up everything from last night's feast before I got down there this morning."

"That's just great," Fornax complained bitterly. Then turning to Sam, he said, "How is it that you know Agent Cornwall?"

"He was upstairs sleeping at my house the morning I was kidnapped."

"Describe him," Fornax demanded, just to be sure.

"Well, let's see, he was young, clean-cut, about so tall, had piercing blue eyes . . . "

"Yep, that's him," Fornax agreed, remembering the man he had suspected of foul play back when his suit malfunctioned on the moon.

Having listened quietly to this exchange, Carina said, "Fornax, honey, if anyone knows where BC is, I imagine that this nice Mister Cornwall does. Why don't we contact *him?*"

"Carina's absolutely right," Fornax said, looking Harsha in the eye. "Cornwall would never have sent you here on an assignment this important without first setting up some sort of way for the two of you to make contact."

"You're a quick study," Harsha said. "Each day at 1400 hours Greenwich Mean Time, Nicholas promised to listen in on the narrow-band. We agreed to use only Seussarian codes in our communiqués."

"Seussarian?" Sam questioned.

"Named after a twentieth-century madman," Harsha explained. "The message units are composed of trite little rhyming passages."

"Like what?"

"Oh, I don't know. Mary had a little lamb, fleece as white as snow; Sam likes green eggs and ham, but caterpillars don't snore, ya know."

"Land's sakes! What the heck does *that* mean?" Sam pressed, more confused than ever.

"It doesn't matter," Fornax intervened irritably. "So long as we can reach him, that's what's important."

"Only we can't," Harsha interrupted nervously.

"I don't understand," Sam said.

"What I mean is, I haven't been able to raise him since before we left."

"I see," Fornax answered unhappily. "But that still leaves us with just one little problem doesn't it?"

"What's that?" Harsha queried.

"Assuming I'm right and this was a murder, and assuming you didn't do it, we have a very short list of possible suspects. Saron, Marona, Lotha . . . "

"Marona was with me," Sam confessed bashfully. "There's no way she could've slipped out of bed during the night to murder this poor bastard without me knowing it."

"Dad!" Carina protested. "She's young enough to be . . . to be . . . my *sister!*"

"I suppose you think you're the *only* one in the family who gets horny?" Sam retorted, a little miffed.

"Let's give it a rest, shall we?" Fornax said. "Without Navi's wine glass this is all a little tenuous. However, I do believe your story, Harsha, and so far as I'm concerned, you're off the suspect list. In fact, I'm inclined to leave you in charge here while I'm gone.

"And as for you, Sam—until I get back, why don't you make a point of keeping your pants zipped. I'm warning you to be careful around this Marona. She seems just a little too eager to jump into bed with a man old enough to be her father."

"Well, I'll be!" Sam stammered, trying to sound indignant.

"And as for you, my sweet," Fornax said, directing his attention to Carina, "keep your door locked and Sandy at your side."

"And just where do you think you're going?" Sam asked.

"With Jenny out of commission, I'll need to scrounge around in the armory for a suitable weapon. After that, I'm going to visit my good friend Chou Kim in Sri Lanka. He'll know where BC is being held."

"Don't be a hero," Sam chided. "There are no Purple Hearts for dummies."

"Yeah, I know—heroes die stupid deaths."

8
Rescue

Even as a young man, BC had always been a pretty tough character. Not tough so much in the sense of mean, but rather, tough as in the sense of resolute, able to withstand pain.

And it was a good thing too, because since his capture, Chou Kim's thugs had been using him as a human punching bag, subjecting him to repeated beatings, whippings, and the occasional hallucinogenic drug.

But none of it had fazed BC because the man was unyielding. He took the abuse like a stoic, in time even earning the grudging admiration of his habitually-drunk captors.

Knowing that he was on his own, that no one from Commonwealth Intelligence would ever bother to come and rescue him, BC had accepted it on faith that if there was to be any hope of escape, he would have to figure it out for himself. And with that in mind, he had watched each day for an opening, hoping to exploit it.

Disoriented and confused by the drugs and by the light deprivation, he couldn't say with certainty just how many days had passed since his arrival. Still, after what seemed to have been about a week, he spied the *Tikkidiw* parked outside in the compound just beyond his cell. Although it was later moved indoors where his captors could presumably study it more closely, he was secretly delighted to learn from the guards that the ship had to be flown to Sri Lanka under conventional propulsion. Apparently, his sabotage of the power coupling was as yet unremedied!

Then too, judging by the tempo and severity of his subsequent lashings, their failure to figure out how the Fornax Drive operated must have infuriated the Chinese to no end. His stoicism had served only to incense them further.

And yet, much to his surprise, they had stopped short of killing him. It occurred to him that what had probably kept him alive was a decision he'd made that day just before vacating the ship. At the very last minute he'd had the presence of mind to hide the O-ring in his shorts.

Threaded on its innerwall with tiny grooves so that it could be used to join together two cables, the round power coupling looked superficially like a broad wedding band. Snugged up around his genitals as it was, the cold metal ring had grown mighty uncomfortable these past few days, but thus far, it had remained undiscovered. Being a student of human behavior, BC had counted on the fact that the manlier the guard, the more squeamish he would be to inspect a prisoner's privates. He had been right.

The next day, when Chou Kim came to his cell—his fat belly jiggling with every step, and a big, sick grin plastered across his greasy face—he was armed with the news that Sam had been kidnapped and would soon be brought to Sri Lanka for interrogation. BC was horrified by the prospect—*Sam could never survive the kind of punishment he himself had endured!*

When, a couple of nights afterward, an intrepid company of bandits broke into the compound and stole the ship, BC made up his mind to bolt. Two nights later he saw his opportunity.

As had been their custom from the start, once the goons were done beating him up for the evening, they would retire to a corner of the cell, break out a flask of tortan, and proceed to drink themselves into a stupor. Despite his status as their prisoner, BC had been pestering them for days to join in. Up until now, he had been refused.

This evening, however, before passing out, they relented. Perhaps they felt sorry for him or perhaps they knew his days were numbered, but for whatever the reason, they handed him the flask.

BC was overjoyed. He downed enough to get a buzz, but stopped well short of becoming as delirious as the two miscreants charged with overseeing him. Once they were comatose, the rest was easy.

Unshackling himself with one of their skeleton keys, and donning one of their kevlar tee-shirts for protection, BC slid silently towards the door of the building. Transferring the O-ring from his undershorts to the pocket of his trousers, he slipped out into the night, hoping to sneak away unseen. He had no idea of the predicament he now faced.

With the moonlight glistening off his stooped and sore frame, BC made an excellent target for the tentative young man positioned at the fenceline, a high-powered rifle slung over his shoulder. Silhouetted against the corrugated aluminum walls of the quonset hut he had just exited, BC should have known better than to stand still. But, by the time he recognized how foolhardy it was not to keep moving, it was already too late!

Suddenly a wild shot rang out, its report reverberating throughout the spaceport! At the sound, BC dropped to the ground, searching desperately for a shadow to burrow into. Finding none, he bolted for the perimeter fence, unaware that he was running directly into the sights of his would-be assassin.

Emboldened by this stroke of good luck, the sniper again took deliberate aim, and for the second time tonight, pressed his forefinger reluctantly against the trigger. Hating himself for what he had to do—for what he had been *ordered* to do—Cornwall exerted just the hint of downward pressure on the trigger as he prepared to squeeze it home. Engrossed as he was in tracking his quarry, the young man was oblivious of the figure creeping up the hill behind him.

The newcomer was Fornax, and when he saw what Cornwall was about to do—and to whom—he was stunned! Calmly leveling his weapon on Nicholas's head, he sternly ordered, "Drop your gun or you're a dead man!"

More relieved than frightened, more appreciative than scared, Cornwall humbly obeyed, laying his rifle down on the ground at his feet. "Okay, mister," he replied, not realizing that the intruder was Fornax. "Take it easy," he said, raising his hands above his head. "Don't shoot."

"Give me one good reason why I shouldn't blast you to smithereens!" Fornax exclaimed just as BC reached the moonlit bluff where the two men were standing. "Just one good reason."

Cornwall stood there numb, trying to imagine what must have been going through BC's mind.

For his part, BC didn't know what to make of the scene before him. Through the fence and to his left—his arms pointing to the sky—stood Cornwall, the prospective assassin BC had thought was his friend. And to his right—his blaster pointed at Cornwall's head—was Fornax, the blond reincarnation of a man he had thought was dead.

"You're *alive?!*" he blurted out, bewildered by this turn of events.

Before Fornax could answer, the sound of a klaxon began blaring out from the compound below. At the same moment, a pair of menacing search lights started fanning their beams across the grounds.

"They've discovered that I'm missing," BC groaned, still plagued by the pain of his last beating.

"Well then, let's get the hell out of here!" Fornax ordered as he cut a hole in the fence big enough for BC to pass through.

Focusing his attention on Cornwall for the first time since he arrived on the scene, and seeing the rifle in the dirt at his feet, BC formed the logical conclusion.

"J sent you here to kill me, didn't he?" BC shouted, grounding Cornwall with a left hook.

"And you agreed to do it, didn't you?" he growled, walloping Cornwall again.

"Not actually," Cornwall groveled as he struggled to his feet. "I was just supposed to wing you."

"*Wing* me?" BC repeated, towering over the man. "He sent you here to wing me?"

Infuriated as much at J for proposing such a lame scheme as at Cornwall for agreeing to go along with it, BC slugged him again, this time knocking him cold.

"Now what?" Fornax demanded. "We can't just *leave* him here."

"Oh yes we can!" BC quarreled as he limped off into the night.

"No, this way," Fornax directed, motioning with his hand. "I think the ship is parked over yonder."

"I'm confused. How did the ship get back *here?* I disabled her."

"So I discovered. And to get her back running again, I had to scavenge an O-ring from this special gun I built. Now the only problem is, without the part, my *blaster* won't work," he explained, pulling Jenny from his pocket.

"Here. Will this help?" BC asked, handing Fornax the coupling he'd been carrying around with him since the moon.

"You mean you had it with you in your pocket all this time?" Fornax bubbled excitedly as he fumbled in the moonlight to resurrect Jenny.

"In a manner of speaking."

As they melted into the jungle, making good their escape, the gnashing of the Overlord's teeth could be heard all the way to Mars.

It wasn't a pretty sound!

9
Escape

"They can't be very far behind us," the fair-skinned man advised as the faintest hint of dawn shone in the distance. "If we don't reach the ship soon, we're both dead men!"

"Oh, relax, BC," Fornax said. "I know I parked it around here somewhere. Don't forget, it was *dark* when I landed. Haven't you ever misplaced anything?"

"Nothing that big, I'm afraid. Now listen, you fool, as thick as this forest is, you're gonna have to do a little better than 'somewhere'."

"That ridge looks familiar," Fornax declared, pointing towards a hillock a few hundred meters in front of them. "Let's head thataway."

"We're lost, aren't we?" BC said as the sun peeked above the horizon. "Just what kind of a rescue is this anyway?"

Although the events of the past few hours had drawn the two men closer together, their association had been slow in coming and could hardly be described yet as friendship. For the moment anyway, it remained an acquaintance laden with taunts and jibes.

"Why you unappreciative limey! Lost suggests bewilderment or confusion. I assure you . . . "

"Damnit, old chum!" BC shouted, pushing aside a branch as he picked his way through the dense woods. "Why didn't you just flip on a locator beacon before you left the ship to come looking for me?"

"Well, if you must know, I was in such a hurry I forgot."

"You forgot?!" BC scolded in an exasperated tone, his ribs still bruised from last night's beating. "You forgot?" he repeated, no less annoyed. "We have an entire squadron of goons out combing the woods, searching for us, and you tell me you forgot?! Just how the hell did we get into this mess?"

"Carina insisted I come looking for you," Fornax said, trying to divert the blame. "I think she's soft on you."

"That meddling woman? Don't be silly," BC laughed as he fought his way through the underbrush. "I was her plaything for a couple of hours, that's all. Deep down, she wants you. But be careful," BC warned, "you may discover that her only interest in you is clinical."

"What do you mean, clinical?"

"Genetic, then," BC explained, his close-fitting shirt revealing his muscular build.

Fornax answered him with a blank expression.

"It's your *genes* she wants off you, not your jeans," he asserted. "She's got this crazy theory about evolution and . . . "

A tight smile inched across Fornax's countenance. "Yes, yes, I came upon her diary," he confessed, a bob of the head signaling that he concurred with BC's assessment. "But can't we just forget about Carina for now?" he suggested, his dark eyes bearing witness to his brooding mood.

"Fair enough," BC replied. "What if Chou Kim's soldiers find the *Tikkidiw* before we do?"

"What of it? Even if they locate her, they'll never be able to *fly* her."

"How can you be so sure? I thought you told me you fixed her?" a curious BC inquired, narrowly avoiding a protruding root.

Proudly recalling his handiwork under fire, Fornax nodded. "That I did."

"What, then?"

"I locked the door."

"You locked the *door?*" BC repeated, nearly choking with laughter.

"They won't even be able to climb onboard!" Fornax announced confidently.

Still chuckling, BC said, "So all we have to do now is *locate* the ship."

"And I've figured out a perfectly good way to do just that."

"How?"

"Soon enough, their airchops will spot our vessel from the air," Fornax explained. "And when they do, they'll hover over it, giving away her position to us. All *we* have to do is listen for the sound of the airchop's rotor, then follow it to the *Tikkidiw*."

"As will *their* soldiers," BC reminded Fornax. "And lest you forget, *they* will be carrying automatic weapons. What do we have?"

"Jenny," Fornax answered simply.

"Jenny may work wonders blasting down dungeon doors, but that thing won't do us much good out here in the forest—there's just too darn many *trees*," BC argued convincingly. Beneath his blond mop, the furrows in his forehead deepened noticeably as he frowned.

"Heh, enough already!" Fornax shouted. "Instead of *thanking* me for coming all the way back to rescue your sorry butt, all I've heard is complaints! I should've left your . . . "

"Shush!" BC ordered, his keen ears perking up. "I hear an airchop," he said, pausing to listen at the foot of a giant cedar.

"I told ya they'd come," Fornax chided.

"Yes, yes, so you did," BC confirmed in an exasperated tone, "but if they spot the two of us before we reach the shuttle, your being right won't save us from a firing squad."

"They don't want *you*," Fornax explained, "they want the ship. That's why they didn't shoot you right off the bat—they hoped to trade you . . . "

"Shush! I think the airchop has stopped moving," BC announced, his well-trained ears focusing like an antenna on the whirr.

"I'll bet they've found her. I *told* you I left her parked on that ridge," Fornax declared, proudly pointing in the direction of the circling airchop.

"Let's move in a little closer, just to be sure. But exercise extreme caution—these woods are bound to be crawling with soldiers before long."

"Heh, Mister Smart-Aleck-Secret-Agent-Man, let's not forget who broke you loose!"

"Whisper, Fornax. Whisper!"

His dirty hair matted down by the morning heat, Fornax acknowledged BC with a nod.

Drawn by the whine of the hovering airchop, Fornax and BC advanced stealthily through the forest, their sharp eyes alert to any sign of the enemy.

All of a sudden, Fornax pushed aside a branch and there she was, gleaming in the morning sun, just as he had left her.

Instead of being elated, he swore under his breath. "Damn! We've got a problem."

Not only was an airchop circling ominously overhead just as they expected, four beefy infantrymen stood in the clearing separating them from their vessel. Two of them held force guns.

"A problem indeed," BC remarked in a noncommittal tone. "Well, what do you suggest now, Mister I-came-to-rescue-you-Man. If you blast them with your Jenny from here, you'll undoubtedly blow our ship to kingdom come right along with the four of them."

"Either we'll have to draw them away—or else we'll have to give ourselves up," Fornax declared as he rose from behind the bushes.

"Give ourselves up?" a stunned BC yelped without meaning to. "Are you *crazy?*"

"Crazy like a fox," Fornax replied as he tucked Jenny into his pants at the small of his back, then raised both his hands high above his head.

"Please don't shoot," he pleaded to the gun-toting sentries.

Keeping an eye on them as he spoke, Fornax walked calmly out into the clearing where the armed men had been standing watch. Still hidden by the foliage, BC held back.

"I'm unarmed," Fornax continued, "and I'm sure your bosses would prefer you captured this airship with its pilot intact."

Keeping his back to the forest, Fornax slowly drew nearer to the menacing soldiers, his arms still raised in the classic gesture of surrender.

"It is wise of you to give yourself up without a fight," one of the men shouted over the din of the airchop.

"I'm not a brave man," Fornax admitted. "I prefer wealth over martyrdom," he added as he slid laterally across the clearing. He was trying to work himself in closer to the *Tikkidiw*.

"You lie like a dog!" the tough-looking soldier retorted, powering up his weapon. "You came here to free an enemy of the state!"

Fearing that the end was at hand, Fornax took a deep breath. "True, but your enemy happens to be *my* friend. Certainly you would've done the same, had you been in my shoes."

By now, Fornax had positioned himself so that the ship was no longer in his line of fire.

"Heh, fella," the not-so-bright guard observed, "for a bloke who's trying to surrender himself, you sure do move about an awful lot. Now, stand still or else I'll drop you right there."

"Why threaten me?" Fornax questioned humbly. "I'm willing to deliver the missing prisoner to you, no questions asked. All I want is my ship."

As if on cue, BC burst from his thicket-covered hiding place. He was fuming. "You're turning me *in?*" he cried out. "Why you son-of-a . . . "

At the sound of BC's angry voice, the guards instinctively spun to face him, and that was all the time Fornax needed. Over the course of the next instant, he reached behind his back, yanked Jenny from his belt, and blew the four of them to atoms! It all happened so swiftly, they never knew what hit them!

Only, the confrontation wasn't over yet!

Without a warning, automatic fire rang out from a gunner perched in the airchop hanging overhead. Narrowly avoiding the tracers, Fornax dashed for the locked door of the *Tikkidiw* even as BC dove back into the woods for cover.

Realizing the danger his buddy was in, Fornax whirled around and let loose another volley from Jenny, this time aiming it directly at the airchop.

Spellbound by the outcome of his shot, Fornax studiously listened as the pitch of the rotor dropped an octave. Then, the entire vessel disintegrated before his very eyes!

As he watched, Fornax was reminded, not only of his short-lived military career, but also of his lingering guilt for deserting his country that very same day. How could he ever repay the debt?

Doing what he could to dodge the chunks of metal raining down upon him from the sky, BC raced to join his cohort onboard the ship. "Next time, you might warn me what you're up to," he exclaimed.

"*Next* time?" Fornax asked, his hands skillfully working the dials on the nav-console. "There had better not *be* a next time!" he declared as he punched the Drive button for the jump to orbit.

• • •

They say timing is everything, and it was an unfortunate quirk of fate that they should lift off without spying Agent Cornwall's arrival in the clearing below. They never saw him frantically waving his hands at them to stop, nor did they ever hear him yell out a warning to beware of Marona Savitar.

Pity.

10
Ajar

A light rain was falling outside when Fornax set the ship down near the Mars station. He had already stowed Jenny away in one of the galley cupboards when BC cleared his throat to speak.

"I'm flattered that you risked your life to save mine, but frankly, I think you made a big mistake coming after me. With a killer on the loose, you never should've left the others alone."

Extracting the tiny bottle of white powder from his pocket, Fornax remarked, "Except for this vial of what I imagine is some sort of vicious toxin, I have no actual proof of anything. I meant to have this stuff analyzed while I was back on Earth, but we booked out of there so fast, I never got the chance. Besides, I left one of your people in charge of things here until I returned. What could possibly go wrong?"

"One of *my* people?" BC asked flabbergasted. "What are you talking about?"

"After Sam was snatched, your buddy Cornwall hired a fellow to watch over us—a young man by the name of Harsha Gandu."

"Never heard of him," BC said, a worried look on his face. "Let's hurry," he urged, bounding out of the ship and into the rain. "After the incident at the spaceport, I'm not sure anymore whose side Cornwall is on!"

Entering the landrover-bay through a side door, they were greeted by a ghostly silence. The ceiling lights were turned down as if it were nighttime, when, in fact, it was nearly noon. Fornax hadn't expected a welcoming party, but since this was the largest room in the place, he had expected that *someone* would be milling around!

Squinting his eyes as he crossed the threshold, BC remarked, "It's awfully dark in there—maybe I should leave the outside door open to give us some light."

"Good idea."

Despite the overcast conditions, the natural lighting gave substance to their shadows. Reaching out, Fornax touched the landrover with his hands. It was dripping wet as if it had just come in from out of the rain. "Curious," he mumbled under his breath.

"Where is everyone?" BC asked in a worried whisper.

As if to answer his question, suddenly the bank of oversized halogen lamps hanging directly over their heads was turned on.

Temporarily blinded, both men staggered backwards, their hands shielding their eyes against the incandescent brightness.

"So, you're back," the husky female voice acknowledged without emotion.

"Yes," Fornax answered, one eye riveted on the large gun Marona held gripped in her hand. His breathing quickened as he spied Carina cowering in the background with three or four of the others. They were huddled nervously together as if they had been repeatedly threatened with bodily harm. Harsha was not among them. The dog, Sandy, scampered back and forth across the concrete floor, his untrimmed nails making a most annoying scratching sound.

"Where's that fancy blaster of yours?" Marona asked, approaching cautiously.

"Onboard the *Tikkidiw*," Fornax answered without flinching.

"You won't be offended if I don't believe you," she declared, framing the question as if it were a statement.

"Where's Harsha?" Fornax inquired, afraid of the answer.

"I took him for a little ride in the landrover," she snickered sinisterly. "He won't be coming back."

"I know what you're here for," Fornax said as she frisked him.

"Is that so?"

After confiscating his blade and slipping it inside her boot, she moved on to BC. Satisfying herself that both men were now unarmed, Marona smiled.

"Well since you're so smart, that'll save me from having to tell you what I'm going to do next."

"But you can't have it," Fornax retorted defiantly, guessing she meant to abscond with the shuttle.

"And who's gonna stop me?" she countered, finding pleasure in toying with the man. "*You?* Your little secret agent buddy? Hah!" she laughed, cocking her gun and swinging it over in BC's direction.

"He killed my father, you know. Hell, you should be happy if I kill him *for* you," she cackled, pulling back on the trigger and letting BC have one in the shoulder. "When you had your head turned, he did your little girlfriend, you dolt! And he'll keep on doing the little tart until . . ."

"Little *tart?*" Carina exploded, angrily advancing across the room. She was revolted by the sight of BC writhing around on the floor, blood pouring from his wound.

Sam stopped his daughter and grabbed her firmly by the arm before events could spin further out of control. He stubbornly challenged Marona. "You slime, you can't kill us all!"

"And why not?" she threatened, now leveling her weapon on Sam.

"No!" Carina screamed, rushing to her father's defense.

"Get outta my way, you tart!" Marona demanded, shoving Carina to the floor. "Cross me again, and I'll fry your stupid little dog!" she spat, kicking Sandy in the ribs.

At the crack of her boot, the dog yelped and flew whimpering out the open door with Carina close on her heels.

"Don't go out there!" Sam hollered after her.

"Let the mutt go or else your father's dead! Anyhow, the dog'll die out there in a matter of hours," Marona callously observed.

"Leave Sam and Carina out of this," BC gasped, struggling to arrest the flow of blood with his free hand. "You came for me, so take me already."

"Oh, don't worry, you little piece of Brit-shit, I will not be denied my full measure of revenge," Marona cackled hideously. "I plan on doing to you just exactly what you did to my daddy—killing you, then discarding your worthless butt on the moon."

Staring back at her in disbelief, his eyes pleading for mercy, BC got up on one knee.

"Commonwealth Intelligence sure does like to hire them young and stupid, don't they?" Marona giggled.

"He's my friend," Fornax said. "And I won't cooperate with you if you harm him." Not since Vishnu had he been close enough to anyone to even care.

Ignoring him, Marona spoke in a savage tone. "First, you'll fly me to the moon so I can dump off the remains of this poor limey, then the two of us'll go to Hong Kong where we can have a nice long chat with *my* good buddy, Overlord ding-a-Ling. He's quite mad, you know, but then he's been waiting a good long time to get his hands on you and your machine."

Waving her gun at Sam and Lotha like a baton, she said, "You two—help get this wounded man outside and onto the ship."

Kneeling over BC, Lotha said, "This man needs a doctor."

"Do as I say, ya big oaf, or you'll be the one needing a doctor!"

Hoping to save his friend's life, Fornax started to argue. "Why bring him along just to kill him later?"

"You would prefer I finish him right here?" she questioned, an inhuman, mean-spirited grin spreading across her face. "Suit yourself," she shrieked, again discharging her weapon in BC's direction.

This time, he fell to the floor with a painful thud.

Enraged, Fornax lunged for her, but she deftly turned him aside with a fierce karate jab to the hip. Cringing, he buckled to the ground next to the motionless BC.

"I need you alive," she explained, "but if you make one more stupid move like that, I'll blow you away along with the rest of these Afghan mongrels."

"No more killing!" Fornax entreated as he surrendered. "I'll do whatever you want, just no more killing."

"Now that's a good little boy," she sneered, helping him to his feet.

"Heh, King Kong," she shouted, directing her stream of vitriol at Lotha. "Toss this stiff aboard the ship. And strap him down in one of the back berths. I don't want his dead carcass floating all around when we're in space."

Growling, Lotha did what he was told.

11
Vile

As the ship's egg-shaped orbit took them around to the marbled, unlit side of the moon, the darkened viewport doubled as a mirror, reflecting his brooding face back at him. Guilt and failure were on his mind. Like a demon, Marona's evil countenance shimmered in the background.

Though Fornax wasn't sure what he could have done to prevent it, he couldn't escape the feeling that he was to blame. BC's death, like that of Vishnu's before him, had been his fault, and the rage was seething up inside him!

Since before they left, Marona had been making fun of him. Now, as he stood there at the window, fatigued by her harangue, Fornax swallowed hard. He understood that this could only end one way—either it would be him or it would be her. There was no way both of them would be getting off this ship alive.

"Why don't you forget about Carina?" she whispered, trying to read his thoughts.

"I'm not sure I can," he replied, confounded by her question. There had always been female spies, and the young and the pretty ones had always used the same tools. So help him, the inner workings of the female mind never ceased to delight and astound. They always figured they could cancel the score and start over with that one trump play—sex!

"Don't you want to take me?" she cooed in a haunting tone, undoing her top as she spoke. "I promise you, I'm much better, and oh so much more athletic, than that prissy, half-breed concubine you've been hanging around with."

"No doubt," Fornax acknowledged, wondering if Carina would forgive him.

Struggling not to feast his eyes on her chiseled figure as she fondly cupped her breasts, one in each hand, Fornax valiantly tried to change the subject.

"How 'bout a toast to your victory?" he suggested, reaching into the cooler for an unopened bottle of tortan-wine. "To *our* victory!"

"And what victory are you so proud of, cupcake?"

"Surely you must've been aware that I've been working for Overlord Ling right from the beginning," he pointed out, wrestling for control of the conversation.

"How's that?" she cross-examined, provocatively stroking herself.

"Surely, your father must have told you of my deal with Lester, a deal bought and paid for by Ling?" Fornax explained as he stood at the counter, opening the bottle of wine.

"My, but aren't we the nefarious one!" she complimented, genuinely surprised by the revelation. "Yes, by George, I'll have that drink after all. Then, when we've had our fun, perhaps we can renegotiate the terms of that deal you made with ole ding-a-Ling."

"Money is what got me started on this," he wryly admitted as he reached furtively into his pocket for the vial he'd been carrying around with him since Navi's murder.

Slipping a few grains of the deadly white powder into Marona's goblet, he said, "Yes, money is what it's all about."

"A toast, then?" she offered, raising her glass.

"A toast," he affirmed, taking pleasure in watching her gulp down the wine.

Licking her lips, Marona renewed her self-absorbed quest to bed him. "Now you will do me?" she moaned, stripping to the waist.

"Of course," he pledged, suppressing the disgust welling up inside him.

"From the moment we first met in the Corkscrew, I sensed that you wanted to have me . . . Now here's your chance!"

Running her tongue along his ear, Marona egged him on.

Fornax stiffened with fear as he replayed the night Captain Michael was killed. She had been the woman at the bar, the one who had so successfully distracted him.

"You're going to hate yourself for the rest of your life if you pass up this opportunity," she said, pressing her bare-chested nakedness against his back before slinking her arms around his waist.

When Fornax didn't resist her advances, she moaned wantonly. "I need it *real* bad."

"So . . . do I," he gasped, his male impulses unexpectedly kindled by her expert caresses.

"How do you like my perfume?" she whispered lustfully, unbuckling his pants.

"It's . . . very unusual, but . . . I do like it," he revealed, aroused by the intriguing fragrance.

"Do I turn you on?" she moaned, stroking him.

"God, yes," he panted, momentarily forgetting who he was dealing with.

"I must have you now," she begged, tearing at his shirt.

"In a minute, my love," he promised, stepping out of his trousers.

Sensing that she was about to get what she wanted, a thin smile uncoiled across Marona's face, jerking him back to reality.

Enraged by her sick grin, Fornax clenched his fist and walloped her in the jaw with the most powerful uppercut he could muster.

A shocked look shot across her face as she lurched backward, falling awkwardly against the bulkhead. But, like the deadly assassin that she was, the woman bounded swiftly to her feet, deftly reaching for the blade strapped inside her boot.

Still naked from the waist up, her nipples hard as pearls, the sinewy muscles in her arms rippling with power, she approached him, her voice cackling.

"You chicken-shit!" she screamed venomously, the glinting steel blade carving circles in the air as she drew nearer. "You gutless wonder, fists are for *fags!* You shoulda *killed* me, not punched me!"

"I *have* killed you," Fornax retorted calmly, producing the vial he had hidden in the pocket of his trousers.

"Well then, we're *both* dead!" she tittered, lunging at him like a wildcat and slashing his arm with a nasty ragged cut.

Fornax screamed out in pain.

Then, with blood running everywhere, he twisted the legs of his trousers into a rope-like cord and put them into service fending off her blows. Knowing that he had no choice, Fornax retreated in the direction of the cupboard where he'd stashed Jenny earlier in the day.

But he needn't have bothered. Even as Marona lunged at him for a second time, she groaned and doubled over in pain. The chilling effects of the poison had begun to take hold!

Her tongue swelled grotesquely, and—as her blood-laden lungs were deprived of oxygen—she began to choke.

Reaching up with both hands to massage her thickening throat, Marona dropped her blade. It clattered harmlessly to the deck, but not before a gruesome look had blistered her reddened face. It was too late to avoid asphyxiation.

Drowning in her own mucus, Marona sank to the floor in a series of gurgling spasms. After one final involuntary shudder, her life ended.

She was, as J would say, finished. Done. Kaputt.

It was over.

And he was exhausted.

• • •

Staring indifferently out into space, the blood dripping from his slashed arm, Fornax was so numb from his ordeal he wasn't consciously aware of the scratching sound whispering at him from down the hall.

All that mattered to him now was that he had won—Marona was

dead and he was still alive.

For the longest time he just sat there trying to sort things out while the moon's mottled surface spun lazily by underneath. Gazing out upon the misshapen, crater-pocked landscape, Fornax was reminded just how lifeless the moon really was.

Unlike the newly-fecund Mars or her terran mother Earth, the moon had no sound. No life. No wind rustling through a forest of towering oaks on a cool, fall evening. No bouquet of freshly-cut grass after a sultry summer's day. No taste of ocean spray as the crashing waves tumbled upon the sandy shore. No snowflakes against the cheek.

At some point in his brooding, self-absorbed trance, it dawned on him that—without ever meaning to be—he was a hero. Thanks to his discovery, an altogether new realm was about to become accessible to humanity!

Years ago, even before the Great War, mankind's efforts to colonize the solar system had all but been abandoned. The harshness of life on this, Earth's only moon, had easily cracked the will of its eager inhabitants, and, despite a handful of noteworthy successes at the outset, disgusted terraformers had eventually given up on Mars as well. The once hopeful vision of man in space had evaporated, and might well have been extinguished, if not for his own greed and ambition.

Now, instead of a months' long trek, the trip to Mars would take but minutes. Now, instead of being a scientific curiosity, Mars could become a haven from persecution for those bold enough to seek her out. Now, instead of a dead end, space could become a new beginning!

As a burst of sunlight blazed through the shuttle's viewport, jolting him from his coma, Fornax saw more clearly than ever what he had to do—what he was *destined* to do.

Though perhaps not quite in the way she had thought, Carina had been right about the human race all along.

Humans *weren't* all the same. Some *were* smarter and more capable, some *were* dumber and less able. But just because their ideas and their skin color and their beliefs were different was no excuse for exterminating or abandoning them.

And that's what Fornax had done wrong; he had abandoned his country.

He had given up on his own people in their fight to be free. And *that*, he realized now, had been a mistake. *That* was a wrong Fornax Nehrengel would someday have to go back and correct.

Only today wasn't the day. For starters, there was still the small matter of Marona's corpse.

As Fornax bent to hoist her lifeless body over his shoulder, intending to intern it next to BC's when he landed, he again heard the distant scratching sound which he'd tuned out before.

Picking his blade up off the deck, Fornax skulked down the corridor of the ship in the direction of the sound.

It grew louder as he drew nearer. A wicked smell filled the hallway.

Rounding the corner to where Lotha had deposited BC's body earlier, Fornax was stunned to find the bunk empty!

A trail of blood led down the hallway to his left.

His heart in his mouth, Fornax followed it towards the medic cabinet.

"Geez," BC complained, studying his first-aid handiwork in the mirror, "for a moment there, I thought you were going to let me *die*."

"I . . . thought . . . you *were* dead," Fornax stuttered, not believing his eyes.

"The kevlar tee-shirt I picked up in Sri Lanka stopped the chest shot, and this here electric searing iron fixed the shoulder wound," he explained, proudly holding up the very same tool he had once used to save Fornax's life. "Here, let me see that arm of yours. I'm a medic, you know."

"So you are. So you are."

12
Andu Nehrengel

Farah District, Afghanistan
Forty Years Later

Granted, it's been longer than I care to admit, but I remember the details of that day as if it were yesterday.

Marching back to our mountainside hide-out in the midst of the most ungodly rainstorm, I found it curiously ironic that I should be fighting to defend a flag I paid scant allegiance to, or risking my life to support cherished ideals I barely endorsed. I resented being there and desertion was on my mind.

Flopping onto my sagging bunk after having killed that day's quota of the enemy, I lay there, wet and cold, licking my wounds and mourning the death of my buddy. We had just cut a Chinese regiment to ribbons, and even though we'd won the encounter, we'd suffered many casualties.

I'd almost cried myself to sleep that night when, all of a sudden, I was startled by an unfamiliar swooshing noise outside my tent. The sound was unlike any I had ever heard previously.

When I rolled over and opened my eyes, an elderly old man was leaning against the foot of my cot, a man I had never seen before, but one I was unlikely to soon forget. Even to this day—some thirty years later—that amazing old coot still haunts my memory.

Although I was alarmed by his mysterious appearance, the stranger did not threaten me in any way. To the contrary.

Supported by a knotty-pine cane, the bloke hobbled in from out of the rain and handed me a big sheaf of yellowed and tattered papers bound in a frayed, folio of red leather. From their ragged condition, it was evident many of the pages were of great age.

Then, before turning to walk back out into the storm, he spoke to me in a broken, fractured sort of tongue.

"Ma nome is Sven Rutland de SKANDIA," he explained. "Dis is vor vou."

Granted, I was suspicious of this brown-skinned fellow, but I wasn't quite sure what to make of him. Even though his accent was peculiar, he didn't appear even vaguely SKANDIAN to me.

"Heh, old man," I remarked, in obvious reference to the papers he'd just given me, "what is the meaning of this?"

In the worst imitation of a SKANDIAN accent I had ever heard, he answered, "Vo grandmudder vanted vou to 'ave it."

"Drop the fake accent, gramps," I ordered caustically. "Ma grandmudder . . . I mean, my grandmother, has been dead for years. My father told me she died even before I was born."

"Nonsense, Andu," he countered in plain, ungarbled English, calling me by name. "Your father told you that just so you wouldn't ask too many questions about your past. In fact, your grandmother has only just passed away within the week. And that is why I am here today."

The old man dug something from his pocket and tossed it across to me. "Oh, I almost forgot," he said, "this is for you as well."

Resting in my hand was an odd-shaped, custom-made key.

Having said his piece, my guest abruptly pivoted on his cane and tottered out towards the open flap of my tent.

At that point, I became completely unglued. "Heh, *stop!*" I yelled, astounded by this whole sequence of events. "How come you know my name?" I shouted. "And if you knew my grandmother, how come *I* never did?"

Pausing at the doorway of my tent, the prehistoric gentleman clarified, "Because she lived on Mars . . . with me."

I chuckled with disbelief and replied mockingly, "Sure pops, and I'm the Emir of Afghanistan."

Tired of listening to this old duffer, I turned to toss the sheaf of papers he'd given me into the waste can. But before I could act, his bony hand had reached out and grabbed my wrist with unexpected fierceness.

"You stupid *dunce!*" he exclaimed, "this is your *heritage!* You must *read* it, Andu! Do you think I came all this way to have you *trash* it? Indeed! Is every Nehrengel that was ever born a stubborn *jerk?*" he screamed, obviously incensed.

I was startled by his outburst—and just a little bit scared. Unsure what to say, I managed to stammer, "You knew . . . my father?"

"*And* your grandfather," he pointed out, loosening his grip on my arm. "You might say I rescued him from the clutches of the Overlord not far from here."

Regaining my composure, I snapped in a cocky tone, "Sure, you and what army?"

"Just me and Jenny," he made clear, a sphinx-like grin bubbling up on his face.

"Jenny?" I asked perplexed. "What kind of a man takes a *woman* into battle?"

"Andu, meet Jenny," he declared, producing a queer-looking gun from under his coat. "With this blaster you can defeat an entire army without losing so much as a single man."

Considering my own meritorious accomplishments that particular day, I overlooked his ridiculous claim, asking instead, "What are these papers anyway, old-timer? And what is your *real* name? It certainly isn't Sven whatever-you-said."

"These *papers*, as you call them, are Carina's diary."

"And who, my good friend, is Carina?"

"Your grandmother, you dolt!" he spewed forth in an exasperated tone. "As for me, I was once a soldier just as you are now."

"You?" I laughed, confounded by the possibility. "You're a *fossil!*"

"Indeed," he answered simply. "A fossil named Fornax."

"That was my grandfather's name."

"So I'm told."

"He was a hero."

"Yes. I was."

"I don't believe you," I announced, though somehow I did. "And this key?" I asked, all at once curious. "What is *it* for?"

"Carina, that is, your grandmother, inherited a great estate near Auckland, an estate which, for many years, served as a halfway house for fleeing immigrants. Since all of her children, save your father, remained with her on Mars, she wanted him to have it. No freedom-fighter was more tenacious than her son, your father, but when he died in the Indiastan revolt, we agreed the Auckland estate should pass to you instead."

When Fornax finished his spiel, he placed Jenny on the table next to Carina's diary, patted it lovingly as if it were his only daughter, then hobbled out of my tent leaning heavily on his cane.

Too shocked by the proceedings to try and stop him, I just sat there on my bunk. By the time I'd rushed from my tent, cued by the strange swooshing noise outside, my grandfather had disappeared from sight.

Had the setting sun not been unceremoniously shoved aside by the invading night, it might have witnessed the departure of this truly remarkable relic of a man. But to this day, I have no idea how he got there, or by what means he left, nor have I ever seen or heard from him since.

Although I was exhausted by the day's events, I barely closed my eyes that night. Until I set off the next morning with Jenny clenched in my fist, I lay in my bunk, mesmerized by every word my grandmother had recorded during her long and winsome life. I was so riveted by what she had to say about Fornax that when I'd finished going over it, I read it through once more, paying particular attention to the passages devoted to him. And, like a bedside Bible, I have reread those selections several times since.

When I awoke with a start the next morning, I clearly understood why Fornax had come and what he expected of me. As was most assuredly his intention, I put Jenny to work in our battle to be free. She marked a turning point in the war. As my grandfather had promised, his awesome gun *could* defeat an entire army! And with her leading the charge, the two of us liberated our tiny, landlocked province from the clutches of the Chinese for the first time in over two generations!

I was hailed by my countrymen as a hero, but the truth be told, my grandpa Fornax was the real hero. Not only did he save me from making the mistake of a lifetime by deserting, he saved the entire nation. We could never have succeeded without the gift he bestowed upon me that night.

For me, my grandfather had become a mystery begging to be solved, so not long after the truce was signed with the Chinese, I set out for Auckland to patch together the truth about him. I found the key he'd given me hugging the bottom of my footlocker, though without an address, I hadn't a clue where to begin to look for my grandmother's estate.

The provincial land office turned out to be my first and only stop. They knew the place well and were happy to have somebody take it off their hands. The magistrate warned me the property was a trifle rundown, a serious understatement if I ever did hear one.

The buildings were old, and the grounds unkempt; yet, I could imagine that in its prime, without the jumble of weeds and without the tapestry of cobwebs, the manor must have been palatial. Regrettably, the years had not been kind, and the estate was now little more than rotted timbers and decaying masonry.

For a couple of hours I stumbled about the property unsure what it was I was looking for or why my grandmother would have thought she was doing me a favor by leaving me this dump.

And that's when I found her, the *Tikkidiw*, a ship out of another time. She was moored in a woodshed whose peeling white paint littered the unmown grass. A tattered butterfly emblazoned on her hull, the gleaming spacecraft was waiting patiently for my arrival. Inside the ship I discovered the archives chronicling her travels, plus the logbooks tallying the names of the thousands of immigrants my grandfather had carried to freedom.

Only then did I begin to grasp the full measure of the man who called himself Fornax Engels.

Andu Nehrengel
5 September, 2501